Parasites
Like Us

Also by Adam Johnson

Emporium

Parasites
Like Us

ADAM
JOHNSON

[VIKING]

Illustrations by Stephanie Harrell

VIKING
Published by the Penguin Group
Penguin Group (USA) Inc., 375 Hudson Street,
New York, New York 10014, U.S.A.
Penguin Books Ltd, 80 Strand,
London WC2R 0RL, England
Penguin Books Australia Ltd, 250 Camberwell Road, Camberwell,
Victoria 3124, Australia
Penguin Books Canada Ltd, 10 Alcorn Avenue, Toronto,
Ontario, Canada M4V 3B2
Penguin Books India (P) Ltd, 11 Community Centre, Panchsheel Park,
New Delhi–110 017, India
Penguin Books (N.Z.) Ltd, Cnr Rosedale and Airborne Roads, Albany,
Auckland, New Zealand
Penguin Books (South Africa) (Pty) Ltd, 24 Sturdee Avenue,
Rosebank, Johannesburg 2196, South Africa

Penguin Books Ltd, Registered Offices:
80 Strand, London WC2R 0RL, England

First Published in 2003 by Viking Penguin,
a member of Penguin Group (USA) Inc.

1   3   5   7   9   10   8   6   4   2

Publisher's Note
This is a work of fiction. Names, characters, places, and incidents either are the product of the author's imagination or are used fictitiously, and any resemblance to actual persons, living or dead, business establishments, events, or locales is entirely coincidental.

Library of Congress Cataloging-in-Publication Data
Johnson, Adam.
Parasites like us / Adam Johnson.
p.   cm.
ISBN 0-670-03235-2
1. Anthropologists—Fiction.   2. Plague—Fiction.   I. Title.
PS3610.O3P3 2003
813'.54—dc21   2002041181

This book is printed on acid-free paper.   ∞

Printed in the United States of America
Set in Cochin
Designed by Jaye Zimet

For my mother, Patricia,
and her mother, Lavina

Eradicated Mammals of Ice Age North America

American lion
American mastodon
Aztlan rabbit
Banded stalking sloth
Capybara*
Colossus beaver
Columbian mammoth
Dire wolf
Florida (spectacled) cave bear*
Forest-dwelling musk ox
Four-horned pronghorn
Giant armadillo
Giant beaver
Giant short-faced bear
Harlan's ground sloth
Horse*
Jeppson's mega-skunk
Large-headed llama
Long-horned bison
Mexican glyptodont
Mountain deer
New World cheetah
Northern pampathere
Peabody's ground sloth
Red-toothed capybara
Saber-tooth
Scimitar cat
Shasta ground sloth
Southern pampathere
Stag-moose
Stout-legged llama
Tapir*
Three-tusked dhole
Woolly scrub ox
Yesterday's camel

*Genus survives outside North America.

Parasites
Like Us

Chapter One

This story begins some years after the turn of the millennium, back when gangs were persecuted, back before we all joined one. In those days, birds and pigs were still our friends, and we held some pretty crazy notions: People said the planet was warming. Wearing fur was a no-no. Dogs could do no wrong. Back then, we'd pretty much agreed that guns were good, that just about everybody needed one. Firearms, we were all to discover, were feeble, finicky things, prone to laughable inaccuracy.

During this brief moment in human evolution, a professor of anthropology might, for the half-year he worked, fish in the morning, lecture midday, and stroll excavation sites until early evening, after which was personal/leisure time. I was a professor of anthropology, one of the very, very few. I owned a bass boat, a classic Corvette, and a custom van, all of which I lost during the period of this story, the brief sentence I served inside the cushiest prison in the Western Hemisphere, the minimum-security federal prison camp at Parkton, South Dakota.

Camp Parkton, we called it. Club Fed.

As an anthropologist, I had the job of telling stories about the past. My area of study was the Clovis people, the first humans to cross the Bering Land Bridge from Siberia about twelve thousand years ago. As you know, the Clovis colonized a hemisphere that had never seen humans before, and their first order of business was to invent a new kind of spear point, which they used to eradicate thirty-five species of large mammals. The stories I told about the Clovis were not new ones: A people developed a technology that allowed them to exploit all their resources. They then created a vast empire. And once they had consumed everything in sight, they disbanded—in the case of the Clovis, into small groups that would form the roughly six hundred Native American tribes that exist today.

I had a '72 Corvette and a custom van!

Dear colleagues of tomorrow, fellow anthropologists of the future, how can I express my joy in knowing there is only one profession in the years to come, that each and every one of you has become a committed anthropologist? The trials of my life seem petty compared with their inevitable reward: that the turbulent story of our species should end with all its members' becoming experts on humanity.

The fate of the culture we called "America" is certainly no mystery to you. Of that tale, countless artifacts stand testament, and who could fail to hear such a song of conclusion, endlessly whistling through the frozen teeth of time? Yet you must have questions. Dig as you might, there must be gaps in the record. Who is buried in the Tomb of the Unknown Indian? you might ask. Was the hog truly smarter than the dreaded dog? Were owls really birds, or some other manner of animal? So, my dedicated peers, I will share with you how the betterment of humanity began, and let no one claim I slandered the past. I am the past.

I'm not sure I can tell you the exact year this story begins, but I'll never forget the day. It was the season in South Dakota in which the Missouri River nearly freezes over—day by day, shelves of white extend their reach from the riverbanks, calciumlike, until they enter the central channel, where the current rips great sheets free and sends them hurtling downstream.

From my office on the campus of the University of Southeastern South Dakota, I could hear the frozen river wail and moan before a lurching crack tore loose a limb of ice. When the day was clear, I could even see from my window in the anthropology building scattered stains of red on the ice, where eagles had landed with freshly snatched fish and stripped them on the frozen ledges. An eagle was a kind of bird, quite large, and it was famous for the boldness it displayed when stealing another's prey. Most birds were about the size of rats, though some came as big as jackrabbits. The eagle, however, weighed in closer to a dog. Picture a greyhound, then add ferocity and wings.

It was a gray, brooding day when Eggers, one of my star

doctoral students, stuck his head in my office. He was vigorously chewing something, and the odds were it wasn't gum.

Eggers wore goatskin breeches and a giant poncho of dark, matted fur, which he'd fashioned himself from animal hides begged off the Hormel meatpacking plant at the edge of town. I could smell him long before he made his way to the stacks of cardboard boxes that filled my doorway and spilled into the hall.

"Careful of Junior," I said and waved him in. I had just received an exciting new crate of raw ice-core data from Greenland, and Eggers' booties were covered with God-knows-what.

"Life's good, Dr. Hannah," Eggers said, making his way around the boxes. He displayed that impish grin of his. "Life is good," he repeated.

My office in those days was filled with houseplants of every variety, though I found indoor gardening so pointless and sad I could barely stand to look at them. Eggers ducked under the hanging tendrils of plants whose names escaped me, his feet crunching across the layer of flint chips that littered the floor from the hours I whiled away knapping out primitive tools and weapons.

He took a seat, and I was confronted with my daily update on Eggers' dissertation project, which was to exist using nothing but Paleolithic technology for an entire year. More than eleven months into the experiment, some of the results were already clear: the wafting custard of his breath, the thin mistletoe of his beard, the way the oiled gloss of his face had attained the yellowy hue of earwax.

I should have been working on a grant proposal or grading some of the endlessly simple student papers that flowed across my desk. But I couldn't concentrate, because of Glacier Days, a yearly carnival intended to lighten the gloom of winter by celebrating the recession of the glaciers that had carved the Missouri River Valley. They'd set up the midway in the Parkton Square parking lot, catty-corner to campus, and every so often you'd hear the muffled, rising moan and long wail of young people on the thrill rides.

"Okay, Eggers," I said. "*Life's grand*. We'll go with that hypothesis."

Eggers shrugged, as if everything was self-evident. "Oh, it's not some theory, Dr. Hannah. Life is tiptop," he said, moving aside a dusty stack of my book, *The Depletionists*, and settling into a high-backed chair. He slumped enough that his hair left a sheeny streak down the leather upholstery. God, his game bag reeked!

I was about to hear one of Eggers' continuing intrigues with a coed, or how he'd won some prestigious new grant. The anthropology journals were already fighting to publish his story. But I couldn't get that "life is good" phrase out of my head. It's what my stepmother, Janis, kept saying at the end, and it became one of my father's refrains after we lost her. I could see behind Eggers, framed in the window, a piece of ice slowly turning down the Missouri River — it drifted in from the future, caught the sun for a moment, and disappeared out into the past. From the Glacier Days carnival, a slow whoop arose from the next generation of South Dakotans as they mocked their deaths on bloodcurdling rides, and my eyes naturally fell to Junior — nineteen thousand notecards and twenty-seven cardboard boxes of research, all yet to be examined, all those stories waiting to be told.

Eggers shifted what he was chewing and went after it with his molars.

"Is this about Trudy?" I asked.

"Trudy? Why bring her up?" he asked. "Are you feeling guilty, Dr. Hannah?"

"What would I have to feel guilty about?"

"Nothing," Eggers said. "Nothing. Except you did file the paperwork to revoke her Peabody Fellowship and give it to me."

"The school's doing that. That's out of my hands. Congrats, by the way."

"You know me, Dr. Hannah. I yawn at money. Money's obsolete to me."

Eggers pulled something out of his mouth, inspected it, and put it back in.

"Don't gloat," I told him. "Everything will be hunky-dory once I explain things to her."

"Trudy's pretty upset. I mean, I was the one who broke it to her."

"This isn't even official yet."

"She needed to hear it from someone who cared," Eggers said.

"Please," I said. "Anyway, that's only half the story. Losing her Peabody is only the bad news of a good-news/bad-news thing. I'll explain it to her."

Eggers swallowed hard enough to make his eyes water, and then he opened the flap of his game bag. I could see a fuzzy tail sticking out of it, and it hadn't escaped the notice of the school paper that all the squirrels on campus had disappeared during the time that Eggers, an adult omnivore, had taken up residence in the middle of the quad.

"I wouldn't worry about Trudy," Eggers said. "Trudy can take care of herself. She'll bounce back." He removed another sinewy morsel and slid it into his mouth. Though grayish-brown, it crunched like celery. He chewed it contemplatively. "I've got my own good and bad news," he added.

I removed my glasses, folded them, rubbed the bridge of my nose.

"Just the good," I said. "Only tell me the good."

"I found something."

Eggers was always finding things. He was the only person in town who walked everywhere, and over eleven months, his travels on foot had netted him countless arrow points, bison skulls, mastodon teeth, and a brass bell that may or may not have belonged to Meriwether Lewis. Sleeping in the same stretch of sand in South Dakota, you were likely to find a buffalo soldier's pistol, a conquistador's breastplate, the hooves of rhino-pigs from the early Eocene, T-rex teeth, and maybe even a Cambrian trilobite, frozen mid-wriggle at the dawn of time.

"Is it a spear point?" I asked.

"It's a point, all right," Eggers said.

"A Clovis point?"

Eggers shrugged, but in a way that said, *You can bet the farm.*

I threw a foot up on my desk to lace my snow-packs. "Show me," I said.

We tromped downstairs and cut through the Hall of Man, a natural-history exhibit that my predecessor, Old Man Peabody, fashioned himself back in the 1960s out of an empty classroom. The Hall was about thirty feet long and lined with glassed-in exhibits. On one side was a series of models depicting glacial advance and retreat during the late Pleistocene. Peabody had crafted the balsa glaciers by hand, painted them white, and used little stickpins to represent Clovis movement from Siberia to South Dakota during brief openings in the ice. On the other side of the Hall was an amazing series of very lifelike models that followed the ascent of humanity: in a row were displayed *Homo habilis, erectus*, and *sapiens*, followed by Neanderthal, and finally Clovis, all posed in natural settings with several artifacts that Peabody had excavated himself. This hall is where I came to pace and think in times of doubt. Simply to cross the room was to travel a hundred thousand years back in time; it was a place where things always seemed clearer to me.

Out in the quad, Eggers and I walked quietly through the snow. The limbs of the maples had been shorn off, so they were whitened posts against what was for now a clear sky. The sidewalks were sanded and salted, though we veered off through the hackberry trees, walking under their weblike branches and listening to the *tap-tap* of thawing icicles as they dripped constellations into the snow below.

Eggers' shelter was situated in the middle of Central Green, and ahead I could see its snow-crusted dome, made from six curving mammoth tusks draped with a mass of various animal hides that had been confiscated over the years by the Fish and Game Department. Also ahead in the courtyard was a large granite stone that held the plaque I'd placed in remembrance of my stepmother, Janis, and I was faced with my almost daily decision: should I offer a word to her, or should I close my eyes and simply walk on?

The proof of my cowardice was that my decision to talk to Janis always came down to whether or not I was alone. At least I didn't put a bench here, which I'd considered.

Eggers could see the apprehension on my face. "Maybe I'll

just go check my snares," he said, and headed toward the arbor-vitae hedge.

"No, don't," I told him. "I'm okay." And like that, I resolved not to speak to Janis today. As I neared, though, I did look at her face, fixed in the mild relief of bronze. The birds had been crapping again, something I hadn't planned on when I'd commissioned the memorial. But, really, did it matter? How could someone be honored by impressing a face on a plaque or a name to an anthropology fellowship? I couldn't even decide if I should use an image of her from when she was young or when she was older. Eventually, I chose a picture taken on the day she graduated from stenography school, a time before she even met my father. She looks young and expectant in the image, but the ironies didn't escape me: since she left my life, I'd chosen to remember her with an image from before I'd entered hers. So now we looked upon each other as strangers.

My father had Janis cremated, something I'm against, but would it have made a difference if we'd buried her? Ten thousand years from now, when people exhumed her bones, what would they know of her life, her spirit? There would be her rings, traces of gold dentistry, perhaps. Would they know of her love of plants, that she longed to see Egypt, or that when she napped on the couch her fingers would type her dreams on her lap? Would the future know her goal in life was an impossible one: to be my mother after my real mother made a stranger of herself? Should I have put medicine bottles and a bedpan in her grave, so the future would understand her final struggle? Should I have chiseled out her story, start to finish, in granite, and what language will the future speak?

The snow thinned as we crossed Central Green, and it wasn't until you neared Eggers' dwelling, which he called his "lodge," that you realized it was situated, as if by chance, atop the one spot on the whole campus where there was no snow. There were underground steam tunnels that sent heat to the dormitories, and Eggers claimed it was just a coincidence that he had built his lodge over the main heat exchangers. Nearing, we stepped through shards from his flint knapping, and an array of his stone tools was lying around—scrapers, cutters, and percussion strikers. Finally, there was a rather shocking mound of bones that Eggers had accumulated over the year. I nosed through them with my boot—most of the bones were surprisingly small, shining dully from under a gelatinous goo that beaded water away, and though rodent anatomy was technically out of my field, I spotted among the prairie-dog and squirrel skulls more than one feline. Eggers was saving them so he'd be able to calculate his caloric intake, once his year was finished and he could handle lab equipment again. These bones were the cornerstone of his dissertation, and I counted them as a real document, as good a testament to Paleolithic culture as any. To keep scavengers away, Eggers urinated on the heap.

When Eggers pulled back the flap of his lodge, he was greeted by a package, wrapped in red paper and tied with yarn, and there was only the faintest smell of fire smoke. Of the gift, probably left by one of his female students, Eggers seemed to take no notice; instead, after the flap closed behind him, I heard him breathing on the fire, a patient, well-paced stoking that made me look away, as if this was a private moment between man and flame. Low clouds had again passed over the river, and of the Clark Bridge, only the upper trestle was visible.

Eggers emerged with a soft leather cloth that looked exactly like a chamois you'd use when washing a car. "This Clovis point is the cover of the *Rolling Stone*," Eggers said, handing it to me. "This is a feature article in *Archeology Today*."

Through the leather cloth, I felt the weight and shape of the stone. You never forget the feel of a Clovis point. A hint of pink was peeking from under the cloth.

"You know, I've never found an exotic one," I told Eggers. "In all my years of hunting. I've found some things, don't get me wrong, but never a colored Clovis point."

"Well, this one's yours," Eggers said.

I unfolded the cloth, and there it was. About five inches long, broad-headed, and cut from the rarest of materials, a semi-translucent rose quartz. Twelve thousand years ago, this artifact was the height of technology on the face of the earth, and no one in the millennia since has been able to reproduce the Clovis' lost craft. The afternoons I spent flaking flint in my office were merely exercises in humility, for the Clovis concerned themselves with nothing but producing the most dangerous weapons on earth. They left behind no art, no monuments, no shelters, few remains.

I ran my fingers down the dimpled spine of Eggers' pink point—the cutting edge was covered with serrated ridges that fanned forward to cause severe micro-hemorrhaging on penetration, while at the same time the plane of the blade was fluted with a ridge leading backward, serving as a channel to runnel the blood from the wound. This blade could snap bison ribs and still slice tomatoes.

Over the course of three centuries—at the end of the Pleistocene epoch, twelve thousand years ago—three amazing things happened: the Ice Age ended completely, and glaciers retreated from North America; humans entered the hemisphere, and these Paleo-Indians we call Clovis quickly spread across all forty-eight contiguous states, founding an empire that included Mexico and Canada before their culture came to an end; and, finally, thirty-five species of large North American mammals became extinct. All in three hundred years.

Mammoth and mastodon skeletons have been found with dozens of Clovis points lodged in their bones. Many paleo-anthropologists agree that the Clovis people eradicated the elephants of North America, though they tend to believe the other large animals were killed off by climate change.

It was my lone hypothesis, however, articulated in *The Depletionists*, that the Clovis blade was the demise of the North American camel, the giant sloth, the short-faced bear, and thirty-two other large mammals. And here was the very spear point that had done it. I marveled at its color, held it to the light, and saw that the quartz was clear at the surface with a cataract of milky pink veined through the center. Only a few thousand Clovis points had ever been discovered, and they were all logged in the National Clovis Bank. Fewer still of these super-bleeder spear points were cut from the exotic minerals only Clovis had a fondness for: smoky purple obsidian and ferrous chert, from feldspar, perlite, spider flint, or the blue-yellow of anthracite. And here was rose quartz. In the back alleys of anthropology, there was a black market for these points, and what I held was worth more than my Corvette and custom van put together.

"Okay," I asked Eggers, "where'd you really get this?"

"I told you," he said. "I found it."

An anger rose in me. "You found *this* and then removed it from the site? This point doesn't mean anything without context. Haven't I taught you anything? Unless it's *in situ*, where we can see its role in the bigger story, it's just a bauble."

"It's more complicated than that," Eggers said. Students were filing out of Gufstason Hall, and his eyes followed their brightly colored jackets as they descended the slushy stairwell, arms out for balance, in baby steps. I looked at my wristwatch. It was just after noon, and my father would be waiting for me.

"I've got to teach my Arc-Intro," Eggers added. "There's more than this spear point. I'll show you, but I need to ask a favor first."

Doing a favor for Eggers was no easy thing. He didn't use money, ride in cars, or borrow music. He didn't need my fishing pole or want a letter of recommendation. He'd been an unexceptional kid as far as I could tell, one who sat at the back of my classes, dressed like a golf caddy, and probably smoked some reefer. Then he embarked on this project, and somehow he'd become a lean, clear-eyed young man who had no need for anything from you but time, muscle, and wisdom.

"All right, what is it?"

"Meet me here tonight, when the moon is high."

"Surely, you're joking," I told him. "What time is that? Midnight?"

"Midnight sounds right, though I'd have to check the moon."

"Midnight's my personal/leisure time."

"And bring Trudy," he said. His big, shaggy figure was already heading off to teach.

I stood there a moment with the pink Clovis point in my hand. It felt wrong simply to stick it in my coat pocket as if it was a pen or a throat lozenge, and it seemed more criminal to wander the campus wielding it in my hand. I probably shouldn't admit this, but my first, brief impulse was to show Janis, to walk up the hill to the plaque that I tried to think of as her, and tell her all about it.

I admit this because these events happened long ago, and it's more than ironic that a man who spent his career trying to bring the past to life would, around the age of thirty-nine, begin to communicate certain things to the dead.

That's when Eggers came walking back to me. I was still standing there, hand extended with a pink spear point, looking toward the river so as not to look toward my stepmother. As Eggers neared, I for some reason felt that when he came close he would keep coming closer and give me a pat on the back or clasp my hand. He might hug me, I thought.

Instead, Eggers said, "Are you okay, Dr. Hannah?"

"What?" I asked.

"I better hold this for now," he said, taking the point from my hand. "I'll give it back later tonight. And get some rest, yeah?"

Then he walked away again.

I set off through the quad, following the snowed-in cardio-track, with its frozen fitness stations, then tromped past the Carney Aquatic Center, standing like a cube of jade with its steamed-up walls of Depression-era glass. I could make out the silhouettes of dive platforms, could almost smell the endless drizzle of mildewy rain that dripped from the glass ceiling inside.

There was no getting around the fact that I would be late for lunch with my father downtown, but still I cut through the dean's courtyard and the president's garden—the ground winterized with rows of burlap—and it struck me as I passed among the stark colonnades surrounding Old Main that the school paper was right: all the squirrels had disappeared.

The campus opened onto Parkton Square, a one-block park surrounded by multi-story brick buildings erected by people who believed towns like Parkton and Sioux Falls would one day be Kansas Cities and St. Louises. Parking was free during Glacier Days, so I walked past green-hooded meters in front of businesses that were mostly alive, though the Bijou Theater was now an indoor shooting range and the Independent Order of Odd Fellows lodge had been divided into the small apartments where my father now lived. If I looked up to the hill above downtown, I could see the library and buildings of Parkton College, the long-bankrupt Catholic school that was now home to the minimum-security federal prison camp.

I crossed the street at Bank, passed the statue of Harold McGeachie, "The Farmers' Farmer," and watched a roller-coaster car swoop above the trees in the park. It climbed its white scaffolding, paused atop the hump to let its passengers fret and moan before the load of colored hats, thick parkas, and trailing scarves plunged screaming from view. Before I pushed into the brass revolving door of the Red Dakotan, I paused to read the movie marquee next door, which was billing a double feature of "His & Hers Pistol Special" and "Super Scope Sale."

The Red Dakotan had been built long before the dam, back in a time when Mississippi steamboats made it this far up the river, when wealthy passengers needed a place to freshen themselves and pass the time in luxury while military prisoners restocked the ships with coal. Inside, the wool carpets had a red fleur-de-lis design, and there was a staircase banister scrolled in the French style. Silver "smoker's companions" stood astride each chair. By the bar, below the Dakotan's wall-length gilt mirror, I spotted my father's houndstooth sportcoat.

When I joined him, he was holding the hand of a woman who was leaving. He bowed slightly to her, extended a business card between two fingers, and said, *"Enchanté,"* before hailing the bartender with an order of two martinis.

He wore a new pair of eyeglasses with amber lenses, tinted like the safety goggles that shootists wear. He sported a mustard-colored vest, and he'd acquired a pinkie ring that was nothing but a huge nugget of gold. Here was my father, a man who in the six months since Janis' death had managed to liquidate everything they owned together, sell his State Farm office, and reappraise all of southern South Dakota with a look in his eye that said, *I'm ready. Man, I am ready.*

"Enchanté," I said.

He pretended not to hear me.

"Did you bring the Corvette?" he asked. "I may need the 'Vette later."

"Let me see one of those cards," I said, reaching for his breast pocket. "I mean, I take it you didn't just try to sell that young woman insurance."

He brushed away my hand. "You wish," he said. "It happens I will be escorting that new lady friend to the radio theater tomorrow."

I swiped one of the cards anyway. It read, "Frank Hannah," and below, in fine script, "Appraiser of Fine Goods, Objects D'Art, & Rare Beauty."

I said, "I notice you didn't mention the word 'Antiquities.'"

Dad gave me his "wise-sage" look, which consisted of lowering his head enough to eyeball me over the top rim of his glasses. "Son," he said, "every woman has something hidden and valuable she wants to show you."

"Like her underwear?"

He snatched the card back. "This wouldn't work for you," he said. "Look at your limp suit and mail-order spectacles. Who taught you how to shave? I woke up. I stepped out of the fire."

He thumbed the length of his lapels and tugged his cufflinks, as if to say, *See?*

"The fire? You mean the inferno that is marriage, fatherhood, and a career?"

"Hey," he said, "I'm still your father. Don't forget that. But here's a tidbit I woke up to. There's no such thing as insurance. You don't bet against doom. You can't sell policies your whole life and just *hope* disaster doesn't come. You got to tip your hat when it comes, because it's coming. So—send in the tornadoes. Let's have the locusts."

"I hope you've been drinking," I said.

At the sound of the martini shaker, Dad closed his eyes. To the music of ice and frothy gin, he said, "Oh, lighten up. These are just musings. This is only Philosophy 101. If I wanted to give you real advice, I'd tell you to find a young girl, ten years younger, and marry her young. That's as close as you'll come to insurance."

Of course he was referring to the death of Janis, but we had, at some point since then, come to a silent understanding: he never spoke my stepmother's name, and I never said my mother's.

Dad's eyes popped open. "Come to think of it," he whispered, "forget the Corvette. I may need the van tonight."

He smiled for the first time, and I saw that his two front

teeth, which had always been a tad discolored and out of align-
ment, now gleamed perfectly white with new crowns.

The martinis came, both dressed to my father's exact
specifications—a toothpick skewering an olive, then a folded
anchovy, and finally a cocktail onion—so I knew my father had
walked the bartender through a couple trial runs before I'd
arrived.

Dad put some cash in the bartender's hand. "We'll want that
booth over there, by the wall, and we'll need our steaks sent
over ahead of time." He turned to me. "Two or three steaks?"

I looked around for Trudy, who was supposed to meet us
for lunch, but she was nowhere to be seen. "Two for now," I
told Dad.

"Two it is," he told the bartender. "Make them porterhouses, keep 'em rare."

Then my father lifted his glass high, a thin film of fish oil
catching the light.

"To floods and hail and the Great Deductible," he said, and
drank alone.

In the Parkton landfill was Janis' Art Deco cocktail set,
complete with flamingo-pink martini glasses and a tortoiseshell
shaker. Gone also were her Bakelite clutch purses, her collection of dime-store brooches, and a little library of vintage eti-
quette guides, which her mother had taught from in the days of
elocution. Dad had lightened his heart by shedding—the house,
the furniture, the car—and, as if Janis' spirit was small enough
to inhabit anything, nothing they'd shared was spared, not the
nail clippers, the alarm clock, the plastic ice-cube trays. He
even ditched his own glasses, because they had once brought
her into focus. Now my father lived in a tiny apartment, and except for a fair amount of money he needed to give away, there
was no evidence that my stepmother had ever existed.

I had two theories on my father.

The first held that he had fallen out of love with Janis at
some point in their marriage, and that her death, while not
pleasant for him to watch, was an overdue relief. This father before me now, yellow-tinted glasses, raw gold ring, was the man
I'd always have known, had he not been hobbled by some mar-

riage vows, a nine-to-five job, and a conscience as old and guilty as two men's.

I sipped my martini—it tasted appropriately oceany, and though I wasn't much of a drinker anymore, it struck a long, clear note in my head. The second hypothesis had to do with my mother, but it would get no sympathy in this room.

My father looked at his watch. "Okay, so where's this Trudy?"

"She should have been here by now. I told her to meet us a half-hour ago."

"She's not like this caveman guy of yours, wearing pelts and crapping in the bushes? Jesus, let's give the money to that poor fool."

A long-ago ocean, that was the quality of my drink, but shot through with sonar pings of alcohol. On my tongue, the ancient brine of salted fish and olive mixed with the bright light of oniony gin.

"That caveman," I told my father, "has a grant from the Carnegie Foundation. He won an outstanding-dissertation-proposal award from the Academy of Arts and Sciences. Then he goes and wins funding from the state Heritage Council and the Bureau of Land Management. Now my department chair has decided to give him our only graduate fellowship, the Peabody, so Eggers will have to acknowledge us in his book. And this kid doesn't even spend money."

"Does he wear drawers under those skins?"

"I don't believe so, Dad."

He cringed. "I suppose toilet paper's out of the question."

"Eggers used leaves for a while, and I'm sure there'll be a chapter in his dissertation about the poison-oak incident. Now I believe he's winging it."

A waiter in a red jacket beckoned us, and I could see that atop a freshly linened table sat a pair of steaming porterhouses. The steaks had come so fast, they must have been cooked for other people, who would now have to wait longer.

"How much did you tip these guys?"

My father shrugged and began to make his way through the tables, drink high. As I followed, it became clear to me that most of the customers were farmers and ranchers from smaller towns, like Doltin and Willis, people who made the trip in for Glacier Days and were now having a late lunch at the one nice place in town.

My steak was closer to medium, but cooked to perfection, from marbled beef that was probably slaughtered that morning at Hormel. The veins of fat had melted away, and I alternated the meat's flaky butteriness with shocks of warming gin. For a while, the two of us simply ate, and every few bites I had to lean back against the red, rolled leather of the booth to remind myself I was alive. In those moments, with my head near the wall, I could make out the faint *pop-pop* of people firing their pistols in the converted movie house next door. The sounds were no more disconcerting than the faint screaming you'd once hear if you ate during the horror matinee, so my digestion was unaffected. I'd never heard a gun fired in anger, let alone fear, and I had no way of knowing then that before that winter was out, an evening would come when all the people in our great nation would fire their weapons at once.

Finally, I set my fork aside. I hadn't even touched the carrots, let alone the hot rolls, but my father lifted his bone with two hands. "So what do students have to do for this fellowship money?" he asked, and raked his bottom teeth along the underside of the bone.

"Nothing, really. It supports them while they study or research. They just keep doing what they're doing. But this money is going to make a big difference to Trudy. She's studying Paleolithic art. The Clovis is the only known culture in the world that left no art behind. There are just a lot of points and blades. Trudy believes that weapons were their art. It's a whopper of an idea. She's maybe going too far with her feminist angle, but the premise is sound."

"Are you sleeping with her?"

I tossed my napkin on the table.

"Really, Dad. You didn't just say that. This fellowship you're endowing is going to make all the difference for her. She has to travel to the cave dwellings in New Mexico, see the petroglyphs in Arizona. She needs to do comparative blade analysis all over North America, France, and of course Peru."

"Hell, I could use a trip to France."

"*Bon voyage,*" I told him.

Two waiters walked by, carrying a single tray between them. On it was a cut of meat called "The Cattleman." There was no shortage of pomp in its delivery, yet the steak was the real deal—beyond large, it was the size of a saddle. If you could eat it, it was free, and the steak's new owner seemed embarrassed only by the fact that this indulgence was a public event.

"What's she like?" my father asked.

"Trudy? She's pretty dang smart, for starters."

"What's she look like?"

"Physically?"

"Yes, physically."

I had no desire to explain Trudy to my father. Her application for the Peabody Fellowship had given me her racial breakdown: a mix of African, French, Korean, and Japanese. With her height, her close-cropped hair, and those shoulders, I occasionally imagined her as a prototypical Clovis woman. It was an inappropriate fantasy, I knew. Scientifically, it was flawed as well—real Clovis were certainly smaller, more compact, and probably poorly nourished. Yet I couldn't help, at times, imagining her body in motion as she hunted down a giant Pleistocene glyptodont.

"She's big, Dad. Five foot nine, probably a hundred eighty pounds."

He worked the last bit off the bone, so all that was left was the white vertebral shank and the descending postilum.

"Big num-nums?"

I shook my head no.

"So this girl," Dad says, "if she's so needy, how come she can't even show up for a free steak?"

"I think she's a little mad at me right now."

"You are sleeping with her."

"No, no, she has a fellowship, the Peabody, but the school's taking it away and giving it to the caveman. It's just miscommunication. She doesn't know about your fellowship yet, the Hannah."

My father pointed the steak shank at his own chest.

"Well, what do I get out of this fellowship-donor thing?"

"Immortality, Dad. Your name gets to live forever."

I expected him to laugh or smart-ass, but he said nothing, just set aside the bone and reclined, hands on chest, against the plush leather. He ran his tongue along his teeth, then asked, "You ever met anyone who really wanted to live forever, one person who just wanted to keep going and going?"

I shrugged. "I suppose not."

Dad leaned forward. "Then no fucking plaques of me when I'm dead, okay?"

When the moon looked high in the sky, I set out from my little apartment by the river, and made my way to Trudy's. She lived alone in a small graduate dorm by the cafeteria, and you could still catch a scent of fried egg rolls in the air from the meal plan earlier that night. It began to snow as I walked, so softly at first that I couldn't tell for sure when the flakes started coming down, but by the time I stood in her courtyard, there were yellow curtains of snow hanging under the campus floodlights.

When I knocked, the flimsy dorm walls shook, rattling the neighbors' windows, and the sound off the hollow-core door was loud enough that three other students stuck their heads out to see if it was for them. But Trudy didn't answer.

"Trudy?" I called.

"Go away, Dr. Hannah."

"Please listen to me, Trudy. I know you're upset that the university took your fellowship away, but we have a better fellowship for you."

Inside, I could hear her pour a glass of water.

I spoke into the peephole: "If you could just listen to what I have to say."

"There's a fellowship in Arizona I could apply for," I heard her say. "And that postdoc at Stanford, unless Eggers already has it spoken for. I was dragged all over the world my entire childhood. No need to put down roots here, I guess."

My voice raised in pitch as I tried to reassure her. I even took out my inhaler, just in case I needed it. "Everything's going to be okay, Trudy. This is a better fellowship. You'll like it much better."

"Don't tell me 'everything's going to be okay,' " Trudy said. "Don't tell me what I'll like and not like. I want my Peabody back. That's the fellowship I earned."

"You'll be the first recipient of this new fellowship. My father has established the Hannah Fellowship, in my step-mother's name, and after careful consideration, you've been chosen as the first recipient."

Trudy opened the door, her hand holding a tumbler of water, half full. She wore her usual paint-speckled jeans, a sweater of chocolate wool a shade darker than her skin, and she'd had her hair cut even shorter since I'd seen her last. My God, those cheekbones. I stole a quick puff off my inhaler.

"I'm the one who should be knocking on *your* door late at night, telling *you* how I feel," she said. From behind her came a tide of warm air, smelling faintly of turpentine.

"Okay," I said. "How do you feel?"

Trudy shifted in the doorway. She took a drink of water. I could see she'd been repainting the walls of her dorm room with ancient cave drawings and symbols.

"Well, I'm pissed off," she said, sounding reluctantly justified. "I've got good ideas. My Clovis theory isn't even out there in the literature. Nobody's articulated it. And all I hear about is Eggers. What's his idea? He doesn't even have one. He has a gimmick."

"Trudy, I recruited you, remember? I've always believed in you. I don't know how you'll ever prove it, but your dissertation hypothesis is brilliant. For a culture based on making animals extinct, to fuse weaponry and art only makes sense. The part about women carving all the spear points while the men hunted—well, you'll maybe have to gather more data on that."

"I've smelled Doritos on him," she said and paused to let that sink in. "Dorito breath is unmistakable. Did you know he doesn't read the textbooks he assigns? He doesn't even use chalk, because it's 'technology.' He gives his tests orally, and gets one of those girls of his to bubble in the grades on his grade sheets. Do you know how many bubbles I bubble in? And he's

Mr. Primitive? Look at how I live. I steal toilet paper from the faculty bathroom. I'm eating noodles and oil in here. If my car breaks down, I'm the one who has to fix it."

"Doritos, huh?"

"Spicy Taco flavor."

"Look, Trudy, I'm going to need a favor from you."

"I'm not done yet," she said.

I put my hands up, as if to say, *No offense, I come in peace.*

"That was my fellowship," she said, pointing at me. "Mine."

Trudy looked as if she was gearing up for a speech, but then, as if she'd heard her own words from afar and decided she didn't like their tenor, she stopped. "Okay, I'm done now," she said.

I waited a moment, to be sure she was through, then said, "This favor I need, it involves meeting Eggers, but the favor's for me."

Now she waited a moment, looking at me with her head cocked.

"Is that for real?" she asked. "That this fellowship's named after your mother?"

The fellowship was in honor of Janis, but I didn't correct her. I didn't answer at all. Trudy seemed to see in my eyes that this was a subject about which I would not lie. She shook her head, as if disgusted with herself, then disappeared into her dorm room and returned with a heavy scarf.

"Okay," she said. "Let's go."

We crossed the courtyard together, passing a solitary picnic table frosted with white. Trudy steered me around the blanket of snow that hid the sunken volleyball pit. Black slush lined the edge of the Honor Roll Parking Lot, and as we trudged through it, heading for the quad and Eggers' lodge, I couldn't help noting the natural grace and authority with which Trudy moved.

It would be less than ethical of me if at this point I did not confess that I believed Trudy was the ultimate female specimen. Intelligence and beauty aside, and from a strictly professional anthropological perspective, her body was perfectly evolved—tall frame, thick bones, and long muscles—a decathlete's physique. Her back flared into broad, square shoulders that framed a strong chest marked with small and unobtrusive breasts, and she carried just enough fat to optimize insulation and energy reserves without compromising mobility. I'd seen her body articulated once as she swam butterfly inside the jade cube of the Carney Aquatic Center, the points of her rotator cuffs launching each stroke, causing a wave that ran through pectorals, abdominals, and quadriceps before she cracked into a dolphin kick with the cablelike snap of her Achilles tendons. This was not the body of a gatherer. This was a person who could walk into any society, historic or prehistoric, and demonstrate abilities that were absolutely commanding. Of course I kept such thoughts to myself, lest I appear lecherous, or just plain old-fashioned.

We followed a thin column of woodsmoke toward Eggers' lodge, which lay in the darkness ahead. Janis was a shadow in the trees uphill from us, and the whole campus was quiet except for one soul. Out in the quad, a lone student was running the fitness track in the late cold. He jogged in his parka until he reached the pull-up station, where his breath plumed upward each time his chin crested the bar. After a certain number, he ran on.

Eventually, we reached the muddy, snowless circle that surrounded the lodge, and were met with the charring smell of an odd, sour meat. With a lift of the flap, Eggers emerged in a bizarre set of pantaloons and a huge serape of black fur. He saw we were looking at the strange hat of rabbit hides on his head. "It's not finished," he said. "Come on. I spend half my life gathering wood, and the other half melting snow."

"Here we are, Eggers," I said. "What's this favor?"

"It involves our new Clovis point," he said.

Trudy narrowed her eyes at him.

"There are no new Clovis points," she said. "Unless you think you're the one person in the world who can make them."

"I have a real one," Eggers said, "and we're going to use it." He ducked into his lodge and returned with a heavy spear, about two and a half meters long, the pink Clovis point bound to the end with some kind of thin fiber.

"Are you crazy, Eggers?" I asked. "This is an artifact. It's invaluable."

"No, sir," he said. "This is a tool, made to be used, and the only thing I still need to do for my dissertation is bring down a large herbivore. This is your idea, Dr. Hannah. This is straight out of *The Depletionists*. I don't care what your critics think. I read that book ten times. Your book is why I'm doing this." He gestured at his lodge, his clothes. "Don't you want to see if it's true, if this point can really do it?"

"There's no need," I told him. "These points have been found lodged in mammoth and mastodon bones. There is no doubt they kill."

"You can shoot an African elephant ten times with a rifle and it will only get angry," Eggers said, gesturing a little wildly with the spear. Trudy and I backed up a step. "Fifty years later, when that elephant dies of old age, it leaves bones with bullets in them. Maybe your mastodons were the ones that got away. You ever think of that? But how can you know, without re-search and testing?"

Trudy laughed. "And where are you going to find a mastodon?"

Eggers turned to me. "All I need is an animal that weighs at least a thousand pounds. Isn't that right, Dr. Hannah?"

"Well," I said, "I suppose."

My head was starting to spin a little. I kept seeing pink spears flying into the future—where would they land? Most of my colleagues believed climate change at the end of the Ice Age had killed off all the big animals in North America, which caused the Clovis to starve and disband; but I'd staked my whole career on the belief that a Clovis point could take down any animal. Yet Eggers was right—I'd never seen a kill.

"Where are you going to find a thousand-pound animal that no one's using?" Trudy asked. "Those guards at Hormel mean business. They'd grind you up and turn you into an Eggers burger."

"Don't you worry about Eggers burgers," Eggers said. "Eggers has this all planned out."

I put a hand on Eggers' shoulder. "Is this the bad news?" I asked. "You know, the bad part of the good-news/bad-news thing?"

"The bad news comes tomorrow," he said. "This is the celebration part." With that, Eggers began backing into the darkness of the quad.

Trudy and I stood there a moment, looking at each other.

"Did you see that Clovis point?" she asked. "A woman made that. I know it. It took her hours, sitting around a mineral deposit with her friends. She talked and told stories while her hands worked the quartz. She chose the material for its beauty, because this was her art, and the design was taught to her by her mother—the keeper of a thousand years of hunting technology."

While Trudy spoke, I pictured her hands working the quartz, holding the point up to the light to search for imperfections, then testing its edge with her thumb.

We both reached the same silent conclusion, then set out after Eggers, following his tracks in the snow, though the vaporous trail of his body odor left no doubt as to his course. By the time we reached the dean's garden, we were abreast of him.

Trudy stuck her hand out.

"Let's see this so-called spear," she said.

She inspected the spear by pointing it toward the moon and turning the shaft to see if it was straight. Then she examined the blade. "It smells like mint," she said.

"It does not," Eggers said.

"Is this dental floss?" she asked. "You tied this point onto the shaft with dental floss, didn't you?"

I was only half listening. In my head, I was animating Clovis points. They flew and flew, waves of them. What had seemed like abstractions were coming clear. I saw a spear fly from dark hands into a gleam of bright light before passing into the haze of its victim.

Trudy said, "Dental floss, unless I'm mistaken, is made from wax-infused monofilament, which is derived from modern polymers. Did the Clovis use petrochemicals, Dr. Hannah?"

"Listen," Eggers said. "Do you know how long it takes to dry and string catgut? I've done it. I know."

By now, we were in the Old Main's colonnade. Across the street was Parkton Square, and the locked gates of the Glacier Days carnival. Eggers neared the tall fence and appraised it.

With one hand, he shook the chain link, and a shower of ice beads rained down on him. He tried to climb it, but in fur booties could get no hold.

Trudy crossed to the gates and went to work on the lock that held the chain. "This is just a combo lock, like the kind for your school locker," she said. "It would be easier if I had my tools with me. I could just pop it open with a prybar."

Trudy knelt on the cold sidewalk and put her ear to the green-faced lock, while I looked through the fence to the dark carnival inside. From somewhere kept coming the keening of ravens, and though I couldn't be sure, I felt I saw a flash of black wings. The raven was a medium-sized bird, with a great curving beak that drove straight into a heavy brow, giving it a look of constant judgment. I can't think of many birds that were physically dangerous to humans, but to those with a guilty conscience, the raven could be a troubling omen.

"Voilà," Trudy said as the lock opened, and it wasn't until we were through the gate that the stillness of the place gave me the shivers. In the dark, all the funhouse faces were more personal, like people from your distant past. Each game seemed to stand waiting for its perfect customer, which wasn't me. The Hammer Blow sat ready for a stronger man, and the Gypsy dared me to purchase its dark fortune. In the moon, all the overdrawn devils and clowns seemed cut from maroon-and-blue plastic, and I wished someone would shut those ravens up.

Eggers led us down a stretch of midway bordered on both sides by shooting galleries. At counter after counter were rifles and pistols mounted on rods, all pointing into dark tents toward rows of bears who stood when shot, ducks who fell back into nothing, and wolves who would grab their asses and howl at the moon when plinked.

We passed darkened trailers that dealt in Indian fry bread and twin funnel-cake carts that folded up like campers, and then we came to a huge pile of the night's leftover popcorn, which had been thrown out in the snow. This is where the ravens were, pacing in the moon, gulleting down cold popcorn.

"God, I love popcorn," Eggers said. "That's one of the things I really miss."

"Maybe Doritos will come out with a popcorn-flavored chip," Trudy told him.

He said nothing, only steered us under the old roller coaster, the kind that packed up onto a couple of flatbed trailers. Its name was no longer visible, but Dragon or Sidewinder would be safe bets. Underneath, a lattice of shadows passed over our faces, and we could see the stains of oil that had dripped down the supports. When the light filtered down just right, you could make out the occasional flash of the nuts and washers that had worked themselves loose and now littered the ground.

Finally, Eggers came to a stop before a temporary corrugated shed the size of an aircraft hangar, hastily assembled on a bare parking lot. "Here we are," he said, and we all looked at the sign above the great sliding door. It read "4-H."

Inside, a single propane heater kept the room just above freezing, though the asphalt floor was certainly colder. The room was lined on both sides with pens of varying sizes, some with straw on the ground, and others with little shelters inside. Maybe half held animals. We walked down the row in the dim fluorescent lighting, stepping over the hoses that were wound everywhere to spray down the waste. A little llama came out of its shed and nuzzled up to the rail. Its pen had a large blue-and-yellow handicapped-parking icon on its floor, and the furry little guy seemed intent on sucking everyone's fingers. At the end of the room, where the heat barely reached, stood a pen larger than the others with what looked like a child's fort constructed in the back. There was a piece of masking tape affixed to the rail in front of us, and on it someone had spelled "Sir Oinks A Lot" in straggling letters.

"Oh, you're kidding me," I said. "This isn't right."

Eggers clapped twice and whistled.

Something rustled in the fort, and its tiny walls shook.

"This isn't happening," I told them. "This is a child's pet, that's a name a child would think up."

A giant brown-and-gray hog emerged from the fort, its head big as a beer keg. It was a pork-belly hog and must have weighed eleven hundred pounds. It snorted twice, and each time it exhaled, its white breath cleared circles of dust and straw from the floor. Its head floated, cranelike, from Trudy to Eggers to me.

Harder to describe than any bird is the pig. There was no animal quite like it. What defined it most were not its enormous dimensions, but the clack of its cloven feet on hard surfaces, the guttural horn of its squeal, the smack of its jowls bouncing as it walked, and the way the tugging weight of its face revealed the yellow undersides of its eyeballs. But what truly comes to mind when I think of the pig are sunsets over the river after the sky was blackened with the kerosened smoke of towering pyres of burning hogs. It's true that I haven't seen a pig in thirty years, but lately I have turned to petroglyph art in an attempt to document those events, and what I have discovered is that, despite its simple oblong shape, the pig is the most difficult figure to convey to a rockface.

Eggers bent over and touched his toes. Then he held the spear over his head with two hands, leaning forward and back, stretching side to side. Finally, he jumped up and down to get the blood going. "All in the name of science," he said.

"Wait a minute," I told him. "We should talk about this, we should realize what we're doing here. At least let's find some consensus."

I turned to Trudy for a dose of sanity, but there was a wild look in her eyes.

"No one's hunted with a Clovis point in twelve thousand years," she said.

Eggers added, "This is the hunt. This is what connects us to the ancient ones, to the lost peoples of the world."

Trudy touched my coat. "Look," she said, "I know your critics think the last chapter in *The Depletionists* is New Age–y, but when you say that the reason we are drawn to the artifact is to know, without judgment, the heart of another, I believe it. That's the whole reason I look at Paleolithic art. That's why I came here to study with you."

I took my glasses off and folded them. I rubbed my temples a moment.

"Okay," I said. "Okay."

"Wow," Eggers said. "We're joining the elect few."

"Yeah," Trudy added, "we're making history."

"Here you go, then," Eggers said, handing me the spear.

"Me? Wait a minute."

Eggers said, "It's your Clovis point, Dr. Hannah."

"I don't know how to throw a spear," I told him. "You're the one living in the Stone Age."

"That's right," Eggers said. "A pig gets killed with a twelve-thousand-year-old spear. Who do you think they're going to suspect? Yes, perhaps the authorities might consider the Paleolith living in the park."

"He's got a point," Trudy said.

"What was with the calisthenics, then?"

Eggers looked shocked. "We're all going to be running in a couple minutes."

I hefted the spear and watched as Sir Oinks A Lot took a lazy turn around the pen, probably looking for a newer, more comfortable place to sleep.

"This thing's heavy," I said.

"Choke up on your grip," Trudy told me.

Eggers pointed at the pig. "Aim just behind the shoulder blade. That's home to lung, liver, and heart. You'll get at least two out of three."

I took an extra puff off my inhaler, for luck, then backed up a couple of steps, then a couple more. I don't know why, but I scratched the soles of my shoes, one at a time, on the asphalt. I wiped a hand on my pants. The pig started to circle, the way a dog would before lying down, and I started to time my throw.

"Don't miss, Dr. Hannah," Trudy said. "That point's irreplaceable."

I ran at the pen and thrust my arm high, but my arm wouldn't let go.

I stood there with the spear still in my hand.

The truth came to me cold and swift: I was no hunter.

"Oh, give it here," Trudy said, loosening up her shoulders.

"Give the woman the spear," Eggers said. "She holds an all-military-school record in track and field."

"Trudy," I said, "we can't ask you to throw this spear. I'm a white male professor, and you, you know, you're an African American female student."

"Oh, Dr. Hannah," Trudy said, "you're so cute."

She took the spear from my flaccid grip, and Eggers winked at me.

Trudy hefted the weapon, felt its balance point, then raised it high.

"What's the bumper sticker?" she asked. " 'You can have my spear when you pry it from my cold, dead hands.' "

The pig cocked its head curiously.

Then it happened. Trudy rotated her body and, drawing back, charged a throw that began in the ball of her foot. The leg followed, the hip lifting, rotating the torso around so the arm whipped like a sling. The spear launched, and the follow-through was complete enough that it left her facing sideways, hopping on one foot.

Almost as quickly as it was thrown, the spear crossed the pen and landed with a great *thuk* that opened a gaping, pleated wound, from which escaped a gurgly hiss as the lung pushed and pulled air through the puncture. The handle of the spear bobbed with the breath of the hog, and with every little movement, the blade walked itself deeper into the cavity of the chest. The pig let out one faint whine before its front legs crossed, almost daintily, and it went down, rolling to its side so that its final breaths sent up mists of blood that speckled the wall a steaming pink.

Eggers looked stunned. He climbed over the rail and walked cautiously to the pig. He leaned over it. "Holy shit," he said.

"Wait," I called. At any moment, that hog could jump up and slay us all. If one thing was constant in the history of the world, it was the notorious danger of pigs. They were the bane of early Mesopotamia, and in African folklore there is no more dangerous beast. Even the Clovis could not handle them. The Clovis eradicated the American lion, the saber-toothed tiger, and the dire wolf, but the wild boar was one of the few animals to live through that age of eradication.

Trudy joined Eggers. She was still shaking out her arm from the throw as she approached the pig. She crouched above a pool of blood gelling against the cold asphalt. She reached for it.

"Don't," I murmured. "Think of the parasites, the trichinosis, the bloodworms."

Trudy placed her palm in the blood, then, dripping, showed it to me.

"This is the first art," she said. "This is the original ink."

On the wall of the shed, Trudy drew a horizon line in red. Below it, she fashioned a circle, the sun of the underworld. Above the line, she used her fingers to make a set of antlers, pointing down. I recognized the symbol, haunting and primordial. She drove around Parkton with it painted on the black hood of her beater GTO.

Eggers pulled a flake from his game bag and cut the spear point free of the shaft. He brought it to me and placed it bloody in my hands, still warm from the pig.

"Here you go, Dr. Hannah," he said. "One Clovis point, as promised."

Then Trudy came toward me, face flushed from the cold, hands red, that great staticky blue light of death around her, and I thought, *Yes*. Perhaps my father's rakish thinking had infected me, but my hands were shaking for her.

"Are you ready?" she asked, and when I nodded, we all started running.

In bed that night, I woke to a roar from the Missouri as a shearing expanse of ice broke away. It sent a wake underneath the whole ice sheet, so that, when the wave reached the shore, you could hear fifty-five-gallon drums leap from the frozen grip of the river as, one by one, everyone's docks cracked free. I knew a great ice raft, large as a lecture hall, was spinning its way downstream.

I sat up in bed, and slowly, by starlight, began to make out the dark tendrils of all the silent houseplants that hung in my room. I checked my bedside table, and, sure enough, there was the stained Clovis point from earlier, right where I'd set it — beside a plaster cast of my mother's leg, removed just before she left us for good. Though I hadn't heard from her in thirty years,

I felt pretty confident that, with the cast and maybe an X-ray of the break, I'd be able to identify my mother if I ever came across her.

Often when I couldn't sleep, I'd pick up that knee-high cast and trace the shape of my mother's calf, feel the shadows left by the fine bones in her feet, but tonight I reached for the Clovis point. The quartz was smooth and warm in the dark, and instead of its conjuring in my mind the story of a people older than civilization, I thought of Trudy. How natural this point had seemed in her hand, and with what kinship did she speak of its fashioner. Trudy seemed to know its song, and the shameful arousal I felt for her, for one of my students, as I replayed the way she launched that spear was eclipsed only by the horror of where it had landed.

Did the Clovis people know the glaciers were on the move? Did the dinosaurs comprehend the impending comet? Janis didn't know what the universe had in store. I heard the ice again, and imagined white rafts slowly floating down thousands of miles of river, a history of ice, and on these barges in my mind, I saw things and people, floating backward, away from me, into the dark. Our old dog Roamy was on one, and another was piled with the sagging boxes of Junior, index cards and notepads spilling into the current. I looked for Old Man Peabody, for Janis, for the father I used to know. Who floated by instead, alone on a piece of ice big enough for all of us, was my mother, frozen the way I last saw her, the way I would forever imagine her—in a pale-blue housecoat, holding a pale-blue handbag, leaning on aluminum crutches—and the farther she floated from me the less I was sure whether she was facing toward me or away. My imagination took a bird's-eye view as I attempted to follow her into the dark, flat landscape, cut only by the cold river of history. At the edge of sleep, I, too, was on the ice, riding it into darkness. I was not cold on this ice, only seized by the notion that if I floated far enough I'd ride the river back in time, back to the Pleistocene, a place where men and women lined the banks with pink spears. As I floated by, they shouted messages for me to deliver to their ancestors.

Chapter Two

I woke before dawn feeling unaccountably alone. The last of the moon was ghosting through the windows, and as my eyes came into focus, I expected to find myself in a distant and unknown place. Then I recognized the duck pattern of my sheets, realized I knew which dark doorway beyond my bed led to the closet and which to the bathroom. Houseplants materialized around me.

My hand was sore, the one I'd gripped the spear with, and I flexed it open and shut before pre-empting the alarm clock, which was set to go off any minute now. I was due to meet Farley, my old friend and lawyer, at the lake for the opening of the Glacier Days Ice Fishing Derby. The only reason, it occurred to me, to head out to a giant floating ice sheet, slip a silver hook into a cricket's chest, and then lower him into a trillion gallons of freezing water was to remind yourself of the true rarity of warmth in this world. With a thumb, I pressed my palm, and the bones in my hand felt vulnerable and nervy, the way your teeth do after a trip to the dentist.

I washed my face with warm water, rubbing my eyes, holding my breath to avoid the smell of pig on my fingers. I pulled some cold long johns from the dryer and, ducking under some hanging houseplants, ate a bowl of cereal under the kitchen light, my blizzard overalls hanging open to the waist. This is what thirty-nine-year-old professors did in the morning when their careers had basically tanked. I rinsed the sink when I was done, flossed one more time, and into a five-gallon fishing bucket tossed a few tilt-up rods, a handful of split-shot sinkers, and a thermos.

Outside, as I clomped down the stoop of University Village, the USSD faculty housing, I saw that I was mistaken—the faint light was not the last of the moon but a first glimpse of sun. Or maybe the two had traded places. All the other professors and lecturers were asleep as I crossed the courtyard, cutting through campus toward the lake. The new snow moaned under my boots, and I cut a sad figure in the cold—there were no other footprints in the powder, and the purple frost of my breath simply vanished into the brittle stars above.

I had a bucket in one hand, a sandwich in each pocket, and, crossing campus, the air sharp in my nose, I felt outfitted for a lifetime alone. Farley kept setting me up with local women from town—a string of evenings with single mothers that never got past pink wine, balsamic vinaigrette, and, from the other side of the couch, invitations to grab some thigh. Farley meant well, but I couldn't explain to him that if you're feeling lonely and misunderstood it's best to avoid other lonely people who misunderstand you.

Downhill was Eggers' camp, and though I couldn't make out the dark fur of his lodge, I could see a lazy strand of white smoke rising from it, which helped me locate Janis in the dark. Passing through some bare, knuckly tree trunks, I witnessed the quarry-black of my stepmother's granite memorial slowly separate itself from the early black of morning. I came round to face her. A web of ice had formed across the bronze, and with my forearm, I wiped until I could make out her puffy cheeks and the line of her cat glasses.

I don't know why I came out here and stood some mornings. I've seen other people speak to tombstones and urns and whatnot, and though the tears on their faces seemed genuine, it always left me feeling empty. But what else was there to do? What were my options?

"Hey," I said to Janis' plaque. Sometimes I told her how people were getting along now that she was gone, which more and more was "fine." Today, I asked her, "What did you think of my lunch with Dad?"

It was cold out, quiet. To keep the blood flowing, I marched in place, the snow creaking under my feet. I looked around to see if anyone might be watching. How stupid I must look from a distance, a lone figure hunched and shifting, taking counsel with himself.

"He doesn't seem to be making much progress," I said. "If I have to, I'll make like Aeneas, who slung his old man over his back and carried him out of the flames of Troy. Did I ever tell you that story?"

When most people spoke with the departed, they probably stuck to rhetorical questions, but I was trained to interrogate the dead, and it was hard for me to escape that, even if everything I asked was ridiculously stupid. But why ask questions that matter—*Where are you? Can you hear me? Are you alone?*—when the dead won't even offer a fishing forecast.

Artifact Number 2

I looked into the chilled bronze, trying to find some evidence of Janis, but those metallic eyes were fixed on the nowhere behind me. Where was the woman who made sure my father brought me souvenirs from wherever he traveled, the woman who helped me learn Latin, who fought my father over sending me to boarding school, who would never let him say a bad thing about my mother in front of me? Where was the woman who wouldn't stop apologizing, there at the end, for leaving me?

I grabbed my bucket. "Your plants are looking pretty good," was all I could manage without sounding too hollow to myself. "I'm going fishing with Farley, so I'll ask how things are down at the courthouse."

I turned into the snow, crossing the quad in just enough light to make out the edges of buildings. I passed the Liberal Arts Center, whose marble steps were worn by countless students, students whose hands had greased the rail a shiny black. I took no heart in the fact that they had all graduated and found their way in life. Rounding what was once the history building, I encountered a marble arch whose inscription from Santayana I'd read a thousand times: "Those Who Cannot Remember the Past Are Condemned to Repeat It." The school once offered a graduate degree in history, but this was now the agri-business building. After World War II, people simply lost their thirst for the past. There was a day, though, when students roamed this campus with books underarm like *Cradle of the Euphrates*, *The Last Days of Pompeii*, and Knuutsen's five-volume *Maya*.

Who today has read *The Chief Regrets of Wali al-Qu'utar*?

Herodotus, Aurelius—forgotten.

As I passed the empty hall, that Santayana quote began to make me angry. His words had once been my motto, but today they seemed a lie. I thought, Point to the book that will guide the way. Show me the story. Didn't life's real lessons come first-hand, and only once, so that, if you ever gained some wisdom, you'd never get another chance to use it? What man goes to war twice? Who has two mothers, dressed in blue, disappear into the snow, and who then loses two stepmothers? Can any person spend two lifetimes alone?

I turned the corner onto Central Green—there, beyond the final slope of campus, was the Missouri. Normally, white sheets extended far from the banks, so that it looked as if the snowy fields ran right out into the middle of the river, leaving only the creek of the central channel. But all the ice last night had indeed broken free, and this great bicep of water in the breaking light was sparkly black, as if the river cut through banks of pumice. The surface was flashing, roiled with eddies, enough that a stranger wouldn't know which direction it flowed. And there was an odd tincture to the water, unusual for winter, somehow purplish and ruddy. The color had the oily maroon of the tallow smoke that bellowed from the stacks above Hormel's rendering floors. The sight reminded me of a comet's coma, of its sooty, smoking ice, and in the distance, standing before this meteor tail of a river, I made out a lone nude figure.

I trudged downhill toward the water, my boots leaving long tracks in the snow, but I knew already it must be Eggers. I stopped and looked around to see if other people inhabited this world. I searched for dorm lights turning on, for cars humming over the bridge trestle, even for the contrails of jets crossing the sky, but there was no one.

Out on the dock stood Eggers, half lit by dawn, the clump of his skins on the pier timbers beside him. I thought he might be doing some kind of experiment on exposure. Then he jumped into the water. A spray rose in the air, and a moment later came the muted sound of the splash. I waited for that great whoop of icy pain to follow, but it never arrived. Eggers executed a few strong strokes, swimming in place against the current, and then he grabbed a ladder, letting his body swing round in the pull of the river. I couldn't make out the bar of soap he was using, but I could clearly see the milk of sudsy water that flowed away from him. Soap was a pretty clear violation of his nontechnology pact, but I understood his urge to scrub down. Killing that pig had made me feel dirty, too. I decided to leave Eggers to his own conscience. A morning of ice fishing with Farley, I hoped, would help me with mine.

The river trail is a path that originally linked USSD and Parkton College to Lewis and Clark Lake, a mile or so upstream, so students could shortcut up to swim and row. Throughout the summer after my mother left, I practically lived along the water's edge: during the hot days, I'd race down this hill on blocks of ice, sometimes making it to the water, usually careening past couples who lay back in the high grass, shorts turning green as they lazily kissed and slapped mosquitoes from each other's legs. Afternoons brought bowfishermen who stalked through the cattails along shore for the great carp who wallowed there, and groups of old people who pointed canes at particular birds before they all lifted their field glasses in unison. My mother would be coming home soon, I figured, and until then, I meant to run a little wild.

My mother would be coming home soon, I was told and told, and when that didn't happen, Janis appeared, and the three of us would stroll down to the water's edge after supper, Dad swinging a lantern whose mantles hissed the way. Photos from those days show my face fixed in a sour, sullen anticipation. The only thing that would lift my mood was when, in the evening, we bought a brick of fireworks and strolled down this path, waiting for the river to flash with sunset, after which we'd skip rockets off the water's surface, bouncing Black Cats and Roman candles in knee-hops across the river, and occasionally depth-charging a floral mortar that would, before thumping up a smoky mist, flash yellow-gray below. Those were Janis' favorites—that faintly glimpsed percussion, before the water shocked white, gave her more satisfaction than any spray of color.

But now, as I walked up the slushy path, everything seemed different. The trail gradually wandered from the river and rose with the levee toward the lake. Gone were elm trees that had lined the walk. Gone were the benches under them. Where was the spring I used to drink from, and the footbridge over it? The whole idea of a path seemed obsolete, meant for families that no longer existed.

Soon, the rush of the spillway was all you could hear, and to keep walkers from slipping into the outfall below, an epoxy-green handrail appeared, though now it was glazed with ice. I had almost climbed to the level of the lake, and there was now a view. From this height, the trail I was on looked more like a primitive highway that connected a hog-processing plant, a prison, and an expanse of concrete that ran the last great North American river through the jackscrews of modernity. The irony was that these were the best spots to fish: the dam churned up all the rich nutrients from the bottom of the lake so that huge walleye and pike lurked just beyond the spillways, and down-hill from Club Fed was the spot to cast for smallmouth bass, because the runoff from all the prison's fancy fertilizers supported thick reed beds along the banks. And then there was Hormel, whose underwater pipes carried animal waste out into the middle of the Missouri. That's where you caught channel catfish, otherworldly in size, some big and slick as stillborn calves.

But Farley and I were perch fishermen. The perch is a small fish that avoids the light and is only vulnerable in the delirium of winter cold, so you need to go out early, and run your lines deep. The perch weighs in around a pound, so there is no mythic "lunker" out there. In that way, fishing for them is a lot like spending your time flint-knapping Clovis points, the secret craft of which is long forgotten. Because no Clovis chipper has ever cried "Eureka" and no fisherman ever stuffed and mounted a perch, both endeavors foster a certain intimacy with failure. Fishing, anthropology, and indoor gardening seem to exist completely in this space between tedium and futility.

The climb became steeper, the trail more slippery. As I

neared the concrete abutments, gusts of mist flashed over the cap-wall and raced down to frost my glasses. I stopped to puff my inhaler, and you could taste the ozone coming off the turbine generators. They used to repeat a story when I was a kid, a tale about a man who fell in the concrete while they were building the dam, and was entombed alive because for some reason they couldn't stop pouring the cement. It was so-and-so's father who fell in. No, someone else would say, it was so-and-so's. I'm pretty sure the story was apocryphal, but when I looked at those deep, gray walls I always pictured that human bubble, caught mid-tumble within.

Looking down upon the town—the snow-plowed streets, a frozen Ferris wheel, the prison on a hill that would become my home—I became nostalgic, for everything, even the Hormel plant, whose furnace bricks would glow white-hot before the year was out. I can fall, as with the wave of a watch, this easily into the soupy stupor of reverie. I have come to believe, after a life of research and personal observation, that there are two fallacies to being human, one great paradox, and three crimes. The first crime against existence is hope. After that great savager of life, the second crime is nostalgia, generally a lesser offense. Anthropology will teach you there's no such thing as the good old days, but hope—hope drives death's getaway car.

I turned my back on this town and headed for the ice. I skirted the dam's control room and climbed the cement stairs that led over the floodwall, then negotiated an embankment of stacked boulders—bucket out for balance—that led down to the Lewis and Clark Lake. I'll tell you this: When the South Dakota wind kicks up, it'll take your back and, with an elbow around your throat and heels in your kidney, it'll ride you like a mule. But if that wind blows across miles of frozen lake, driving dry snow and blades of ice, it'll first make a chump of you—whistling in your armpits, doing laps around your belly, snapping the back of your scrotum—before the real hurt begins: the dry cuts, tongue swell, lip peel, and eye freeze.

I set out across the ice, baby-stepping the slick spots and holding my arm up against sharp flurries of wind-driven snow that tail-chased my vision. Ahead was a village of wooden warming huts staggered along the ice, each strategically placed above what some fisherman believed must be a point of interest for fish on the lake bottom below. When I was young, you'd see men huddled around their holes as if warming themselves around campfires. Now you only saw fancy huts that men had towed out with snowmobiles, each one surrounded by a half-dozen ice holes with tilt-up fishing rigs. Through the wind, I made out my first glimpse of humanity, aside from Eggers, that morning: as I walked through the field of huts, men took turns emerging to scoop newly formed ice out of their holes, and in the flashes when their doors were open, I caught bits of country music and talk radio, saw men slouched toward the blue glow of televisions. One figure stared religiously into the pulsing screen of a fish finder.

Ahead, only one shadow sat exposed to the elements, and this was Farley Crow Weather, whom I'd known off and on nearly all my life, and who'd recently helped me settle my step-mother's estate. There are only two things you need to know about Farley.

The first is that, in general, he is impervious to cold. It was a different story for me. The wind buffed my scalp to brass, then stropped my ears sharp. Walking amid the scramble of blowing snow, I dropped my head, observing that it was cold enough to freeze the ice clear and colorless—there was enough morning light now to illuminate clouds of lake algae glinting under the surface.

There used to be a fish out here called a white sauger, though they always looked pinkish to me. They loved the light and took little interest in people—if you walked clear patches of ice like this on a cold afternoon, you'd see their moony humps cruising the underside of the ice, occasionally stopping to pick at bits of food trapped in the crags beneath your feet. It was a dopey sort of fish, slow-moving, with fat cheeks and small lips, and when I was about eleven, a couple of jokers discovered that by lowering giant red lights through the ice they could net sauger by the bushel. In one season, they cleaned the lake out, and I haven't heard of one since.

I was endlessly fascinated by this nightly scene, and I con-fess I wasn't thinking about the fates of fish. Each night, after dinner, I'd bundle up and climb the flood levees to watch these fellows work. They coordinated all variety of pulleys and cords before lowering an immense assembly into the dark water, while I waited for the moment they hit the power.

I suppose there was a reason I was drawn to this sight. I was antsy for adulthood to begin. I hoped that when it did I would be dependent on no one, that the weak half of me—the half that needed, that felt something was always missing, that feared anything good could end, without notice or reason— would simply calve away. So I believed my father when he said my body would one day change, and after that, it was only a matter of following instincts. Life was something to squirm through until, easily and suddenly, a switch was thrown and a light came on. Sitting on a winter levee, I was never surprised by this moment. Instead, it felt both ancient and familiar: the entire lake would ignite a luminescent red, deep and glowing, crusted like lava, and it felt like proof of the primal scenes my science books had promised, as if I were witnessing the original cooling of the earth.

Farley hailed me. He was sitting on an upturned five-gallon bucket with an official fishing-derby entrant number pinned to his sleeve. There was an extra bucket sitting there. I'd brought my own bucket, and I wondered if he was expecting company.

"Hey, where ya been?" Farley asked in that accent of his. "Fish're up."

"Took the scenic route," I told him. "How was your big date?"

"What, the other night? I don't know what I was thinking, taking a court-appointed psychologist to dinner. That morning, when I had her on the stand, I thought we had some chemistry. I thought she was giving me more than testimony. But I spent half the night answering questions about my mother, and all I got in return was a dream interpretation."

We sat side by side, staring at six holes, the derby limit, spread out before us. Each hole had a tilt-up reel that would raise a little flag when a fish was on the line. Every few minutes, someone would have to get up and ladle new ice out of the holes.

"You told her your dreams, on a first date?"

Farley shrugged. Below the promontory of his crew cut, his

face was composed of subtle plateaus, capable of evoking a great range of emotion that you rarely saw. It wasn't stoicism, but an acknowledgment that most of what people said was unimportant, and this endeared him to me. And, from time to time, amid some chitchat, the planes of his face would suddenly soften, and you'd realize you'd just said something that mattered.

"Just the fish dream. I guess it wasn't even a date, was how it turned out."

Farley said this, then got up to clean holes. He scooped out the ice chips and dumped them on the icy mounds that formed next to each hole. It sounds like a routine chore, but Farley had his method. First, he'd place his feet wide and bend down, so his face was near the hole. He'd scoop, then peer deep into the water, scoop, then peer, as if he were removing a veil of less transparent water, skimming off the curds of the physical world, so he could behold a sweeter one below. This brings me to the second thing you need to know about Farley:

He believed the king of all fish lived at the bottom of our lake. This fish was small and either golden or orange, depending on the dream. It could speak, was full of wisdom, and would tell you your secret story, as long as you asked its permission before catching it. I didn't quite know what to make of all this. It wasn't a Native American thing, as far as I could tell. Farley said that when he was a boy his mother used to tell him the story of this fish, and after she left he started dreaming of it. I admit I like the idea that we have secret stories, that they might be revealed if we're patient and polite. I asked Farley once, if we were living in another town, fishing on another lake, would his golden fish live there? After thinking about it, Farley said probably.

Farley moved to scoop out another hole, and I pulled my thermos out of the bucket. Unscrewing the metal lid made a dry squeak with each twist, sort of a haspy sound. Before I had it off, the crickets in Farley's bait bucket were answering. They were inside a folded paper takeout carton, the kind with the wire handle you get at Chinese places, and for a moment, I played my thermos lid like an instrument, listening to them sing.

"Out of curiosity," I said, "I was wondering, the other day, what are the laws on killing animals? You know about that stuff?"

Farley looked at me, scooping. "Well. It's illegal to harm a companion animal, though technically they're still property."

"What about over at Hormel?"

Farley came and sat down. "You can't cause intentional suffering to any animal, even livestock, though a violation at Hormel would be USDA jurisdiction, rather than a criminal infraction."

"But you can kill livestock, legally?" I asked, filling a plastic cup of coffee for Farley, the metal one for myself.

"Sure."

"What about someone else's livestock?"

Now Farley eyed me with interest. "I'd have to look it up," he said. "Could be theft, could be rustling, I suppose."

I took a sip of coffee and set it down, trying to seem off the cuff.

"Let's say the pig just got sick, no one knows how it died."

"What pig?"

"Any pig, a hypothetical pig."

"Is there something you want to tell me?" Farley asked.

"What about hunting?"

"Hunting livestock? For sport?"

"Forget that. Let's say a wildcat, a big puma, comes and kills the pig."

Farley nodded. "That could be an act of God."

"Okay. Now we're getting somewhere. Let's say there's a wild man, and he's from a land far away, and he doesn't know our laws, and —"

Farley lifted his hand. "And you were just curious if this strange traveler could legally murder a hypothetical pig? This 'wild man' wouldn't be a student of yours, would he?"

I got up to scoop ice.

"What's he gone and done now?"

"Nothing," I said. I waved the scooper. "What?"

"You fool." Farley said, "That kid has all of you smoked, your whole university. You're gonna give him a Ph.D. in camping. My grandfather was living the Old Way even when I was a kid. And he didn't smell, eh? You know I caught your boy

Eggers drinking out of a hose once, right there on the court-house lawn. My paw-paw didn't drink from any hose."

I asked, "Did your paw-paw teach you the Old Way?"

"No," Farley admitted.

In the distance, a flag went up near one of the fishing huts, but no one came out. And far beyond that, I saw a Corvette, its yellow paint bright against the snow, appearing and disappearing as it negotiated the turns and switchbacks in the hills between town and the marina.

"So what was the interpretation of your dream?" I asked.

I reached for my coffee cup, but it had frozen to the ice.

Farley answered. "She said my dream was easy, that it was about litigation. The fish is the jury. I have to lure the jury on, persuade it to take the bait, and then it will speak the truth. The fish is gold because I value the law."

"What do you think?"

"She wasn't for me."

My eyes followed the Corvette. Sure enough, it was making its way past the fish hatchery, past Mr. Chippy's Fish Ship, and finally to the marina, where it drove down a steep boat ramp and out onto the ice. Lifting a hand against the glare, I tracked my father as he raced across the lake, leading a spinning tunnel of snow.

The tires drummed over old ice-fishing mounds, rocking the chassis back and forth, making the motor sound breathy. The wheels stopped spinning a hundred yards away, yet the car floated, tires brooming snow off the ice, all the way over to us. I'd bought that car, the classic '72 with the huge spoiler, to celebrate the publication of *The Depletionists*, and now, as it careened to a halt before me, making the ice crinkle and talk, the ironies were too much to take.

Dad revved the engine before killing it, and as he was climbing out, he grabbed a motel bedspread off the passenger seat. He wore the same mustard vest as he had yesterday.

"Jeez, you look like hell," Farley said. "You sleep?"

"Christ, it's cold," Dad said. He draped the bedspread over his head and bundled up, so only his face and black dress shoes showed from under the gold floral pattern.

I studied my car, beyond extravagant on the ice. Now we

looked like all the other convenience-addicted jerks out here. Plus, there'd be an oil stain on the ice when we left. There were several empty bottles of airplane liquor visible on the dash. "You didn't hook up with a stewardess, did you?" I asked.

Dad didn't answer. He grabbed Farley's extra bucket and dumped all the tackle out, including the carton of crickets, which fell open. Upturning the bucket, Dad took a seat as a hundred black crickets sprang from us. They got about three hops before they paused and then froze in place.

"Great one," Farley said.

Dad grunted at Farley. "Shouldn't you be defending freedom about now?"

Farley said, "I'm taking the Tribe to court this afternoon."

I looked at Farley. "I thought you wanted to go to work for the Tribe?"

"I do," Farley said. "But they don't want some Indian defending them. They want hotshots from New Jersey, white guys in tight suits."

"So you're suing the Tribe?"

Farley bent to grab his scooper off the ice. "I got to get their attention," he said, and walked over to the holes, quiet and serious.

Dad said, "What's your case about?"

"It's a good one," Farley answered, scooping. "There's this older woman, in a motorized wheelchair. Every day she rides it over to the casino to gamble — slots mostly, and some keno. Fortune is with her, and she wins most every day. People start rubbing her wheelchair for luck before they play. It's just superstition, but the casino gets nervous about these things. Anyway, she up and dies, and her grandson gets this chair. So he picks up right where she left off and starts driving this thing to the casino. The Tribe's like, No way, you're no cripple, and they won't let him in the door. It's a clear civil-liberties violation. My opening remarks to a white jury will be about a once-proud people and so on. Those Jersey lawyers are going to shit."

"Sounds like the story of Senival," I told them.

Dad and Farley were quiet. I couldn't tell if this was out of reverence for the stories I sometimes told, or an effort to not encourage me.

"Senival was a warrior king, and before the third and final battle for Scali, he asked the oracle what sacrifice was needed for victory. In those days, wars took years, and soldiers brought their wives, kids, goats, everything. Senival brought his mother, who got sick on the way, and she was like this bad omen. Her wails filled the camp, and the moaning was driving everyone crazy. A cloud of death hung over the campaign, and the oracle was clear: Senival had to—"

"Oh, don't tell me," Farley said. He meant it.

Dad said, "He had to kill his mother?"

We all shook our heads in disbelief.

"What happened?" Dad asked.

"Senival was victorious, of course. He enjoyed a long and prosperous life and turned out to be a pretty good king, too. But when Dante and Virgil visit him in the fifth circle of the *Inferno*, Senival's torment is to drag his ancestors into hell with him, connected by a chain of umbilical cords."

I paused while Dad and Farley tried to wrap their heads around that picture.

"Where does the chain end?" Farley asked.

"It doesn't," I told them. "It goes mother-child-mother-child, all the way to infinity."

Farley's face slumped, and I immediately felt bad. It struck me that I hadn't been thinking how his mother had left them when he was young. He'd been raised by French Catholics who, in the way of life skills, taught the girls to sew, trained the boys to fix shortwave radios, and provided them all with Canadian accents.

Farley said, "It would be something, though, to see all your ancestors lined up like that. You could see what manner of people they were, who you took after."

An ironic smile crossed Dad's face. "So the fathers didn't go to hell, huh?"

"Not because of their sons," I told him.

Eventually, a little flag popped up, and Farley went over to reel in the fish. I had sunk into a mood, and I started to feel bad for that fish. I imagined its point of view—feeling the draw of a silver hook on an unseen line that pulled toward a circle of light. What perch wouldn't contemplate the afterlife: Farley's face, appearing walrusy, gleams down through a hole in a sheet of blue, broken only by the great shadow of a golden, winged vehicle, waiting amid a field of deliciously helpless crickets to whisk you away.

While Farley reeled in the tugging line, I tried to imagine the afterlife of crickets, but, looking at their black husks lying crisped on the ice or flipping in the wind, I couldn't come up with anything. I stood and picked up my bucket. I didn't have to teach just yet, but I suddenly didn't want to be around when Farley landed that fish and, before the skin froze solid, scaled it alive.

"I'll see you guys," I said.

"Take 'er easy, eh," Farley said.

My father, nodding off in the cold, perked up. "I'll run you back."

A man couldn't look sadder than sitting on a bucket, wrapped in a gaudy, snow-dusted motel blanket, making a spectator sport of ice fishing. How pathetic his hours must be since Janis died if this counted as living. "No thanks," I said, "I'll just catch you later."

By the time I'd climbed below the dam, I was sadder than I'd been all day. I stopped again at the spillways, the green safety rail now dripping in the morning sun, and I turned to regard the dam. The wall of concrete stood giant and blank as a drive-in movie screen, and I imagined the dam was made of ice, that instead of cement there was a curving window of ice, clear as glass, and my vision could penetrate straight into the lake. I looked deep into the standing water, ice-hued and shot through with beams of light from fishing holes, my eyes swimming like fishes that roved the dark channels.

My vision followed a long, submerged valley, then narrowed into a dramatic, dim canyon whose floors were littered with car axles and upturned outboard motors. A rusty shopping cart stood sentinel over grounds on which people after people had documented their lives with petroglyphs: spanning the walls were hands, palms open, carved one after another, a whole history of hands. A herd of bison, suggested merely by the curves of their humps, ran beneath a spear, in mid-air above them. A peccary was carved on his back, legs up, spine twisted in pain. Higher on the rockfaces, above it all, were spirals, chipped deeper in the rock, holes in the sky to the next world.

Farther up the canyon, way ahead in the water, I saw a flash of gold, layered and shimmery, as if off many scales, and amid the cold and dark, this was clearly the light of the living. Like eyeshine glimpsed on a night's drive along a country road, you know when something's alive and interested in you. The gold flashed again, more faintly, then was gone, and I was left only with the sensation of having been seen.

Back at the university, life seemed so normal as to appear foreign. The sky was clear and sunny, the wind subsiding. Students wandered campus with their hair exposed—parka hoods hanging loose against their backs, unneeded. I walked past a couple students puffing menthol cigarettes as they hung colorful crepe-paper decorations on the kiosks, and ahead, near the anthropology building, young people had gathered in some kind of forum.

When I got closer, though, I saw the students were circled around a large brown van, illegally parked below my office. The van was extended, windowless, and the thing that you immediately noticed, aside from the yip of little dogs inside, was the way it was weighed down, the rear tires almost rubbing the wheel wells. The nose of the van seemed almost to levitate. Then I walked round to the front of the vehicle and saw what had drawn the students' attention.

The van's front windows were slathered with blood, and inside, a whole brood of furry lapdogs were going wild. They leapt over the captain's chair, running along the dash and gauges, and the dogs were soaked in blood, their fur syrup-streaked, their whiskers drooping with it. One lapdog was desperately pawing red streaks on the glass, so that the driver's window was greasy with a thick, dirty paste.

This dog looked into my eyes, its baby-sized tongue darting in excitement as its tiny breaths pompommed the window. Was it begging for help, or wild with savage frenzy? What had someone done to these poor miniaturized beasts? All I knew was this: dogs arose here on the North American plains during the Eocene epoch, and they managed to get along just fine in the twenty-eight million years before they finally met a creature named *Homo sapiens*. If dogs had an afterlife, I hoped for their sake it was void of humankind.

In my office, a sheriff's deputy was inspecting artifacts on my desk. Though his back was to me, I instantly recognized his incredible physique, even through a winter uniform. He was a tiny man, about five foot one, but with a brawny torso and powerful, knotty forearms. His small hand passed over the items in my flint-knapping kit and landed on an antler-handled adze. He picked it up, swung it a couple of times, and seemed surprised when a hanging trailer of ivy fell to the floor. He turned the tool in his little fist, and I remembered the strength of those bully hands. This was Gerry, my nemesis from Mactaw High, though back then he was "Chief Gerry."

The Mactaw People were eradicated by either the Mandan or the Arikara—each claimed the honor, in the days before they, too, were eradicated. After Parkton's city councilmen bulldozed the Mactaw's burial grounds to build our school, they paid tribute to the land's former tenants by preserving their likeness in the form of a mascot. "Chief Gerry" was famous for his ballgame antics, which included the War Whoop Kickoff Run, a Flaming Spear routine, and the ever-popular Firewater Dance, in which Gerry stumbled over to the other team's bench, dropped his buckskin breeches, and mooned them.

And here he was in my office. Small though Parkton was, I hadn't seen him in probably a decade. I looked at Gerry's blue jacket, a size too large, then eyed his snub-nosed pistol.

"Hey, Gerry," was all I could muster.

Gerry turned, adze in hand. "Hey, Hanky," he said. "Man, is this thing sharp. You could kill someone with this. What's with all the plants?"

From below rose the constant yipping of dogs, but Gerry seemed not to notice.

"What can I do for you?" I asked Gerry.

"Dang, how long has it been, Hanky? Sheriff Dan and I

were just talking about you—that got me telling all kinds of stories from the old days. I see you keep a tomahawk on your desk. *Go, Tomahawks.*"

"It's an adze," I said.

"Sure it is," Gerry said, smiling. "Gosh, remember how you used to slick your hair down?"

"People don't call me Hanky anymore."

He smiled. "Remember how you were the only guy in the Hot Rod Club without a hot rod?"

"Times have changed," I told Gerry.

His laughter subsided. "I suppose they have," he said.

Over a hail of dog yapping, I said, "I'm pretty busy right now, if you don't mind."

Gerry glanced at the fishing bucket in my hand. "I'm sure your time's important," he said, "so I'll get right to it. I was just over at Glacier Days with Sheriff Dan, and he has one sad little girl on his hands. Sheriff Dan said you were the only one who could help."

All day, a spear had been hovering in my mind, and now it floated past me, sailing toward the Parkton courthouse, poised to land at the feet of a judge whose every pronouncement over the years had been recorded by Janis and rebutted by Farley, a courtroom where a small, weeping girl would learn that I'd conspired to murder her hog.

I felt a little light-headed. I needed my inhaler. Gerry gave me a concerned look.

"Hey, sorry about the hot-rod joke," he said. "You're not still sore about high school."

He stepped forward, reaching up as if to pat my shoulder. I took a step back. This little guy looked unassuming, but I knew better. During football games, he'd run the field in his headdress, swinging a giant tomahawk, executing incredible gymnastics—successive back springs strung together with double flips, sailor rolls, and pommel leaps higher than you could believe. This guy could be on your back in a heartbeat.

"Look," Gerry said, "high school's ancient history. We're mature adults now. I'm not the kind of guy who goes around sticking people in cafeteria tubs anymore."

A chorus of howls rang out. Irritated, Gerry opened the window. "Shut up," he shouted.

Below, students backed away from the van.

"McQueen better not be getting into my evidence," Gerry said.

He lifted his eyebrows and mimed the sharpening of a knife.

"I'm going to perform a little autopsy," he said, in a braggy, conspiratorial way.

"So—those are your dogs?" I asked.

"If you can get McQueen to shut up," Gerry said, "then they all shut up."

"McQueen?"

"You know, Steve McQueen from *The Great Escape*," Gerry said. "McQueen's my stud. Can't breed him fast enough. This batch is headed to the airport right now."

"What are you talking about?" I asked. "Fast enough for what?"

"What planet are you on, Hanky? You haven't heard of *Impossible Journey*?"

"Is that a movie?" I shook my head. "Didn't they turn the theater into a gun range?"

Gerry couldn't tell if I was joking or what.

"You've never been to the outlet mall?" Gerry asked. He was gesturing all over the place. "There's a brand-new multiplex out there. *Impossible Journey* is showing on half the screens. My ex–old lady's kids are crazy for this movie. It opens with a circus plane crashing in Canada, and these little dogs have to make it all the way back to Orlando. But an evil French fur-trapper catches the dogs and makes them drag this miniature sled piled high with traps and icy with blood. All these Pomeranians have are their tattered and burned circus uniforms to keep them warm. I'm telling you, when the little ones see those sad stripes and polka dots, they bawl their eyes out. I bought a dozen of these dogs through the mail the next day. Right away, I sold four to the ex–old lady. Covered my costs and—bang!— I'm in with the kids again."

Gerry went on and on about his Pomeranian mill, but I was in a daze. I know you can't unthrow a spear, but in my mind, I was running the lawns and streets of Parkton, racing across intersections and tennis courts, in the open door of the library, running through stacks of books before leaping out an open window, running until I ran up the steps of the courthouse, into the rotunda, where I hoped to catch my own spear.

"Hey, are you listening?" Gerry asked.

I had to sit down.

Gerry came up and patted me on the cheek. "Lighten up, Hanky," he said, smiling. "I didn't mean to pull your chain about the old days. Me and Sheriff Dan just want you to explain this."

Gerry took out a napkin and handed it to me. On it was drawn a horizon line. Below the line was a circle, the sun of the underworld. Above it was a set of antlers, pointing down.

I slumped in my high-back chair, a row of *The Depletionists* staring at me.

"Sheriff Dan just wants to know if this thingy on the napkin is Indian."

"I don't understand," I said.

"It's an Indian symbol, right?"

I shook my head. "You mean, is its origin Native American?"

"A simple yes will do," Gerry said, then leaned forward, smiling. "I can't discuss a case in progress, but . . ." He mouthed, *Gangs.*

Gangs? I mouthed back.

"An Indian gang. There've been other signs. Beer runs. Vandalism. Some serious joy-rides. All the trouble you'd expect with this new Indian casino."

I sat there, shaking my head *I don't believe it,* Gerry nodding *Believe it.*

"Well, I've got all I need here," Gerry said.

"Wait a minute," I said. "Just hold on here."

"Gotta go," he answered, sharpening an imaginary knife again. "Lunchtime."

Gerry turned to leave. He began climbing through the boxes that blocked the exit. But then a thought seemed to strike him. He looked back at me. "Hey, before, when I said 'autopsy'—you didn't think I was going to do an autopsy on a person, did you?"

"No, no," I assured him.

He was standing on a box of pluvial-silt studies from local late-Pleistocene lakes. It gave him the stature of a full-sized man. He asked, "Then what did you think I was talking about?"

I had to think fast. "I thought it was a metaphor," I said.

Gerry cocked his head. "Right," he said, "a metaphor."

Because of an interdisciplinary program in place at the university, my department forced me to teach an occasional class in a related field. I was currently instructing Pop Culture, a course I interpreted as "popular culture through the ages." We were doing a unit on mid-glaciation lithic figures of the proto-Inuit, and things weren't going so well. Gerry had rattled me a little, so my lecture was off, and before dissension set in, I decided to show some slides.

The projector's rotary tray dropped fertility figure after fertility figure into the light, and I did not narrate the stories behind images I hoped would speak for themselves. On the screen flashed a palm-sized female idol, all breasts and buttocks and belly, the ivory worn dark from rubbing. Next flashed a blackened birthing totem that had, at some point in the last twelve thousand years, been burned. Then came the image of a kneeling woman, etched in obsidian, her almond eyes lowered in contemplation of her swollen abdomen.

At this same time, three days a week, Trudy taught her Arc-Intro across the hall from me. We both conducted class with our doors open, and though the wooden floors in this building had been replaced with carpet, and the plaster ceiling was now acoustic tile, I occasionally made out bits of her lecture, noted the tone of her voice when her teaching grew passionate, heard when her students chuckled at her jokes.

As the frames silently clicked forward, I began pacing, keeping an ear tuned for Trudy while timeless female forms lit my room in their advance and retreat. The projector was on auto-repeat.

"Notice how sexuality and maternity are captured in the same image," I said to my students when they'd seen enough images to note patterns. "Also observe," I continued, "how small they are. This is personal, portable, perhaps even mass-produced art. This is the art of a people on the move, a people who, in only a few centuries, traversed three thousand miles of Siberian and Aleutian coastline before populating North America by shooting the gauntlet through the two largest glaciers of the late Pleistocene. Now, that's an impossible journey," I added, trying to sound hip.

"How come the carvings didn't get more realistic?" a student asked, a young man in back.

It was hard for me to keep their names straight.

"They're more difficult to make than you think," I said. "But what's important here is the conservation of culture. These people had a belief system that worked, and their art expressed those beliefs. Experimentation in art happens when old systems of meaning fail and new forms are needed."

I paused in the light, the pink marble of a sleep goddess projected on my chest.

This young man cleared his throat and spoke again.

"I understand what you're saying, Dr. Hannah, about their beliefs staying the same. I just think they'd get better at carving. You're always saying those people are no different than us. Well, I'm a music major, and after the fiddle became popular, we had the Stradivarius within a hundred years."

Another voice came from the back of the class, an older man's. "What Brad's talking about is simple progress," he said.

"Who are you?" I asked.

"I'm Brad's father," he said.

I went over and turned on the lights. "How long have you been here?"

"Since the beginning," he said.

"Of the semester?" I asked.

Everyone laughed.

Brad's father continued: "I think what Brad's trying to say is that these fertility people don't show any signs of progress, which is what sets us apart from the more primitive cultures. There's a tribe in Borneo that hasn't even discovered fire, and, you know, we've been to the moon."

I stopped the slide projector and wound the cord while I took a good look at Brad's father. He wore a polo shirt and a gold necklace, and you could tell that, despite his hard features, he'd led a soft life. I headed for the lectern, and the students groaned as I placed a foot casually on the podium's rung. They knew what was coming.

"That is a thoughtful contribution, sir, but I would modestly propose in response that the concept of progress is a lie. Certainly, technology improves, but the state of being human is constant. When it does change, well, we'll be something other than human. It is because we don't change that the Grecian urn speaks to us."

My blood was up. I flexed my hand open and closed, then glanced into the hall to see if, in the sliver of her class that I could view from my lectern, Trudy was visible. She wasn't.

"Of the twin fallacies of humanity," I continued, "the first is that people invariably believe they live in times of great change and significance. Eighteenth-century England believed it. The pharaohs believed it. Turn-of-the-millennium America believes it. How about living through a great plague—say, 1348 Europe or 1521 Mayan Mexico. Is that significant? Perhaps a few centuries of bondage for a people? A hundred-year war?"

Brad's father sat with his arms crossed.

"Verdun," I announced. There was no response. "Birkenau, Bhopal, Black '47."

I eased forward to one of the front desks, which always seemed to be empty, and rested a foot on its seat. "Pompeii," I said. "Apartheid. If these are times of great significance, why isn't the hair standing on your arms? And if the Trail of Tears is not such a time, then what is? I ask you—can anything that happens to one part of humanity change the sum of the whole?"

I whipped off my glasses for effect, a trick they were used to. A lone student produced an exaggerated yawn, and in the blur of the room, I couldn't make out the culprit. True, I was getting off the topic with my world tour of tragedy, but the students looked ignorant and scared, the desired effect, so I rolled on past plagues and wars and lectured on torturous despots and senseless disasters.

Yet, after a while, the real truth became evident—the fates of strangers had little impact on us, and I was angry not because I felt connected to anyone in Dresden or Hiroshima, but because I'd witnessed a single disappearance and a single death, and I'd been changed by them. My pity pony wanted to trot the ridge where my pain was visible to those who inhabited both the valley of friends and the mountain of strangers. But you can't just quit a rant. I'd started something and, like it or not, I had to play it out. I described the backstroke we cut before the waterfall of time, paid some lip service to the bellows of injustice, and finally sketched out the raven of Regret.

I shook the podium one last time, and, before dismissing class early, admonished them: "All life offers us is the moment. There is only the ravishing spontaneity of being, then nothing more. Moments, people—enhearten them, for they are fleeting."

We all waited to see if I was done, including me.

Then someone asked, "Is that going to be on the final?"

I was the first one out of the room. A queasiness tightened my ribs, and I stared at my feet as I passed Trudy's door. But I couldn't resist glancing in. The desks, as I'd imagined, were empty. Walking down the rows of faculty offices, I endured the looks of cartoon characters taped to teachers' doors, felt the dour, accusing stares of jazz musicians glaring off tacked-up black-and-white postcards. *Moments are fleeting?* I sounded as dramatic and fake as the romantic poetry glued to English teachers' in-boxes. Was "enhearten" even a word?

At the end of the hall, my office stood open, as it always did, because of those stupid boxes of research. There were raw ice-core data from Greenland and summaries of nitrogen levels in the air pockets of late-Pleistocene volcanic flows. I'd accumulated diatomaceous readings from glacial loaming and summaries of paleo-pollen samples extracted from amber. Junior had started as an appendix, a small response to critics of *The Depletionists*, a junior answer to their junior minds. But as my critics grew over the years, so did Junior, and now I was looking at constructing a unified-field model, one that incorporated every variable in the disappearance of the Clovis, if I was ever to rescue my reputation.

I stepped awkwardly over the boxes, adding another set of dirty footprints to these smudged reams. When Peabody was a young professor here, he became fascinated with the ancient petroglyphs lining the canyons around the river. He'd always planned to map those cliff carvings, tracing each one and its relation to the others. Such a comprehensive survey was a big job, but there was no other way to understand the hands that carved them. "I always thought I'd have time," Peabody told me. "I thought there'd be time." But he waited too long—they built the dam, and everything was lost underwater.

What a fool I was. In my office, I grabbed my blizzard overalls and left.

Winding down the old staircase, I made out Trudy's voice, faintly at first. She had her whole class crammed into the Hall of Man, and when I crossed the foyer, she was leading a discussion. Her face was visible over most of the students. I glimpsed her shoulders and recalled our dark work last night. Her eyes were serious, and this display of passionate teaching made me suddenly ashamed of the desire that had animated my imagination before sleep last night.

"That's a good point," she was saying to a student, "which brings us to the reason I call this place the Hall of Hoochie. Let's look at *Homo habilis*, the earliest hominid represented here. Notice that the person who created this exhibit chose to depict her as lone female. She's also made older, with droopy features and saggy, flattened breasts. An older ancestor is depicted as an older woman, past child-bearing, and therefore of lesser use."

Trudy left behind an artwork of smudges and fingerprints where she'd gestured against the glass, then moved on to the next diorama, in which two *Homo erectus* females sat next to a fire, suckling, while behind them on the wall Peabody had painted, with an amazing sense of perspective, two men in mid-hunt. This was an exhibit I'd always loved. Peabody had captured the meditative way people stare at flames, and I somehow recognized my own gaze in their eyes, which was the best that anthropology could hope to do—in some small way, connect people to the past.

Trudy asked, "What message can be gained from this anthropological display?"

A young woman spoke immediately. "The women are stuck at home with the babies while the men go to work."

"They're kind of fat, too," a young man added.

"Big jugs, though," Trudy amended, "and less hair. Which brings us to *Homo sapiens*."

The whole class shifted over a few steps.

"Here two males carve spear points," Trudy pointed out, "while the females lounge like supermodels, one of them sucking on a bone. Their breasts are perfect, bodies lean, and they're unencumbered by offspring. My favorite is the touch of bouffant to their Pleistocene hairstyles. Anachronistic though their coiffures may be, the message to those who view this exhibit is clear. Males provide. Females consume, and the closer we get to modern times, the more women evolve into sexually desirable and available beings."

Trudy turned toward the Clovis display, the place where Peabody had housed nearly every major Clovis artifact he'd discovered, and I decided to move on before Peabody's life's work took another blow. But before I could move, Trudy and I locked eyes. She kept speaking to her class, but her gaze was directed at me. "Beyond the sexism, I ask you to notice the Nordic features these Clovis are imbued with. I needn't remind you that when we speak of the Clovis we're talking about the original Asian Invasion. And, of course, all of humanity came from Africa. In the end, this exhibit is more about the Northern European male who created it than the culture he thought he was depicting."

I stomped down the stairs. Near the front entrance, I leaned against a vending machine and pulled on my blizzard overalls. My shoe wouldn't go through the pant leg, and I hopped, frustrated, in place. Had I taught my graduate students no respect? Had they learned from me to mock their predecessors? I fell against the gaudy machine and nearly tore my pants.

The process shook a Snickers down from one of the racks, and I pocketed the candy bar.

Outside, the weather was changing again. Above, like a bank of fog, a snow front was baby-crawling toward us, like the drunk who would have to spend the night. I set off to find Eggers and his "bad news," but my mind conjured the way Peabody had once described the sandstorms that swept across North Africa, weighty curtains of wind, laden with gypsum and bone dust and clay, these storms that hid Rommel.

Before he retired to Florida, Peabody and I spent some time in the field, walking old riverbeds and alluvial terrain. On such excursions, he described the great sites of Alexandria, of Egypt and the sub-Nile. This, to a person who as a boy, when his house felt lifeless, went down by the park and used a stick to wheedle through old Lakota mounds. There was nothing left of value, of course, but with every shard of stone or flute of bone, my imagination took one more step into a past world where a family like mine got along fine without soap operas, insurance meetings, and sales junkets. In this world, when a father went off across the plains to trade, his goodbye meant something, because he might not return, and he'd have to use every skill in his power to ensure he didn't let his family down. And in this other mother's eyes were signs she considered the unthinkable every time he left; in that way, he could never really leave her.

So I was a sucker for Peabody's khaki pants and walking stick, his head of swaggering gray hair. He was a man of the field, restless in the classroom, perhaps restless in South Dakota, but he wasn't leaving this place without a legacy. Like my own father, Peabody was probably a loner at heart, but he spoke my language and paid attention to me. In the semester between my arrival and his departure, Peabody dropped in on my digs and looked over my shoulder, out of sheer curiosity and camaraderie. He asked my opinion. He approved of my book. So, after his Hawaiian-shirt retirement party, and his plane flight to Tampa, when we never heard from him again, not even a postcard, it was in the Hall of Man that I felt he resided. I've tried to picture him on a Floridian pier, fishing in that blue aloha shirt we gave him, cigar in mouth, but I can't really conjure it. He must be over eighty now, most likely dead, and I suspect I'll never know his fate. But as you pick through the bones of the past, you have to keep in mind that you'll never really know another human's story. The point of anthropology is not discovery, but learning to tolerate the unknown.

By the time I reached Eggers' lodge, the first flakes were dropping—so heavy and thick they seemed to stand in the air and let their shadows fall. Eggers didn't exactly have a doorbell, and there was no place to knock. I cleared my throat a couple times. There was a rustling around inside, and then Eggers emerged.

"I've been waiting for you, Dr. Hannah. You won't believe what I'm going to show—" Eggers stopped and stared at me. "You okay, Dr. Hannah? You look like you've seen a ghost."

His long hair was completely frizzed from the bath that morning, and his skin whistled of Irish Spring. But in his eye I detected genuine concern.

"Oh, I was just getting nostalgic," I said. "The past is a trap, my young friend, and we should only go there armed with shovels and torches."

"Sure," Eggers said, "sure."

He was nodding his head, but the look of concern hadn't gone away.

Suddenly the flap to his lodge opened, and a young woman appeared, face sooty. Her parka was wide open. She didn't suppress her smile.

"See ya, Brent," she said, and dashed off through the snow.

We didn't say anything for a moment. Then I put a hand on Eggers' bison poncho. "I understand that you've got this technology pact, but you are using condoms, aren't you?"

"Dr. Hannah, please," he protested. "She's a journalism major. She writes for the school paper."

I gave him one of my father's grunts, and we set out across campus for my excavation van, which was a beauty—blue-and-white striped, with rear doors and blue-curtained windows all the way around. It had the total package—luggage rack, air-cushioned captain's seats, and cup holders everywhere. I kept all my digging gear in it, and I had the thing rigged so I could live out of it for weeks.

Of course, going somewhere with Eggers meant driving three miles an hour while he walked beside. I found that turning on my hazard lights and driving on the opposite shoulder worked best. That way, my van shielded him from errant cars, and I could roll down my driver's-side window and conduct a fairly normal conversation.

We crawled out of the university, and I had to honk ten times to get us safely through the downtown. Near the defunct mall, Eggers pulled out a piece of chert and began pressure-flaking some design, using a percussive back-cutting technique common to the Clovis of our area. My headlights were on, and there was enough snow to hit the wipers every now and then.

"God, turn the station," Eggers said.

This was a familiar refrain. The country was too country, the pop too pop. I tuned the radio to a gospel broadcast and found the call and response soothing.

"You're killing me," he said, doing some delicate strikes with the antler tip. "Try KROK, eighty-nine-point-one."

I turned it off.

"Eggers," I said, "do you think Old Man Peabody was a sexist?"

Absorbed in his carving, he wasn't even watching where he stepped, his furry boots trudging through snow and slush alike. "You mean the guy who made the Hall of Man and filled it with naked women?" Eggers shrugged. "I never met the dude, but you have to admit that he *was* an ankle man—that's one thing that didn't need to evolve, in his opinion."

We crept along for a while, passing the farm-equipment dealership, and after this it would all be frosted fields of broken stalks and strands of corn silk frozen to the fence lines. Cars shot past us on their way to the casino.

"You ever try to make a fertility idol?" I asked.

"Clovis weren't really into the fertility thing, were they? Isn't that more up the Inuit alley?"

The visibility kept dropping. I had the van in low gear, so it idled at just the right speed. All I had to do was steer. I threw a foot up on the dash.

"Yeah, I tried to make one, a long time ago," I told him. "It came out more like a rabbit—you know, short arms, big legs. Without the ears, of course."

"This here's a whale," Eggers said. "You wouldn't think it, but it's hard as hell. A whale's just an oblong thing, kind of formless. What's to carve?"

"What're you making a whale for?"

Eggers examined it closely—its shape was blocky and vague.

"It was going to be a gift, but it looks like shit," he said.

He took the thing and tossed it off in a desolate cornfield.

"Hey, I wish you wouldn't pull stunts like that," I said. "A tractor will plow that under the soil, and it'll really screw with the mind of whoever finds it. Without any context, they won't know that carving isn't ten thousand years old."

"It's a whale," Eggers said. "We're in South Dakota."

"All the more reason."

At some point, without my noticing it, the crunch of wheels on shoulder gravel had shifted to the shush of tires on snow that had given a new coating to everything. Ahead, in the flurries, appeared one of the new billboards the Tribe had put up, welcoming us to the Reservation, Home of Fun!

Neither one of us said anything as we slowly passed it.

"Eggers," I said, "it was none of my business, what I said about the condoms. It's just that there's no way you can live a hundred percent Clovis, and I was concerned."

"Don't worry about it, Dr. Hannah. I didn't take it personal."

"I saw you taking a bath this morning, so I know your technology pact suffered a little. But I understand your reasons for cleaning up. I've been struggling with it myself."

I was thinking about the pig, about the poor girl who'd lost her hog.

Eggers looked at me funny. "You've been struggling with Parents Weekend?"

"Parents Weekend?"

"Yeah, you know, banquets, speeches, the big game," Eggers said. "You know, my parents have no idea. I started this whole thing right after they came out last year, so they don't have a clue how I've been living."

We drove for a while in silence, the heater blasting on high. The glorious Thunderbird Casino began to materialize, in all its flashiness, on the horizon.

A quarter-mile from the casino's central parking lot, Eggers said, "We're here."

I killed the motor and set the brake. Though the heavy snow had mostly subsided, enough had fallen to coat the van. When I opened the door, a wedge of snow dropped into my hair, packing my glasses and ears, slushing down my neck.

Eggers tightened the strips of leather that held his poncho closed.

"Ready?" he asked.

Above us stood a vast billboard advertising Phase II, which boasted an architectural sketch for a second casino that looked exactly like the first one—hazy, then clear—in the distance. We walked under the sign's great legs, and at the fence Eggers stomped down one strand of barbed wire while bowing up another so I could duck through.

We set off across a field, fallow under snow that shone in the afternoon light with the bluish, old-wool hue of manganese. A few rabbit trails crossed the powder, suggesting they'd bolted as we arrived, and ahead, a small creek babbled through the snow. The cold air made your nose whistle, your breath plume glinty before you, and the light was enough to narrow your eyes.

I turned to Eggers. "Okay," I said. "What's the big deal?"

"Shh," he said. "Listen."

In the distance, a couple of charter buses dieseled in the casino's main lot. An occasional car chugged its way down the half-frozen road. Other than that, the only sound was the sleepy-talk of the little brook. I was about to ask *What's the big deal?* again when it struck me how odd it was to hear running water in this intense cold.

I began walking toward the water, Eggers following, giving me the lie of the land. "This is runoff from the casino," he said, and, sure enough, you could see how the creek wound all the way back to the parking lots, where a pair of corrugated culvert pipes dumped their meltwater.

We neared the little channel running through the snow. The water was only an inch or two deep as it tumbled lazy and black-hued over a bed of silica sand that had washed down the culverts. Sand gives cars traction in the winter, and they mix it with rock salt to fight the ice.

"So it's salt water," I said.

"Which is why it doesn't freeze," Eggers added, "and why it excavated this in the middle of winter."

A stick had been pushed into the sand, and where it rose

from the water, a ribbon of corn silk had been tied. "Is that some kind of marker?" I asked.

"Yeah," Eggers said. "That's where the Clovis point was."

"Did you touch anything else?"

Eggers shook his head no.

"I don't suppose you're going to tell me what you were doing out here."

Eggers shrugged. "Just walking."

I sunk my hands into my parka and scanned the surrounding terrain.

There was a slight slope to the land. This suggested an alluvial plain, and a small ridge in the distance could have been a glacier's terminal moraine—both ripe settings for fossils. There were no boulders in the field, which comes from glacial plucking, a likely clue that any artifacts were deposited from someplace else. The creek strata revealed a foot of topsoil, and below that, a layer of diatom, followed by a striation of shale. Again, ideal settings—alkaline and unmolested.

Eggers didn't speak. He silently studied the terrain with me, and if I'd taught him well, he'd hear everything the land had to say.

I knelt at the edge of the creek. There was something in the sediment. I went to all fours, and then I lay down. Plainly visible at the bottom, downstream from the stick, was the ivory loop of a shaft straightener, a common Clovis tool. Time had eaten away the pockets of cellulose, leaving only the stronger honeycomb of bone. And half sunk in the sediment was what looked like the sacral bone.

The oldest human remains in North America that had been dated *in situ*, with strata and artifacts, were those of Kennewick Man, from Washington State, at ninety-six hundred years. If these bones were associated with these artifacts, in this soil, it could be two thousand years older, making it the definitive site on our continent.

I looked a few feet downstream. Rocking in the current were several tiny metacarpals, all trapped from washing farther by the protruding fin of a human scapula. I slid down into the ditch, so I was close to these minnowlike finger bones, schooling in the shadows.

How old are you? I asked them.

They wiggled quietly in the stream.

Who are your kin? I whispered. *Are you all alone?*

Eggers finally spoke. "What do you think, Dr. Hannah?"

I looked up from the water.

"What will you name him?" I asked.

"You think it's for real?"

"He's got to have a name," I said.

"Tell me it's for real," Eggers said.

"I think it's for real."

Eggers' gaze drifted to the casino. He studied its endlessly scrolling marquee: "Welcome Parents—Blackjack—Keno—No Hold 'Em—Slots."

"Keno," he said.

"Keno," I repeated.

I sat up, dusted the snow off my overalls. My boots had soaked through, but I didn't feel it. My eyes scanned the scene—blank snow, an ivory tool, and the bones of the hand that had made it. Keno's hand. I listened again. The stream seemed to talk a little, nothing I could make out, though I could almost see a set of footprints, faint in the snow, the trail of Keno's last steps before he lay down and sank into the soil. I wanted to look into Keno's eyes, note their wetness and intention, maybe hear the clip of his speech, but I could only see his tracks, barely, and that was half-dream.

"I think you've really found something here," I told Eggers. "Something amazing. It'll be a battle, but don't worry, we'll get permission to dig."

Eggers was still looking off to the casino.

"Permission?" he asked, turning to me. "We don't need permission."

I thought he was trying to be funny or something.

"Of course you're joking," I said. "We can't do anything without authorization."

"Nobody owns history," he said. "There's no monopoly on the past."

"But someone owns this property."

"Keno needs us," Eggers said, as if that were all there was to it.

"This is tribal land," I explained. "We have to get permission from the state Antiquities Board, the lieutenant governor, and the Bureau of Land Management, which operates under Federal Land Trust law. Then there's the Tribal Council, and even if we get their permission, we have to find a judge who'll grant us an exemption from the Native American Graves Protection and Repatriation Act."

Eggers looked unimpressed. "I'm gonna start digging tomorrow," he said.

There was something both childlike and heroic in his obstinacy. He almost made me believe it was possible to dig in full view of all the authorities, in the middle of a South Dakota winter, exposed to ice storms and white-outs. On the horizon right now, a brooder of a storm was cooking—fat clouds ass-scooted toward us, pushing gusts of wind that groped their way through stands of trees, coaxing snow from limbs and stealing it back to the sky.

"So you're just going to set up shop right here?" I asked him. "You don't think anyone's going to walk out of that casino and ask questions?"

Eggers didn't have an answer.

"Look," I said, stomping the snow, "the ground is frozen solid. You couldn't dig here if you wanted. Even when it thaws, you'll be dealing with serious mud till spring. Trust me, son, you're in no rush. By the time you're done applying for a dozen permits, you'll be thankful for the extra time. Then there's a fleet of funding grants to be written. Have you stopped to think how expensive this will be?"

"I have a plan, Dr. Hannah," he said, "one that doesn't need money or permits or judges. All it needs is you and Trudy."

"Are you listening to yourself?" I asked. "How will you authenticate the find? You can't get published without proper excavation method. You've got to keep meticulous records to pass peer review. You have to win the esteem of your colleagues if you hope to sell your book and speak at the top universities. Anything less, and you can kiss the lecture circuit goodbye."

"I don't care about any of that," Eggers fired back. He stomped the ground himself. "Will you hear me out?"

I looked into the approaching clouds.

The storm was rolling in faster than I'd thought. Its leading edge was beginning to sweep by us, lifting as much powder as it dropped, driving old snow chips that pricked your face. Locks of Eggers' bison fur stood sideways. My boots now sang with cold.

"Okay," I said, "let's hear it."

Eggers waved an arm, as if to erase an imaginary slate between us.

"This has never been done before. We excavate with Paleolithic technology."

He studied my face for a reaction, but I had none; I was caught completely off guard.

"We grid the site with homemade string," he continued, "and we dig with stone tools. Our maps and site sketches—all charcoal. We cut our own measuring sticks and carve our own spades. Tonight, I'll light some fires to get the ground thawing. Tomorrow, I'll sharpen a couple bifaces and flint an extra adze. Wait till I show you the screens I've been weaving. Instead of using gravity to sift dry dirt through the air, we submerge the screens in the creek here, and let the water dissolve away the strata. If we cancel a few classes, I figure we can do the whole thing in a few weeks."

I had to admit that digging with stone technology was sort of brilliant. Old Man Peabody would have kicked his heels at the challenge. There was just one problem.

"It's illegal, Eggers. It's against the law to remove these things."

Here he beamed large, snow dusting his sparse beard.

"Oh, but that's the beauty," he said. "We're gonna put it all back."

"Eggers, don't even say things like that. Talk like that could cost you your reputation, your whole future."

"Reputation? This isn't about reputation, Dr. Hannah. I'm not in this to become a star. My future doesn't include driving a macho car and lusting after students."

"That was uncalled for."

Eggers said: "Paleo-anthropology is about shining the light of inquiry into the darkness of prehistory, about unearthing the truth of who we are."

Of course, those were my words he was quoting.

He stared at me, waiting for a response.

"That trick won't work this time," I said. "This is different. Other scholars need our research, and they need to be able to trust it. Even a rumor of you tainting a site like this would finish your career."

"I don't care what anybody says," Eggers told me. "Think about it, Dr. Hannah. You, me, and Trudy. No red tape, no money, no attention. Just the joy of discovery, of hearing Keno's story. We put everything back, and if you want to get your name in the paper, then you're welcome to dig him up later."

Finally, the real snow began to fall, the kind that was in for the long haul. It flurried our field, making the casino vanish behind weighty, billowing tracts of white. The flakes fell like reams of paper, confident as propaganda fliers. I imagined these snowy leaves as the now worthless pages of every Clovis article we could debunk with Keno. I put my hand out, the flakes falling sure and steady as outdated books from the shelves of libraries.

"Stop this," I said. "Stop it. There is a *system*, and the system exists to prevent grave-robbing. We invented the red tape, Eggers, we did, the scholars, to stop grave-robbers."

Eggers didn't reply.

"I won't go along with this," I told him. "If Keno's for real, he's been sleeping for a dozen millennia. He can snooze another couple months."

"That new casino breaks ground in a couple of months," Eggers said.

In the distance rose a muted roar, a dull clapping that made Eggers stop and listen. Slowly we began to make out the cracking blades of a helicopter, swooping in low and fast from the east. It thumped heavy in the damp snow, the sound growing sharper as it neared. I figured it was just some high roller choppering into the casino, or maybe Club Fed receiving a new batch of white-collar criminals, but Eggers couldn't stop scanning the snow-dumbed sky.

When the pitching blades whacked violently above, I, too, craned my neck back and squinted to catch sight of it. With a shock, the helicopter broke from the clouds, swinging round and past us, showing the green-black of its belly, and only when it had flashed on toward town could you hear the roar of its jet turbines.

"Shit," Eggers said. "My parents are here."

Chapter Three

A note from Dad was waiting on my kitchen counter.

"Pooped from ice fishing," it said, "but meet you later at the Parents Weekend mixer. Might be a few minutes late, so don't tizzy your feathers. Your dear old dad."

The keys to the 'Vette were still missing from their peg on the wall, a sign that Dad's activities from the previous night—silver dollars and song requests, ice buckets and aphrodisiacs—would truck on into this one.

I'd hung Janis' portrait over the key peg, so he'd have to look her in the eye every time he took the car. The photo was taken on the day we surprised her with a cat to replace Roamy. It was a handsome, broad-headed Burmese that would in a matter of days spray every piece of plastic in the house, pull down a half-dozen birds from the feeder, and make a latrine of the shower stall. Janis had spent several nights searching the farm roads for Roamy, and in the photo, her eyes still seemed focused on the horizon, so the arrival of this cat was a too-sudden conclusion to the last holdout of hope in her expression. *What could be* had been tempered by *what would do.* At the time, a part of me was glad she finally knew how it felt. I'd hoped this feeling would transfer to my father, but he'd long since developed an immunity to that.

A lone glass stood in the sink. I sniffed it—bourbon—and tipped it up so the ring of liquor that had settled in the bottom ran toward my lips. The bourbon rang in my teeth, finding all the old fillings and the sites of a couple cavities to come. I knew about bourbon—it was part of the reason I was never invited on the lecture circuit anymore. Another couple sips, and it would start to gruff your voice. Then it would muss your hair, pull your shirttails out, and finally settle into your real soft spots—ego, adolescent urges, and the fear that at any moment your fraud would be discovered. In my case, this all translated into a talent for boring people, unintentionally belittling them, and failing to get laid.

After *The Depletionists* came out, I was invited to speak at all the big universities, places where I pulled up in a classic Corvette, greeted everyone like chums, then lectured endlessly about the against-all-odds drive of the lone scientist and the self-sacrifice of the maverick fossil-hunter—anything but the six years I'd spent in a library researching the book. Naturally, there'd follow the reception: I was the one eating all the shrimp, copy-righting my wit, and saucing my talk with me. Even now, as I stood at my sink, the thought of the two graduate students I managed to sleep with sent me looking for a drink.

I found the bottle, three fingers gone, in the cupboard, and though I was no longer much of a drinker, I poured myself a glass, examining its smoky color through the swirls of my father's fingerprints. I'd bought the bottle years ago, on a whim really, not long after Peabody left. I had this notion that he'd begin to miss me and sometime soon invite me down to fish under that warm Florida sun. After we'd rigged our poles and thrown the first cast, I imagined pulling this bourbon from my pack. Old Man Peabody and I would have a high time of it: sipping from the bottle in turn, arguing anthropological theory until night came on, and as the stars rose, maybe pulling out cigars.

I dropped a couple cubes of ice in the bourbon, then added a splash of water. I leaned against the counter, noticing how Janis' houseplants were drooping from their hanging pots, thinking there was something particularly suspicious about the way my father was excited to attend a university function even I had forgotten—he could already barely stand them when Janis was around. After I considered it, though, I figured Dad would feel right at home in the savanna of a university-sponsored social event, a watering hole where the sheepish wolfed the liquor and the catty dogged the meek.

A copper watering can sat at the end of the counter, and I picked it up. I held the can under the faucet, felt it take on weight. Normally, I'd just slop a little water on each plant, never enough to drip down to the carpet, trying to get the whole thing over with before the fertilizer turned my fingers blue. Tonight, though, I played some Latin jazz, then turned the shower on full-blast, leaving the curtain open to steam the house.

Moving from pot to pot, I watered each plant till blue fluid ran from its weep holes to a bucket below. Then I began misting the plants, dabbing the dust off their leaves in rhythm with the music. As I sipped my bourbon, I began examining the plastic tags tucked into the soil of each pot. Here were the care instructions for *Perisporus clavinerum:* plant in southern subtemperate conditions under canopied light, allowing room for wandering roots. *Genopedia cordoba*, native of Bolivia, needed pumice for drainage, potash for alkalinity, and, for optimal pollination, I should plant near a colony of kissing bats.

I studied the raised veins of *Genopedia cordoba*, felt the bristly hairs that frosted its tiny blossoms, each one smeared with amber pollen, thick as resin, that stained my fingers the yellow-brown of nicotine. Somewhere in the world, a bat was seeking out this bloom—I pictured a dark rain forest, warm fruit drooping, bright birds asleep, their colors muddied by night, and I tried to hear the navigational singing of a bat I could not see or feel. It sounded near.

I'd always seen these plants as ferns and ivy, as interchangeable creepy things of the dentist's-office variety. I never looked past the ironic artificiality of growing them here in South Dakota, where they wouldn't last a minute without climate control, constant care, and their precious blue food. But suddenly I saw something miraculous in their journey. They'd evolved in the Cenozoic era, in the long isolation before South America crashed into North, and then they'd made the rest of the migration by jumbo jet, five thousand miles in a Federal Express evening, simply because someone desired them.

In the year before she began to decline, Janis became obsessed with these plants, and now I saw them as she would—

as snapshots of jungles and mountains she would never see, as souvenirs from a journey she wouldn't get to take. In the face of fate, when people see a last opportunity to change their lives, Janis didn't fly to Mexico or climb Mount Fuji. She wanted to be near us, to continue her life as it was—working as a court stenographer, inventing home improvements she and Dad could tackle together, reading books at my excavation sites in the afternoon light.

In the shower, I began wondering what I'd do if I knew the end was coming, if I was about to fall into a lake of concrete. Junior would be an orphan—the university would simply fork-lift my research into the shredding bin. Soon, my book would be as dated as the Hall of Man. And, of course, if I slipped through the Missouri ice or was mauled by a breeder hog, there'd be people in this world who'd never even know I was gone—my mother, Peabody. To them, I'd always be the first chapter of a book they set aside and never finished.

I toweled off and dressed. By the time I'd snapped the ends of my shirt cuffs through the arms of a sportcoat, I was thinking about legacies, mulling over what a sad inheritance Peabody's Hall of Man was. I splashed on too much aftershave, and the sting somehow made me think of Trudy. In the mirror, my hair had started slimming to a widow's peak, the lines on my fore-head seemed a little deeper, but I was still young. I downed the last of my watery bourbon, then picked up the phone.

I dialed Trudy's number. I needed to tell her about the dis-covery of Keno, but when the line connected and her phone rang, I knew I would first ask her to help me update the Hall of Man. Perhaps she could chair a committee for student input on the renovation. It was a chance to change history, as all the stu-dents saw it, and a chance to change Peabody, for those who never knew him. Her line rang and rang.

I quietly flossed my teeth, then made my way down the frozen steps to the van.

The motor was slow to warm, and I waited in the dark, win-dows whited over, with only the dim yellow glow of the dash lights for company. Keno could change everything, I thought. The human clock would be set back a couple thousand years.

My phone would start ringing. There'd be a profile in *Anthro To-day*, another book, and I might even ride Keno's back out onto the lecture circuit again.

When the defroster had thawed two small circles in the windshield, I made out a snow-coated raccoon in my headlights. He was balanced on the lip of the garbage Dumpster, scavenging a meal from our trash, some of which was scattered on the ground below—a cellophane wrapper, aluminum foil, oil-stained paper plates. *Bon appétit*, I said and dropped the van into reverse. The raccoon's ears swiveled; then its yellow eyes came to bear on me. A shimmy of snow lifted from its fur as it ducked from view.

I made a left out of University Village, heading to the Parents Weekend mixer to see what dark trade had engaged my father. I passed the empty courtyard of Graduate Village, the sad row dorms where Trudy lived. The metal tops of the picnic tables looked galvanized through layers of frost, the volleyball nets sagged with ice, and the windows in her upstairs room were dark.

The mixer was being held in the new student art gallery at the end of the quad. I cruised through the faculty lot, hunting for a parking spot. I kept an eye out for my yellow Corvette, but as I scanned the rows of cars, something was wrong: though the night was cold and clear, the cars I passed looked storm-battered—dirty snow was driven into their hoods and grilles, while twigs and trash stood frozen to windshields.

I backed into a handicapped spot and climbed out of the van. Everything had been pelted with grubby snow, and it only took me a couple steps to realize that the twigs stuck to car fenders and sunroofs were actually little bones, as if someone had eaten buckets of chicken and tossed the remains so their half-frozen grease glued them to cars. A Doritos bag, chips still loitering in the bottom, was skewered on an antenna.

I pulled one of these bones from a windshield and, wincing at its texture, examined it. In my hand was a tiny skull, its sockets filled with a gelatinous gristle, its fine cartilage stubbed from impact. I was no expert on comparative rodent anatomy, but I was pretty sure this had once been a squirrel. Holding the bone to my nose, I sniffed—urine.

I turned toward Eggers' lodge, shielding my eyes from the parking lights. In the middle of the quad, I saw the menacing green fuselage of a tremendous helicopter, its great blades drooping under their own weight, tail rotor spinning casually with the breeze.

Moving toward it, I crossed from slush to powder, my dress shoes plunging stiff, flat holes in the crusted snow. I came across an animal skin in the half-dark. I threw it over my shoulder. In a few more yards, I found a copy of my own book, wet and battered, but I could clearly see through the running ink that Eggers had underlined dozens of passages.

The helicopter loomed larger and larger—its intake cowlings flared like haunches, and the landing gear raked forward, suggesting a sinewy brawn. I admit I'd never been this close to a copter before, but encountering it could have been no different from wandering out to this spot an eon ago and stumbling into the five-meter tusks of your first mastodon, or chancing upon a short-faced bear, claws long as speed skaters' blades.

I swung wide of the copter. It was frightening how the campus security lights glared off its lifeless windows, how the throbbing hum of its engine heaters made a digestive noise. When I reached the site where Eggers' lodge should've been—there was nothing. The helicopter had blown everything away. All that remained was an open patch of muddy clay surrounding a ring of hearthstones. It looked like every site I'd ever excavated—a few surface artifacts, a dusting of charcoal, and the anonymous stains of humanity. It could have been ten thousand years old. The irony was that I was glimpsing the future. When I look back, it is to this image that I return as I reflect on what became of our culture. Of all the things I had yet to behold—a night sky lit by the laughter of muzzle fire, a river changing gear, the day that dogs would forsake us—this empty ground would prove to be the oracle.

Across a field of white, I made out a lone figure in the dark. I headed that way, walking downhill toward the Missouri. The snow was deeper here, my shoes sounding as if they punched through sheets of aluminum with each step. Ahead, I made out Eggers, toiling to find the remains of his shelter. He had fashioned a litter using two mastodon tusks as skids, with a pallet lashed between them to carry all the skins he'd rescued. He picked something out of the shadows, shook out the powder, then tossed it on the pallet, which he pulled like a rickshaw toward the next outline in the snow.

I fell in behind his footprints, framed by the twin tracks of the litter.

I waved a copy of *The Depletionists* at him, but if he saw me, he gave no notice.

"Hey," I called, "I found your book."

"That's all right," Eggers said. "I already know how it ends."

When I caught up, his face was serious. He wore a poncho cut from a shaggy dark pelt that made him appear broad-shouldered and stout.

"Look, I'm sorry about what happened to your lodge," I told him.

I tossed the animal skin atop the others.

"It's okay, Dr. Hannah," he said bitterly. "In case you forgot, I'm a nomad."

"You're upset about the bones," I said. "I understand that. But this won't mess up your dissertation. We can extrapolate your caloric intake through other means."

Eggers turned to walk away.

"Wait a minute," I said. "This isn't the end of the world here. Think of it as a second chance. How about we go to the party, and in the morning you can rebuild your lodge over at University Village. It'll be a better lodge, and we'll be neighbors."

Eggers was silent. Standing with our backs to the school, we were spared its harsh light and concrete, its trees planted in perfect geometry. Instead, we gazed upon a river valley of dark farmland, our only company the rising white of our breath. High above, the jet stream pushed tight clouds against a backdrop of stars, making it look as if our breath reached the heavens and raced toward the horizon, as if there were some distant place it was meant to be.

I put my hand on Eggers' shoulder. "So—what do you say?" I asked him.

He shrugged me off. "It's getting a little crowded around here," he said. "I'm going to bunk with Keno."

"Don't be like that, Eggers. What about your parents?

They're probably up there right now, waiting for you." I pointed toward the school. "You owe it to them to at least say hi."

"I don't owe anyone anything, Dr. Hannah. I use nothing and spend nothing."

"But they came all this way," I said. "You took a bath. You even brushed your teeth. I mean, don't you want to see them?"

Eggers leveled his eyes at me, in sadness or anger, I couldn't tell.

He said, "They're not really here to see me."

"Nonsense," I told him. "It's Parents Weekend."

"Dad's old accountant is in Club Fed," Eggers said, nodding uphill to the prison. "My parents have a big interest in keeping him happy. If they're in South Dakota, it's to sweet-talk him."

I held my hands out, as if to say, *Come on.* "Eggers, they practically landed their helicopter on the party. Of course they're here to see you."

"Wardens don't take kindly to private helicopters landing in their prisons," he said. "And what you're not getting, Dr. Hannah, is that I've chosen to live in a time in which people don't have the luxury of only pretending they care. In my world, relationships aren't about lip service or social calls. In my time, family is all that matters."

"But you're all alone," I told him. "You're the only Clovis on earth."

Eggers picked up the ends of the tusks and held them at his waist. "We'll see about that," he said.

Now I was angry. "You don't walk away from people who care about you," I told him. "No Clovis would ditch his parents this way."

Eggers leaned forward, breaking the sled loose from the snow. "My parents are wonderful people," he said over his shoulder. "Three gin-and-tonics and my father'll fund any fellowship you want. A couple rum runners to wash down the mood pills, and my mother will—"

"Stop this," I said, grabbing his pelt. I yanked him close. "You only get one mother," I told him. "You only get one father."

He pushed me away, then turned to the snow. In a moment,

there was nothing but his footprints, framed by the twin lines of his sled, heading off into the night.

When I reached the door to the student art museum, my lungs were cold from breathing heavy, and my hands were shaking — that's how worked up I was about Eggers.

Inside, occasional people loitered the corridors of the high-ceilinged, overly white gallery, and a quick scan for my father yielded nothing. A table at the door offered a fleet of wine-glasses, prepoured with red and white. I knew better than to mix my liquors, but I grabbed a red, wondering how anyone could say such bitter things about a mother.

I felt the hot glow of burgundy in my mouth, and pictured Eggers out in the snow, heading to a campfire that he would share with a story he couldn't tell. If there are ghosts on this earth, they are formed by the things you cannot utter, and they'll outlive the black in your teeth, burn hotter than any hole in your stomach. Untold stories take on lives of their own. They silently eat dinner with you. Still as shoe trees, they stand over you, watching you sleep. They'll make you pace all-night Laundro-mats or hunker down to a marathon night of bottom fishing — back to back in a boat with a ghost who mimes you with its heatless limbs. It's what makes Farley stare down an ice hole, what put the tailwind on Trudy's spear, what made Eggers' litter so heavy as he dragged it alone. The title of my father's untold story is *Janis*, and though he may want to tell it, it's what keeps the ice in his drink from melting, what keeps him nervously turning his new ring. It's the reason I went to a funeral alone.

I puffed my inhaler to ease my breathing, then downed the wine. I grabbed another glass and crossed the gallery's hard-wood floor. Descending on long wires from the rafters were small artsy lamps that cast tight cones of light on stray people, making them appear to be mingling. There were no rich people here, and certainly no millionaires. A few students avoided their poorly dressed professors, while a farmer or two in work bibs squinted at the art. I realized Eggers was right — his parents had other plans tonight.

Everything about the gallery was making me uneasy, and I didn't know how long I could wait for my father. I read the exhibition placard on the wall. It said the exhibit—entitled "We: The People"—was sponsored by the Thunderbird Casino, and, sure enough, all the student paintings depicted Native Americans. There was a young warrior drinking a can of Lakota-Cola, a council elder playing bingo, and a team of mounted scouts pointing binoculars toward the viewer, in the lenses of which were reflected blonde girls in bikinis, upside down. Everything hinged on the irony of culture clash, and it sickened me that none of the students had tried to tell the story of a people who, for all practical purposes, were gone.

I polished off most of my wine and made for the back door, averting my eyes from paintings that invariably included eagle feathers, trusty palominos, and cloudy-eyed braves with washboard stomachs. I was almost to the exit when a woman stepped right into my path. To keep from knocking her over, I put a hand out for balance, and it landed on her shoulder.

"Careful," she said as I juggled my glass, nearly sloshing wine on her.

I felt the cool, silvery fur of her coat, which was made from a patchwork of rabbit pelts, and, realizing I'd let my hand linger a moment too long, I pulled back. She had pale, pale skin and dark hair, and her eyebrows lifted in a wry way, as if my touching her was a gesture so unexpectedly forward that she found it entertaining.

"Sorry," I told her. "You okay?"

She smoothed the collar of her coat, then checked the state of her own wine. She regarded me over the rim of her glass, as if deciding what to do with me, and after finishing the last sip of white, she narrowed her eyes as if she'd made a decision, though something told me this look was for my benefit, that she'd made a decision before she crossed my path.

"You must really love this painting," she said. "But there is room enough for everyone to enjoy the artwork without running people over."

The way she unabashedly appraised me was commanding—there was some hunter in this woman—and though she was too skinny for my taste, though her posture was pitiful, something rose in me, and I decided to see where things might lead.

"What painting?" I asked.

"This painting," she said. "This painting is not so bad."

She pointed toward a large canvas, on which was a simple depiction: in a hammock made from an American flag, a woman snoozed under a blue stand of summer sun, surrounded by an atoll of prairie grass.

"The other paintings have too many people in them," she said. "It is my experience that people come and go. I prefer landscapes."

There was a slight honk to her voice, and an accent I couldn't quite place.

She turned toward me, as if for my opinion, and the downy rabbit fur made her seem charged somehow, made me want to study the portrait more closely. Looking deeper, I saw how delicately the artist had captured the carefree recumbence of a woman in slumber: the way an ankle hangs in the air, how light cascades through hair, making it look as if the hammock swung with the wind.

But I didn't want to seem uncritical, either.

I shook my head in minor disgust. "The artist seems completely unschooled in the depiction of mountainscapes," I told her, pointing at the brown bumps on the painting's horizon. "I suppose these are supposed to be the igneous formations common to local grasslands. The work is not without merit, however. I like the way the flag cradles the woman and rocks her to sleep. It lacks the irony that ruins the other pictures for me."

"Perhaps," she said, smiling. "Observe, however, that the hammock is strung between two saplings. These are birch trees, very brittle. And there is wind. I predict the woman will soon be on the ground. Though the artist may not intend this. It is my opinion that people rarely know their flora."

Now I studied her more closely. Again, she was not my type, but I noticed how full her lips were, how her eyelids lowered when she spoke. "I don't believe I've seen you before," I said. "What brings you to USSD? Parents Weekend?"

She said, "Tomorrow I deliver an academic paper. This

I have been with fever to finish. Now is time for personal amusement."

"Really?" I put my hand out. "I'm Henry."

"People call me Julie," she said, though she didn't shake.

I took a step closer. "So, Julie. What's the topic of your paper?"

"Corn."

"Corn?"

"Well, corn mostly. There is some talk of beans, especially the lima."

There was a silence. I scratched the back of my neck.

"How fascinating," I said, nodding. "The lima is one of my favorite beans. What's your thesis?"

"There is no actual thesis. The paper is a summary of early migration and cultivation of Mesoamerican starches. I teach the history of agriculture at the University of Northwestern North Dakota."

I nearly spat up my drink. I'd gone to UNND once on the lecture circuit. Talk about the middle of nowhere.

"I know this is not a glamorous university," she said, pulling out a tube of nasal spray. "But where else may I do my research? North Dakota is also kind to my allergies, and the countryside reminds me of home."

"No, no, corn is fascinating," I said.

She proceeded to block a nostril before administering a whopping blast of saline spray. She then craned her head back to let it penetrate.

She stood there a moment, eyes watering, and I grabbed her empty wineglass.

"Here, let me freshen this for you," I said, and beat it across the gallery, into the hall, and out the back door to the parking lot. The old "refill" move was one of my smarmy maneuvers from those dark *Depletionists* days, and it shamed me how easily it came back.

I ditched the plastic wineglasses in the snow and made for the van. Before I'd even found the right key, I looked over my shoulder to that helicopter, silently looming in the dark snow. Through the smoked bubble glass of its windows, I thought I saw the glow of a cigarette burning, like the tiny red brain behind the eyes of a giant insect. It was probably just a blinking instrument light, but the thought that Eggers' parents could be sitting comfortably inside such a craft while their son walked alone made me want to go up and pound their windows. Yet what would I say to Eggers' parents? What had I ever said to my own?

I climbed in the van and drove to the old Odd Fellows building, where my father now lived. Downtown, the commotion of Glacier Days seemed to roost in the trees—lights shot grotesque shadows high on brick buildings, and the mixing sounds of humans and carnival machinery keened through the streets. The midway throbbed near the gates—that huge 4-H building outlined beyond—and the plunge of a coaster sent a shiver through me. I would forever hear in any scream that skittish, porcine whine.

The Parkton chapter of the Independent Order of Odd Fellows had gone the way of the Masons and the Moose and the Elks. The customs and rituals of their aging members were dying with them, and their brick buildings were now being parceled into apartments. I parked in the street and entered through the great hall, its wide expanse still filled with the same red couches, elbow-worn and smoke-darkened. I made for the elevators across a marble floor inset with a ring of the order's symbols: the lamb and rod, pyramid and sun, eye and rook. In the center was an owl, body facing away, head swiveled back to eye you.

Instead of numbers, the elevator had buttons that read "Mezzanine" (which housed all the social halls), "Lodging," "Executive Council," and then a final, unmarked black button that brought me to the top floor, where all the order's secret business had once been conducted. This was where my father lived, in a loft converted from their former initiation room.

His apartment had a massive, reinforced door, hung on industrial hinges. Instead of a key lock, it opened with a large combination wheel, the kind you see on safes. He never locked it, though. He'd repeat some insurance-industry baloney about more people dying from fires than from burglaries, but this door bothered him, and even though I knew the secret combo, it was always open. Did he hear his own heartbeat when it was locked? Did it speak of the crypt? I placed my palms on the door, felt the faint rumor of music vibrating within, and then swung it open to a sight I have never forgotten:

The apartment was a large studio with a high, vaulted ceiling that arced from wall to wall, firmamentlike, and my father was in the middle of the room steadying the base of a ladder, head craned back, looking straight up a woman's skirt as if contemplating the mystery of the heavens. Dad wore a loose double-breasted suit and sipped a gimlet almost phosphorescent with lime. His head bobbed with the beat of a rumba, and as I followed his look of conjectural joy up the rungs of the ladder, I realized the woman was Trudy, stocking-footed in a black, skintight cocktail dress, straining atop the steps to inspect the ceiling. Her rhinestone earrings were shimmering, and in her hand, a cosmopolitan glowed as opaque-pink as Chinese jade. Beads of water condensed on the glass—when a drop ran down the stem and fell on my father's forehead, he closed his eyes and smiled.

Then Dad noticed me. He turned away from Trudy's powerful legs, and in his eyes was not so much surprise, or even shame, as the sparkle of a challenge.

"There you are, my boy," he said. "We've been waiting for you."

Trudy smiled down, surprised to see me. "Hey, your father said you were going to meet us later, at dinner," she said. "God, have you seen this ceiling?"

I walked closer. With each step, my view began to resemble my father's, until I, too, stood under Trudy, an arm's reach from the mid-thigh cut of her dress, beholding the way her tidy breasts rose with each breath. I could feel my lungs constrict. I hadn't seen a woman's body in some time. In winter, women wore everything from parkas and pantaloons to sweaters and socks. After entering a building, they'd remove a powder jacket, blizzard bibs, a long coat, and a scarf, only to reveal they were dressed in fabrics like flannel and denim, with the bitter promise of long johns below. So, as Trudy stepped down from the ladder, I could see perfectly outlined in Lycra the powerful breadth of her back, her padded torso, and then those hips— articulated, capable, thick with possibility.

My father smiled. "Bourbon, right?" he asked as he folded the ladder.

"Sure," I said, only half hearing him. "Trudy, what are you doing here?"

Dad carried the ladder off across a room furnished only with a stereo on a stool, a set of chairs—black leather, chrome tubing—and a Japanese screen that cordoned off a makeshift bedroom. He leaned the ladder in a corner and made steam for his "bar"—a line of bottles along the windowsill.

"Well," Trudy said, scooching her dress back into place. "Your father said our reservations got pushed back at the Red Dakotan, so we decided to have a drink in the meantime."

"Reservations, at the Red Dakotan?" I asked.

"Look," she said, "I know I kind of blew off our lunch yesterday, and I guess I owe you an apology for that. I wasn't sure about this fellowship thing, but I checked with the USSD Foundation, and it's for real. I feel pretty stupid. I mean, once I talked to your father, it was obvious how interested he was in my dissertation. I brought some of my research abstracts, and he was really into them." She nodded to her briefcase on the floor. "Then I saw this ceiling. Have you seen this thing? I could write a whole paper on it. It's a complete history of an all-male secret society, half of it in code. I bet I'm the first woman who's ever set foot in this room."

I didn't say anything to that.

Trudy went on to describe how the entire ceiling was covered with finely printed initiation rosters, membership rolls, and codes of male behavior, but I refused to look up. It was to her briefcase that my eyes were drawn. I'd never seen it before. It was simple and businesslike, with a faux gold handle and spring-loaded hasps, the kind your aunts and uncles chip in for when you go off to college. It spoke of the dreams of many, riding on the success of one, and knowing that it was filled with all of Trudy's ideas made the bourbon in my stomach flare.

"Trudy," I said in a stern whisper, "can't you see the way my father's leering at you? He doesn't care about your ideas. Looks like I came over just in time."

"Oh, please, Dr. Hannah," she said. "Remember my master's thesis topic?" She put a hand on her hip.

"Sure, sure," I said. "You compared symbolism in tribal tattoos to gang tattoos."

"I've walked the entire length of Sec-Ward in Angola Prison. I took five hundred Polaroids in Marion Penitentiary." She cocked her head and looked at me. "Don't think I don't know when a man is leering at me, Dr. Hannah," she said.

"Ice?" Dad called to us, clicking a set of tongs over a silver bucket. It was a rhetorical question. Beyond him, in the window, spread the blanketing flicker of town, bordered by the ropy dark of the river valley. Past that was Hormel's flashing smokestack and the sodium glow of Parkton Prison. In my mind, I began following Trudy down cellblocks made from epoxy-sealed cement and bars painted maritime-green. I imagined her walking past inmate after inmate without fear, even as they pointed their wrought hands and small mirrors at her.

"All I'm saying," I told her, "is thank God I came over when I did."

"This fellowship is for real, isn't it?"

"Of course."

"So I'm ready for my dinner at the Red Dakotan."

Dad cruised back with a bourbon and a business envelope. I took the drink as he showed the envelope to Trudy. On it, in script, was written "Gertrude Labelle."

"It's empty, of course," he told her. "The real fellowship check will come in the mail from the University Foundation, but this is what the dean will present you in front of the photographer at dinner tonight."

"*Dean?*" I asked.

There would be no photographer. The dean was not coming. It was even an accident that I showed up—Dad had ditched me, asking me to wait all night at a place he wouldn't show, so he could scheme an intimate dinner with Trudy.

But there was no way to tell Trudy this—the excitement was unmistakable on her face; she beamed at the prospect of real recognition. I knew what a library basement was. I'd done time with carbon paper and computer punch cards. And I'd come to understand that the only real reward you got was the respect of your mentors and peers, that, years later, it could all come down to a colleague like Peabody saying something as simple as *Well done.* This was how you learned to respect your own work, after years of doubt, and it sickened me that my father would exploit this in the name of a stepladder peep show and the longshot of nooky.

Oh, that cocky smile of his.

A sip of bourbon gave my voice the timbre of false concern.

"Gosh, Dad," I said, "the dean might be pretty busy with Parents Weekend and all. We might want to give him a call to confirm."

Dad threw me a disapproving glance—it said, *Hey, now. Work with me here.*

"Let me use your phone," I told him. "I've got his private number."

"No need to call the dean," Dad said. "If he says he'll be there, he'll be there."

"Never hurt to check," I said. "It's an important night."

Dad waved this off. "Why bother the man? We'll see him soon enough."

Trudy looked with wonder from me to Dad and back. She assumed a nasal, documentarian's voice. "The alpha males lock horns over the feeding ritual," she narrated. "Has the presence of a female threatened their respective roles?" Dad and I didn't say anything. He just nodded toward the screened-off bedroom, where the phone was. I had no intention of calling the dean, a man I'd personally seen fire a toothless poetry professor just to get his parking spot.

My father's room consisted of a small chest, a bed made with crisp black sheets, and a window with a view of the carnival. I grabbed the phone's handset and lay on his bed, extending my legs down its black comforter, heavy and stiff as canvas. Beside me, on the pillow, lay a flower, presumably for Trudy's sniffing pleasure. Above, an owl, body facing away, looked back at me from a metal plate set in the ceiling. Here and there on the walls, you could see vague symbols and writing ghosting from under the fresh white paint.

I stared at the ceiling a moment, listening to the murmur of Dad and Trudy talking. Their exact words were lost in all that space, yet it seemed natural that people should feel close and far at the same time. Then I examined the phone's amber-glowing keypad. I was about to call Information to get the number for the Red Dakotan, to see what kind of reservation my father had made, but I already knew the truth: he'd booked a table for two. Instead, I pressed the redial button, which would call the last person my father had contacted. The line rang and rang until a woman answered. "Gi-Gi's Go-Liquor," she said. I hung up.

There was a set of speed-dialing buttons. The first one was programmed for Shanghai Express. "Sweet and sour, half an hour," was their greeting. Other buttons connected me with Speedy Taco, White Glove Laundry, and an establishment called Bam-Bam's. My phone number wasn't there.

Then, for reasons I can't explain, I dialed their old number, Dad and Janis'. A recorded voice told me the party I was attempting to reach was no longer available. The message repeated, without urgency, and nothing seemed reconcilable: I couldn't imagine my father sleeping by himself, under these black sheets. Nor could I conjure him sleeping with Trudy, obviously the climax of his pathetic plan. And here I was, in my father's bed alone, waiting for inspiration like so many Odd Fellow initiates who had come through this room, young men who knew nothing more than that the black button in the elevator had finally been pushed, the combination wheel spun, and here they were, on the cusp of secret knowledge, with the promise of unconditional acceptance ahead. Above them, the owl who sees tomorrow looked knowingly back.

When I returned, I decided to trump my father's little plan.

I took a lick of bourbon, cedary and sweet. "Turns out the dean can't make it," I said.

"Well, looks like it's just the three of us, then," Dad said, eyeing me.

"Except that something else has come up," I said. I turned to Trudy. "Remember Eggers' little Clovis point from last night?"

We were immediately locked in our own nuanced world, one that excluded my father as much as he wanted to exclude me from his "Awards Dinner."

"Of course," Trudy said.

"Well, Eggers showed me where he found it. And there's more where that came from."

"Remains?" Trudy asked.

"*In situ,*" I said.

"Where?"

"I'll show you. Out by the casino."

Trudy picked up her briefcase. She grabbed her coat.

"Hey, hey," my father said, "what's going on here? What about the Red Dakotan?"

"You don't mind if we take a rain check, do you?" Trudy asked, and I realized she'd seen through his little ruse all along. "Or, better yet, why don't you come along?"

"I don't dig," Dad said.

Trudy said, "My car's downstairs, Dr. Hannah. We'll stop by my dorm so I can change and grab my digging gear."

"Eggers wants to excavate with primitive technology," I told her.

"Like hell," she said.

In a courtly manner, Dad said to Trudy, "A rain check it is." Thank God he didn't try to kiss her hand.

The two of us took the old elevator down, cinching our coats as cold air rushed us through the open, scrolled metalwork of its walls. Old checkered floors whisked by, and you could have kissed the counterweight as it swooshed past. In the underground garage was Trudy's GTO. The quarter panels had all been patched with Bondo, much of which had fallen off, and the whole undercarriage was crummy with rust. She was planning on fixing it up and giving it a cherry paint job, but till then, the gray coat of primer was hand-painted with details of cave art. Grand on the hood was the same symbol she'd drawn in blood: a red horizon, the low-slung sun, and those antlers, pointing down.

It took a while for Trudy to fire the engine up. I knew the sound of a souped-up GTO; I kept waiting for that joyous GTO rumble, but all I heard was the grind of the starter.

"Sorry," Trudy said. "The flywheel's missing a few teeth."

When the motor caught, I felt more sorry for it than anything. Blue smoke started filling the garage, yet we had to wait there, choking, till the thing warmed up. Finally, we groaned out of the smoke and, lacking any real suspension, were pitched sideways as we pulled out of the garage. You could hear the wild jangle of Trudy's tools being thrown in the trunk.

I waited in the car while Trudy grabbed her gear and changed. Then we hit the road, heading out of town on the same road Eggers and I had walked. In the dark, we passed empty fields where the ridges of buried corn rows were echoed in the snow, making the pastures seem raked with black and indigo. Near the casino, we scanned the fields for Eggers. One fire burned out there, small as a tiger moth against the night. It had to be Eggers. I shuddered to think of him alone and angry as he took counsel with a litter of poached animal skins and an open grave.

Trudy parked the GTO on the side of the road, under the "Phase II" casino sign. We could make out a figure by the feeble fire, stirring it with a twig.

"That must be him," I said to Trudy.

"Let's do it," she responded.

We got out and walked a few steps down the embankment. But I stopped. I'd almost convinced myself that I wanted to come out here, but Eggers' sullen silhouette reminded me this was just a ruse to thwart my father.

"Why don't we get a drink up at the casino first?" I offered.

"Didn't you say this was a Clovis site, *in situ*?"

I nodded.

"What's wrong with you, Dr. Hannah?" Trudy asked. "This is the Holy Grail. This is what anthropologists dream about. If I wanted a drink, I'd be at the Red Dakotan right now, being leered at."

I looked at Eggers out there, feeling abandoned and needy. I'd dealt with one father tonight. I thought, *Let Eggers deal with his.*

"I'm going to take a rain check, too," I said. With that I showed her my back, then crunched off into the snow, walking through slush and grit toward the neon glow of the casino.

The Thunderbird parking lot, when I entered it, was beyond full: vehicles stretched horizonward in orderly rows, industrial lights muting their paint jobs to variations on blue, the frost making windshields appear yellowy and sandblasted.

Inside, the bartender was a lean young man from the Tribe. He wore heavy glasses that were partly obscured by bangs, and as if in acknowledgment of the poison he was handling, he poured my drink carefully, holding it directly in front of his face.

He set my bourbon on the bar, gave change in gaming chips. "Party on, Dr. Hannah," he said and returned to folding some napkins. The kid's name tag said "Tommy." I figured he must be a former student. In khakis and a polo shirt, with that haircut all the boys wear, he could have drifted through any of my classes.

"Party on, Tommy," I said.

I set off across the casino floor, where scores of people, transfixed as if by fire, crowded around gaming tables, three and four deep. Green and illustrated, the tables resembled small sports fields, above which hung round lights that illuminated glowing cones of cigarette smoke. I moved like a ghost—all eyes were focused on the turning cards—while smoky clouds rose toward the lights as if being sucked.

Here were all the missing people from Parents Weekend— students and out-of-towners, teachers and administrators, as well as local folk, from farmers and aldermen to barbers and prison guards. They sat with their backs to me, yet I was greeted by colognes and perfumes, by a matrix of smells who'd left their original owners: the creamy stink of hog tallow, the tanky musk of a grain silo, and the pink ammonia of aircraft de-icing fluid.

I came upon a table at which only one man sat. He wore a warm-up suit cut from fabric so fleecy and sheened it obviously cost hundreds of dollars, while his wife stood behind in a T-shirt spangled with gold. His jowls were ruddy, his manner was expansive and chatty, and on his finger was a grand square-cut diamond. A passionless dealer attended him, and their parlay was conducted in black chips—a huge denomination, I assumed.

Immediately, I imagined them as Eggers' parents, people who swooped into town to yuck it up with billionaire friends in prison, but couldn't resist kissing off a couple pillowcases of cash at the casino before choppering on to paint the next town red. All while ignoring their son.

Childs and Lizzie Eggers, I named them, though they could easily have been Reece and Sabrina or Lattie and Pearl. I looked at their bloated excess, and the irony struck me that these were the real Clovis: people who used for themselves the resources of many, who exploited their environment to depletion, and, once everything they wanted was gone, would skip town. I felt sorry for Eggers at this moment. The boy was a romantic, his dissertation an exercise in nostalgia. Eggers was no Clovis. The Clovis took and took and took, leaving six hundred generations of descendants to fend for themselves in an impoverished world, a place without horses to ride, elephants to tame, or camels to burden.

"Childs" laughed deep at the turn of a card, and "Lizzie" raked the chips for him. I wanted to throw my drink on these fat cats, but there wasn't much left, and they surely weren't Eggers' parents. Like I had the guts anyway.

I examined my glass of icy bourbon. I hadn't drunk this much in years, yet I didn't feel a thing. Why didn't the damn stuff work?

Then something on the other side of the casino caught my eye. Through an acre of lights, I noticed a flicker, beckoning me. I cruised through rows of slot machines, squatting like silver monkeys before the old people who tormented them, and I followed runners of red carpet until I reached another bar, a horseshoe of padded booths below a cul-de-sac of windows. Through them, I could see a ring of fire in a distant, frozen field. I neared until my face entered that layer of biting air that always hugs glass in winter.

Eggers had five fires gong out there, the flames making the snow incandesce a sooty orange that penetrated the powder, traveling under the surface till it dulled pale yellow. Or were there six fires? The flames seemed to sway, separate themselves, rejoin as one. Could be a trick of the wind, I thought. Or maybe the bourbon had kicked in.

I held up my glass, ice winking. "I'm sorry I doubted you," I said.

I became aware of someone staring at me; in the window, I could make out the reflection of a woman at the bar. When I turned, she turned, but not before I recognized her—it was Julie, from the art show. She feigned interest in her drink, a fuzzy colada or something.

She sat, hip ajut, on a red barstool, looking very available in a foofy blouse, black leather skirt, and dark hose. Peeping from her handbag was an issue of *Horticulture Today*.

Hers was the sole face I recognized in the entire casino, and despite her flinty knees and frizzed-out hair, I needed to be near someone, so I went to her.

"Julie," I said, taking the next stool.

"Get lost," she told me.

Her eyes narrowed to dismiss me. Her accent was strong—*"Gyet loss."*

"Julie, please," I said. "We're academics here. Let's be civil. Let's talk."

"It is Dr. Nivitski to you," she said. "You have been drinking much."

She leaned away and waved her hand—*what, from my breath?*

"Perhaps I looked like a bit of a cad earlier," I said. "But I can explain."

She slurped the bottom of her drink. "When I saw you in the art gallery, I am thinking, He is sort of cute, he is my type. But I am wrong. You are like the rest."

She set aside her glass as if to leave, and I felt a pang run through me.

"Please," I said. "Stay. Let me get you another drink."

It was maybe not the best thing to say.

Julie's eyes widened in outrage—she had fire in her.

"So pathetic, your tricks," she said. "I am not the rube. You are the rube."

She scooted over to the next stool, showing some serious thigh as she did. I was left with her empty glass.

"Julie," I implored, "just listen to my side of the story."

"*Julie?* I am in disgust of you," she said. "You do not listen. I am a doctor, and I will have you know that I have traveled around the world, all the way from Vlotovnya, to rid myself of a man such as yourself."

I moved to the stool beside her.

She stood to leave.

A current of panic went through me. I needed to explain that I did like corn, that lima beans were important, that it was wrong of me to walk out on her.

"Don't go," I said.

She reached for her bag. "I have a self-defense spray," she said.

I dared not speak as she pulled on her rabbit-fur coat.

She took her sweet time shouldering the bag. "I am leaving now, and you will stay away from me. Tomorrow I lecture, then return to North Dakota, and I never see you again."

She casually left the bar, exaggerating the toss of her hips, and, without looking back, turned the corner into the casino.

I wandered the gaming floor in a kind of daze—dealers pushed chips across bolts of green felt, waitresses lofted trays of small dirty glasses, and an old man accidentally activated his panic button. It seemed everyone in the world was here, bumping me, talking loudly, knuckling me with their breath, jabbing me with elbows of body odor. Everyone was here but the people who mattered.

In a scene out of the Old Testament, I watched as old people lined up to spin a great wheel. Their heads slowly turned as they watched the word "Cadillac" circle past, and the thing I couldn't stop thinking about was Julie's husband, ditched on the other side of the world. I named him Ivan, and I figured he and Julie had been professors in the same Soviet agriculture department. The poor bastard, I thought, stuck in some Siberian icebox of a university, wondering where was his Julie. His office probably reeked of untold test tubes of pollen samples and crawled with a zillion spore cultures. I pictured him driving one of those sad, communist-made Ladas. What scared me, though, what made my knees go weak with speculation, was the way Julie was certain that Ivan deserved to be left, that he just wasn't good enough to merit her presence. This is what sent me looking for fresh air, though I wasn't fast enough. Before I even reached the casino doors, I was thinking about my mother.

Outside, the cold hitched in my lungs, and it seemed the

backhand of winter had struck while I was inside: a dry, fuzzy frost coated cars whose bellies dripped black icicles, while the panels of pickups appeared haloed, their iced-over fenders glowing gray in the stupor of industrial lights. I tromped past a tour bus dieseling in the dark, its driver reading a paperback by the running lights, and as I walked between rows of cars, the night became quieter and blacker, and all the more cold for it. It was on a night like this that my mother broke her leg, and I had always thought that it was those weeks of housebound convalescence that gave her an opportunity to rethink her life, that allowed longing and regret to take hold. Some great adventure called to her, I'd always assumed. Something out there completed her, and without it she could never be happy. This is what sent her down our driveway, swinging aluminum crutches.

The truth is certainly less romantic: at some point, my mother realized she'd married a small-town rogue, and, sitting at home with an elevated leg, she must have also understood how needy and fearful her son truly was. She seemed happy during her convalescence. She had me dramatize scenes from my *Marley's Great Moments in History* reader. She volunteered to play the instrument-handing assistant in my chemistry-set experiments. Yet I realize now that some part of her wasn't really there. She knew she was about to leave, and as she orated Cleopatra's lines, as she handed me the beaker of sulfur, her imagination had surely made the advance passage.

I made my way among the cars, turning sideways to squeeze between recreational vehicles that filled six spaces apiece. You could feel the slope of the blacktop here, and runnels of salt water cut through the tire-packed snow, making their way toward the storm drains ahead. I would never get my mother back. I knew that. Even if I found her—and I wasn't looking—you don't just make up thirty years. All I wanted to know were the details of her life. What color were her fingernails, and did she still bite them? Did she like anchovies? Did she still wear that amber ring?

The stars shone clear and stark. Out in the far reaches of the lot, I began wondering what had become of all sorts of people. Where was Jim Toggleson, my lab partner from school?

Where was Susan Preston, who tutored me in statistics and always stapled tracts on Mormonism to the homework she returned? If you don't know what became of someone, if you don't attend a person's funeral or hear word from a friend of a friend, these persons who float from our lives attain a kind of immortality, always hovering around the next corner. By closing your eyes, you can attach to them any set of attributes: the various chairs he reclines in, the soda she might sip from, the dreams they have of you they can't remember in the morning. This brings me to life's great paradox: for someone to truly be a part of you—to live in your thoughts, roaming your memory and vision, occupying planes of hope, nostalgia, and speculation in your mind—he or she must be wholly inaccessible to you.

Twin corrugated pipes jutted from the end of the asphalt, and I followed the sound of black water to their mouths. In the dark, I lowered myself down an embankment and began walking toward Eggers' fires, my legs sinking in powder that refused to pack. I thought I heard the plush thumps of an owl's wings as it ghosted the snow for white rabbits. Is there a spookier sound? There have been many nights in the years since that I have heard such wings and doubted they're truly extinct. I began walking faster, kicking my feet free from deeper snow; suddenly I ran into a three-wire fence.

It bounced me backward, landing me flat in the snow. I sunk into the powder, my breath rising, and then, clear and obvious as the stars above, I had a vision of the afterlife of *Homo sapiens*: I saw a galactic ice sheet so vast and barren that, stumbling through the cold, you might only encounter another soul once in a lifetime. But this is eternity, a billion lifetimes, and though you walk endlessly alone, eventually you'll cross paths with everyone you lost touch with, every person who stood beside you in a grocery line, every distant uncle and forgotten friend, every human that's ever been. You walk and walk and fall and walk again, and when, at last, you near the warmth of another human heart, regardless of their race or language, age or appearance, you clutch them for all you're worth.

The stars looked away from me.

Then I realized a face was staring down, oily and fire-blacked.

"Dr. Hannah," Eggers said. "I knew you'd change your mind."

When my eyes came into focus, I asked, "What are you doing here?"

"You were yelling for me," he said. "I came running."

Eggers helped me out of the snow. He threw an arm around me.

"I'm warming Keno," he said as we made for the fires. "Soon those tired bones will sit right up, and maybe he'll tell us a scary story."

Trudy was sitting by the fires. "Did you get that drink, Dr. Hannah?" she asked.

I sat where Eggers had a large, matted skin spread across the thawing mud.

"Trudy's finally taken me up on an invitation to spend the night," Eggers said.

"The GTO's out of commission again," Trudy said. "It might just be the throw-out bearing, but I won't know till I drop the tyranny. I removed the license plates, which keeps the wreckers from towing you right away."

The ground was steaming. I reclined. My whole body relaxed in the old fur.

Eggers squatted beside me, crossing his legs. His face was exuberant, glowing with firelight. "I've been doing some thinking," he said.

"If you ever held any esteem for my opinion," I said, "you will quit this farce of science."

"This is serious," he said. "Wait till you hear this."

I asked him, "You didn't go see your parents, did you? You didn't listen to me."

Eggers endured my entreaty, smiling. "Ready?" he asked.

He gestured a large headline in the air above us. "Pleistocene World," he said.

Trudy said, "You're going to love this one, Dr. Hannah. Talk about half baked."

I reclined across the fur, tuning the boy out. Part of me was still on that galactic ice sheet, and I let my eyes go heavy with it. With focus, I might return.

"Get this," Eggers said. "We reintroduce tigers, elephants,

sloths, and so on, maybe in some kind of park, or maybe just wild. Tourists go crazy for this stuff—lions chasing camels, here in South Dakota. Can you believe it? We'd get a tram, maybe."

"How about a gondola?" Trudy said.

"There'd be giant bears everywhere, and maybe, in ten thousand years, things will have taken their course, things will be back the way they were before."

"Before what?" I asked, pulling an animal skin over me.

"You know, *before*," he said. "What do you think, Dr. Hannah?"

"Sounds like you're talking about a zoo."

"A zoo is where you store animals that are going extinct. Sticking an animal in a zoo means you've given up on it. My idea is the opposite of depletion. I'm talking about *re*pletion." His face shifted gears. "No, no, wait. How about Pleistocene Times? That has a ring, no?"

Eggers went on and on, describing Pleistocene Whatever in great detail, with Trudy plugging in her two cents, both of them slumber-party punchy. I pulled the skin close around my face—it smelled of both the human and animal worlds. From this window of fur, the casino was reduced to a hypnotic plane of light, high-strung and out of focus. In the Cretaceous period, a meteor traveling twenty-one kilometers per second eradicated 93 percent of life on earth. Mammals at that time were nocturnal, burrowing rodents, so when the sky turned blue-white with fire they were safely underground, happy to snooze through the resulting nuclear winter.

When I was at the edge of sleep, cocooned in dark fur, my eyes opened and closed, focusing on a bleary mobile of flame, stars, and casino lights. How alluring the night sky must have been to our tunneling ancestors, to whom the only glimmer on earth was a snatch of starscape, glimpsed on a nightly foray. Their fossilized nests exist today, still packed with ancient shiny things—teeth, micalike flakes of petrified scales, and hardened, amberized corneas, all scavenged from billions of newly dead dinosaurs—proof we have always been attracted to flashy things, that we were born to dig graves and line them with souvenirs of the dead.

Chapter Four

In the dream, I am walking through valleys replete with white, save for a few lichen-covered boulders and an occasional island of frozen grass whose brown tufts poke from the snow. Iced-over saplings lean one way, then another, in the meter of the wind, and I watch as a shaggy ground sloth, big as a backhoe, lumbers up to an extinct Uinta tree. Using its stumpy tail, it rears up to strip the top branches, and when its black claws get behind the bark and tear, it sounds like husking corn.

I traverse ice hummocks and pressure ridges. Though I am in an unknown land, I move under the illusion that below the fresh powder are unseen sets of old footprints, showing me the way. The sun is strong, though diffused through clouds, and I don't feel the cold. Ahead, on a leveling plain, I spot a team of humans, a black huddle against the horizon. It takes forever to near them. Are they grouped around a kill? Lighting a fire?

Nearing, I see they've cut a hole in the ice, and they are cradling, like a baby, a fish whose yellow scales are graying with each moment it is out of the water. Recumbent on their mittens, the fish knits its brow and speaks—it sweeps a fin past their fur-shrouded faces and tells a story in a tongue I do not know. What I feel in the dream is an amazing sense of continuity. I suddenly know that the story Farley's mother told him is true, that it was faithfully handed down through six hundred generations, and I feel connected, almost electrically, to twelve thousand years of oral history, to every elder who repeated it on a winter night.

The fish, as if tired, pauses to fan its gills for air.

Then it points its fin at me. "Now you," it says.

I jolted awake. Opening my eyes, I found myself in the warm belly of a mastodon. Great ribs met above me in a line, and a yellowed membrane stretched between them, which must have been its stomach lining. I sat up, shaking off an animal skin. A crack of light met my eyes, and I pulled a flap and stepped outside. Only in the blinding light did it come clear that those ribs were really tusks, that Eggers had erected his lodge around me during the night.

Artifact Number 4

The day was both occluded and bright, a sign of snow to come, and not a stone's throw from the lodge were the mounds of discolored snow that marked Eggers' latrine. Along the ditch where Keno rested, I noticed a grid system had been erected: at intervals, sticks protruded from the sooty mud; these were laced together with strips of knotted leather. Amid this tangle, Eggers and Trudy lay on their sides, meticulously excavating something from the mud.

"Water," was all I could say.

"I bought coffee up at the casino," Trudy said. "But yours is probably cold by now."

My eyes hurt. My mouth tasted like oily hair, and I was itchy all over. I had to have fluids and aspirin, and the need to urinate was approaching desperate.

But as I stood, I glanced over at Keno, and for a moment I forgot the madness of Eggers' project, Trudy's foolishness in joining it, and I could only think that I was in proximity to the oldest skull in North America. I took a couple quick steps through the wet remnants of last night's fires, then leapt across the stream, where I dropped in the mud beside Eggers and Trudy, the three of us face to face.

"Morning, Dr. Hannah," Eggers said.

When Eggers spoke, the poo of his breath nearly finished me—his puffy gums and furry teeth fumigated me with a writhing, larval cloud of vinegary yeast. Hadn't he just brushed his teeth?

It instantly ignited my hangover.

Still wincing, I turned to Trudy. "What have you found?"

"Tell me about it," she said. "Wait till he farts."

She whispered, "I think he's been eating trash."

This I pretended not to hear. "Find any hematite?" I asked. Hematite is the source of red ochre, which is commonly found sprinkled over gravesites.

"Not yet," Trudy said. "There's no sign of whether Keno was buried or if she died alone."

For some reason, I winced at the pronoun.

With what looked like a sharpened antler, Trudy pointed to a section of exposed earth. There, embedded in a plane of thawing mud, was a saucer of bone that, even half sunk, glowed with the vellum of prehistory. I couldn't look directly at it. I'd hoped all my life to find the remains of a Clovis, the most elusive Paleo-Indian on earth, and now, when I was so near, I froze up. My mind got distracted, and all I could think about was the slipshod nature of the excavation. I suddenly hated Trudy's antler. Anger welled over Eggers' stupid dissertation stunt and all his ridiculous theme-park plans. I should have recognized fear when I felt it, known that I was somehow afraid of Keno, but all I could muster was disdain for my students.

I reached out and plucked one of the flimsy leather straps that served as a gridline. The stake it was tied to flopped in the mud.

"What kind of sorry grid system is this?" I asked.

Before they could answer, I said, "It's worthless. I can't even tell what scale you're using." I yanked another strap of leather. "The squares are smaller than a meter yet bigger than a foot. The whole point of the grid is to map the site. Haven't you two learned anything?"

Eggers looked stunned. "You know I can't use the metric system," he said.

"Hey," Trudy said. "He made his own. You have to give him credit for that."

I looked at Eggers. "You made your own what?"

From the muddy snow, Eggers produced a stick.

"This is one eno," he said, handing me a fresh switch of mulberry whose edges had more or less been rough-planed square. There were eight hash marks on it.

"What is this?" I asked him.

"It's an eno. You know, as in 'Keno.' That's where I got the name."

I could tell Trudy's heart wasn't completely into defending Eggers. Still, she said, "We're using our own measurement system. An eno is the length of a Clovis femur."

My jaw dropped. "You found a femur?"

"Not exactly," Eggers said. "I measured mine."

"An eno's about sixty-three centimeters," Trudy said.

"Let me get this straight," I said. "You're going to document a groundbreaking discovery by dividing your leg into nine sixty-thirds?"

"It's not how you're making it sound, Dr. Hannah," Eggers said. "The beauty of the eno is that you can divide it any way you want—tenths, sixteenths, whatever. The eno leaves all the old systems behind."

"Give him a break, Dr. Hannah," Trudy said. "Don't you see what we've found?"

"Yeah," Eggers said. "Check this out."

With a twig, he indicated the piece of bone. "We defined the edges but decided to stop, choosing to get more data from the surrounding strata. Over here we found some soil calcification, and closer to the water, more finger bones. Trudy thinks the torso is oriented this way."

With his hand, Eggers made a sawing motion that ran parallel to the ditch.

Trudy raised her eyebrows. "Don't you see," she said. "This is the birth of a whole new field. This is *paleo*-paleo-anthropology. We're not dragging bones into the cold light of the modern age. We're going back to Keno's time. We're entering the context. *We* are *in situ* with the bones."

I shook my head in disapproval, but still I leaned close to examine the bone.

Lightly, with the pads of my fingers, I gave it its first human touch in twelve thousand years, and that shiver of fright ran through me again. Cold and mud-slick, it was like making contact with your greatest fear: that humans could live, love, and die without a trace, vanishing as if they had just slipped the earth's mind. But of course the opposite is true: the ground never forgets. Only humans punish each other with amnesia. Unremembering another's name and story is strictly a human pastime, and only we have learned that, to truly get the last word, you must give silence.

So you had to get the ground to talk. I'd come to believe, after a career of study, that justice leaves no mark on history, let alone the soil, and the longer a story lies buried, the more unsavory you'll find its moral. Go back far enough, and you'll no longer know the heroes from the villains. All we had of Keno's story was a dark conclusion, and only science could tell us its middle and beginning. Trudy and Eggers needed science. They needed to tease out the terrain of Keno's final day with striation-and-sediment analysis. With chemical spectography, they could get the soil to whisper the menu of Keno's final meal. They needed to run his remains under ultraviolet light, the best rumor mill for old injuries, illnesses, growth spurts, and malnutrition. Radiocarbon is solid scuttlebutt on clan and friends. Dental morphology would tattle on Keno's age, diet, health, and kin. To get a story as old as Keno's, my students needed to gossip with fluorine isotopes, pillow-talk with electron microscopy, then, finally, name names with DNA.

Invariably, however, you will be left with some degree of mystery. Beyond science is an area of not knowing, and to get past that, you must enter the story yourself, filling the blanks with your own past, splicing the helix of your own narrative into the gaps of another. You must enter the play before you, becoming a minor character, the ambassador or court jester who appears in the final scene to satisfy the audience's need to know how everything worked out.

My students had always shown good digging instincts — at a Mandan site last year, Trudy had worked with patience and method, while Eggers had shown an uncanny instinct for nosing his way through the soil. But this slapstick before me evidenced neither science nor intuition: They had none of the equipment from our lab, so there was no way to measure anything, not even alkalinity or leaching. There was no way to acid-bath the remains or coat them in hardener — they couldn't even tag the bones, let alone make casts of them. And for all Eggers and Trudy may have learned about reading rock matrix and soil strata, they had no clue how to coax bones into sharing their secrets, let alone telling your own in return.

I closed my eyes and turned away. "You two don't know enough to do this yet."

Trudy looked at me. "You're the one who taught us."

"Yeah," Eggers said, "you've taught us everything you know."

"No," I told him. "No, I haven't."

"But—" Eggers said, then stopped. Something had caught his eye in the distance beyond us. I followed his gaze to the road, where a sheriff's cruiser was coasting to a stop on the side of the highway. It was far enough away that you couldn't hear its tires in the slush, and the ghostly part was that the squad car seemed driven by no one.

I rose, as did Trudy and Eggers.

In the distance, the cruiser's door swung open, and a tiny man emerged, flanked by a posse of small, jumping dogs. He tripped over one of them, falling into the snow. A moment later, he stood, yelled something we couldn't make out, then headed our way, dusting the powder from the seat of his pants. This was clearly Gerry marching toward us across the field, his team of Pomeranians leading the charge.

"Shit," Trudy said.

Gerry trudged, head down, through snow deep as his knees, and something inside me said to get the hell out of there. "I got to use the bathroom," I told everyone, and wincing at the place where Eggers had been doing his business, I turned, to make my way through the mud toward the casino.

"You're not running away, are you?" Trudy asked.

"I have business to attend to."

"Dr. Hannah, you can leave a place—I've had to move away from more cities and army bases than I can count—but you don't quit people who need you."

Gerry was almost in our camp. A legion of lapdogs was now upon us. You couldn't even count them—a ball of tumbling fur would suddenly split into two dogs that leapt, tail-spun, then blurred into other yipping tangles. One dog began tugging at the fur of Eggers' lodge, while another attacked something in the latrine.

Gerry came to a stop in front of Eggers and Trudy. The fur-rimmed hood of his sheriff-brown coat gave his face the pinched, beady look of one of his own dogs.

"Hey, Hanky," Gerry said when he recognized me. "What're you doing out here?"

Eggers smiled, opened his hands. "Why, what can we do for you, officer?"

"Yes, officer," Trudy said, "how can we help you today?"

"Well, I was looking at that GTO over there," Gerry said, still looking at me quizzically. "Any of you folks see somebody messing with it?"

The Pomeranian that had been rooting for feces in the latrine's foul snow raced up to Gerry and began springing in place, looking for a treat. Whatever it had wolfed down was gone, though flecks of matter speckled the tips of its ears and whiskers.

Old Man Peabody would have vomited at this sight. He couldn't stand to see any contact between humans and dogs — he once nearly had a breathing attack when we passed a girl on the street whose face was being licked by a poodle. Peabody believed that all of humanity's Old World diseases came from the domestication of animals, but in the New World, he was sure dogs were to blame for bringing humans into a thousand parasitic cycles: dogs' coats were host to fleas, mites, ticks, chiggers, scabies, and lice, all of which made dog blood a medium for dozens of encephalitics and hemorrhagics, not to mention beauties like rabies, Borrelia, rickettsiae, and Chagas. Their eyes weep toxoplasmotic larvae by the million. Their mouths drip with cystozoans, and their anuses are home to flukes, proglottids, cysticerci, and of course the worms: tape, round, heart, pin, thread, seat, and hook.

Eggers tried to shoo the filthy cur with a giant mitten.

"That car?" I asked. "I hadn't even noticed it. I didn't even know it was there."

Gerry pulled back the hood of his jacket. "Looks like our little Indian gang struck again, Hanky. Sheriff Dan thinks they may be running a chop shop." Here Gerry made a little tomahawk chop with his hand.

"Maybe someone just had car trouble," Trudy said. "And

what makes you think it has anything to do with Native Americans?"

"The car's been painted with well-known gang symbols," Gerry said, shrugging.

Eggers added, "The hunter-gatherer 'gang' is the oldest social structure on earth. We all came from gangs."

Trudy put her hands on her hips, making her shoulders broaden under the gray of her sweats. "Maybe a bunch of middle-aged white guys stole that car," she said.

"Oh, no," Gerry said, more than half offended. "The perpetrators who did this are cowards, I can assure you. I've seen their work before, miss. Innocent motorists don't remove their license plates when they're stranded. Innocent people have a healthy respect for carnivals and farm animals. Regular folks don't go around fingerpainting with the blood of their victims."

Trudy's eyes went wide. Eggers froze, even though the Pomeranian called McQueen was leaving a trail of urine as he headed toward the lodge entrance.

Gerry went on: "I gave that hot rod a good once-over. Looks like those punks went for a joy ride until the transmission gave out. There's a sock in the glove box stuffed to the stitches with condoms, so who knows what else they're up to. Sheriff Dan's got a couple boys from the South Dakota Bureau of Investigation coming in from Sioux Falls tomorrow. They'll get to the bottom of this."

Eggers cut McQueen off at the pass and was looking to give the lapdog a taste of buckskin. Gerry intervened. "Hey, careful with the Poms," he said. "Those things have papers, you know. These here are purebreds."

"Gerry," I said, "can you call off the hounds already?"

Another darted into Eggers' lodge and began rummaging around—it emerged crunching something that sounded suspiciously like a potato chip. That's when Trudy noticed that a pair of Pomeranians were digging like mad in the matrix that held Keno. We heard her gasp and followed her eyes to a fury of paws that spit mud everywhere.

"That's it," Eggers said, and grabbed from the lodge his rodent stick, a savage piece of technology if ever I've seen one. Its shaft was cut from willow, so it was flexible enough to follow the curves of any rodent burrow. Its three-pointed tip was armed with sharpened bird bones. This Eggers rooted down every hole he passed, fishing around till he jabbed something — once I'd seen him pull up a trio of baby rabbits, hanging from the barbed gigs by their baggy skin.

Only when Eggers hefted the rodent stick did Gerry seem to realize what was happening. "Hey, hold it right there," Gerry commanded. "Put that thing down."

"Call your dogs," Trudy told Gerry.

"Hold on," Gerry said. "You can't hurt those dogs. They're already sold. We're headed out to the airport right now."

"He'll do it," Trudy said.

Gerry stopped. He cocked his head, seeming to notice, as if for the first time, that Eggers was dressed in animal skins. "What the hell is going on around here?" he asked. "What's with the crazy getup?"

Nobody said anything. We all looked at Eggers, who lowered his rodent stick.

Gerry took a step closer to Eggers. "Just who the hell are you supposed to be?" Gerry looked at the cold firepits, the wallows of mud, all the stone tools lying everywhere. "What are you yahoos up to out here?"

I looked to Trudy, then Eggers.

"Well, it's complicated," Eggers said. "This is very scientific. What we're doing here is . . . Well, it has to do with truth and discovery."

"Yeah," Trudy said. "And humanity."

Eggers added, "We're shining the light of inquiry into the darkness of prehistory."

My words had never sounded so stupid.

Gerry turned to me. "What the hell are they talking about, Hanky?"

Suddenly, a sharp, pain-stricken yelp sounded at the edge of the field. We looked in time to see the bent-over trunk of a sapling spring upright from a snare. The motion pulled a cord of sinew that sent a Pomeranian high into the air, high above the tree. I cringed as the dog rounded the pinnacle of its arc, and I was already backpedaling before its fall was cut short by the snatching grip of a noose.

Gerry took a couple stunned steps toward the dangling Pomeranian, then broke into a run. Eggers dove inside his lodge, and for a moment there were only Trudy and I. She stood there, a true calm to her. She picked up a sack lying near the site and handed it to me. She made sure I held it, her hands clasped over mine. "Remember—we're a team," she said, then lifted the flap to join Eggers.

I headed off through the snow, carrying her sack, and, believe me, I was picking up the feet. I marched on, the casino looming larger and larger, the beeping of delivery trucks and the air-brake hiss of tour buses coming to me as I jammed my hands in my pockets and leaned into the deeper drifts. Why look back?

The giant marquee flashed the Thunderbird logo above a scrolling banner that had changed from "Welcome Parents" to "Welcome Meat Wholesalers." I looked at the giant bird. Its wings flashed red, white, then blue, and its neon head swiveled left and right, nervously. There was no such bird as a thunderbird, really. It was a mythological creature that in Native American lore was the source of doom and destruction.

At the wire fence, I paused to let my bladder go, a piss so fantastic I saw sparkly yellow lights at the edge of my vision. I pissed the ice off a green-and-silver fence stake, beyond which was the snow angel I'd made after falling the night before. You could see Eggers' footprints, and frosted in the snow was an empty highball glass.

Climbing over the culverts, I scrambled up to hardtop and came eye level with a frozen lake of dirty American cars. I couldn't help looking back. I could see, far past the lodge where my larcenous students hid, a little man by a little tree, and I knew Gerry was cutting down his dog. Why don't snow clouds ever swoop down when you need them? Out there was the scientific discovery of a lifetime, and instead of a full-scale excavation, all I could see were stains in the snow, students hiding under poached animal skins, and a man bent over his dog. Where was the cloud large enough to white out this scene, to obscure the havoc I had made?

I passed the fat trunks and dented bumpers of sedans that seemed iced in place, as if their owners were inside drinking and gaming away the time until spring thawed those tires loose again. An unmistakable waft of burning meat floated toward me, making me think of the stockyard east of town, the way thousands of animals were corralled into their own lot of tight pens, icicles of snot hanging from their muzzles, frozen mud locking their hooves in place. I was hoping to find Bill Hasper, Parkton's lone taxi driver, for a ride back home.

Ahead was a modest commotion, centering on a column of smoke, and the black slush at my feet soon became littered with rib bones. I came across an old water tanker, which had been fashioned into a gigantic truck-sized grill, in the manner of those oil drums people cut lengthwise to turn into smokers. A man in a chef's hat stood upon scaffolding over this thousand-gallon grill, scalding entire racks of ribs and briskets. He leaned to shuffle great mounds of meat over heat that rose a shimmery silver-black. The raised half-dome of the water tank read "You've Got a Friend in Beef!" and I was pretty sure that, if the dome slipped off the stick that kept it propped up, it would cut this man in half.

As I walked past one gritty vehicle after another, it was on Julie that my mind settled. Sure, she was stuck-up and aloof, and her hair was a fright, but I couldn't stand the idea of her going out into the world thinking I was a buffoon of a man, a scientific huckleberry. In universities across America were departments that had had only one encounter with Hank Hannah, and they will forever remember him as the jerk at the shrimp bowl, the ape at the lectern. But I wasn't the same man who once entertained a dean with a cocktail-napkin diagram of the sacred Mactaw fertility dance. I wasn't the same person who wore Highlander aftershave and walked around with a copy of my own book in my back pocket. I simply couldn't let Julie return to UNND with such a skewed portrait of a guy who had since caught sight of some of his problems and was really trying.

In the extremities of the lot was recreational-vehicle land. Here streams of RVs were parked in parallel lines, rather than rows. It was like walking down industrial alleys, colder somehow in these corridors of motor homes, and when the wind kicked, you could see lines of them rock like train cars. That's where I caught sight of Farley Crow Weather, eating ribs from a Styrofoam container, admiring a WindReaper Mark V.

Farley nodded, mouth full, at the sight of me, and beckoned me over. I could tell he'd just had his flattop trimmed—fine bristles dusted his forehead and ears.

"Jeez," he said, "where a guy couldn't go in this rig."

Together we studied the camper. It was a three-axle model, with outriggers and built-in tow bars. A satellite dish pointed toward the Arctic.

"You planning on a trip?" I asked.

Farley tossed a bone under its rear bumper, grabbed another rib.

"Never know," he said. "A fellow thinks about it now and again."

"It's a pretty big outfit for one person," I said.

"I suppose," Farley said. "You think it could take the hills?"

We examined the vehicle's size and length. We bent to inspect the rear differential, and when Farley pointed toward the exhaust pipe, whose mouth was nearly six inches wide, we nodded that an engine that big probably could.

"Out here for business or pleasure?" he asked.

"Oh, both," I said. "You?"

Farley gave me a quick once-over, noting my wild hair, my jacket, the general animal hide of me. He eyed the raggedy gift-shop bag I held.

"Serving some writs," he said. "Plus, I know a guy out here who cuts my hair."

My scalp was really itchy. "Look," I said, "I could use a ride."

"Yeah, sure, I s'pose," he said, pointing a bone in the direction of his own four-door American sedan. This was his way of saying, *Anything, buddy, anything.*

Farley's back seat held two milk crates of legal briefs, both buckled down with safety belts; the passenger seat was a bin of soda cans and empty boxes of Vicks licorice cough drops. A police scanner on his dash flashed little red lights as it roamed all the emergency channels, looking for trouble. When I climbed in, Farley fired up the engine, then promptly powered down all four windows. He kept looking at me funny.

"What?" I asked.

"Nothing," Farley said. Then, "You got a rash or something?"

"What are you talking about?"

"Nothing," Farley said, but as we turned onto the main road, he eyed me again.

I was scratching behind my ear. "What?"

Farley returned his attention to the road. Cold air flooded the cab, lifting a flurry of cough-drop wrappers as we picked up speed. Trudy's GTO, crusted gray with road-swept snow, sat on the side of the road, but there was no sign of Gerry's cruiser.

"Farley," I said, "it's good that I ran into you. I've got an important question."

The police scanner stopped for some staticky talk, though we couldn't make it out. Farley turned down the squelch, so the red light cycled and cycled in silence.

"Shoot," he said.

I said, "Let's say you have some friends, and these friends are probably doing something bad. You aren't exactly helping, but you know it's bad, and you haven't turned them in, either. Are you in trouble?"

We passed the old skating rink, a gang of crows keening along its saddled roof, probably casino-bound to scavenge all those bones. Farley shook his head. "You know, Hank, I'm your lawyer. You can tell me things, and it's confidential. That's how it works." Farley raised the windows, asked, "Would this have anything to do with an article I saw in the paper that someone killed a little girl's pig over at Glacier Days?"

I didn't say anything. I felt something sharp on my ear, like I'd been bitten. I slapped at it.

"Your school didn't start giving Ph.D.s in hog butchering, did it?" Farley joked.

Beyond the tractor dealership was Parkton's one sleazy motel, the Lollygag, and there, in the parking lot, was my van. How many vans have custom-painted tire covers that read "King of Spades" above a playing-card anthropologist that held a shovel instead of a scepter? Of course, everyone in town would think it was me in there. I craned my neck as we drove past. Was my father really in one of those rooms getting laid? I'd need scientific notation to figure out the last time I got laid. I'd need an Aztec calendar to find that date.

I turned to Farley. "Do you think I'm washed up?"

Most friends would say, *Hey, buddy, what's eating at you?*

But Farley meditated on the answer. "It depends," he said, after a while.

I didn't ask, *On what?* I let the clapboard farmhouses shoot on by.

Farley eventually said, "If you're comparing yourself to the hotshot Hank who got his theory published and started living too high-hog to spend time with his friends—well, compared to that jerk, you're doing pretty good. If you're comparing yourself to the Hank I knew at Mactaw, the pimply kid who drove our sociology teacher crazy, who wrote articles in the *Tomahawk* about making the world a better place, who talked over lunch at Burger King about history and truth in a way that this reservation kid had never heard before . . . Compared to that guy? Well, you tell me."

When we pulled up in front of University Village, Farley held my eye as I grabbed my bag and swung open the door. This meant that he wasn't done with me, and, standing out in the snow, I leaned in the window, because sometimes Farley could say some pretty dang wise things when you least expected it.

His foot rested lightly enough on the brake pedal that the car wanted to pull away. He waited until I'd closed the door, then unwrapped a Vicks cough drop. "Try to avoid those store-bought flea powders," he told me, popping it in his mouth. "Start by bathing in baking soda. If that doesn't do the trick, you'll have to use vinegar and tomato juice."

Then he rolled away.

Inside, there were no messages, no notes, no pets to greet me. Janis' face, when I passed it, pretended not to see the state I lived in. I grabbed a tumbler of water and sat in the living room, the light through the windows frail but clear as I reclined in a chair that had belonged to my father. A parade of hypotheticals overtook me—flashing from Julie to Keno to Peabody to a woman in a motel I'd never met—making it seem as if their lives were accessible, open to influence, coexisting in a realm of simultaneity, of possibility, with mine. In my animation of them, we were all in a room together, or at a picnic bench, laughing, talking, and Peabody could toss peanuts that Keno would catch in his mouth as easily as Julie and Janis might reminisce on fate. But really I was as remote from them as Ivan, in his own chair in Siberia, wondering why he was all alone.

I absently tugged at the gift-shop bag Trudy had given me. I pulled out clear baggie after clear baggie, each of them containing a bone. Most looked like metatarsals and phalanges, though one cracked section might have been part of the radius. Each bone was tagged with a numbered marker and individually sealed with an instant photo of the bone *in situ,* next to a metric ruler. At the bottom of the sack was a receipt from the casino gift shop for a Polaroid camera, a roll of toilet paper, and a box of Ziplocs. On the back of the receipt was a note in Trudy's handwriting:

> *Dr. Hannah—I need your help to pull this off. Eggers can never know.*

I got up and walked to my bedside table. Here was the Clovis point Eggers had given me, and his battered, annotated copy of my book, as well as the cast of my mother's leg and a pair of Janis' blocky eyeglasses. I placed Trudy's note among these things. I knew Trudy and Eggers' excavation was still wrong, that the whole project was undertaken in bad faith, but I must admit that a feeling of well-being had spread over me at the idea that Trudy had learned a thing or two, that I'd taught her something.

I flossed and shaved, and in the shower I used double the shampoo, going after my scalp with a hive of fingernails. I put on a spiffy sportcoat while I steeped a cup of tea, though all I had was an herbal brand called BabyDreams, the only kind Janis could drink near the end. It tasted a little like candy canes, but I didn't mind. I stood there a minute, sipping it. Her plants draped the room, and in the sideways light you could see the veins in leaves that look X-rayed.

Then I took off the sportcoat, the slacks. I suppose I'd been planning all along to attend Julie's lecture. In the back of my closet was a suit I'd worn only once, when I was invited to sit on a panel at Harvard. It was chocolate-brown, cut smart, with a faint windowpane pattern and a three-button breast. For a while, I'd lacked occasions to wear it again, and then, as time went by, the more I thought about that day, the less I wanted to remember it. The best minds in anthropology were there — Stanford's Hatitia Wells, the Rogers-Klugman team from Princeton — but all I could think about was how the other panelists kept interrupting me, cutting me off, and when I finally got my chance, my mouth became a device whose sole purpose was to blab about my theory, my book, me. I honestly can't remember one thing anybody else said. Maybe now, I figured, I could meet a new day in that suit.

I didn't so much put it on as step into it. The jacket hung perfectly — shoulders snug, vents loose, buttons custom-fit — and the slacks looked creased by cardsharps. "Julie," I said, snapping the cuffs. School was only a block away, but I fired up the 'Vette. There'd be no parking, of course, but I could usually squeeze into that little zone reserved for motorcycles.

On campus, I was struck by the void where the helicopter had been. Its absence was overwhelming. I had Trudy's bag and about thirty minutes to get to work before Julie's lecture, but I stood in the quad, just staring at the snowless zone where that chopper had been.

Inside the anthro building, I needed a secure location to study Keno. The answer, when I nosed around a little, was obvious: the Hall of Man. It was the only place with serious locks on the doors, and students, unless forced to enter, avoided the place like the plague. Peabody had also installed temperature and humidity controls to maintain his exhibits. The lighting was great. From my office, I grabbed a fine-work kit, complete with detail tools, most of them dental, and a couple of bottles of light acid for etching.

With all my gear, I crossed campus for the biology department. The white lawns were nearly empty on a late Saturday morning. A lost Frisbee lay half exposed in the rotor-washed snow, and a pair of moon boots hung from the bough of a diseased elm, slowly turning in the bright light reflected from the newly iced river. This side of campus was home to all the "hard" sciences, like engineering and physics, and all the buildings had been constructed in the sixties with the same lust for broad expanses of cheap, overly red brick.

I used an old master key Peabody had left me to get upstairs into the dissection lab, which was also where they stored all the veterinary pathogens. I needed a gurney, and, luckily, lined up at the edge of the room were several stainless-steel autopsy tables. Any of these would be perfect for storing Keno, as Eggers and Trudy unearthed him piece by piece. I'd begun to wheel one away when I spotted one of those tall, rolling stools that lab techs use; I'd always wanted one of those, and this baby was chrome. I sat on it, lifting my legs to push off the cabinet. I rolled across the room toward the bovine-virus freezers, where I came face to face with a pair of big orange biohazard signs that warned of imminent, deadly contamination. I liked those swirly, spiky biohazard symbols — so threatening! — and when I pushed off and rolled back, I had these signs in my hand.

The biohazard signs, when I'd taped them to the doors of the Hall of Man, had quite an effect. No one was going to bother Keno in there. He'd be safe on his personal autopsy table, though I didn't like to think of it that way — we were reconstructing Keno, not the other way around, even though all we had of him were some bones from his left hand, half a forearm, and a shoulder blade. Ninety percent of his skeleton was still missing, and somehow I loved the knowledge that the other pieces would come, that he'd no longer be lost as the three of us brought him in from the cold. When I looked at those six empty feet of brushed steel, I didn't see the metallic void where a person should be but, rather, the place where we were going to make the remotest of humans materialize.

It was in this state of mind that I made my way to the agribusiness building, which was really just the old history building, gutted and renovated. I walked under that Santayana quote, shaking my head, and I couldn't help noticing how watery and colorless the building had become since agri-business took over, since history had become an entertaining elective, not a subject that merited a major. Entering the alcove felt more like striding into a dentist's office—pastel carpets now covered the old wooden floors, and the lath and plaster had given way to expandable, accordionlike walls that could accommodate any conference or team-building session. The old water fountains, copper with malachite basins, had been replaced by a lone blue cooler. It was as if they'd tried to remove the history of the building itself. But history isn't so easily glossed over. I could feel the past fixed here by a century of storytelling in these rooms. The meditations of Sor Juana seemed woven into the banister's scrollwork. The fate of Darius felt cut in the ceiling's frieze.

There were about twenty students in the auditorium, a normal crowd for one of these lectures. Waiting for events to begin, I couldn't help coveting agri-business's new ergonomic seats, not to mention the sound system and splashy modern-art panels on the walls. I sat in the rear of the hall and endured a long introduction from some lame department head before Dr. Yulia Terrasova Nivitski came to the lectern. She carried a sheaf of paper, a wad of tissue, and a bottle of water as she strode before us in a charcoal suit that was all business, except for a V of ultrawhite skin that plunged deep into her num-nums.

But her hair! The endurance of a Russian perm seemed limitless.

"Good morning," she said when she'd adjusted the microphone. "I am many times asked how is it I became interested in paleobotany, and today I thought I will open with a humorous anecdote."

Julie spoke as if she were addressing a group of children, and you could hear people shift in their seats, settling in for the long haul. "As a little girl in Vlotovnya," she continued, "I suffered terrible allergies. Always my nose was running. A new specialist came to town. This man was very dashing. Who was more excited, my mother or I, I could not tell. Always when we are walking to the specialist for our visit, Mother is telling me, 'Smile, smile.' Behind the specialist's office was a greenhouse where he cultivated the botanicals, even when the snow was deepest. My mother admired this handsome doctor. She would praise his work as he held me firmly and abraded sores into my skin with a file he wore like a thimble. Then he would rub a different compound in each little wound.

"After these tests, I would be sent to the hothouse while my mother and the specialist waited for the inevitable results: rows of welts that rose and spotted my body. My limbs would inflame. There was the inevitable wheezing. Week after week, the specialist could not believe it: I was allergic to everything. Soon I ran out of skin to make his abrasions. Then he ran out of compounds to rub in them. There was no point, anyway, he said: You are allergic to everything. Yet, after all the experiments were over, I kept coming to this hothouse. I finally knew the names of the things that had been hurting me. I began to recognize their forms. As I realized we were bound together, these plants and I, I became fond of them."

Julie went on, cataloguing those plants in botany-talk before moving on to the lecture's topic of plant domestication. I didn't need a bunch of Latin names to feel I was there, in Russia with Yulia, surrounded by aromatic botanicals destined to touch her skin. I could smell them—I was there! Before me were milkweed, columbine, horehound, and aster. I pictured feverroot, foxwort, myrtle, and brax. Then there was mandrake, nux vomica, cattail, and all the conifers. The students around me were taking notes on the fourth millennial diaspora of Mesoamerican starches, but my mind wouldn't leave that Russian hothouse.

Sitting in my ergonomic chair, I heard an occasional moan from the Missouri outside, straining under a new load of ice, and I pictured this hothouse on the banks of a great river, the Volga maybe, a place where the glare of a short-lived sun made glass and ice indistinguishable. Here a girl moved through rows of green, and I clearly saw the copper watering can she touched, heard the rustle of coat sleeves as she combed all the leaves. It felt like my secret, this atrium by the river where a girl was banished once a week by her mother and some doctor of debonair. I bet Ivan didn't even know about this place. If he'd ever pictured it the way I had, he'd have understood Julie better, and maybe she wouldn't have left him. Was this "specialist" a witch doctor or a man of science? Was Julie's mother sleeping with him? Was either of them really interested in Julie's well-being? For the moment, I didn't care. I only saw panes of Siberian light illuminating a young woman as she learned to love the thing that caused her grief.

When the time came for Q&A, I raised my hand.

Julie tentatively pointed my way, though I doubted she recognized me in the back row. I wanted to ask, *Did Ivan both thrill you and hurt you, too? Is that why you were drawn to him?*

But that's not what I asked. "Dr. Nivitski," I said as I stood, "most grains and starches from the Pleistocene era survive today, do they not?"

"Yes," she acknowledged, though I could tell she smelled a setup.

It didn't deter me, though. I needed to wow her with a couple of my ideas.

"And yet," I concluded, "the animals which fed on those plants do not survive. Wouldn't you see this as evidence for the hypothesis, articulated in my book, *The Depletionists*, that the extinction of North American mammals was caused by Clovis hunting, rather than starvation due to climate change?"

I leaned forward, waiting for an answer.

"I must say this is not my field," she said. "But I was just reading a new article by Hatitia Wells in which she speculates that if Clovis had brought just one diseased animal with them from the Old World a virus could have decimated North American mammal populations."

Everyone turned to look at me. For effect, I removed my glasses and twirled them once. "Well," I said, "I'd just point out to Stanford's Hatitia Wells that South Dakota is pocked with the skeletons of young, healthy animals that bear the marks of some big ol' spear points."

"Hatitia Wells is at Harvard now," Julie said. Instead of waiting for a response, she scanned the room, as if to say, *Next question?*

Some idiot agri-biz major asked the difference between corn and maize.

I sat back down, gripping the leather armrests for support. Had I ever been cut off like that before? I watched Julie take question after question, treating all comers with equal gravity. Why did my blood boil for her? And why did my mind keep wandering to Ivan? I saw him clear as a bell, sitting on a stool in a room fashioned from Siberian slump block, above him a buzzing electric wall clock. *Where has everything gone?* he asked himself. Outside his window was another brown building, just like his. Beyond that was another town, just like the one he was in.

Those ergonomic seats weren't so great, I decided. The fabric was terribly itchy.

When the Q&A was over, I waited for the usual circle of sycophants to clear. The smart students wandered off first; the sticky new teachers hung on a little longer, trying to gladhand their way toward tenure. Last to leave were a couple downtrodden administrators I recognized only from their filibusters in the faculty senate.

I approached Julie, strolling down an aisle. I tried to act cool, like I was chummy with all the famous anthropology professors. Julie was reaching for a carry-on suitcase stashed behind the curtain. When she saw me, she extended its handle with a snap.

"Dr. Nivitski," I said, climbing the steps, then strolling onstage.

"You," she said.

I leaned an elbow on the podium, casually, as if my guts weren't made of soup. I didn't know exactly what I was going to say, but I needed to straighten her out about me. I needed to make her understand some things.

"Now, hear me out," I told her.

But Julie cut me off. "First you are rude to me?" she asked. "Then you accost me at a casino? Then you follow me here and use my discussion time to plug your book? Now you make demands."

I couldn't stop looking at that V of skin. I was not normally a breast man.

She tossed up an arm. "Unbelievable," she said.

"I'll have you know," I said, "that I happen to personally know Hatitia Wells. We were on a panel together *at Harvard.*"

Julie just glared at me. I started to cave.

I said, "I do apologize if I dampened your discussion, however. That, perhaps, was less than professorial of me."

My apology was so fiberless that even I winced. Where was the new Hank Hannah, the guy who was trying to redress old wrongs and be a better person?

"Have you been drinking again?" she asked. "Because I know about drinking and apologies. First he gets drunk, then there is a thousand 'sorry's, and after is sex. Then he gets drunk again."

"Please," I said, "I'm not like that."

She planted a hand on her hip and flipped her wild hair back to address me. That fist on her hip clearly meant business, but she hadn't walked away this time, and I felt good about that. "I will thank you," she said, "to direct me toward the nearest taxi stand or place of public transport."

How a zing went through me when she got bossy!

"There's no such thing," I told her. "You'll have to call for a ride, but why do that? Please, let me drive you. A courtesy from one professional to another."

She shook her head. "The telephone," she said.

I led her off the stage and down into the fancy new agribusiness lobby, her rolling carry-on clanging down the steps. That suitcase looked so battered, so airline-tagged, that it might have spent a lifetime traveling the world with Julie as she abandoned men all over the globe.

But where the old coin-operated pay phone had been, there was now a new one, with no slots for change. Instead, it required some fancy type of calling card, probably common in places like Boston or France. When I lifted the receiver to speak to an operator, there was only a computerized voice. Julie stared out the window while I diddled with the buttons. Then that fist went back on her hip.

The look she was giving me was wicked. God, when she clenched her teeth . . .

"The less you have to lose," my father always said, "the more you stand to gain."

So I turned to her. "Just tell me this," I said. "What the heck made you walk up to me in the first place?"

Instead of answering me, Julie nodded out the window to

the arched façade above us. "Do you know these words?" she asked, pointing to the Santayana quote — "Those Who Cannot Remember the Past Are Condemned to Repeat It."

"This is a popular saying where I am from," she said. "In Russian, this word 'past' is feminine, so they translate it as 'He who forgets the past must dance with her at the harvest.'"

I thought about the past being feminine. Of course it was. Even without the idea of being condemned, the Russian quote was more foreboding, more sinister, for making destiny a feminine engine.

I asked her, "Was that some sort of coded answer to my question?"

"I was just thinking," she lamented, "how always in Russia the sayings come down to sex."

Why did she keep bringing up sex?

"My office is this way," I said.

Outside, the light off the snow was blinding; it made mirrors of the sharp, clear ice sheeting the marble entrance and penetrated the cloudy slush at our feet, making it look frozen from pulpy lemonade. Across the quad, new snow had erased in one night all traces that Eggers had ever lived there. Downhill, ice on the river was complaining under the sun. It chattered and creaked, and when a chunk snapped free, the newly exposed water steamed in the glare.

I suddenly recalled that the University of Northwestern North Dakota was in the town of Croix, also located on the Missouri, near the borders of Montana and Canada. This river was something Julie might look at from her office on campus. Suddenly, the Missouri was a ribbon that connected the two of us. If she were to write a message, and cast it upon the water in a bottle, it would float seven hundred miles, all the way to me. Well, all the way to the dam, at least.

"Isn't the river wonderful?" I asked.

Julie's suitcase bobbed behind us as we made for the anthro building, her breath, then my breath, alternating white before us. She looked over her shoulder, regarding it. "The river is bitchy with ice," she said. "It will soon crack free, and then — is anything more beautiful than open water in winter?"

Inside the anthro building, Julie's attention was immediately drawn to the flame-orange biohazard signs on the Hall of Man.

"I'm doing some important work in there," I said.

Half aloud, she muttered the words "Hall of Man," not without a little bitterness, as if she saw all of the Dakotas or Russia—all the world, even—as an outdated, hazardous Hall of Man.

Upstairs, mine was the only office that stood open, Junior spilling into the hallway, and it looked to me like someone else's mess, as if this heap were so many years of someone else's life.

"Don't mind this crap," I said, slogging through the papers, trying not to slip on the slick covers of iceberg surveys. Entering the shambles of my own office, I saw it as another professor would, had one ever come in here. Julie would be the first in years. Flint chips littered the floor, along with crates of anonymous bone casts, and the shelves were stacked with Tupperware containers of dirt, each masking-taped shut with excavation information. The hoary chair where Eggers always sat was sheened with grease, and either it was my glasses, or a small cloud of fruit flies had taken up residence. Then there were the plants.

Looking back, it's easy to see how little things lock into place. I'm not a man who believes in Destiny. Sure, I would soon be called upon to act in ways that bordered on heroic, and it's true that superhuman tasks awaited. Yet not too much should be made of Fate. Would Determination really determine me to be its hand and sword? Would Destiny leave the inheritance of humanity in the hands of one so petty? No, life, such of it as there is, is spittled with moments that feel absolutely inevitable only because they are completely surprising, as when a student finds a spear point and instead of putting it in a museum decides to use it, or when an ordinary man invites a beautiful botanist into an office full of tropical exotics left him by his stepmother.

Julie followed me into the office, and I turned to her, ready to help drag that suitcase over Junior. I also needed to explain that there was only one cab driver in town, that his name was Bill Hasper, and that he was likely to speak the word of the Lord—starting with his alcohol troubles, tracing his entire third marriage, and ending with his minor successes at the lottery—all the way to the airport if she dared summon him. When I turned, however, I saw she'd let go of the suitcase. Already she was reaching for the mustardy fronds of a fanlike plant and the drooping stalks of a red-veined something-or-other.

Already that V of skin was prickling red.

She turned to me, trying to catch her breath.

"My word," she said, "I had no idea."

She approached the skinny plant on my desk, touching its spiky ends.

"A *Brophilia porsophoa*," she said. "Rare cousin to the *Redendosa familia*. These specimens are sensational. How do you keep them in this climate?"

I couldn't exactly tell Julie that every once in a while I whacked off all the hangy parts, including the brown, fuzzy chutes the bush by the window kept sending up, and the rotty white cones its neighbor was always opening.

I told her what Janis was always saying:

"The secret, Dr. Nivitski, is love."

Julie's breathing was hoarse, labored. Her hand found my arm—completely without her knowledge, it seemed—and she looked into my eyes. "How is it you have gathered them here?"

"There was no more room at home," I said. "So I had to bring the overflow here."

Of course, this wasn't the answer to what she was asking, but it had the desired effect: her eyes widened, her throat grew flush, the rims of her nostrils flared—though that may have been her sinuses, I suppose. At some point, passion and allergies are indistinguishable.

"I have to get out of here," Julie said. "I have to get to the airport."

I took hold of her shoulder. "I'll take you."

"Let's go," she replied. "Let's go."

If those ferns set the hook, the Corvette drew blood.

When we walked up, Julie did a double take as she realized which baby was mine. Sure, some of the yellow fiberglass was cracking through, and the racing spoiler drooped to the right, but Julie let out a little *woo* when the engine fired up. I had a loose motor mount, which caused the whole rig to rumble and vibrate, so revving the engine sent some serious quakes up our tailbones.

I goosed it out of the lot, the tires sizzling some ice before they found traction. They caught with a lurch, causing a couple baby liquor bottles to roll from the dash down to Julie's lap, and soon we owned the blacktop — glassed-over postboxes flew past, along with the cocooned rumps of family sedans and an occasional swing set, sinister with icicles. The Eagles were in the cassette deck, but unless things reached critical, I figured I'd hold off.

I looked over at Julie — she had her nasal spray out, and she was trying, without success, to land a few blasts. Her cheeks were swollen, her lips puffy red.

"Are you cold?" I asked, pointing a heat vent her way, though the warm air carried the faint waft of my father's cologne, which smelled too much like Highlander for my comfort.

She kept looking at me like I was real trouble, like drunken, swashbuckling botanists were her weakness. "A *Pittisporum chrebus*?" she asked me, shaking her head in disbelief. "It's a good thing I'm leaving this state. It's a good thing I'm getting away from the likes of you."

"What?" I asked. "Why?"

"On you are all the danger signs," she said. "Can you see what happens to me? Do you see how I suffer?"

Julie tried to swallow through a constricted throat and swollen glands. She snuffed at me. In futility, she dropped the nasal spray, then turned to the window, to the barren whiteness streaking by. The edge of town had given way to open road, the slats of snow fences flapping as we passed them. Hormel grew in the distance.

"There's something special about you, Dr. Nivitski," I told her. "Join me for a salad at the Sky Lounge, would you?"

She didn't say anything.

I said, "Look, if this is about those little liquor bottles, I assure you I had nothing to do with them."

"I've heard that one before," she said, and I could tell that was the end of it.

Soon the blue-lit runway was pacing the road beside us, and I became melancholy. Airports had always disturbed me, especially now. It wasn't the fact that, from time to time, planes fell flaming from the sky: that seemed pretty normal. What got me was the idea of crossing a whole continent and simply dropping in someone's lap. The idea is, you just ambush this distant stranger, chum it up for a while, and then you're gone, probably forever. Maybe that person doesn't want you dropping in. Maybe that person doesn't want anything to do with you — does anyone ever think of that? Maybe that person lives far away for a reason.

And on an airplane, you don't even have time to think about what you will say to this stranger you're jumping, how you'll act, whether you'll pretend to know the "real them." It's just over: one minute you're looking at the high-altitude rat maze of their city, and then you're landing, and the next thing you know — *How do you do!* — you're there. Does anyone want to look at his own hometown from that height? The whole of the Dakotas, seen from a window at thirty thousand feet, looks not unlike the pale, pointless patterns strewn through acoustic tile, or the smattering of brown flecks amid a catbox of white.

I pulled into the white zone and left the motor running. Through the glass I saw ticket counters for all the major airlines, though only prop-driven planes landed here. Bill Hasper's lone cab idled in the loading zone, waiting for the next fare or the rapture, whichever came first.

When Julie climbed out of the car, she looked as if she was still vibrating. She jerked her bag from behind the seat, slammed the door, then leaned in the window. I was still hoping to come into the terminal with her, buy her a snack or something, and, I hoped, talk.

Instead, she simply said "Thanks" and was gone.

No *See you later* or *Catch you soon.* Julie didn't say *Until we meet again,* or even *Looking forward.* I would have settled for *Aloha,* but what could I do? I turned on my emergency lights and bolted for the airport. The terminal never changed: a blast of air hit me when the doors rolled open, followed by the must of snow-sogged carpets, and that fried-metal smell of overworked space heaters. I trotted through the terminal, its pitted windows showing foamy pink puddles of de-icing fluid that blew into clouds when a turboprop kicked up. Alone out on the frozen flight deck was a large aluminum crate. Did I hear a faint barking?

I caught her at Security. She'd just fed her carry-on into the X-ray machine, and she was about to step through the metal detector. She held a belt by its silver buckle.

"Julie, wait," I said. "You've got me all wrong. I'm better than you think. I'm not some guy who throws out empty pickup lines. I'm no college-mixer Casanova."

She stopped short of the security scanner. "In that house of yours," she asked, "you don't have a *Draculunus vulgaris*, do you?"

"Of course," I said. "Absolutely."

Julie put her hands up, flat-palmed, to keep me from going on.

"Please stop," she said. "No more talk of plants, and put sex out of your mind."

"I love *vulgaris*es," I said. "I have two of them."

This sent a visible shiver through her.

"Enough," she said, and spun on her heel, passing through the metal detector, toward the gates, and beyond.

Chapter Five

How invigorating! I felt like a new man.

The first thing I did was head straight for my office, where Junior was calling. Somehow that old *Depletionists* fire had stoked itself again, and I'd regained the drive that had sent me down into the library basement every night for six years while writing it. This was the energy I'd thrived on before I received any acclaim, before I made friends or had students, back when the world wanted nothing to do with me. Funny how quickly that scientific magic can return. I didn't have time for agri-business lectures or fancy plants, let alone pussyfooting around with stuck-up women. I had work to do! Julie's brush-off, far from setting me back, had been a real boon—now I could see what really mattered. Rejection always had a way of rejuvenating me, making me feel like my old self!

I tore into those boxes and began sorting knee-high stacks of paper, creating a skeleton of the multivolume project ahead. By evening, my office was filled with high-rises of paper, and I decided that if I got cracking, there was no more than three years' work here, tops. My "junior answer to the junior minds of critics" had amassed itself into a unified-field theory on the disappearance of a people. The task was daunting, but I had a vision. I believed 100 percent in my theory—that an entire people had been selfish, that they'd lived solely for themselves and they'd left their offspring nothing.

When you're a student, they teach you to be slow and skeptical, to gather data patiently, analyze them, and only *then* form a hypothesis. But that's not how it really works, not at all. In real life, it's just the opposite. You take a position you know in your heart to be true and then support it for all your worth, no matter what colleagues desert you, no matter which journals show you their backs. The dust from all those boxes was making my skin itchy, but did anyone care? Was *Anthropology Today* the least bit interested in my sneezing fit? Did Hatitia Wells give one titty about my scalp? Of course not. That's what being a scientist was all about.

I was leafing through deep-core glaciology results from Greenland's mid-rift when the telephone rang. It droned on forever before it finally quit and I could concentrate again. The Greenland data confirmed all the other studies: the earth suffered ninety thousand years of ice-age weather, then ten thousand years of warm, in a loop that repeated over and over, as far back as there was ice to record it. The Clovis appeared at the end of the last Ice Age, inaugurating an era of warmth that ushered in agriculture, the birth of civilization, and the ascendancy of *Homo sapiens*. But the Clovis simply plundered the first sunny days of humanity, just as we, a thousand years overdue for the next Ice Age, were plundering the last.

Artifact Number 5

REACH

Oh, the caprice of history was limitless, and it was my job to tame this bitch.

The phone went off again—where was that blasted thing?

When I answered, it was Trudy, breathless, on the other end.

"What are you doing calling me here?" I asked.

"We tried you ten times at home," she said. "We need you out here, Dr. Hannah. We've found something." Gaming machines trilled in the background.

"What do you mean you've *found something*?"

"Eggers is the one who actually came across it," she said. "We don't know what to make of it—it's like nothing we've seen in any of the journals or textbooks."

I sat down at my desk, scratched the back of my neck. Certainly I was interested, but look at the towering stacks of Junior. I'd just recommitted myself, and you don't go running off every time something sparks your fancy. You don't just up and quit when someone new comes along; you don't pack your bags when some distant mud city appears golden under scientific light.

"Dr. Hannah?" Trudy asked. "Are you still there?"

"Trudy," I said, "I'm afraid I'm going to have to pass."

"*Pass?*" Trudy asked. "What do you mean, *pass*? You don't even know what we're talking about. We were out in the field, Eggers was digging away, and then—there it was, right *there* before our eyes. You've never seen anything like it."

I paused a moment, then said, "I have my own work, too, you know."

Now she paused a moment.

"You are some kind of teacher," she said. "You're one piece of work. Do you know what I'm putting up with out here? It's cold as hell, and all day I get to listen to Eggers' theme-park ideas. You know he wants to start a Clovis Channel on cable TV? Twenty-four hours. I thank God every time he goes to the latrine, but then I have to race around sneaking off Polaroids for my professor, who, after a year of secretly lusting for me, takes my fellowship away and then won't even help me. Do you hear me?" she asked. "You aren't even listening," she said, and hung up.

I leaned back in the chair and exhaled deep. I'd momentarily lost my thirst for science, but that was to be expected. It was simply the ups and downs of the investigative process—the same force that drove a man into the library basement would, eventually, scare him right out again. I replaced my Greenland-glaciology surveys on the tallest stack and, stepping out, closed my office door for the first time in memory. But the key to lock it, I discovered when I thumbed through my key purse, was long since gone.

I sat in my car, engine idling. The thought of my own dark house gave me the willies—the leather of my father's chair grown cold under drapes of blind, creeping plants—and I just couldn't go there. When the motor warmed, and the defroster had cleared the windows, I saw that someone had spat all over the windshield. As the mucus thawed, it began to run. Some clown was obviously jealous that I'd snatched the prime handicapped-parking spot on campus.

I dropped the Corvette into gear, the trademark headlights

popping up. The power steering whined in the cold as I rolled toward the end of the lot. The plow had been through earlier, pushing up hard, crusted mounds of snow. In my headlights, the heaps glowed like glazed crap. When I got to the exit, for some strange reason I circled back for another loop, parking again in the same handicapped spot, one hand on the shifter, a thumb tapping the wheel.

Of course, I could go hang out with Farley—I was always welcome there—but when I thought of his house, bright and warm on top of the bluffs, I wasn't so sure. I pictured the steam of his laundry machines venting into the night, smelled the jerky he was always making in his basement dehydrator, saw his nieces' drawings taped to the fridge—stiff construction paper, watercolors. Farley was on the couch, I was sure, talking long-distance to his grandmother in Mobridge, eating cookies in the blue of the TV. No, he probably had some lady over, was cooking up that soufflé of his, the one with the mushrooms that never failed to impress the babes. Santana was playing on the turntable.

How could I barge in and interrupt him like that? Stars, if you'll notice, burn dimly and alone. Once in a while, two ignite together. Never three.

I couldn't think of a place in the world I belonged that night. Then, prickly and chilling as a whiff of gin, my father came to mind, and it seemed the evening I deserved included him. I slipped out of the lot and cruised a couple of blocks, rolling past a bank marquee that still read "Glacier Days Awaits," though the sign had lost a lot of bulbs.

Past the victory grove of oak trees that lined Parkton Square, Glacier Days was simply gone, leaving precious little evidence it had ever been—a few latrine-blue puddles of ice where the Porta Pottis had stood, the flapping of junk-food wrappers exposed by melting snow, and the petroleumlike smell of butter where they'd dumped the nightly popcorn tubs. Glacier Days had only rained stuffed animals on the city of Parkton, given its citizens a safe taste of death, and fed the crows.

I suspected my van might be sitting in the red zone outside

the Odd Fellows, as it was some nights, but when I cruised up, it wasn't to be seen. It was probably still parked in front of that cheap motel. In the lobby of the former lodge, I could see a gauntlet of old men, sitting on sad red couches, watching televisions suspended by chains from the ceiling. These gray-haired men were the Odd Fellows themselves, guys who'd lost their place of congregation, yet still gathered here in the after-supper hours to reminisce, smoke, and watch TV in a marble lobby whose symbols used to be theirs. Through the dirty windows, their faces were hazy enough that I could picture them all as my father, five years down the road.

I couldn't sit there a minute longer without getting all soupy. There was nothing to do but cinch my parka, crank the heat, and power down the windows as I drove out of town, heading for Keno through fields whose low spots were puddled with indigo. Above were clouds more meant for a summer afternoon. Big and singular, they sailed against a clear night sky. Backlit by a hefty moon, they glowed at the edges like chips of obsidian. If there were other cars on the road, as there must have been, I did not see them.

I craned my neck to look into the howling wind. Pinpoint stars, fixed in a galactic vise, stood fast in a sky as slick and intense as midnight vinca, the flower whose small hemlock-blue petals Janis wanted spread with her ashes in the Missouri, a wish Farley and I honored one evening last summer. From the back of the boat, I broadcast bone dust that chalked the surface of the water before heavier chips—femur, pelvis, teeth—sank like tiny comets. Farley spread the midnight vinca, beyond blue as it landed and turned in the gas slick behind his outboard.

It would be easy to look back upon myself, at the wheel of my Corvette, and say that *this* was the night, that along this road the resolve formed in me to become the leader of the Keno excavation, that, after a silent, contemplative drive, I opened my car door a changed man, a captain. But the truth was that such a moment of clear decision never came. I simply couldn't be alone a minute longer, and I sought only the company of other humans, the sound of their voices, a place beside the fire with my kin.

I rolled to a stop by Trudy's hot rod and fished a flashlight from under the seat. Then I headed across a field that grew lighter and darker as small, fat clouds crossed the moon. I scanned the bare branches of windbreak trees with my flashlight, checking for owls. All clear.

A path had formed from our trips back and forth—a streak of tamped snow scribbled through with Pomeranian tracks. Nearing the lodge, I found Eggers and Trudy down in the mud, exposing artifacts amid the stagger and play of torchlight. Fire smoke had blackened the oil of their faces. The casino backdropping them looked like a grand nineteenth-century painting of Byzantium.

Rib bones littered the site.

Trudy was sitting cross-legged, hunched over something I couldn't make out by firelight. Eggers was on his knees, moving dirt with a crudely fashioned spade. He looked up, smiling smugly, as if he'd known all along I'd be out here tonight. "Dad always said I'd be a ditch digger," Eggers announced. "If only he could see me now."

His beard in the torchlight looked thin and tangled as fishing line.

I kicked a rib bone toward him.

"What?" he asked defensively. "Can't a guy even gather?"

"Scavenge is more like it," Trudy said.

I picked up another bone. There was still some sauce on it.

I asked him, "Won't this contaminate the site?"

Eggers shot back, "I think we can manage some things on our own—like telling a Pleistocene-era artifact from a barbecued baby-back rib."

I gave him a look that said, *I have my doubts,* but I wasn't out here to give anyone a hard time. I'd been rough on them earlier. Now, standing under the stars with them, I found it hard to remember what the fuss was about. Here were my students, dedicated, ambitious, and in need of guidance. Here was an anthropological site begging for serious inquiry. I rubbed my hands together, watching everyone's breath in the dark. If other people didn't prefer my company, if some folks didn't even have time for a simple salad at the airport, well, so be it.

I tossed the bone into the fire. Sparks streamed from the flames like the words of an ancient story. We watched them plume orange, cool, and vanish.

I said, "Are you going to show me what you found, or what?"

Eggers smiled. "You won't believe it," he said.

He led me to the excavation pit. The earth was peeled like a cadaver, and amid the carefully exposed striations of soil, I could see a set of gypsumlike forearms—radius and ulna—their joint sockets sheened oystery where they'd worn smooth from use. And beyond that, as if the arm had been reaching for something, was a shape in the dark. I fixed my flashlight's beam. There, nested in a bowl of exposed soil layers, was a sphere.

"We found it below the finger bones," Trudy said. "Like she died holding it."

Eggers and Trudy looked nervous, wild-eyed.

"Is this for real?" I asked. "Are you two playing some kind of joke?"

I knelt to examine it, my breath glowing amber in the flashlight's path.

The sphere was a little larger than a melon and seemed formed from unfired river clay that had, over the eons, mineralized as hard as cement, capturing in its surface the impressions of fingers and palms, the very prints of the hands that had formed it. God, were they Keno's? Little divots and grooves pitted the surface, probably the result of river grass and seeds that were patted into the mud and had long since rotted away.

"Trudy," I said, "is it heavy? Is it hollow? Report."

"We haven't touched it," she said. "When we first encountered it, we thought it might be the skull, but, exposing its surface, we realized it wasn't bone. We figured you'd know what it was."

I handed the flashlight to Trudy, who focused the beam as I lifted the ball. It was cold in my hands, absolutely hard, though it looked as slick and wet as the riverbank from which it was shaped. And it weighed a fair amount—heavier than a bag of sugar. When I rotated it to inspect the underside, I felt something shift, though it could have been my imagination.

"Is it some sort of vessel?" Trudy asked.

"Clovis Tupperware?" Eggers asked.

"I don't know," I said. "I don't like it, though. There's no evidence of Clovis being associated with pottery. Hunter-gatherers in general didn't use clay. It's heavy and bulky, and it wasn't employed until people needed it, until they'd started agrarian lives and had things to store for long periods."

"It could be some sort of funeral offering," Trudy said. "Maybe something for Keno to take with her to the afterlife."

"The problem is," I said, shielding my eyes when Trudy pointed that light at me, "that the idea of taking material things into the next world really only comes about with the rise of agriculture, when people settle down and begin to accumulate things. That's when cultures first start wanting to take it with them. It wouldn't even occur to a hunter-gatherer to bring stuff to the afterlife. I have to say, this discovery bodes ill for the authenticity of this as a Clovis site."

"But we found a Clovis point," Eggers said. "What better proof is there?"

"Let's say Keno was sort of an anthropologist, like us," I answered. "A thousand years ago, Keno runs across a ten-thousand-year-old spear point, which she, I mean he, picks up and carries around until an untimely death."

"We'll just radiocarbon the bones," Trudy said. "If we get a Pleistocene date, then we know the Clovis used primitive pottery."

"What lab in the country would test artifacts without proper paperwork, especially if they just happen to turn out to be the oldest in the hemisphere?"

"Enough mystery," said Eggers. In one hand he lifted his torch, eyes shining from the fire, and in the other he hefted that spade. "Let's crack this nut."

I pulled the ball close. "Don't even joke," I said.

Trudy pointed the flashlight at the ball. "Maybe it's filled with wampum," she said. "You know, beads and shells. Or maybe even precious minerals, some raw quartz or obsidian, a cache of materials to flint-knap blades with."

Eggers said, "What if there's a head in there?"

We all stared at the ball. Nobody said anything for a moment.

"We haven't found the skull," Eggers added. "It could be Keno's mummified cranium."

We spoke in a flurry:

"The shape's too round," Trudy pointed out.

"The weight's all wrong," I said.

"Plus, the size seems a bit too small," Trudy added.

"There's no head in here," I declared, holding the sphere away from me a little.

Despite our efforts to convince each other to the contrary, there was suddenly no way to look at that ball without imagining a severed head at its center.

"Look," I said, "it's time to be realistic. This job's too big for us. This is a job for an entire research team, for Hatitia Wells at Harvard."

Trudy switched off the flashlight. Eggers just stared into the fire—the flames were low and clear as they wagged and popped above the coals. It was hard to believe he had made it from one spark, tindered from a stick and bow. There was nothing I could do about their disappointment.

"Trudy," I said, "let's have that camera."

She pulled it from a bag in the snow and handed it to me. I didn't even look at Eggers. I set the ball back, surrounded it with the contents of my pockets—change, nail clippers, as well as my watch—to provide scale, and then burned off all the Polaroids, getting the ball *in situ* from all angles. The bones were an important find, but all I wanted was a look inside that sphere. "I better get this back to campus," I told them, hefting the ball again. "I'm going to be up all night."

"Wait, Dr. Hannah," Trudy said. She touched me on the shoulder. "There's one more thing," she said.

"What?" I asked.

"I need your help."

Eggers pointed to a dark patch in the snow.

"I think it has to do with that big set of chains," he said.

"The thing is," Trudy said, "I have to get rid of that car. That cop said some detectives are coming tomorrow. I don't have time to fix it. I don't have anyplace to hide it."

"Sinking it in the lake was my idea," Eggers added. "That water's a hundred enos deep."

Trudy opened her mouth to make a plea, but already I knew I would fall for it. She could play up the mentor thing, or speculate on the many ways that car could jeopardize Keno. I nodded, and the next thing I knew, I was following her across the snow, carrying a petrified mudball that might or might not contain a human head. Within minutes, Trudy was wrapping a chain around the rear axle of my Corvette and securing it with a grappling hook, the kind you'd use to scale the walls of a bank. And then, like a dream, I was easing my car forward to take up the slack. I felt the tug of the GTO behind me, and I pulled away from Eggers and his fire, pale against the casino's dazzle. Trudy ran the GTO without lights. Tractionless, it was a black ghost behind me, sleek and flat in the rearview mirror, floating side to side in the lane.

When I turned left onto the river road, Trudy swung wide behind me, the haunch of her GTO busting a snowdrift high into the air, sending her shooting out of my mirror, into the other lane. Without a transmission, Trudy could only steer with the handbrake, and, trying to compensate, she pressed the brakes hard, making it seem as if my front tires were about to wheelie off the ground. When I hit the brakes, the chain went slack between us, sparking along the pavement like the Fourth of July.

Heading toward Lewis and Clark Lake, I saw, every so often, the signal beacon of the Parkton air-traffic control tower. Alternating white and green, the beam seemed to sweep in vain. What was that lamp seeking with such seriousness, such ceaseless vigor? Of course the airport made me think of Julie, doing an about-face in the terminal, showing me her back. Oddly, though, my mind landed on that aluminum crate of little dogs. I pictured it still out there, forgotten on the pink runway, the airport grown dark and empty, no signs of life but the white breath of dogs through the vent holes.

I eased off the gas as we neared the marina. We passed the old fish hatchery, its abandoned cement ponds lurking like pitfalls under snow, and then coasted along a field of empty boat trailers that looked in the moonlight like the graveyard of elephants they were always searching for in those old Africa movies. The chains rattled the ground as we passed Mr.

Chippy's Fish Ship, and the boat ramp's speed bumps nearly tore the rear end out.

The ice, when we put our wheels to it, was so white in the moonlight that it seemed like morning. Empty warming huts glowed blue-brown, and a layer of hoarfrost gave the lake ice a ruddy, purpled-over look. As we drove on the ice, everything changed. The GTO in my rearview mirror somehow coasted faster than I could drive. It kept closing on me, and the only way to avoid getting bumped was to speed up. I didn't know which direction to head, the lake was so vast. But each time I sped up, that black car closed, the slack chains playing hell with the GTO's undercarriage. Soon we were moving nearly fifty miles an hour, and when I sped up again, it only drew Trudy closer. To avoid the impact, I turned my wheel slightly to the left. When her car floated past me, I knew we were in trouble.

Slowly, my car began to turn. Suddenly I was traveling at highway speeds—backward—as we began spinning in tandem, slowly rotating counterclockwise like a giant bola, which is the weapon ancient humans used to eradicate the large, flightless birds of Tasmania, Australia, New Zealand, and Madagascar in the mid-to-late Pleistocene. In great revolutions, our cars swooshed round each other. Tufts of loose snow fleeced my windows, while the tires kicked up fits of ice that riddled the fenders and hood.

When we came to a stop, I was half in the passenger's seat, sharing it with Keno's mudball. I sat there a minute, the windshield a cataract of frost and snow, waiting to see if I would barf. I pushed off the passenger seat and leaned back, putting both hands on the wheel.

I looked in the mirror. The rear window was clear enough so I could see Trudy in the moonlight, examining the interior of her car one last time. She had a glove in her teeth, held by a fingertip. She flipped down the visor to remove her registration, then policed all the personal possessions from the glove box. She popped the trunk and got out.

Trudy startled me by knocking on the window, which was so sheeted with ice I needed two hands to roll it down. She leaned her head in. "This'll go pretty fast."

I got out and watched Trudy slide under the 'Vette.

"You got some rust under here," she said after she'd crammed her head and shoulder under the rear end. "You really should invest in some fresh undercoating."

I heard some clanking around under there, the rattle of links running over the axle, and then the hollow clunk of the big hook hitting the ice.

"Shouldn't we unhook the other end of the chain?" I asked.

"I don't need that chain anymore," she said from under the chassis. "Do you?"

"No," I told her. "No, I guess not."

She wasn't even greasy when she slid out. She walked to the open trunk of the GTO, where she pulled out a chain saw. She tugged its starter cord once or twice in the cold, adjusted the choke, then tugged some more. Blue smoke puffed as the saw tried to start, filling the air with the smell of unburned two-cycle oil.

Almost instinctively, I began backing up.

Right then, the saw caught, and Trudy opened the throttle, racing the little motor till the smoke blew out. Then she put the saw to ice. Where was my inhaler? I patted my pockets.

The saw, when Trudy sank it, drew from the ice a jet of material that kicked high and low, depending on how she rocked the blade—a curtain of water ran from the bar when she plunged deep, and a sleet of ice chips kicked when she got the saw to bite. I scanned the horizon, taking in the slate-white lake, limned with an intangible shore that could be dark green or purple, depending on how you squinted. The noise from the saw was like radiation in the cold; it penetrated all things, fled all directions, and there was no echo.

I wrung my hands as the saw raced and stalled in the thick ice. The teeth bucked and dug while Trudy cut her way around the passenger side of the GTO. She worked the blade into a turn when she reached the trunk, and I was ready to leap into my two-seater and speed away from this dark business. The whole scene was straight out of the old whaling days, a scrimshaw tableau where a figure traversed the white expanses of whale belly sinking a blade into an upwell of fluid that wallered his boots and oilskins.

Then it happened. Trudy had cut around three-quarters of

the car when the saw froze up, bound in the ice. Things suddenly went quiet, and there was only the sound of her huffing and straining to pull the blade free. Then the great cracking came, like a limb cleaving from a tree.

The ice breached, and Trudy ran. Behind her, a great rectangle of ice tilted back, the GTO rearing with it like an old cowboy showboating his horse. The slab of ice heeled higher, grinding loud as a manhole cover, and almost lost in the noise was the cracking snap of a chain and the clanging as it hooked something in the undercarriage of my Corvette.

The GTO began to go down. A surge of water washed out of the hole in all directions, an ankle-deep wave that turned the frosted ice clear black. Only as the water soaked my boots, making them seem perched atop a sheet of smoked glass, did I realize that something else had happened, that, as the black of a hot rod slipped into the abyss of the lake, my Corvette had started to baby-crawl backward toward the hole.

Silently, the GTO slipped from view until there was only an oily froth of bubbles and a Corvette following in a strange, halting dance across the water-slicked ice. In the moonlight, the 'Vette sashayed backward in starts and fits, the rear end stuttering one way, then reversing, the headlights sweeping this way and that across the ice. When its tail reached open water, and the chain hung straight down, the car stopped. Below, we knew a beast of metal hung by its nose ring in the black static of the lake. There was only a steady bubbling of air as the GTO filled with water, making it heavier and heavier. The ice let out a low, patient moan as the burden grew on the back of the 'Vette, the rear tires flattening, the front end threatening to rise up.

"Keno's head," I shouted. "Save the head."

Trudy started running toward the 'Vette, half slipping in the skein of water.

"Come on, Dr. Hannah," she called, skidding to the car. She put her weight on the front bumper. Still the car wanted to rise, the shock absorbers becoming visible in the wheel wells. The ice around her began to grimace under the strain—fractures shot out that prattled and chatted. Over the years, I'd become comfortable working shoulder to shoulder with the dead, but how it stunned me to see Trudy leap into the lap of death itself.

I had no intention of hopping into a Corvette to ride shotgun with the reaper. But what was I to do? I can't say I ran, exactly. It was more like a trot. There was only an inch of water over the black ice, but this film somehow magnified the well of black below, made it feel as if the ruminant deeps were intent on me.

At the passenger door, I paused.

Trudy was bent over, her arms brought to bear on the fender, while, below our feet, the ice seemed to glow with stress. If you could see microwaves or hear nerves fire, that's what it was like.

"Open the door, Dr. Hannah," she told me. "Save Keno's sphere."

I pulled the handle and swung the door wide, the interior looking small and sad: the Eagles poked from the tape deck, my keys dangled from the ignition, and with the clutch and yawn of the ice below me, a sermon on impatience, it was as if I could see the whole history of my car at once—from the salesman in Sioux Falls who first showed me the yellow "lady slayer" on his showroom floor to the linger of gin my father had left two nights before. I felt the rumble of the engine, smelled the hot gear oil, heard the kiss of the clutch. Oh, my willing V-8! Those worn leather seats, the custom dash, the heated glove box where I kept the old trowel Peabody'd given me, ready for any emergency!

"Dr. Hannah," Trudy groaned.

"Right," I said. I scrambled into the passenger seat and reached under the dash, where I found Keno's ball, still warm from the floorboard heater. My inhaler was in the driver's-side console, but I couldn't reach it. I grabbed Keno's ball, locked the door, and slammed it shut.

Trudy let go. The Corvette executed a perfect backflip into the water, showing us its dingy belly before crashing white and vanishing. We watched through the black ice as a twirl of head-light, fractured and swooshy, illuminated mushrooms of surfacing air. Ropy umbilical cords of motor oil floated up and pooled under us. Then the lights dwindled as two hot rods, their fates linked forever, raced to their graves.

We just stood there, looking past our wet feet, waiting, I suppose, for the crash as they hit bottom. They ghosted silently through my imagination, spinning ancient and celestial. If they struck the bottom of the lake, this hammer and mace, we didn't hear, and they were left turning in my imagination.

"My car," I exclaimed. I dropped to my knees in the cold, a ball of mud under my arm. I just sat there, looking through the ice, though there was nothing to see. When Trudy put a hand on my shoulder, I shrugged it off. "It was more than just a car," I said. "It was a part of me."

Trudy took my arm and helped me up. "Come on, Dr. Hannah," she said.

She straightened my collar and dusted imaginary snow off my parka.

I didn't want to be consoled.

"That was crazy," Trudy said. "No one could have predicted that."

"That wasn't crazy," I said. "You sank my car."

"It was a fluke," she said, softly. "The way that chain popped up and caught the axle—one in a million." She looked me in the eye. "But what matters is, you were there for me, Dr. Hannah. I needed you, and you were there. Warrior peoples like the Bantu, the Cherokee, and the samurai know a debt like this can only be repaid with an equitable act of heroism. I trace my lineage back to the buffalo soldiers on one side and the Kaesong Brigade on the other, and I just want you to know this: whenever I can be of service to you, *anytime, anyplace,* and no matter what engaged, I will assist you."

Trudy's pledge, ringing like an ancient warrior's call to arms, humbled me. She deserved more than a washed-up professor who ogled the breadth of her shoulders. She deserved a mentor worthy of her code of honor. There, on that dark, frozen lake, my Corvette sinking to its final resting place, I couldn't even meet her fierce gaze. To acknowledge such a pledge was to commend myself worthy of it. Instead, I stuffed my hands in my pockets, leaned back in my wet shoes, and turned into the wind.

We began walking, cinching cuffs and turning up collars against the cold. My boots were freezing stiff already. There was no conversation as we headed for the marina, our eyes trained on the brief stretch of skiddish ice before our feet. We grabbed each other every so often to keep our balance, but there was nothing sexual in this sudden groping. Rather, we were merely two people reaching out to steady one another.

It was as if I were crossing that galactic glacier I'd imagined the other night, except I was not alone now; my fate was not to bump into humans once a decade, but to move with them. *Anytime, anyplace.* No one had ever said those words to me, and it's laughable how quickly they solidified in my heart, like the notes to posterity kids write in wet cement. On my personal glacier, when I was lost in a crevasse, there was someone who would come looking for me, *no matter what engaged.*

When the moon went behind the clouds, the ice seemed underlit somehow. When the moon appeared again, the water once more darkened. There was something reassuring in this rhythm. At the boat launch, the ice clawed into the grooved incline of the ramp like the first ooze that pulled itself from the seas, and, as we crossed from ice to cement, the footing felt a little too trustworthy for my taste. Buildings appeared abandoned in the late indigo, as if summer would never come, and no one would ever rent a paddleboat again or ever lie back in the itchy grass, waiting for the Coney Dog Hut to open. Past the igloos of upturned canoes and a two-man ranger station, we moved single-file through this ashen woodcut of summer, Trudy, then me.

The road rose toward the two-lane highway, and there was nothing but the frictiony *shush-shush* of our nylon parkas, the far-off civet of skunk, and the silent companionship of things half exposed in the plowed shoulder—various bits of refuse, a fan of radial-tire belts, rows of fallen icicles stuck in the snow. The empty cups of horse hooves walked out of the woods, pacing us awhile before vanishing.

At the junction, you could see the tracks of big rigs that had blown through not long ago, and the only other signs of life were rectangles of light from Tyler's Bait & Go. Inside the bait shop, we opened our coats to take in the heat and then headed straight for the junk food. Trudy hit the nachos hard, then switched to little breakfast biscuits, the kind with double sausage patties. I dug into some cellophane-wrapped bologna-and-cheese sandwiches, the ones that are cut diagonally both ways. I folded open a carton of milk so the top was wide-mouthed and square. That way I could dunk the points of my sandwiches and get them down that much faster.

A guy came out from the back room, carrying a case of toilet paper. He was wearing a hunting cap, driving gloves, and a walkie-talkie in a holster. He almost dropped the box when he saw us. "Jesus," he said, veering toward the register, "I didn't hear the bell."

He looked back, suspicious of the petrified ball of mud under my arm.

I didn't say anything to him. Had I ever been so hungry? I knew better than to cap things off with grape soda and salted nuts, but after chili, cheese, bologna, and milk, what did it matter? I took a swig of soda, the nuts fizzing in my mouth as I inspected a wall covered with photos of folks posing with trophy fish—shovel-faced sturgeons stretched the scales, and men held up trot lines of crappie, strung like Chinese lanterns. Two catfish, black as vinyl, lay on a dock like body bags. One photo showed an old man at the water's edge, cleaning fish assembly-line style on a rusty ironing board.

Under the food station's bright lights, I looked at Trudy anew. She had a sprinkling of freckles across her cheeks and nose, and even in fluorescent lighting her skin looked the color of roasted almonds. Her brow seemed weighted, as if she viewed the world through the parted curtains of what had been. I suddenly had a surge of fondness for her which I could only describe as fatherly. We'd witnessed something fabulous and dangerous, something that, by the laws of brashness and foolishness, should have gotten us dead. I nodded and saluted with my grape soda.

Fiesta concluded, we took the empty cans and containers and carried them to the counter, where we piled next to the Lottery machine. The man working the register obviously wasn't the regular cashier. He flattened some wrappers, punched some numbers, then squinted across the store for prices.

He looked up. "How about twenty bucks?" he asked.

I treated, glancing out the window as I opened my wallet. The cashier looked out the window as well. He scanned the empty lot.

"You folks have some car trouble?" he asked. "I drive the wrecker around here."

Trudy said, "We might could use a lift."

"I'm no taxi," the driver said. But then he shrugged, asked, "Where to?"

"Almost to the casino," I told him.

"*Almost?*" the driver asked.

We followed him out back to the tow truck, brand-new, painted cream and trimmed with chrome. On the door, instead of a sign or logo, there was an airbrush of a Lakota dancer, underlit by fire, his arms upstretched to the great Cangleska, or Medicine Wheel, of the sky.

I turned toward the driver to see if I'd missed some Sioux in his face.

"It's my brother-in-law's truck," he said. "He owns Pride Towing. Ty's my other brother-in-law." He pointed to the Tyler's Bait & Go sign above us.

The driver had probably been hoping to get mashed in next to Trudy but got stuck elbowing me instead. He flipped on a row of toggle switches, and then turned up the police scanner, though there was nothing to hear, and off we went. The diesel knocked so loud you'd think it ran without oil, and the headlights were insanely bright. We trucked in silence past the airport, the downtown, the prairie prison on a hill. We were almost to the casino when we passed the Lollygag.

Most of the cars were parked around back, beyond the view of the wives, husbands, and general citizenry of Parkton. Only my van was prominent, glowing pink under the Lollygag's neon signs, and it was parked before a room with all the lights on.

"Hold it," I called. "You can let me off here."

The wrecker clanged down through gears, slowing to the shoulder, the tires fighting for traction as they slogged through frozen gravel.

"Trudy, it looks like my father has procured a room here. Are you going to be okay going out there with Eggers?" I asked, as if she had not just wielded a chain saw.

We came to a stop, and I opened the door, swinging myself down by the big side mirror. Trudy slid over to get some breathing room, and I paused on the running board.

"Sure, Dr. Hannah," she said. "You okay here?"

"Don't worry about me," I said.

"Maybe we'll see you tomorrow at the site," she said.

"Maybe," I said.

I turned to face the Lollygag, which flagged under a northerly wind that would have cut us down out on the ice. Twin aerial antennas sang with the gusts, and riding the air was a medley of empty-swimming-pool smells—exposed plaster, old chlorine tabs, the frozen fiberglass of a diving board.

When I knocked, my father answered in an undershirt and shorts.

"Hey, there's my boy," he said, and smiled, though he looked as if he was expecting someone else. He stuck his head out and looked both ways down the row of motel doors. "Come on in."

The place was like a sweat lodge, the tinny room heater set to fire-hazard levels. All the lights were on, as was the TV. Taking a seat on the empty twin bed, I noticed the carpet was oddly worn in front of the full-length mirror. I set Keno's ball on the bedside table and leaned against the headboard.

Dad offered me a can of vegetable juice, but I waved it off.

"This is all I can drink today," he said. "My stomach is killing me."

"Mine, too," I said.

Dad eyed me, then seemed to determine that the source of my trouble was different from his. He looked back at his TV movie. "You're welcome to stay," he said, "unless something comes up." The film was *Jeremiah Johnson*, starring Robert Redford as a guy who gets fed up with things and goes to live by himself as a mountain man. Nobody talked to anybody else in the movie, and from what I could gather, it was one of those plots where a guy's on a journey to find growth and inner peace, but in reality fights everyone he comes across, including several large animals.

"I'm taking the van back," I told him. "So you'll have to get your own car."

"Key's on the ring there," he said.

"I'll need the house key, too."

"Suit yourself."

As a nod to our father-son thing, I tried to watch the TV.

What could ruin my mood more? The only television programs I remember enjoying were the Winter Olympics—God, those lady speed skaters!—and a nature show I saw at Farley's about how certain bears, when they get old, refuse to hibernate. They just wander around all winter causing trouble. Lonely and cranky, they pull down baby trees for no reason and tear the bark off logs. The narrator said these were the most dangerous bears to film.

I was starting to get sleepy. It was hot enough that I unbuttoned my shirt.

"Okay," I yawned. "I'll bite. What are you doing here?"

"They're painting my place. The fumes are awful."

He said this in an offhand, exhausted way.

"What color?" I asked.

"White, I guess."

"White? Your place is already white. That apartment's not even a year old."

"Believe me," he said. "It needed it."

"Oh, it did, did it?"

"Those walls were driving me crazy," Dad said, reaching for his vegetable juice.

Robert Redford tromped on and on through the snow, giving shit to all the Indians. His Hollywood buckskins never got dirty, and the scenes started to blend together. At some point I drifted off, shirt open, dozing on top of a motel bedspread, the antennas on the rooftop above whistling the soundtrack to my life, and this was how I spent my last night of freedom in the land we used to call "America."

Chapter Six

Which brings me to the second great fallacy of life—the notion of "climax."

This is how it supposedly works: You're going about the normal business of living when an event occurs that forces you to drop everything and cast a long glance toward the approaching brakeman of fate. A moment of sudden definition has arrived, a point at which life's manifold possibilities narrow to one true course, and grand decisions must be made. Destiny beckons, and the future falls clear as the scythe through the field. Common side effects of climax include tunnel vision, loss of balance, hearing voices, and occasional bladder or bowel failure.

Climax, of course, is an illusion. High powers suddenly call us to action? Mundane days spontaneously become epic? Don't make me laugh. It's understandable that people are drawn to moments in which they feel like actors in a larger drama; it's only natural to let such moments stand in for all the days that slip away. But there's no shorthand for existence. Time spars with no stunt double.

The need to have life rise to a higher plane is strong enough, however, that history is littered with examples of "false climax":

After the last battle for Persia, Alexander declared that crossing the Hydaspes River had been the glory of his life, the reason he was born. Little could he know he was still to conquer Egypt, Media, Scythia, and India.

Rome didn't crest and fall with the ascension of Nero, as the armies and Senate expected, but with the conversion of Constantine centuries later.

John Wilkes Booth told reporters in 1860 that performing *Hamlet* for President James Buchanan was "the greatest role of his life."

In N'Gosa's biography of Nelson Mandela, we learn that, on the eve of his incarceration for life in the Kittleton Afrikaner

Penitentiary, Mandela ordered his followers to hold a funeral for him, complete with coffin and song. How could he know that his life would "climax" five more times, Moses-like, before he became the leader of his people twenty-seven years later?

So, the following morning, when I woke itchy and nit-ridden in that oven of a motel room, my life was not without historical precedent for the day ahead. A feeble light penetrated the heavy drapes, setting aglow the nappy fibers of my father's bedspread,  which he'd neatly made, folding and tucking the corners. I wasn't about to go hunting him down, though. My scalp was on fire. My armpits, too, were aflame, and I'd rather not talk about the troubles I was having down below.

I took a shower so fierce and scorching that my skin puffed red, and my hairline felt as if it receded an inch. To no avail, however—the nits had incubated and hatched, and a good scrubbing only served to work them up. How I'd have killed for a Q-tip! I don't want to go into it, but my underwear turned out to be a lost cause, and I was forced to proceed with my day in the French manner.

Still flushed from the shower, I dressed and stepped outside, where my hands steamed in the crisp air, as if the cold were trying to burn off my fingerprints. Except for my van, every car in the lot was gone. On the horizon, the Thunderbird Casino went through its morning calisthenics—its flashing banners pumped up and down, while neon fountains of light climbed, climbed, then dropped and gave us twenty.

I had Keno's ball in one hand, the key to my van in the other, and I told myself just to forget my father and go. But I smelled coffee brewing, and I couldn't help wandering past the bleak, tarped-over swimming pool, smelling of frozen leaves and granulated chlorine, to the Lollygag Lounge. Inside, dark corkboard lined the walls, its surface quilted with tacked-up photos of patrons, mugging for immortality in this hall of good times. Twin TVs broadcast at each end of the bar, in the middle of which my father sat alone. While one television broadcast news images of faraway fires, typhoons, and sundry disasters befalling remote points of the globe, my father watched the other television set, the one showing muted interviews with pop stars.

I took a stool next to my father.

He opened his mouth to speak, but I cut him off:

"There you are, my boy," I said, mimicking his fake-cheery voice.

"Good morning to you, too," he said.

I looked around at the empty bar. The corkboard had been darkened by an eon of cigarettes, and the thousand faded photos stuck to it formed our Greek chorus. Above, I was drawn to the TV footage of cattle with blistered lips and cracked hooves, to the chicken fires that were lighting the night skies of Hong Kong.

"What are you doing here?" I asked.

Dad rapped on the bar. "Best breakfast in town," he said, though I'd never even heard of someone eating here. Respectable adulterers left this place long before first light.

"The biscuits," Dad said, "are celestial. Light and buttery as love."

That bitter note of irony was my cue not to take him too seriously. It was meant to throw me off balance and invite me into our usual rapport—a well-trodden mode in which we avoided all topics of consequence. I'll admit I was in the mood for a day like that, where we drove around without talking, slowing to look at places we knew already, or just staring off the dam at the turbulent water below.

I looked at the bottles of booze, some of them plastic, lined up in front of the bar mirror.

"I'm serious," I said. "What are you doing here? You want to go on a bender, why not stay at the casino?"

"I don't know," he said. "The T-bird's the best place to crash in town, but it's not so good to wake up there."

"Who is she?" I asked.

He pretended not to hear me.

A waitress came out of the kitchen area. She was about my father's age, and she held three empty coffeepots in one hand.

Dad and I were the only people in the place, so when she saw us she looked surprised, then just shook her head. She came over, her face looking steamed from the kitchen though it was just past dawn and the bar hadn't even opened. She set the pots down.

"You again," she said to my father. They held each other's eyes a moment.

She stuck a ballpoint pen in her hair. She casually leaned toward my father, and together they regarded me. "That him?" she asked.

My father had this strange expression on his face, as if he were seeing me through her eyes, as if I were a stranger he was interested in getting to know.

"He's the one," Dad said.

The waitress looked at me, as if to confirm some aspect of a story she'd been told. "The professor," she said, then pointed at Keno's head. "What's with the paperweight, Professor?"

Dad answered for me. "Probably some petrified dinosaur egg," he said. "The boy likes to dig things up. He roots around in the past."

"A dinosaur," she said to me. "You gonna bring it to life, like in the movies?"

She said it in a friendly voice, as if I was an outsider she wanted to include.

"If I could bring things back to life," I told her, "I'd start with my old man here."

She followed my gaze to Dad.

"Don't you worry about him," she said. "Don't you worry."

"Hey, are we going to eat or what?" Dad asked. "I'll take the usual."

When he said "the usual," there was some sauce on it. Either he'd never eaten here before, or they were lovers. This woman pulled on a towel that was draped over her shoulder, then wiped her hands. She went into the kitchen, set something sizzling on the grill, and began fixing us two Virgin Marys while more coffee brewed. Before I knew it, we were knee-deep in breakfast, the real proof that something was up between these two. First came sausage links, seasoned with anise and sage, then home-style potatoes, fried in butter and rosemary, and finally eggs, salty and fried crisp at the edges, all flanked by triangles of toast.

I dusted my eggs with black pepper and dug in. There is nothing like the eggs of birds—yellow-white, quivering with flavor, and light as the nests they were plucked from. Eggers always boasted that a reptile egg is just as good. He even claimed to like that ring of brown oil around turtle yolks. That morning in the Lollygag, though, the black pepper on my eggs had started to creep me out. Those little bits seemed to shift and twitch on my plate, hopping in my peripheral vision. Soon my skin was crawling, and I tossed my napkin on the bar.

Dad was crunching the celery stick from his Virgin Mary.

"You ready to roll?" I asked. God, my armpits were burning.

"Something wrong with the food?" he asked.

"Everything's fine," I said. "Let's just get out of here."

I was still thinking we'd go fishing, maybe just sit around and not talk. We hadn't played cards in a while. He used to love to play cards.

Dad shrugged. "I'm in no hurry."

"Well, grab your coat," I told him. "I can't just leave you here."

"You go on. I'll finish watching my show."

I looked up to the soundless television, where celebrities in strapless gowns were auctioning each other for charity.

"Look, I'm taking the van back, remember?"

Dad said, "We'll do lunch later. How's that sound?"

"Well, I'm not going to just leave you. I won't do it." I put my coat on and grabbed his off the stool. "Take it," I told him. "Because I'm not going to abandon you here. You get some other son to do that. Find some other offspring for that shit job."

This was when Dad was supposed to give me a winner smile and sweet-talk me with that salesman voice of his. But he didn't. He just looked at me as if I was a curiosity. He took a nip of bacon. Whatever he was about to say would wound me, I felt it coming, and before that could happen, I dropped his coat on the floor and turned to leave.

When I reached the door, a voice came from deep within the kitchen:

"Nice to meet you, Professor."

It was a sweet voice. I heard it over and over as I drove away—in my head the words were clear, but they seemed to come from far away.

Inside the Hall of Man, I set Keno's ball on the autopsy gurney, just above his upturned hands, making Keno seem to shrug about his missing body. The phone in my office upstairs was ringing like mad, but I didn't have the key and I didn't care. The campus was deserted—was it a weekend, a holiday?—so that my phone was the only sound in the building, and I could hear its faint plea through the corridors, even in here.

I sat on my new silver stool, absently scratching at my crotch as I wheeled up and down the Hall of Man, Pleistocene glaciers advancing and retreating in the exhibits like some flip-book of history. Humans evolved and devolved with each shove of my feet. I'd push off one wall, and in a blur one hundred thousand years would pass, evidenced in the posture of a Clovis, reflected in the eye of a Cro-Magnon. Everywhere in these dioramas, I felt the hand of Peabody—in the blood-tinted authority of his cave paintings, in the way his depiction of a sunset over glaciers turned the ice below the color of watermelon meat, or the way runty dogs cowered, conniving, in the periphery of humanity. Peabody was the constant as millennia flew past. He was proof that people could transcend time, that no one was ever lost, if someone was left to tell your story.

I rolled back and forth until he was a presence in the room. Not that Peabody was standing there talking or anything. I just felt him, the way he cocked his head when you spoke, that indulgent smile he cast while he listened. I heard the rubber tip of his cane going *cush, cush*, as it helped him up stairs, saw his pediatrician's hands turn a bone, carefully, as if there was only so much patience an artifact had before it got stubborn and fitful.

And then there was a faint, low sound in the room, much different from the stool's casters, or the thud of my boots off the wall. I stopped rolling. "Peabody?" I whispered.

The lights hummed. Air circulated in the vents. I wheeled to the autopsy table, my eyes fixed on Keno's ball. Leaning over the cold steel, I put my ear to the fossilized mud. At first, there was only a staticky sound. Then there was fluctuation, rhythm, like blood in your ears, and I began to hear what sounded like weather, elemental and faint, some ancient meteorology. There was wind buffeting, and the pepper of gust-driven snow. A human call came from this cloak of snow, an urgent whisper held in an eternity I saw as white. I closed my eyes. All was preservative-white, the white that spins forever inside a souvenir globe, the kind you give a kid who didn't make the journey, who was left at home, and I didn't need a translator to understand Keno's lonesome tune.

The phone was still ringing when I left, and I knew where I must go. I dropped the van in gear and sidled out toward the casino. It was a perfect day for digging—the sky clear, the temp above zero—and as I passed grid after grid of snowed-over fields, I could imagine great finds under all of them. All the lost answers, all the missing pieces, were out there, I felt, waiting for me to find them. I looked for that black GTO when I coasted off the casino road. Then I remembered it was sitting at the bottom of the lake, rump to bumper with a Corvette, their dull headlights illuminating the petroglyphs above like some ancient drive-in movie.

I parked the van on the side of the road, and set out to dig. As I crossed the fields toward Keno, wind-driven ice crystals cut at my skin. Maybe I'd been rolling around a little too much in the Hall of Man, but I half expected to see herds of woolly camels hoofing up the snow in search of roots, or great teratorns circling the sky above. I followed the now worn path from the highway to Eggers' mastodon-tusk lodge, squinting into the distance to catch sight of my team. Spades of mud flew from the excavation site, surely the work of Eggers' arms, and a figure squatting, square-shouldered, her profile noble, was Trudy.

I stepped carefully through the detritus of humanity—old bones and burned sticks, camp scraps and lumpy latrinecicles—until I stood at the edge of the pit, now knee-deep in places.

I put my hands on my hips and addressed them: "Today, we are scientists."

Eggers planted his makeshift spade and leaned on it. Trudy lowered her digging antler.

"Life is full of rituals in which people celebrate the living," I continued. "Today, however, we commit to the dead. Today, we show allegiance to the missing. We declare that the departed matter, that the absent, the unaccounted, and the truant walk alike before science."

My team fell silent while I surveyed the dig. The long shadow of a human was beginning to emerge. Various bones had been felt out and left *in situ*, and I cast my eyes upon the yellowed Pixy Stix of a *Homo sapiens*. Mentally, I tried to identify these fragments as those of a gravesite, a crime scene, a last stand, or a lost soul. I noted the flat back of what had to be a femur, knuckle pointing south. Did Keno die on her stomach? Would the Clovis bury her this way? Did they believe in the heavens or the underworld? Was showing your back to a god a sign of trust, as the Anasazi people believed, or an insult, as most cultures agreed?

"Trudy," I said, "dig over here. That's where we'll find the torso."

She rolled her eyes, as if to say, *But we found the fingers over there.*

"Dr. Hannah," she said, "there's something—"

I lifted my hand. "Eggers, forget the earthwork. I need you sifting over here for foot bones. I'll take care of this femur." I eyed them. "And let's not fall victim to laxity and sloth, people. We have a mission here. She's depending on us."

I clapped my hands together. "Chop-chop," I said.

No one moved. "What?" I asked. "Just what is the problem here?"

Trudy leaned forward and grabbed an animal skin that was lying in the pit. When she removed it, there was another sphere, just like the last one, half exposed in the mud. She lifted her eyebrows. "It's not that simple," she said.

I dropped to my knees. "Who found this?" I asked.

Eggers gestured with his spade. "Trudy had the honor this time," he said.

I examined the sphere, though it was obviously of the same variety—similar shape, palm-printed texture, pitted striations from river weeds. It was electric to the touch. "Do you know what this means?" I asked.

Eggers smiled. "That we've found a two-headed Clovis?"

"Curb that insolence," I said. "This means we have a grave on our hands. No hunter-gatherer would carry two of these heavy, ungainly things. These spheres were placed here, with great significance, by the people Keno left behind."

"Why here?" Trudy asked. "What's significant about this place?"

Ignoring the casino and the highway, I tried to see the landscape as it was twelve thousand years ago. Distant bluffs marked the final reach of a great glacial hand, its long fingers of ice clutched in a last grip — reaching southward, yet receding north. Mist and fog would have been constant, with curtains of cold whipping off the ice, and all around were places where the retreating glaciers deposited their icebound cargo — boulders, bones, and minerals, all churned up from a thousand glacial quarries. Might this have been a place of reverence to Clovis, a place of connection to a hundred thousand years of icy past? Or was this where the ice handed them pink quartz and obsidian, carted here from Canada?

"Trudy," I said, "Keno will tell us. If we ask the right questions, she'll let us know."

Her eyes lacked focus. She didn't seem to be listening.

"Trudy?" I waved my hand in front of her face.

She lifted her hand and pointed toward the road. Gerry's cruiser was pulling up, followed by Sheriff Dan's Blazer and a powder-blue sedan from which emerged two men in matching yellow parkas. The four of them consulted, then inspected my van, the men in yellow shining flashlights in all the windows, even though it was broad daylight.

In the distance, we saw Gerry gesture wildly, then point in our direction.

"That's not a good sign, is it?" Trudy asked.

Eggers fell in beside me. The three of us stood in a row, shielding our eyes. "Things don't look so bad," Eggers said. "The cops never talked it over before arresting me before."

"Arresting you for what?" Trudy asked. "Speeding in that pink Porsche of yours?"

"It's *champagne*," Eggers said.

"Let's keep some focus here," I told them.

Did Eggers really have a Porsche?

That's when Sheriff Dan kicked the tire of my van and nodded his head, and the four of them headed our way, one of the men in yellow talking on a radio as they marched in the cold. I know it's hard to believe, dear colleagues of tomorrow, but history was once governed by the laws of private property, and anthropology, more often than not, was a crime.

Eggers clapped once and rubbed his hands together. "Trudy, you go on. Dr. Hannah and I will take care of things. We'll cover for you."

Trudy laughed. "Cover for me? You're the one who snared the deputy's dog."

"Come, now," I cautioned them. "We're a team. Both of you better hit the road quick. I'll face this menace alone."

Eggers wouldn't budge. "Some team," he said. "What happened to 'Today, *we* are scientists' and 'Today, *we* commit to the dead'?"

"Yeah," Trudy said, "don't *we* have a mission?"

"Would you two just get out of here?" I asked. "I know how these guys operate. I know their language."

"I fear no authority," Eggers said. "Growing up in the guest quarters of your own house will teach you that. So will weekly boxing matches with a father who never, never let you win."

"I'm not scared of them," Trudy added. "I've come up against North Korean MPs."

"Get out of here," I told them. "Now."

Eggers pushed off and began walking away. Trudy fell in behind.

I turned to face our new guests.

When Gerry was close enough to shout, he pointed at me.

"That's him," he yelled. "He's the one who killed my dog."

Sheriff Dan entered our camp, flanked by his team. He strode up to me, his eyes gray and dry in the cold, his voice down-homey yet formal.

"Morning, Henry," he said, the crop of his jacket flapping in the wind. "How's your father? I haven't crossed paths with him in some time."

By "crossed paths," Sheriff Dan meant the funeral.

"Dad's fine," I said. "He's coping."

"Dog killer," Gerry said.

Sheriff Dan ignored him. "Things sure haven't been the same down at the courthouse without Janis. Everyone feels your loss."

Sheriff Dan was my father's age, so when he said this, sounding as though it came from the heart, I had to nod, even though I barely knew the man. He hailed from the upstanding side of town, lived on a street where people didn't pirate cable television, didn't clear their sidewalks by snowblowing the drifts into neighbors' yards. The Sheriff Dans of the world paced off the jurisdiction of their existence with passes through the Rotary Youth car washes, Sunday Fellowship pancake breakfasts, and the occasional ant line out to the cemetery. I kept my distance from them: they'd smile and tell jokes as they cinched people's handcuffs; they'd affably discuss church events as they evicted the poor. They were happy to go through the motions of life, seemed to connect truly to no one, and were therefore capable of anything.

I eyed the men in yellow parkas. They both had broomy mustaches and thinning hair. I couldn't tell them apart behind their sunglasses. One of them pointed to the figures walking away toward the casino, their forms sharp, then dull in jets of wind. "Are those your associates?" he asked.

"Not at all," I said.

He just stared at me.

Then his partner handed me a photo of a black Subaru, up on blocks in front of a corncrib. "Do you recognize this car?" he asked.

I shook my head no.

He produced another photo, held it close to my face. "What about this one?"

This picture showed a warehouse floor filled with mechanical parts, some of them spray-painted black. "I'm not sure I see a car," I said.

Knowingly, he asked, "How many transmissions do you own?"

The question struck a philosophical note in me. I thought of my Corvette at the bottom of the lake. Was it still mine? Wasn't it now in the public domain, like Keno's spear point or the bell Eggers found from Meriwether Lewis' lost boat?

"Give me a minute, would you?" I asked him.

He smiled, then pulled out a notepad, jotted something down.

"Look," I said, "what's this about?"

"These fellows," Sheriff Dan said, "came down from Sioux Falls to look at something. And now it's missing."

"Gone like something you love," Gerry said through his teeth. "A little fellow you'll never see again."

Involuntarily I looked over to the stretching hoop next to Eggers' lodge. On it, pulled tight with sinew, was a fresh pelt.

A radio squawked, and one of the men in yellow reached to his belt. Without looking, he clicked it off, then said, "Tell us about the moniker King of Spades."

"Moniker?" I asked.

"You know," he said, "a street name. Are you known to your acquaintances as the King of Spades?"

I knew what a moniker was, but before I had a chance to defend myself, the other one asked, "Do you have any tattoos?" He toed his boot through several stray baby-back ribs, inspecting them, while his partner began nosing around the site. "Do you like pork?" he asked me, though I was watching his sidekick pull back the flap of Eggers' lodge—he winced at the smell, shone his flashlight around inside, and asked, "You're sympathetic to the Indian way, aren't you?" Together, the two of them bent to examine a frozen segment of feces. One popped on a rubber glove and picked it up. The frosty crust shined in the light. Very closely, they studied it.

The one wearing the glove pointed the turd toward me.

"Would you like to explain the fur in this object?" he asked.

Gerry looked horrified. "Lord, no," he said. "Not Spark!"

"That fur's not *in*," I told them. "It's *on*. Those little mutts were running everywhere. They were the ones rummaging through the latrine. We don't do our business in camp. We're scientists!"

"Who, exactly, is 'we'?" Sheriff Dan asked.

Gerry was trembling with fury. "His name was Spark," he said, "and he was a Pomeranian, not a mutt."

"Look, Gerry—" I said, backing up.

"Pomeranians are an ancient and noble breed," Gerry said, nearly stammering. "They were miniaturized by the Norse from Icelandic sledding dogs."

With each step backward, Gerry came closer. I looked to Sheriff Dan for support, but he just shook his head. The duo from Sioux Falls was heading for the excavation pit. "You gentlemen can't go over there," I called to them.

Gerry reached up and poked me in the chest.

"Hey," he said, "we're talking about Pomeranians, here. As if you even care. I could loan you a couple videos on the topic, in case you're ever curious about the animals you kill."

A yellow blur flashed across the ditch. One of the men knelt in the mud and pulled out a pen that telescoped into a pointer or some kind of prod. Then his partner joined him, walkie-talkie in hand. "Looks like we've got some human remains," he radioed in.

"You officers are going to have to go," I called. "I'm not joking—there's serious science going on here."

Sheriff Dan tensed at the word "remains." He lifted a hand to quiet Gerry, then took my shoulder. "I've got a thermos of coffee in the squad car," he said to me. "What say we wait in the cruiser while these boys do their work."

The look in his eye scared the crap out of me.

It was here that I felt my first climactic moment. Within Sheriff Dan's calm voice of concern lurked a possible new life, one laden with shame and disgrace. In this other life, I was not a man of science but a fast-talking pilferer of antiquities. It is not until you're old that you come to realize there's no such thing as real climax at all—such cairns on life's journey are only monuments to your thirst for drama, markers to guide the trailing nostalgia. But you can't know that at the time. As Sheriff Dan offered me a cup of coffee, my spine glassed over. It would not be the last time I felt weak in the face of climax's threatening illusion: soon the river would deliver to me teams of corpse-eating dogs, and within weeks, the time would come for me to hunt down the last Russian boy on earth.

I looked around. Everything was moving in slow motion. The men in yellow were kneeling in the mud. They went straight for that strange orb, their hands getting grubby with matrix, and then came that sucking sound as they pulled the orb from the muck.

"Do not touch that object," I yelled, but it was too late.

Did I really shout that warning? Were my hands about to become "savage instruments," as the judge later described them? Gerry reached for his cuffs. Sheriff Dan gave me that warm, parental smile, the one I was always a sucker for, while two men from Sioux Falls rapped the butt of a flashlight on a twelve-thousand-year-old grave offering, listening for anything that might rattle inside. It was as if I was there, and I wasn't there. Something went quiet and still in me. My limbs felt ghostly. There was Eggers' rodent stick, leaning against his lodge. Suddenly it was in my hands.

"Get away from Keno," I warned them. "Return her ball to the pit."

The four of them stared curiously at the long, willowy stick I was brandishing.

I jabbed the rodent stick in the air, its three sharp tips hissing, but none of them seemed afraid. Looking around, I realized there was no one, anywhere, to help me.

"I've seen these barbs driven into a badger," I told them. "When they were jerked out, braids of intestines looped from the holes."

That's when everybody's handcuffs came out, and they started closing on me.

Gerry advanced, shifting his cuffs from hand to hand like a switchblade, shaking them here and there to get me to strike.

"This one's for Spark," he said, and faked a charge.

Instead of flinching, I flashed that rodent stick, whistle-quick, near his face.

"I'm the dog killer, huh?" I told him. "I'm the bad guy? *You're* the one who butchered a little girl's hog. *You*, chief, are the one running a puppy mill. Breeding them in that school bus of yours. Shipping them in unheated containers."

I saw Gerry wince and glance fearfully at Sheriff Dan, whose jaw tightened in determination, as if right then and there he'd put Gerry on the roll of ex-deputies.

In my peripheral vision, a man shrugged off his yellow parka. He began waving it to distract me while his partner slipped to my rear.

"Son," Sheriff Dan said, "come, now, son." With both hands, he cautioned me to drop the stick, though he could have been asking me to lie down, lie at the feet of what was to come. Nothing could have tempted me more.

This is what my life had come to. There were tears in my eyes.

"My students had nothing to do with this," I yelled, then threw the stick and started running. I hadn't gone ten steps before I felt something spring onto my back, little legs clamping my sides. A hand slipped round my throat, ending in a scissor-lock choke. Then my face hit the snow. The lights dimmed, and my vision went sparkly, as if a snowstorm were dropping layers of powder that covered everything—burying cars and hydrants, erasing hovels and headstones alike.

A voice, a disembodied whisper, reached me through the muffled cold, through my prickling, snow-filled ears. "Maybe you haven't heard," it said, "but I don't live in a school bus anymore."

By noon, the state of South Dakota had charged me with attempted assault of one of its officers, and a Seventh Circuit prosecutor from Omaha had phoned in a federal charge of grave-robbing—which had local "cult implications" that Sheriff Dan was looking into. The sheriff's station was no larger than the Dairy Queen next door, and it was filled with several small booking desks, most of them empty. The deputies were out patrolling town in the pathological loop called law enforcement.

Only one young deputy was there to book me in, a flat-topped kid who wore, beneath his uniform, an oversized bullet-proof vest. He was familiar in an awkward way that made me suspect he was a former student. He took a little too much pleasure in smashing my fingers into the inkpad, and he smiled a private little smile as he plucked out hair samples for the evidence kit. All the while, I could see Sheriff Dan, recumbent in a big chair as he phoned other agencies to consult about rarely enforced statutes like "ritualistic dismemberment" and "crimes against nature." On the corner of his desk was a little pile of dog collars.

I had to fill out a gang-affiliation card and submit to a tattoo search, and I was being digitally photographed and logged into Gangbank, the national archive of street affiliation, when Sheriff Dan raised his office window and called to the Dairy Queen drive-through across the way.

"Three double specials," he yelled, and while the burgers were being fried and the malts were being mixed next door, Sheriff Dan fielded calls that, judging by the expectant look on his face, meant he was hoping for grand charges against me. I could hear him pronounce words like "mutilation" and "conspiracy" to parties unknown, but by the time the food arrived, he looked a little pissed. There was no chitchat with the delivery boy about Parkton High football. Sheriff Dan simply grabbed the grease-stained Dairy Queen bags and sauntered to the bench where I was shackled. He dropped a bag on my lap.

He said, "The County of Parkton, South Dakota, hereby charges you with trapping out of season and two counts of class-three cruelty to animals."

He held the chocolate malt near my lips and took some pleasure in watching me strain for the straw. I sucked for all I was worth, but the malt was too thick, and I got nothing. Sheriff Dan grunted once, as if this confirmed his suspicions of me.

"Let's go, son," he said, removing my cuffs, leading me to a large, insulated door at the rear of the station. From behind its reinforced surface came volley after volley of low, gargly cries.

When Sheriff Dan put his key in the lock, I saw him wince in anticipation, and as the door swung wide I nearly gagged from the smell. Before us were three cells, constructed of bars painted mint-green with epoxy. The walls and floors were slick with an industrial sealant designed for easy hose-down.

The cell on the right contained nothing but a few children's toys scattered across the floor; the walls were covered with doodly crayon drawings.

The middle cell was completely empty.

And the cell on the left contained a pack of dogs, a dozen at least, circling with frenzy, leaping on each other's backs with scat-covered paws.

Sheriff Dan pushed me through the middle door. As soon as it swung shut, a great Dane in the next cell stood tall, rising a full head above me, his paws hooking in the upper bars so he could show me his big red one. Steam rose from it.

I grabbed the bars. "This isn't funny," I said. "This is no kind of joke."

"The dogs are temporary," Sheriff Dan answered. "It's just till they finish the new wing at the dog pound. Wait till you see it," he added. "The Humane Society's going to double its capacity."

"This is intolerable," I told him. "I've got dander issues. I can barely breathe."

"You'll get used to it," he said. "It's just till morning. They'll be gone by morning."

I rattled the steel door. "This is my life," I said. "I've got some serious thinking to do. I can't have some parade of puppy adopters coming through here. I won't tolerate big-eyed girls staring at me as they shop for poodles."

Sheriff Dan gave me a knowing nod. "Nobody's getting adopted around here," he said. "You know what really happens to all these strays. A deputy will be in here to take care of them in the morning. The whole thing is over in five minutes, and then—hello, peace and quiet."

This shut me up. When Roamy disappeared, it was a while before Janis finally found him on the roadside, and I have to admit that, in those couple days, I imagined Roamy had worked his way into another family's heart, that he'd found a nice white farmhouse with lots of children, a swing in the tree, and some-one always around to push you. Now I saw that sad dream for what it was. That pickup or semi did Roamy a favor, because he'd have really ended up in the hands of a human like Sheriff Dan, in a place like this.

Sheriff Dan leaned in close, shoulder against the bars, looking as if he had something serious to say. He jutted his chin, thoughtfully.

"Henry—you spent any time with the Good Book?" he asked.

I, too, leaned close. "It's Dr. Hannah," I said. "And don't I get a phone call?"

Sheriff Dan shook his head. "Think you know it all, don't you? You think you're above justice." Here he tapped his boot against the bars, as if to remind me which side of the iron I was on. "The second you waved that little spear at us, I knew you were the one who killed the McGeachie girl's hog. Two hundred years of prize hogstock, wasted, and for what, some twisted thrill?"

"You mean *McGeachie,* as in 'The Farmers' Farmer,' the founder of Parkton?"

"Don't play the fool with me, *Doctor.* The boys are going through your office right now, and the word over the radio is it's full of bones. Piles and piles of bones. And Gerry's been keeping us posted on what you've been doing to the small animals of this town. You think these squirrel disappearances have gone unnoticed?"

"Gerry's the real criminal here," I said. "He's the one who—"

Sheriff Dan lifted a hand. "Gerry's got his own mistakes to answer for. And he will, believe me. You worry about yours." Here he stared deep into my eyes and then rumpled his nose. "Innocent squirrels? Lapdogs? What makes people like you tick?"

I said, "I'm an anthropologist."

His smile said I was the saddest thing he'd ever seen.

"Allow me to get your precious phone," Sheriff Dan said, then turned and left, clanging the heavy door.

I pinched the bridge of my nose to help me breathe and took a seat on a metal bench welded to the bars that separated me from the dogs. I tore open my Dairy Queen bag and spread out the food, placing my double burger, napkins, and salt and pepper packets all in a neat row. I went for the fries first, squirting them with ketchup.

I had to figure a way out of this mess. I needed to do some serious thinking, but right away one of the filthy little buggers next door stuck his snout through the bars and grabbed my hamburger. The burger was then stolen from him, and a melee followed that sent bits of wax paper floating above a frenzy of wild-eyed dogs who—teeth flashing, ears folded—clawed up flanks and popped each other's tails. When a dog's hackles went up, you could see its nits lift.

Once the burger was gone, the dogs returned for more, licking the bench, nosing through napkins. They all sat in a row, like a wet-eyed boys' choir, watching me eat my fries, following my hand with their noses as it traversed from the greasy container to my mouth and back.

I turned from them to the other cell. On the floor were various toys: a red rocket ship, an assortment of plastic zoo animals, and a laminated chart of the solar system. I walked over and slipped a foot through the bars. With it, I was able to scoot a coloring book close enough to grab. I pulled it through the bars. It was called *Impossible Journey*, and its pages were filled with roughly colored images of circus dogs, interspersed with scenes of an evil French fur-trapper.

Suddenly I realized that this cell had been used as some kind of day care for Gerry's kids, and it was the saddest thing I'd ever seen. My mind flooded with memories of all those days I sat alone, mother gone, father off on insurance junkets, days I spent inventing yarns in which I was part of a great tribe of people. I was usually the medicine man or the priest, a person the village couldn't live without. I'd climb the temple steps and spread messages of love and family; to help them sink in, sometimes I performed a few sacrifices. From time to time, in an empty living room, my ten-year-old voice announced the will of the gods. "Burn the crops," I demanded. "Fill my room with gold."

I turned to the dogs. Their ears lifted in anticipation. What sad, abandoned beasts. Unwanted, unloved. I showered them with the last of my French fries. They went mad, lunging and snapping, obviously making Sheriff Dan nervous as he returned with the cordless phone.

I glared at him. Putting an anthropologist in prison is one

thing, likewise crating up all the strays in town, but how could this man allow his deputy to put his own children in here?

"You make me sick," I said.

He gave me a fake little smile that suggested he didn't know what the heck I was talking about. Then he passed the phone through the bars, along with a tiny rice-paper edition of the New Testament.

I took his phone and shook my head.

"Being a child is prison enough," I said, "without people like you in the world."

Then I tossed his silly Bible on the bench, where it landed in some ketchup.

Instantly, some cur stuck his snout through the bars and nabbed it. Now the whole murderous lot erupted, raising a cloud of tissue paper—gospel-white and ketchupy.

Sheriff Dan couldn't quite hide his shock. He tried to act cool.

He said, "Looks like you and the hounds found some common ground after all."

I pressed against the bars. I could feel cold metal on both cheeks. Then I beckoned him close with my finger. "You want to know about common ground?" I asked him.

I planned on really zinging Sheriff Dan with a good comeback, a put-down that would smart for the rest of the day.

With a cocky sidestep he neared me. *Closer,* I motioned to him. *Closer.*

When he was near enough that I could smell the burger of his breath, I decided to really zap him with a one-liner, but all that came to me was *Sit and spin,* a line I used to use in high school. My brain was totally crapping out on me. Where was my Ph.D. when I needed it?

Then something unexpected happened: a single flea hopped from my scalp, and without Sheriff Dan's even noticing, it landed on his cheek. The black speck whirled, vibrating in a little dance, then disappeared into the man's silvery hairline.

A large smile crossed my face, a look that totally unnerved Sheriff Dan.

"What?" he asked, but I just smiled bigger.

That's when he glared at me and stalked out.

When he was gone I clasped the phone. I needed to call Farley to get me out of there. I needed to contact my father, so he could post bail, but, for reasons I can't explain, my finger dialed Directory Assistance for the state of North Dakota. I asked for the number for one Yulia Terrasova Nivitski, paleobotanist, resident of the city of Croix. The line was faint and staticky, as if I was calling through a snowstorm, but right away, before the first ring was over, a boy answered.

"*Da*," he said. The voice couldn't have been older than eleven.

A Russian greeting, of course, yet I couldn't shake the feeling that he'd addressed me as a father. I cleared my throat. "Dr. Nivitski, please."

"Who is telephoning?"

"Tell her Hank is on the line. Hank Hannah."

There was quiet.

I said, "Just tell her it's Hank. She'll know."

Again, quiet. Was he covering the phone while he spoke to her?

"Hannah," I said. "Dr. Hannah from Parkton. Parkton, South Dakota."

Nothing.

"Hello?" I asked.

Then the boy spoke again. "Do you have many canines?"

I looked up and suddenly became aware of all the dogs, snarling and yapping around me. I guess I'd gotten used to them.

"Look," I said, "I'm calling for Dr. Nivitski. Is she there or not? Who is this?"

"This is Vadim," he said, pronouncing his name *Vah-deem*. "I greatly dislike canines. They used to chase me on the way to school. They would hide in the woods and wait for me."

"Is Julie there?" I asked. "Are you alone?"

"No," he said, "I have many friends over. We are working on a grand project."

"Seriously," I said. "Is anyone else home?"

"Yes, there are many of us. My friends and I will one day be scientists. Our project could be a tool for peace or a weapon of mass destruction, depending on whether or not the world appreciates us."

Now I was the one who was quiet. A shiver went through me, and I experienced this strange illusion that I was calling back in time, that a blizzard had messed up the phone lines and I was talking to myself, twenty-five years ago. I didn't like it.

Vadim asked, "Do you work your science on canines?"

"No," I said, "they're just pets. I'm sort of dog-sitting. Look, will you just tell Julie I called? Can you write that down, that Hank Hannah called?"

"In Russia, my father works his science on rabbits. He is very famous."

A sickness was coming over me. I had to get off the line.

"Just tell Julie," I said.

"I will write a sticky note," Vadim said.

"Goodbye," I said.

"What sort of science do you work?" Vadim asked.

I hung up.

Toward afternoon, the heavy door burst open and in walked Gerry, a cardboard box under his arm, anger and determination on his face. He walked past a height chart painted on the wall — five one in boots, I noted — and headed for the cell with the toys.

Without looking at me, he unlocked the cell door, then dropped to his knees and crawled this way and that as he picked up toys and tossed them into the cardboard box. He scooped up balls and brightly colored zoo animals. He chased down crayons that had rolled to all quarters. I neared the bars so I could peer inside the box — also there were his own possessions, from his desk and locker, from his old police cruiser.

Finally, he stood and looked around, registering not me but the book in my cell.

"Give me the dang coloring book," he said.

I grabbed the *Impossible Journey* book, a bright-eyed Pomeranian on the cover, and passed it through the bars. "Hey," I said, "no hard feelings."

"*Hard feelings?*" Gerry asked. "They're going to feed you shit pizza in prison, and I only wish I was there to put the cherry on top."

"You're angry," I said. "I understand. I was out of line with the school-bus remark."

"The school bus. You guys'd never leave that alone, would you? You'd never let that go. Well, my parents happen to be dead now, so the school-bus chapter of my life is over." With two fingers, Gerry pinched some air. "I was this close to getting back with my ex–old lady. She gets out of the hospital next week, and we had this big party planned. We're talking helium tanks, Bundt cakes. I've had those kids eating out of my hand all week."

I nodded toward his cardboard box.

"I know you think this was my fault," I said. "But it wasn't. You break the law, you take the consequences, right?"

"Don't you sad-sack me," Gerry said. "I got some serious side projects going on, real entrepreneur stuff. You think I give a turd about being fired? I work nights at the prison. I work weekends at the casino. I'm a survivor, Hanky. I'll have a new day job by tomorrow, my friend. I've worked every day of my life. But you wouldn't know anything about work, would you?" Gerry hefted the box, tucked it under his arm. "By the end of the day, tomorrow," he repeated, then took a long look at those dogs, as if this was all he'd miss about the Parkton County Sheriff's Station.

Evening came. My breath turned white. Darkness blued the corners of the room. The dogs huddled in the center of their cell, sleeping as one, their nit-lined coats rising and falling in a patchwork of snores and dream-whimpers that kept the cold at bay. It seemed those dogs knew something we humans had forgotten. In the next cell, all that remained of Gerry's ex–old lady's kids were crayon drawings on the walls. In the muted light, they resembled ancient cave paintings. Across the cement was depicted an arcing dog team, purple and brown in the near dark, towing a great sled that seemed to lift and take to the sky. It was like some mythic story, or an interpreted constellation, an arm of the Milky Way tamed by humans, man and animal jumping the hoop of the North Star.

I couldn't stop thinking of Vadim.

The hardest thing in life is to see beyond the known. What I knew was that there was a little boy seven hundred miles away, and he was alone in a room I couldn't picture. He liked science, feared dogs. And that was it. He would stay that way in my mind until I knew otherwise. His mother worked—in a lab, a classroom, an office?—on campus, and unless I knew where she picked up fried chicken on the way home, without knowing the rights and lefts of her drive, whether she entered through the front door, the side, through the garage, I'd never be able to put them together in my mind. That boy would always be alone.

As it grew dark, I could see, through my one mesh-reinforced window, the red safety lights come to life atop the smokestacks of Hormel. The towers were hard at work, pluming steam vented from the rendering floors, where hogs danced their way into sausage casings, where pigs poured their hearts into patties and links. It was easy not to think about the grim work that went on twenty-four hours a day in the meat factory below. The simplest thing in the world was not to visualize the hydraulic slaughter line or picture the busy air knives and cauterizing belts.

As the moon rose, a soft light illuminated the smokestacks, setting to glow the lime in their mortar, giving the giant towers a mosaic look—like the pattern of fish scales, or the blue-and-white weave of old maize. The bricks glinted with bits of silica that had baked to glass in a Kansas City kiln a hundred years ago, and the blinking crowns of the towers were glazed maroon with a buildup of carbon. The towers made me think of the minarets of Herat, pillars that stood tall during the sacking of the year 1222, hovering blue and floral above the executions of all Herat's 160,000 inhabitants.

I decided, lying on my metal bench, to drop this tidbit into my next pop-culture lecture, maybe let my students jaw on the jerky of perspective for a while. A hundred and sixty thousand, I'd tell them, is a fair guess as to the sum of people you meet in life, the number of humans you make eye contact with, the tally of beings who accidentally brush your shoulder in the hall or unintentionally knuckle the back of your hand in a tight elevator. I'd ask my students to imagine that many people disappearing. Picture them missing. See that birth-to-death chain of every person you would've met—broken. See yourself walking alone, moving through life without each of the thousands of human moments that confirm you're alive.

I thought of all the people I'd hoped would come visit me, and the list was ridiculous. They were the people that I'd never see again, that I probably wouldn't recognize if I did. Peabody was dead. He had to be. Janis' face, when I conjured it, was now the stranger on the bronze plaque. My mother had never been anything more than a crumbling plaster cast and a yellowy X-ray.

Then it struck me that I probably wouldn't be lecturing tomorrow.

The room grew cold, and as I drifted toward sleep, I'd have lain down with the dogs if I could have. A bird landed on the perch outside my window. It was a pretty thing. I wish I could tell you which kind it was. Except for the noteworthy birds, all the rest have merged in my memory into a representative variety, a catch-all composite: medium-sized, pigeon-color, grainy beak.

This bird flapped its wings and pecked twice at the glass.

Did I mention that birds were supposed to be symbols of freedom and liberty?

As quickly as it had arrived, the bird startled and was gone.

Before bed, I, too, urinated on the floor.

Chapter Seven

Sheriff Dan woke me in the morning. He extended a paper cup, half full of coffee, through bars that were white with frost. "Reveille," he said.

His breath shone crystalline in the morning light.

Like many people, I sleep in a fetal position, with one hand in my drawers. And I'm not used to doing anything before my morning ritual—I hadn't stretched or flossed, let alone gargled, and who would greet visitors before enjoying that heavenly, cottony, first Q-tip of the day?

Shirttails out, wet spot on my collar, I shielded my eyes, calling out, "What?"

The light was painfully bright. As I stood wincing, I located its source: A loading-bay door stood open at the end of the room, a rolling steel shutter that I hadn't noticed before. Through it, a parking lot glowed afterlife-white.

Sheriff Dan shook his head. "You can snooze through anything, Professor." He glanced at his watch for effect and handed me the cup of coffee.

I spit the first sip all over the floor. "It's ice cold."

"Get used to it," he said.

I was getting a little tired of Sheriff Dan's tone. As far as I could tell, he possessed no special attributes that qualified him to boss around his fellow man. But I hesitated to say anything. I imagined, behind him in the stationhouse, a desk on which sat Keno's second ball. I pictured a spare handgun or maybe a nightstick as the only thing that blocked it from rolling off the desktop and smashing open on the floor. How could I get my hands on that ball? I sweetened my approach:

"I'm willing to meet you halfway on the coffee," I said, very politely. "A little warmer-upper would do."

"The teat of Christian tolerance has about run dry, my

friend," Sheriff Dan said. "And I'm not about to let you scald the face of peace and justice."

His voice was more than a little snarky.

"What are you talking about?" I asked. "I'd never throw coffee on anyone."

"This from a man who defiles scripture?" he asked. He pointed to the dogs' cell next door. "The deputy who took care of these dogs this morning was a Christian, and he didn't take kindly to hosing Bible pages down the sewer, not on his first day of dog duty."

I followed his gesture to the cell in question, to where the dogs had shredded that ten-cent Bible, and I saw that it was empty, hosed clean except for a few soggy, uneaten biscuits. Those sad, stupid dogs, I thought. All that remained of them was a series of wet streaks on the floor, leading from the cell to the back door, places where their fur had mopped comet tails of filth as their limp bodies were dragged out back to some pickup, waiting to haul them to the dump.

"What'd I tell you?" Sheriff Dan asked. "Peace and quiet."

"What happened to them?"

With his thumb and fingers, Sheriff Dan mimed a hypodermic injection. "We do things the civilized way around here," he said. "We don't set traps for little dogs. We don't skin them warm and eat them. Law-abiding folk don't fingerpaint with animal blood."

Sheriff Dan passed a sealed plastic bag through the bars. It contained tampons, toothpaste, and a few other travel-sized toiletries from manufacturers I had never heard of.

"They'll probably hold you in one of the state facilities after this," he said. "We'll be parting company. I doubt you've been to the lockdown in Sioux Falls, but I'll give you this advice, and if Janis were here, she'd give the same: speak to none of the prisoners, and no matter what, never join one of those gangs." He looked at his watch. "If you want to brush your teeth, you'll be thankful for that coffee. Your lawyer's here. It's time to pull yourself together."

After Sheriff Dan left, I brushed my teeth alone, spitting the green-brown foam on the floor. A tiny bottle labeled "Bucolave Fresca" turned out to be an awful lemon-flavored mouthwash, and the jail-issue floss was like deep-sea fishing line. My gums bled as I used it, staring at that empty cell next door.

Farley entered in a blue suit—almondy tie, French cuffs, level in the shoulders—his haircut flat as a New Mexico mesa. In one hand, he balanced a slim manila folder and a cup of coffee—his was steaming—while the other held an all-purpose suit, wrapped in plastic. This he hooked in the bars by the hanger, then handed me the coffee.

"Look at you," he said. "Taking fashion tips from that student of yours?"

I wanted to ask Farley if he'd viewed any evidence from the excavation site, if those yahoo deputies were playing bocce ball with Keno's grave offerings. At this very moment, were they bowling down the DQ drive-through with the head of an ancient one? But did it really matter if they did? I kept seeing Sheriff Dan's invisible needle, and I couldn't shake the feeling that it would come for all of us, that tonight, while I slept, some deputy would back his van up to the side door, creep into my cell, and—and my story would conclude alone, without witness, without comment, the cell simply sprayed clean again, my few possessions thrown into an evidence bin like Keno's.

"Are Trudy and Eggers okay?" I demanded.

He pulled a tie from his pocket, unfurled it. "You're a mess, my friend."

"I appreciate the help, but I don't need it. Just tell me, did they find the Polaroids? What about the Hall of Man—have they been sniffing around there?"

Farley reached through the bars. He tapped my chin to make me look up, then pulled the tie behind my collar. "I tell you, I thought you were coping pretty well," he said. "But you're not. We got you fishing again. We played some serious gin rummy. There was that night we talked late. But it's worse than I thought. You're still trying to punish yourself."

I stared at the ceiling. Preserved in the cement were patterns of rings and knots, a life history of the timber that had been used to form it. "I don't need a lawyer, and I don't need a psychologist," I told him. "I need to know if they've disturbed the dig."

Farley just kept talking, his eyes on his fingers as he looped the ends of the tie.

"Someone you care about is gone," he said. "And the hurt is real. It must be somebody's fault, right? I mean, someone must've messed up royal. But you're the only person around to take the blame. Suddenly it's like you're the one who failed. And to move on, to do something good for yourself, well, that's giving up, that's quitting a memory, and now you're the one who's walking away. You become the one pretending someone didn't exist."

Farley cinched the knot and snapped my collar down.

"Look," I said, "aren't you listening? I'm guilty. I don't need a lawyer."

Farley pulled his hands back. "And so you start driving people away." He peeled the plastic off the suit and passed the coat and slacks through the bars. When I took it, he opened the folder and read from a piece of paper: "Quote: 'Before abandoning his weapon and fleeing, the perp declared, *My students had nothing to do with this.*'" Farley closed the folder. "You get queasy scaling fish, Hank; you're afraid to uproot houseplants; yet you think a judge will believe you killed an eleven-hundred-pound hog with your bare hands?"

How could I explain that Eggers and Trudy were the best things that had ever happened to me? My tenure at USSD would soon be forgotten. My book was chaff. But Trudy and Eggers would go out into the world and train the next generation of anthropologists.

Farley tried a different angle. "You know he's a billionaire, right? Certainly you've taken a moment to type his name into the Internet. So you know Brent Eggers can speak Japanese. You've heard about his fat book contract."

"I believe in my students," I said, with an undertone of *Do you believe in me?*

Farley looked unimpressed. Still, he reached through the bars and patted me once on the shoulder. "Sure, sure, of course you do," he said. Then his face became grave. "But make no mistake, my friend. There's no nobility in accepting the title 'convicted animal abuser.' Need we even speak of 'grave-robbing'? Don't punish yourself by weaving the words 'cruelty' and 'desecration' into the story the future will forever tell of you. You just put on that suit, do something about your breath, and pull yourself together. They'll have you in the courtroom in twenty minutes, and I'll do the talking."

By the time he left, the coffee was cold. I put on Farley's jacket, baggy in the shoulders and chest, then slicked down my hair with a product called Señor Pompo.

On the drive to the county courthouse, Sheriff Dan cracked all the windows, whistled "Western Wind," and seemed oblivious to a snow rabbit that darted from a culvert and got lost in his tires. Before I knew it, I was in the building where Janis had spent her life.

The same fat man worked the metal detector in the lobby. The same little security badge dangled from everyone's blue shirt. The lustrous marble floors were buffed to the sheen of burnt sugar, and the mahogany panels smelled of linseed wax. Sheriff Dan led me into the main hearing room, plopped me behind the defendant's table, and, after cuffing me to a ring in the banister, headed off in search of coffee.

I looked around the room, and nothing I'd hoped to see was there. Missing were Keno's artifacts, which I'd imagined would be spread across the discovery table. Where was the evidence against me—the dog pelts, cat skulls, and squirrel tails? No parade of Dorito bags, barbecued ribs, and dental-floss fibers? Where were Trudy, Eggers, and my father, not to mention my friends and neighbors?

Didn't I have any friends and neighbors?

There were some retired folk in the rear gallery, the same group who haunted the benches back when I was in high school, back when Dad would leave on his weeklong sales circuits. I'd come here after classes let out rather than do my homework alone, in an empty house. Spreading my schoolwork—book reports, history outlines, workbook quizzes—on the gallery benches, I ate sandwich halves and daydreamed as dramas unfolded below. You'd be surprised how much of court life is spent searching for papers, rereading testimony, and stalling for time. There were lots of recesses, points at which Janis would make for the restrooms or slip down the hall to brew more tea in the bailiff's kitchenette. Sometimes, she'd hydraulically descend to Records in the basement—a place that everyone, out of laziness, accessed with the wheelchair lift—so she could tend to a night-blooming cereus plant she had growing down there.

When a woman heads down the hall, do other people wonder if they'll ever see her again? When a father "goes for a drive," when a mother walks out the door and into the snow, do other people think: *Is this it, are they ever coming back?*

To have been left is to know that anyone can leave, at any time. But that morning in the courthouse, I felt its opposite effect—the illusion that a person could return, that she might have a change of heart and emerge, at any moment, from one of these magisterial doors. It didn't matter that Janis was dead, her ashes washed to the Gulf of Mexico. Hope doesn't give a crap about facts like that.

Crystal pitchers of water were placed at the witness box and jury stand. Someone turned on the judge's microphone, which filled the room with a light buzz. Beyond the bar, the room was alive with clerks and bailiffs, gesturing with color-coded folders, typing, and talking as they geared up for the morning's docket. These were Janis' old co-workers, and though they ghosted through varying realms of familiarity in my memory, the routine of their motions only furthered the illusion that amber rings from Janis' tea must still stain that stenographer's table, that a lost Lean Cuisine lunch or two yet haunted the back of the kitchenette freezer. Did her little lotus tree still spruce the Mediation Room?

I began to feel her presence—her pain-in-the-ass, can-do spirit, her maddening humming of songs too soft to make out, her stupid need to hug every human she encountered in the state of South Dakota—and I felt it physically, in my arms and knees, how much I've missed her since she died, six months before, in the guest room of my father's house, even as he was packing her upstairs belongings for the dump.

The room grew colder. I felt as if I were sitting at the center of a merry-go-round, the world in motion viewed from the calm. My eyes, when I rubbed them, burned from the Mexican hair pomade on my fingers, and I watched through bleary vision as civil servants went about their business. Could none of them feel Janis in the room, the person with whom they'd eaten Chinese buffet twice a week for twenty years? Did none of them feel the parts of her that remained?

My father believed the dead lived on in their possessions. To him, Janis dwelled in the latent heat of an old curler set. She sighed in each exhale of a Tupperware lid, and spoke through the curled strips of trial transcripts she brought home and hung ribbony from refrigerator magnets. Trudy was partial to the notion that people preserved themselves through the images they left behind, and Eggers believed the dead were bound to the soil through which they'd trod their days.

It was by watching Janis here in this courtroom, as I read my history books and peeled bananas, that I came to see that the dead reside inside narrative, that something immortal was happening as Janis documented everyday people swearing to the truth of their lives. Husbands and bosses, grifters and orphans testified to broken promises and failed bonds, to randomness and surprise, to the unexpected turns life took, and Janis was there to give evidence, not for or against them, but *of* them. She was the repository of our town's stories. Is there a more noble trade?

Farley swung into the courtroom, smelling suave in cologne and clicking a gold pen, a lozenge tucked in his cheek. He gave me a wink, then proceeded to glad-hand the prosecutor's assistants before he worked the whole room in a counterclockwise circuit. My hands were trembling. An announcement was made, something I couldn't make out. The judge made a joke, and everyone laughed. Through the doors came a clerk, balancing a stack of briefs. It was a clerk that Janis had mentioned before, the one with the stammer who grew angry whenever old people took the stand.

I heard the courtroom doors swing open again. When I turned, it was the new stenographer instead. She wore wire-rim glasses and carried a roll of tape. "Sorry, Judge," she said, making haste for her seat.

I leaned back and stared at the courthouse ceiling, where there was a grand oculus whose natural light filled the room. Craning my neck, I studied the leaded glass dome and the great circular mural surrounding it. Chiseled from marble was a series of vignettes depicting the history of South Dakota: In quartz-veined stone, a red man in feathers offered an ear of corn to a loose-shirted fur-trapper. The next panel showed three buffalo kneeling, their horns pointing down, as a horse, returning after ten thousand years, approached through the wheat. A sodbuster yoked his plow to the rising sun as a row of boys, standing in descending order, observed and learned. A locomotive named Progress—its caboose a covered wagon—split the state in two. And in the final panel, an owl sat under an Indian moon, looking not at pilgrims or prairie schooners but down through the vault of justice, to me.

People were talking. Farley was talking.

"I have that right here, Your Honor," Farley said, and the bailiff came to take a sheaf of paper from his hand. This bailiff was the guy who dressed up like a Civil War cavalryman on the weekends, who was known to eat hardtack and jerky at lunch, who made his own soap and smelled of lye. All of these people Janis had spoken of now played a role in my arraignment, but I don't have the heart to describe them, to give their names or render the look in their eyes. They're dead now, every last one of them in that room, every person but Farley, and how can I bring the entire courtroom to life as mere backdrop, as window dressing to my one morning there? There's no such thing as doing quick justice to the deceased. To speak of the dead is to conjure them, and it would be a crime to beckon them from their graves, to prance them around in some conga line of history before vanquishing them back to the cold, as if their lives were no more than footnotes in the tale of another.

The more you learned about life, the more it seemed an engine of little design, and to survive its queer lottery was what we called living. You could choose to celebrate this survival, as my father did, or you could mourn the misfortunes of others, which I figured was the least we could do. But the future would prove us both wrong—to live when others do not, we were to learn, isn't survival, but being left behind.

The next ocular mural of South Dakota, assuming you rebuild the courthouses, my friends of tomorrow, will not be chiseled with images of clerks or bailiffs or little people like me. Were the million Lakota who died of smallpox included in this one? No, the marble of the next history of this land will be inscribed with flames leaping to the sun, chains of dogs lashed together, and, of course, a great red hand.

Because the charges were federal, Farley managed to get me transferred to the federal prison camp at Parkton while I awaited a trial date. Before the sun was high in the sky, I'd been remanded to Club Fed, formerly Parkton College, a moderately religious school that had gone bankrupt some years earlier. I was "processed" in what had once been the main cafeteria, now filled with the old-carpet odor of bureaucratic cubicles and the scent, like aspirin, of copy toner in the air. The dining-hall windows, however, were still stained glass, and their luminous depictions—an anointing of grape leaves, the multiplication of fish, a last supper—cast a fruit-bowl light across the correctional system's laminate desks and morguelike filing drawers.

They handed me receipts for all my property, and then I was placed in a white room that had once been part of the vast kitchen—still visible in the floor were marks where the old industrial freezers had been bolted down. Here I was forced to watch an orientation video. Following that, I had my head and nethers shaved, and was ordered to drink a chalky liquid, then made to urinate into a paper cup. Next, I was briefly violated, and before the rubber gloves even popped off, without so much as a glass of orange juice to calm my nerves, I was dusted with a delousing powder that tasted, in my nose and mouth, bitter as vitamin C.

Wearing only a towel, I was shown another video, this time focusing on the parasitic cycle. The only place to sit—no thanks—was on a freezing metal table. This video focused mainly on head lice and genital crabs, but as I stood there alone on the examination floor, my mind wandered to ticks and fleas, lamprey and ichneumon larvae, to all the flukes of the world, each leeching off the life of another, so desperate to exist they called the scrotum home, the colon cathedral. In that cold white room, I lifted my feet in turn off the icy floor, wondering what manner of beast could make it through life alone. I thought of Alexander Pope. A hunchback, a cripple, he once said,

Man, like the weedy vine, supported, lives.
The strength he gains is from th'embrace he gives.

The video screen went blue, and then the tape began to auto-repeat. I walked over to the rolling metal cart and turned it off. I thought, *Do we cling any less tightly than the suckerfish, and without it, doesn't the shark swim alone?* I returned to where I had been standing, tried to find the spots where my feet had warmed the floor, but couldn't.

"Hey," I yelled to the ceiling, "it's freezing in here."

My voice still echoing off the ceramic-tile walls, I began to pound the metal door.

I pounded and pounded until, finally, I heard footsteps.

When the door opened, a little man stood there. He wore a tiny jumpsuit, khaki with a black stripe, and his wiry hair was filled with what looked like sawdust.

"Small world, Hanky," he said. "Here's your boots and bibs."

These he thrust in my chest. It backed me up a step.

"Gerry," I said, taking in his uniform. "What are you doing here?"

He grabbed his ID tag and aimed it at me. "It's Officer Gerry," he said.

"This is some kind of joke," I told him. "Gerry, tell me this is a charade."

"Officer Gerry," he said. "That's a week of toilets."

Gerry was enjoying this, I could tell. I shifted strategies.

I said, "I'm terribly sorry about what happened to your miniature dog."

"Laundry detail."

"We're old friends," I reminded him. "You're not mad about

getting fired, are you? You know I'd never purposely try to get you fired."

"Now you bought yourself twenty. Let's have 'em."

"Twenty what?"

"Push-ups, shitbird," he said, pointing down. "Drop and give me twenty."

My skin went goosepimply under the white powder.

I looked down to my waist. "I'm only wearing a towel," I said. "And there was nothing like this in the orientation video. The video said there were no violent offenders here." The video had depicted the campus—that's what they called it, a "campus"—as integrated into the community, with a montage of townsfolk using the grounds as a park, walking their dogs, checking books out of the prison library, and watching one of those old 3D outer-space movies in the theater. There was even footage of the high-school swim team holding a meet in the prison pool.

Gerry glared at me. "Keep pushing me," he said. "Go ahead and keep pushing."

With as much dignity as possible, I let my towel go and crouched down to the cold floor. The first couple were easy, but then my elbows started to shake, and soon my chest was burning! I wanted to scream every time the tip of my manhood touched the icy floor.

Gerry mimicked my moans, trying to make me sound like a pussy. Still I kept pumping, and when I got to push-up number seven, Gerry counted out "six."

That little "miscount" trick was one they had persecuted me with during my mandatory physical-education class at Mactaw High. Always there was some jocko like Gerry to count off your calisthenics, and always they would horse around with you in the middle of your squat thrusts and T-bones, when you didn't have the wind to tell anyone off. Even if you had a good comeback ready, even if there was a put-down on the tip of your tongue, you were wheezing too hard to say it.

"What's that?" Gerry said, putting his finger to his ear. "You want more?"

I put my head down, arms quivering, to squeeze out a last

push-up. Instead, I collapsed. I'd done only thirteen, the last few girl-style, using my knees.

Completely pooped, I just lay there, face-down on the floor. That's when Gerry removed a large tool from one of the steel cabinets. The device looked like a big set of bolt cutters. He stood over me with it.

"Working nights," he said, "I never got to orient the new inmates. On night detail, I never got to use this device. But now this is my day job."

Then Gerry sat down on me. At first, I thought he was going to choke me again, but then he positioned himself atop my bare buttocks and turned his attention to my legs. This was not in the video! Gerry grabbed a foot and tweaked it back. I felt cold metal on my calf, and then, with a flash of pain, I heard a pneumatic clamping sound.

Gerry stood. "Get dressed," he said and kicked those new boots and baby-blue coveralls toward me. I looked down, and there, on my ankle, was a hard metal band lined with rubber, a wispy wire antenna hanging down.

Outside, Gerry led me across campus toward the extradition wing, where I was to be housed in a mostly empty unit. The air was cutting, and because the campus was on a hill, currents of mist swept through the buildings. Newly bald, I felt as if I had no scalp, no skull even, as if my brain were out there, wind whistling through the hemispheres.

I followed Gerry along a sidewalk inset with grates to fight the ice, and something about the metallic rasp of our footsteps made me think of ice climbing.

Gerry glared back at me. "Shoe's on the other foot now, isn't it, Hanky?"

I didn't say anything, not after all those push-ups.

"You're used to sitting up there on your throne, laughing at the little guy. It feels different to be the one who gets pushed around, who always gets crapped on. What, you want me to do some tricks for you, so you can be amused? You want to laugh at my backflips? Fat chance."

Gerry turned around, so he was walking backward. Every

time he gestured I winced, as if he was going to jump on me again.

"Your fat Corvette," he said. "That cush job. What do you know about life? When have you ever lived? You've obviously never been arrested before. I bet you never even been fired from a job. Well, get ready to pound the pavement with a felony on your record, get ready for doors slammed in your face and the unemployment line, 'cause you're the poodle now."

"Actually," I said, "I have tenure."

Gerry stopped and looked at me funny, as if he had an idea what the term meant but wasn't completely sure. I wasn't about to explain it all. I only said, "I won't be losing my job. Things will be inconvenient, sure. I suppose I'll have to direct student dissertations during visiting hours, and my classes will have to make do with handouts for a while. But with full tenure, I could work from anywhere, from France if I wanted. And I'd have to do something pretty bad to get fired."

"Worse than animal mutilation and grave-robbing?"

"Look here," I said, then paused. "Well, yeah, it'd have to be worse than that."

Gerry stared at me. Maybe the idea of tenure offended him, or maybe it thrilled him. I couldn't tell from the way he shook his head, like now he'd heard it all. He used his teeth to tug off a glove, then pulled a watch from his pocket. He said, "We have to make a pit stop."

Gerry veered off the path, and we pushed on through knee-deep powder toward a cluster of buildings beyond the dean's residence, which was now called the Warden's Residence. There weren't any guard towers or Cyclone fences at Club Fed—the only security was a wire, buried along the perimeter of the school, which would trigger an alarm if an ankle monitor crossed it. Still, the place no longer felt like the Parkton College I'd visited over the years as a guest lecturer. Gone were the benches and fountains. Missing were the kiosks and bike racks. No coffeehouse. No food court. This was how a university must look in Russia.

We passed groups of middle-aged white men in blue thermal jumpsuits, their faces pink with cold. They smoked in tight huddles, avoiding the icicle-laden eaves of buildings whose names had been sandblasted off. Branner Hall was now named G-4, and Peterson Auditorium, where all the seniors of Parkton College had graduated, was simply H-1. Yulia and Ivan probably met at a school like this, an unadorned bunker of a campus, an institution where people studied radiation technology and weapons development.

Outside the Warden's Residence was a winterized rose garden that resembled, on a smaller scale, the President's Promenade at USSD—beds of frozen, thorny stalks were surrounded by heaps of mulch and burlap, all ringed by circles of brightly colored rocks. One stone I recognized as obsidian. When we got closer, I saw that there were large pieces of quartz and feldspar. Stacked at the foot of an irrigation box were chunks of Siberian marble—mint-green shot through with pearl. Suddenly I realized these stones were mineral samples, commandeered from the college's old geologic collection, which had been housed in display cases in the library's concourse.

Gerry stopped and checked his watch again.

"So this tenure thing," he said. "What about sleeping with a student? Does tenure let you do that?"

"Do you mean *a* student, or *my* student?"

"What's the difference?" Gerry asked.

"Well, the practice, in general, is frowned upon."

"So you've done it."

"They weren't *my* students," I said. "I'm not proud of it."

Gerry shook his head. "Pitiful," he said. "What a shameful abuse of power. That's twenty."

I didn't argue. I knelt in the snow and began my push-ups, though I could barely do any, especially staring at what was once a college's prized geological cache. Before me were amethyst clusters and batholite cores. There were azurite, fluorspar, and bitumen. Oh, what a Clovis wouldn't give. Straining on rubbery arms, I realized I was staring directly at a meteorite, an escapee from the very ovens of creation, an object marooned on our planet after being orphaned by some ancient star extinction or distant galactic collision.

I did a handful of push-ups, leaving a face print in the snow, and then we pressed on down the hill, to the old industrial-arts building, its aged brick façade reminiscent of times when hands-on manufacturing was a proper university subject. At the door, we could hear the muted whine of machinery.

"Wait here," Gerry said, and disappeared inside.

I danced in place for a little bit, clapping my hands to keep them warm, but then my curiosity took over, and I slipped inside to see what was happening. The door opened into a dark work area filled with idle industrial-arts equipment. It was empty except for four preadolescent children running power tools by the glow of a single droplight. Shop-goggled and saw-dusted, they were hard at work: one fed wood into the whiny teeth of the bandsaw, while another stabbed the lathe with a spoon chisel that spit wood shavings directly into his face. A third child was precariously perched atop a stool that allowed his short arms to feed strips of lumber all the way through the ripsaw in a single swipe. The last boy ran a drum sander that turned at such revolutions that it burned the wood, sending up curls of cedar smoke, a spicy smell, thick with resin, that instantly cleared my sinuses.

Gerry approached them and began sorting through what looked like a pile of miniature wooden skis the kids had made. He picked up one of the tiny skis, sighted down its crown. This he repeated several times. Then he lifted a finger to his throat and mimed, *Cut*. One by one, the kids shut down their machines and lifted their goggles, revealing pale skin and rabbity, bloodshot eyes.

"These are all lefts," Gerry said. "Tell me you've been making the rights, too."

The kids looked from one to another. Slobbers of glue had dried in their hair, on their cut-off shirts. Bursts of blue-and-red marking powder splotched their arms and backs, so you could tell there been some pitched battles earlier with glue guns and chalk boxes. Now, however, none of them spoke.

Gerry asked them, "What will happen if you only make left skis?"

His voice sounded more instructional than angry, though the kids looked used to being punished. They stepped from behind their machines, reluctantly, and lined up as if it was an old drill. Side by side, the boys looked like quadruplets, with a couple of inches in height the only thing separating them. How could they all look eleven? Who could ever tell them apart?

Gerry asked, "Won't left skis make everything go in circles?"

The kids were wearing prison-issue visitor name-tags clipped to their cut-off shirts, and I watched as Dana looked to Kelly, who looked to Rene. Standing at the end, a hair shorter than the rest, was Pat.

The biggest one, Dana, said, "We figured it would be faster to cut all the lefts first and then cut all the rights. That way we don't have to adjust the saw blade after every cut."

"Right," Gerry said. "Okay. Good idea."

Pat pointed my way. He asked, "Who's that guy?"

Gerry looked over and noticed me for the first time since I'd entered.

"That," Gerry said, "is the man who murdered Spark."

I suddenly realized that the bigger boy still held a glue gun. The second wielded a rat-tail file. "That," Gerry continued, "is what happens when you horse around too much and don't listen to directions. He's what happens when you think you're better than the other kids in school, when you hide in the restroom to gang up on them. This man is what you get when you won't stop pestering people about your mom."

"What are you talking about?" I asked Gerry.

Little Pat approached me, cautiously, with sidesteps. His lower lip was downturned in anger. When Pat was a couple paces from me, he threw a handful of sawdust in my face and ran.

My eyes, my nostrils!

Gerry turned to the boys. "See how he cowers? This is the kind of man who hurts animals. Go ahead, ask him how many push-ups he can do. Let's see how tough the animal abuser is."

The kids all took a step forward. I tried not to show any fear.

"Please," I said, "I won't even dignify that."

Gerry looked at the boys, as if to say, *What are you waiting for?*

All four of them hit the deck and began banging out push-ups at a feverish pace, their noses making greasy dabs on the dusty floor.

Watching them exercise, Gerry suddenly seemed overtaken with pride. He leaned toward me as though we were confidants, as though he hadn't just insulted me seven different ways. "You know, they've never had any discipline," he said. "Last week, when I picked them up — Jesus, it was like that movie *Lord of the Flies*. I opened the trailer door, and it was like Indians had attacked. The furniture was stacked up in fortresses, and the twins had raided all the food. Nobody was getting past Kelly to the bathroom. Little Pat was sleeping with a sharp stick at night. Now look at them."

The boys pumped in unison. They all had that same rail-thin body, the same wiry biceps and pointy elbows. They all sported identical mullet haircuts, dustbin-blond, and they even wore matching silver studs in their right ears. Later, I was to learn that these kids could run for days on end through unpacked snow. And eventually I would discover they weren't even all boys.

"What is going on here?" I asked.

"This," Gerry said, indicating the pile of skis, "is my latest project. I'm going to increase my sales sixfold. It'll take the Midwest by storm. You know they're already filming a sequel to *Impossible Journey*?"

"No," I said. "I meant, what's going on with these kids? Where's their mother?"

"Oh." Gerry looked down to the kids doing push-ups. Every time they reached another increment of ten, they pushed off hard enough to clap their hands and sound off — "Thirty!" — so when Gerry spoke his voice was a mix of pride and sorrow. "The ex–old lady, she's having some health issues. I'm kind of watching the kids till she rebounds a little, at least until she gets her short-term memory back. They're good kids, though, you know? They grow on you. I mean, do *not* lay any free time on their hands. Do *not* let them out of your sight. But, you know, you get used to having them around."

"Even if you have to keep them in a jail cell?"

Gerry was in another place. He didn't even hear me. "My ex–old lady, she was making the kids breakfast, like every other day," he said. "I warned her about that toaster trick a hundred times."

I watched his eyes closely. It was like he was there, watching it happen.

"What?" I asked. "Did she put a knife in it or something?"

Gerry shook his head. "You think that woman'd learn."

"She was shocked? And it had happened before?"

Gerry looked off, as if all those fancy machines could help him craft the words. "I never thought I'd get her back," he said. "She took off for all those years — I thought she was gone for good. All I did was work and work. You know, you get into this loop where you only let yourself look forward. I had two night jobs. I begged Sheriff Dan for extra shifts. I've arrested everyone in town — two, three times. She was the best thing that ever happened to me. And this is how I get her back. This is how she returns to me. Don't get me wrong, though. I'll take it. If this is how it has to be, I'll take it."

I put my hand on Gerry's shoulder. "I hear what you're saying."

He slapped my hand away, as if I'd offended him, then took it out on the kids. After one of those piercing two-finger whistles I could never do, he yelled, "Double time."

The kids clutched the cement for all they were worth, elbows knocking as they drove it home, clapping twice between sets. When they chanted "Fifty!" Gerry sensed he'd made his point. He called "Cut!" and the kids popped up, faces glowing as they looked to Gerry for approval. By way of praise, Gerry brushed the dust off all their painter's pants and lined them up again. Little Pat came up and hugged Gerry's leg.

Gerry turned to me. "Look," he said, "this project is taking longer than I thought. We've got a quota to fill, and then I've got to get these kids to their first hockey practice. Can you find your cell on your own?"

"Yeah," I said, "I suppose."

He pulled a map from his pocket. "You're in Building C-3." He pointed to the old freshman dorm. "Your room's on the second floor. Go straight there, and do not cross the perimeter wire. If you step off campus, the alarm sounds, and then they hunt you down. Then you get transferred to a *real* prison."

Outside, the sun shot purple halos through bilevel clouds, and a mist raced between the buildings, furling like parachute silk, smelling of the chinaberry hedges it passed through. The light, indeterminate and bright, made my eyes weep in the corners, where bits of sawdust had lodged.

Before me, the prison campus was a series of mirror-bright fields punctuated by old-timey buildings whose bricks had leached whiter with each winter. The current freeze held broken branches fast in the trees. An aerial antenna slumped under a baggy suit of ice. Clutched by a trellis of brown ivy was a yellow T-shirt, still looking summery and surprised. I couldn't quite make myself move toward any of these buildings. How could I sentence myself to some teeny dorm room? How could I resign myself to slacking off the remainder of my days on a freshman bunkbed? I had no way of knowing it, but as I stamped my feet with indecision, the annals of primitive technology were rewriting themselves. A new day had dawned in science, and though I didn't understand it yet, I was the Adam of anthropology. There was so little time.

Then it came to me: the Unknown Indian. I hadn't been on this campus in years, since long before it'd become a minimum-security prison, but I suddenly realized there was a place I needed to go. I pulled up the hood of my prison-issue blizzard overalls and tucked my hands inside the jumpsuit's sleeves. I gauged the wind, dropped a shoulder, and set off for what had once been Parkton College's humanities building. Down in the basement there was an exhibit called the Tomb of the Unknown Indian, a collection that began with some ceremonial graves discovered during the school's construction, and had over the years expanded into quite an archive of death ephemera.

Despite the tithing wind, the prison's population of white males was out in full force, clustering in groups of ten to fifteen, showing the cold their backs. The puffy eyes of billionaires tracked me as I passed their chummy cadres, smoking Canadian cigarettes under a work-detail awning, or gripping foam coffee cups in the lee of a laundry van. There was something ganglike in the way they huddled, and I decided I'd take Sheriff Dan's advice: I wasn't going to speak to any of them.

Heading downhill past the gymnasium, I passed a group of older corporate types, all wearing their blue prison bibs, all sporting military crew cuts. And in front of the library stood a group of young lions, hair slicked down, glasses lean and wiry, which was probably the look on Wall Street when they were arrested for crimes like price fixing and securities fraud. Beyond them, through the library's windows, I could see the shelves were still loaded with books, bolstering my faith that the Unknown Indian exhibit would still be there.

I cruised by the old Memorial Union, whose little collegiate movie theater was hosting a monthlong Hitchcock film festival for the viewing pleasure of the titans of white-collar crime. Perhaps at this very moment, the moviegoers included Michael Milken, Charles Keating, Fife Symington, and Ivan Boesky. The matinee was *The Birds*, a film whose paranoia and hubris were laughable. As if our feathered friends were the ones conspiring to eradicate *us*. Tonight's screening was *Psycho*, the most frightening movie ever made. What sick freak could think up that story line, what kind of person would leave his decaying mother's corpse in the basement?

Finally, I came to the old humanities building. The main doors were inset with dark wood, and heavy shocks hissed them open and closed. I made for the basement doors at the end of the hall. Passing rows of classrooms, I noticed through the little windows that all the old rooms had been converted into sound booths. Through the security glass, you could see blue-bibbed inmates using the old language-lab equipment to record books for the blind. In room after room, men wore pastel plastic headsets and read works like *White Fang* and *Beloved* into outdated, modular microphones. Lord, how would I make it through a day here, let alone a month?

I headed downstairs, where a repository of regional grave paraphernalia was on display. Though I'd viewed the artifacts before, there might be something I'd see in a new light, something that would help me understand Keno. The collection was famous for a set of seventeenth-century Nakota coup sticks and a primitive polished-shell mirror used only by Ojibway men who'd completed a rite-of-passage ceremony called "The Life of the Long Body." The exhibit also boasted a Mandan breastplate made from rose sea coral. Most famous of all was a set of twenty duck decoys, hand-woven from bulrush reeds, discovered during the dam's earthmoving phase. The decoys carbondated back three thousand years.

Of course, compared with the Hall of Man, the Tomb of the Unknown Indian was an inferior installation, hastily assembled, poor of theme, and though the exhibits were ethnographically accurate, they lacked the little flourishes—track lighting, dioramic painting, mood music—that truly ignite the imagination. Still, I took the steps two at a time.

When I pushed through the fire doors at the base of the stairs, I encountered not a portal into humanity, but a room full of vending machines. Strips of fluorescent tubing hung from a low ceiling, illuminating a room ringed with all manner of snack and soda machines. Glowing panels advertised sodas I'd never even heard of, like Splash and Quirst. One soda was named Jolt, and took as its logo the universal icon for accidental electrocution. LED panels flashed, and metallic dispensing screws gleamed. I had to turn in place to take it all in. I approached a tall, ominous machine that sold snacks called Bugles, Bangles, and I swear, Curdles. I peered into the machine. Hanging there on a rod, admittedly alluring, was a bag of those Doritos Eggers and Trudy were always talking about. Alas, I had no change.

In the center of the room was a pair of twin vinyl benches that had been pushed together, the way they do in an art museum. I took a seat and studied the machines, each a climate-controlled, perfectly lit gallery of goods. On an ottoman of vinyl, I reclined. Above me, pipes lined the basement ceiling, some color-coded, some crusty with fireproofing, all of them wound through with fiber-optic cable and coaxial cord. This room had been a repository of the meekest of cultures, a few tattered remnants of now extinguished peoples, saved as tokens by the people who had vanquished them. Now they were gone. I wondered if, in a thousand years, a perfectly preserved soda bottle—tinted green, curvy, slightly opalescent—wouldn't speak as much about us as an Algonquian baby rattle, made from the amber-clear shells of baby turtles, or the translucent horn ladles the ancient Manitobans drank with. Wouldn't a Mars Bar candy wrapper, cut from silky, shiny Mylar and printed with the planets of our system, speak as much of us as a Spokane baby swaddle, handwoven and dyed the Five Colors of the Universe?

But who had use for ancient things? What had happened in this room was all too common. What had been done here was repeated the world over whenever one group came into possession of something that was burdensomely sacred to another. The Midwest was full of stories of construction crews unearthing mammoths, or city contractors trenching up burial mounds, only to till the artifacts under so that building wasn't halted for the troubling process of investigation and "repatriation." Here's what the prison had surely done: one night, a backhoe opened a hole somewhere on campus, a truck backed up, and a few unlucky inmates were forced to shovel out Aleut spirit totems, Lakota "tomorrow" suits of heavenly buckskin, Crow death masks made from beetle wings, and a hundred other accouterments to the afterlife of native peoples. This was what would probably happen to Keno if the casino had its way.

Two inmates came into the room to stock up on candy bars, but I didn't look up. Blackfoot fireboxes were sparking in my mind. Narragansett death flutes sang in my ears. After death, the former lit your way to the other side, and the latter whistled you back if you weren't ready. Reclining, I heard my fellow inmates drop quarter after quarter, followed by the whir of the dollar-bill changer, and finally the mechanical twisting of the selection screw that sent a run of Milky Way bars into the pan below. Perhaps they were headed to see *The Birds*.

Dear anthropologists of the coming millennium, when you come across the grave of the Unknown Indian, dumped to the brim with unwanted artifacts, what will you make of this grave of graves, filled with the soup of a hundred cultures? Perhaps you have already encountered this oddity and developed a complex theory, the source of much debate among the common people. Don't let it become another footnote in the literature of yesterday. If the site is yet undiscovered, the resting place of the Unknown Indian shouldn't be hard to find. The prison was on a hill above the river, right near the forty-third parallel. I charge you to locate this grave, liberate these objects, and place them in a hall you shall name the Hall of Humanity, which will also house all the artifacts you can find from the eradicated peoples of the earth. This Hall of Humanity should be climate-controlled, tasteful in its lighting, "hands-on" in its general approach, and perpetual in its charter.

Someone entered the room and began messing with a vending machine.

I was still trying to picture this new Hall of Humanity, up on a mountain, with lots of pillars perhaps, or maybe in the center of a great plaza. But someone's interminable banging on a vending machine was ruining my concentration. I sat up. There, squatting in front of the potato-chip machine, was a man in a filthy fur coat, feeding a stick up the receiving door of the drop bin.

"Eggers?" I asked.

Eggers turned to look at me.

I asked, "What are you doing here?"

"I'm here to see you, Dr. Hannah," he said. "What happened to your hair?"

"Don't change the subject. Just what are you up to?"

He looked at the rodent stick in his hands, half swallowed by the gleaming machine. "Gathering," he said.

I pulled myself together and, nearing Eggers, crouched beside him.

What the heck was he doing? Soda spearing? Chip fishing?

"Hold this," he said.

I grabbed the switch, freshly cut from green willow, as Eggers pulled off his heavy parka in preparation for some serious concentration. "They took my other rodent stick," he volunteered. "I spent all day making this one."

He took the stick from me, then continued worming it up the dispenser flue, working the thing by instinct and feel, the way you floss a hard-to-reach crown. He nestled his cheek against the glass, wrapped his free hand around the machine. Through finesse, Eggers sent the barbed head of the stick rising, cobralike, up through the rows of gum and mints, past the candy bars, toward the top row, where the real calories hung—in bags and bags of potato chips.

Eggers grunted and muttered to himself as he coaxed the stick, and I must admit, there was something sexual about the process. How long had it been since the poor boy'd known a woman? I'd never questioned his reputation as the campus paramour, but there was certainly something desperate here.

"What happened to Keno?" I asked.

Eggers scrunched his face at me, as if I was breaking his concentration.

I said, "I'm in jail here, in case you haven't noticed. Nobody's exactly taking the time to keep me posted."

Eggers returned to his delicate work. He began twisting the stick, to help it clear the rungs of Twinkies and HoHos. Through the glass, the stick was right before our eyes, threatening to snag on the plastic rim of a Ding-Dong package.

Easy, I kept thinking. *Easy.*

Eggers gave the stick a little jiggle, and, simple as that, the triple-barbed head slid up to the next level. Then he spoke again. "I crept back to the casino last night," he said. "Everything was gone. They confiscated all my tools. They impounded my lodge. They took my rodent stick. Can you believe it? Everything. There was only an evidence receipt, staked in the snow."

Eggers shifted, and his buckskin shirt raised enough that I could see his exposed ribs and the hollow of his stomach. Under all those thick pelts, the boy was skin and bones. His midriff was also covered with circles of scaly red skin—an advanced case of ringworm. Eggers had the stick poised below all those potato chips, and he kept trying a little push-twist-jerk motion to make the bags drop. They'd shimmy a bit, swagger with a good strike, but none would fall.

"So—what about Keno?" I asked. "What about his ball? Don't tell me they're gone."

"Show a little concern, would you? I lost *everything.*"

"You're a nomad," I said. "You *take nothing and use nothing,* right?"

My tone was a little snotty, enough that Eggers looked at me like, *What's eating your ass?* "I lost all my stockpiles," he said. "Have you ever woven your own rope? Made bags out of sheep bladders? I had an entire pouch of sinew. Do you know how many roadkills you have to raid to get that much tendon? It takes a whole deer carcass to harvest enough sinew to make a single snare. You have to cut out the hamstrings, scrape the whole vertebral column, then strip the neck. You have to take the tendon, beat it into fiber, dry it in the sun, and weave it into cord by using glue made from hooves."

Eggers was sounding pretty sore.

"Sorry," I said. "Take it easy, would you?"

"Take it easy? Have you ever made glue from hooves, Dr. Hannah?"

I didn't say anything.

"Have you ever been to the dog-food plant south of town, where Hormel dumps its hooves in those huge mounds? Have you seen the size of some of those raccoons? They travel in packs, you know."

Now Eggers was totally worked up. He took his rodent stick and began slashing it around in the vending machine. The barbs tore holes in the bags, sending down a rain of Ruffles, Doritos, Fritos, and Funyuns, so that the dispensing bin filled with chips, and empty, torn bags hung from the racks. Eggers reached in and began devouring chips. I'd never seen someone eat like that, shoving them wholesale into his mouth, masticating them into an orange ball that he shifted as he chewed.

Eggers turned. "Look at me," he said, lips shiny with spice. "Look at how I live."

His eyes were a little wild. I put my hand on his bony shoulder.

"You've done enough science for one day," I said. "You better get out of here before they catch you."

He laughed, like I was an idiot, like I didn't understand anything.

"I said I came here to see you. I brought you this."

He opened the flap of his game bag, and from it removed

one of Keno's balls. This he handed over, then began scooping chips by the armful into the bag. The ball was warm and weighty in my hands. It was like being handed a baby.

Eggers said, "Trudy and I got this out of the Hall of Man this morning. We figured you put the first ball in there."

"So Keno's gone?"

"You know what happened to Keno," Eggers said. "Some guys from the casino came out in the middle of the night, and they started shoveling him up. Right now, Keno's probably in some cardboard box in the casino basement, never to be seen again. *Ancestor? What ancestor?*"

"How'd you get in?"

"To the Hall of Man?" Eggers asked. "We picked the lock. Though afterward, of course, the combo was obvious—your birthday. You know some freak put biohazard signs all over the place?"

I shrugged in a way that said, *What can I say—I'm a Virgo.*

Eggers took a long look at that ball in my hands.

He said, "You're in jail, right?"

This I had to concede.

"And the cops trashed your office?"

"I suppose," I said.

"Your career's basically shot."

"What's your point, Eggers?"

"My dissertation is shit," he continued. "All my work is gone. I'm talking a year of my life. And my parents? Forget it."

"Eggers," I said, "you're worked up about the loss of Keno. That's understandable, and I'm willing to pretend I didn't hear the sauce on a few of your earlier remarks. But never forget this: out of sight is not out of mind. No one is ever truly gone, as long as someone out there still cares. It means nothing that Keno was shoveled into the trunk of a police cruiser or stuffed in some box in the basement of a casino. We specialize in bringing people back, across far greater distances, through geologic time, so the patience of an anthropologist must be limitless."

"You really interrupted me that time, Dr. Hannah."

"Sorry."

"I was about to make a point."

"Of course," I said. "My apologies."

"I was going to say: Give me one good reason why we shouldn't open that ball, right here, right now."

I looked at the ball, at the petrified handprints preserved in the surface. My hand, when I placed it atop a print, fit. "Come on," I said. "Follow me."

Without speaking, we made our way back across campus to the industrial-arts building. We were men of purpose, moving with a silent mandate, and when we reached our destination, we opened the door without hesitation. Inside, the place was empty, the machinery still. The floor had been swept, the tools returned to their places, and I have to say I admired Gerry for teaching his kids the proper respect for public property. Eggers and I walked among the machines, silent as totems in the dark hall.

"Which one should we use?" I asked him.

"Beats me. Why not just drop it on the floor?"

I grabbed a pair of shop goggles off a peg. When I put them on, the world grew cloudy. I adjusted the elastic straps as snugly as possible, for safety's sake, and the dangling tails kept tickling my cheeks. Then I approached the bandsaw. I wished that Trudy were here. She'd know how to work these things. When I hit the power switch, the saw raged to life, the cement floor vibrating from its torque. I set the ball on the cutting table and turned to Eggers.

"What, should I just cut it in half?"

"Dude," he said, "there is no Clovis orb-cutting manual. You're writing it."

Dude?

I studied him as he leaned against the table saw. He pulled a dry river reed from behind his ear, then opened the flap of his game bag and withdrew a little buckskin pouch, from which he extracted an herblike substance. After packing the reed full, he stuck it between his lips, and, James Dean–like, looked at me.

"What does it matter?" he asked. "Open the thing already."

"What does what matter?"

Eggers withdrew his little firebox, which contained a single coal wrapped in corn husks, a fireproof material with great insulating power. He peeled back layer after layer, till he found the ember. This he blew on. "We dedicate our lives to anthropology," he said. "And for what? To get crapped on? To have your shit rummaged through and stolen? I bet the Clovis had their version of the Fourth Amendment. In the late Pleistocene, there was no illegal search and seizure, I can tell you that. If someone's sinew turned up missing, you can bet there'd be hell to pay. In the Ice Age, if you stole someone's rodent stick, you could count on some serious Clovis justice descending on your ass."

With a little effort, the reed took, and Eggers began puffing away.

As soon as I smelled the smoke, I lifted my safety goggles.

"Tell me that's not marijuana," I said, glancing around for security cameras.

He held the reefer out to me. Suppressing a cough, he said, "Homegrown."

"Don't insult me," I said. "Do you realize where you are? Have you no respect for the penal system?" I had the ball poised before the blur of the bandsaw blade, but I needed to get a couple things straight with the boy.

"Eggers," I said, "do you really have a Porsche?"

"Where'd that come from?"

"I'm asking the questions here," I said. "Do you speak Japanese?"

"*Domo arigato,*" he said. "You want some French? *Merci beaucoup.*"

I eyeballed him good. "Are you a billionaire?"

Eggers took a toke of weed.

"You insult *me,* Dr. Hannah. You know I've taken a vow of poverty. I possess nothing but my friends, my loyalty, and twelve thousand years of history." Here his eyes got hot. "And I'll have you know, from direct observation, that a billionaire is the most loathsome thing on earth. It's a person who uses for himself the resources of a thousand others. Worst of all, this wealth makes him think he doesn't need other people, no matter who they are."

"So you're telling me you don't have a fat book contract?"

"Of course I do," he said. "I want to change people. My book will make them reconsider everything that's important in life, the way your book did."

What was there to say to that?

Satisfied, I lowered my goggles in a way that said, *Let's open this puppy.*

A rooster tail of red clay shot from the saw when the ball touched its blade, instantly dulling the ribbon of teeth. Still I cut on, scoring a circle around the equator of the ball, which I cut deeper with each revolution. After I'd worked through about an inch of clay all the way around, the pitch of the blade changed, and it seemed clear I'd hit some softer material.

I shut down the saw and moved the ball to a workbench.

Eggers pulled an antler from his game bag. He worked it into the seam I'd cut, and with a little prying, the clay shell broke loose, revealing an inner core, wrapped in a velum of ancient, hardened tissue that was certainly animal intestine. These yellowed layers of watertight membrane were stiff and crackly to the touch. Picture a head of iceberg lettuce, but with leaves made of hardened rawhide, nearly translucent, tough as bark.

At that point in my life, I had yet to become intimate with the husking sound an animal sternum makes when it's cracked wide—that yawning, almost creaky noise that comes after you stick your foot into a gaping chest cavity, hatchet through the breastplate, then bend the ribs back to the snapping point. But that's the kind of sound we heard as Eggers and I began peeling back layers of velum until we reached the center, which contained a cache of tiny white beads.

Eggers and I both grabbed a handful. They rolled smoothly in your fingers, and you'd think they were little pearls except they weren't quite round. They tended toward a teardrop shape. Too light to be pearls, too.

Eggers sniffed one, then held it up to the light.

"What the hell is it?" he asked.

It struck me suddenly that this was some kind of wampum, that what we'd discovered was the equivalent of Clovis cash, and a wave of dejection ran through me. Certainly there was some anthropologist out there somewhere nerdy enough to study ancient monetary systems, and to him this would be the discovery of a lifetime. Personally, it made me sick—those beads meant that Keno had been a fat cat, bent on taking it with him, that his vision of the afterlife was based on maintaining wealth rather than discovering the infinite, transitioning to the eternal.

The news was going to crush Eggers. I watched him put a bead on the table, but when he went to smash it with an antler, it skittered away. He grabbed another one and inspected it closely.

"What is this made of?" he asked. "Is it ivory? Horn? No one could carve beads so small, so uniform. Who would? And why?"

I put my beads back in the ball. I didn't want anything to do with them.

"Let's get out of here," I said. "We'll worry about it later."

Eggers looked at me like I was insane.

"Seriously, now, Dr. Hannah, what do you think?" he asked. "Are they man-made? Or naturally occurring? Hey, what about freshwater pearls? Or kidney stones removed from game? Weren't the Mactaw known to save the kidney stones of the buffalo they butchered?"

It was so like a grad student to be concerned with the small picture, to get caught up in form rather than function. This time, I was happy to keep it that way.

"Not to worry," I said. "We'll do some tests later this month and get to the bottom of things."

"Month?" he asked. "I don't have a month. My dissertation's almost over."

I leaned against the table, crossed my arms. "Just when *are* you done?"

"Exactly?" Eggers asked. "I don't know, exactly. It's not like I use a calendar or anything. I'll have to check where the sun sets on the horizon."

"You said you started last year, after Parents Weekend, right?"

"Yeah."

"Well," I said, "Parents Weekend is over."

"Let's just get back to work," Eggers said, and moved to put a bead in his mouth, as if taste might solve this problem.

I grabbed his wrist. "Don't be a fool," I said. "You don't know what we're dealing with. Remember the *National Geographic* team who discovered that galleon in the North Sea? They celebrated by drinking a jug of wine from its hold, and everything was one big party until they became the first people in five hundred years to contract the Thames strain of the black plague."

Eggers adopted a look of bemused indulgence. Or maybe it was the reefer.

"Dr. Hannah, my worms have worms," he said. "My amoebas have dysentery. Over the past year, I've devoured frogs, ducklings, and minnows, still wriggling, and I've actually taken a liking to a dish I call 'culvert surprise.' I've eaten eggs straight from bird nests, little blue speckled things that you crunch down whole. I've gnawed on acorns till I shit lentil soup, and I ate a perch straight from the gullet of a dead river eel. I had squirrel fever for three weeks. I've eaten larvae, fungus, crabapples, and sap. I've siphoned blood from livestock, then frozen it into little cubes I could chew on for breakfast. In October, I practically lived on pumpkin meat, and I was the one who stole the candy canes off the USSD Christmas tree. I've eaten old fishing bait, Dr. Hannah. I'm a man who's sucked the sunflower seeds from bird feeders."

That doobie gave him a serious case of the munchies, I thought as Eggers droned on and on about his diet. But then, out of the blue, I said, "Seeds."

"Seeds?" Eggers asked.

Like a thunderbolt, it had struck me. "What if they're seeds?"

"Seeds," Eggers echoed, starting to nod his head.

I grabbed one of the beads, studied it. In the light, it did appear organic. Indeed, you could see a tiny dot at the end of the seed—the growth bud.

"It looks like corn," I said. "Don't they look like miniature kernels of maize?"

Eggers looked dubious. "Sure, it looks like corn, but maize

comes from South America. It's only migrated north in the last few thousand years."

"Bear with me," I said, gesturing largely. "Let's imagine, hypothetically, that maize was indigenous to all the Americas, but then the Clovis came along, and through overconsumption they eradicated it, the way they eradicated everything else they touched."

"But what about the Law of Seeds?" Eggers asked. "Doesn't the Law of Seeds state that the fruit of plants beneficial to humans will be made profligate—not extinct—by them?"

"But not when the food is cooked," I countered.

Eggers looked at me suspiciously. "The Clovis left no grinding stones," he said. "There are no cooking pots, no hearths, nothing. Clovis teeth show none of the wear associated with milled cereals. Yet you're saying the Clovis cooked corn fritters?"

"Look, Eggers," I said, "you let me worry about that. You just meet me here tomorrow with that corn. Right now, I have to make a phone call."

"To Hatitia Wells?" Eggers asked. "You're going to bring in Hatitia Wells, aren't you?"

"That's not your concern. You just safeguard that corn, and we'll finish this tomorrow. In the meantime, no stunts, no improv, and none of that 'Clovis creativity' of yours."

"What?" he innocently asked.

"I know you, Eggers. Do not plant, grind, or ingest any of that corn."

Eggers didn't say anything.

"I'm serious," I said. "No baking, boiling, cooking, or chewing, okay? And do not get anyone else to do it. And no smoking it, either. You bring that corn back tomorrow, intact."

"You really think Clovis could have eaten corn?"

"I'm going to bring in the best paleobotanist in all the Dakotas to find out."

Outside, darkness had fallen. How was that possible?

The only public phone I could find was in the movie house. The lobby smelled of salt and butter and the must of old velvet, and the prisoners working snack-bar duty were watching the movie through breaks in a curtain that had once been purple. I sat in one of those old-fashioned phone booths, and through the door I watched hot dogs slowly turn on the rotisserie as I waited for Dr. Yulia Terrasova Nivitski to accept the charges. A collective gasp rose from within the theater. When Yulia finally came on, I could tell she wasn't too happy about the collect call.

"Hank?" she asked. "From where are you calling?"

"That doesn't matter right now," I said, trying to strike a note of authority. "I have an important question to ask you."

"There is something chaotic going on," she said. "Is there an emergency?"

She must have overheard the movie score in the background—there were a lot of insane, shrieking birds.

I decided to get to the point. "You love plants. That's your calling. You love plants because—"

"I am hanging up now."

"Wait," I said. "I've called for a reason."

"As I guessed. You did not call to talk to me. You only want something from me."

"No," I said. "Yes."

"You do not even speak 'hello.' You cannot even engage in chitchat. Always it is the same kind of man who calls me—one who reverses the charges, then makes no small talk, no foreplay. The kind who wears coveralls and has a crate of motorcycle parts in his bedroom."

I tried to not picture Yulia in another man's bedroom, strewn with oily cranks and manifolds, maybe some weightlifting equipment. "Listen to me," I told her. "We have made a discovery, a grand one. It will shake the foundations of paleobotany. We need your help. I need it."

Yulia harrumphed. "Maybe you need Hatitia Wells," she said. "All of the men fall down for her. *Hatitia, your thesis was brilliant. Hatitia, can I freshen your drink?* I know, I have been to the conferences."

"I didn't call Hatitia Wells," I said. "I called you."

"Yet you do not even talk to me, let alone listen. I happen to be very conversant. But is there any *Have you read any good novels lately, Yulia?* What about *Did you get the committee chair you were hoping for?* Do you say, *I like to karaoke, Yulia; do you? Do you re-*

member speaking to my son yesterday? Do you ask, *How is Vadim?*"

"Please, hear me out. It has to do with corn. . . ."

I waited for the line to disconnect, but it didn't. I knew that would pique her interest. "We have found some maize," I said, "Some very, very old maize, and I need you to catch the next flight to South Dakota."

I waited for Yulia to say, *I just left South Dakota,* but she didn't.

That corn had her. I mean I owned her. It was time to set the hook:

"We believe this corn dates from the late Pleistocene. We need you to verify it."

"The Pleistocene?" Here Yulia laughed. "That is impossible. That cannot be. I see you have been selling me a cartload of dung."

"I know it sounds crazy, but we've found maize, a kilo of it, *in situ* with Clovis remains."

"I am flattered that you would concoct such foolishness on my account, but let me tell you something, Dr. Hannah: desperate men are not sexy. Please, now, stop this. I will thank you to say goodbye. I must return to my evening, which just might be quite scheduled. In fact, I might be watching a rental video at this very moment with my masculine boyfriend."

"The kernels look perfect," I said. "Completely viable. They were stored underground, in even temperatures, wrapped in layers of airtight velum."

"It is just not possible," was all she could say. "This cannot be."

"I need you," I said. "I need you to come here. If you get in your car right now, you'll be here before dawn."

There was a pause. I could hear her breath.

"It is just not possible," she said again.

I was silent.

"Tell me," she said. "You must tell me. Is this about corn? Or is this about me?"

I had nothing to lose. "Yulia," I said, "I'm no catch. No one reads my book. My phone doesn't ring. Though I have heart and good intentions, I ultimately fear I do a disservice to my graduate students by teaching them. They could be someplace else, where real research is being done. Right now, I'm calling you from a minimum-security prison, where I'm being held until jury selection begins on my grave-desecration trial. Now I have found what looks like a kilo of the oldest maize on earth, and I have a grad student who, I fear, might try to eat it. I don't know if this Clovis corn is real or not, but my gut tells me this is the biggest thing ever to happen to me, and all I know is that my first instinct was to include you. When a sheriff's deputy strangled me unconscious, I thought of you. When a pack of condemned dogs ate my hamburger, I thought of you. And now that I've opened a door into the previous eon, I want you to step through with me."

I could hear Yulia breathing. "I'm coming," she said. Then the line went dead.

When I hung up the phone, I could see that a prisoner working the concession stand was preparing for *Psycho* by popping a fresh batch of popcorn. Inside a box of yellow Plexiglas, the smoking metal drum turned and turned, a snow of puffy white falling into drifts below.

I couldn't bring myself to seek out the small bunk that awaited in my "cell."

Yulia, I kept thinking. *Yulia*. This was the time when you were vulnerable. This was when Hope snuck up on you, slipped an arm around your neck, and slapped a sleeper hold on your ass. Still, I couldn't help thinking about her.

Already, I could picture Yulia's hair, frizzy and wind-driven as she descended the steps from the airplane. Her eye shadow was Ukrainian midnight, her lipstick Chernobyl red. Behind her ear was a fresh-cut *Draculunus vulgaris*, a blossom I imagined as flushed and fiery as an inflamed genital. I watched her hips sway under a Soviet-gray skirt as she strode across the pink tarmac, through the hot terminal, and toward a taxi whose driver would speak to her of rapture all the way to the spectral, stained-glass light of the visitor-processing center.

From there, heedless, she would come to me.

I needed to walk around. I had to clear my head!

I stepped outside, let the cold air penetrate my scalp. I inhaled deep enough to bend me over. I stared at a movie poster until I settled my breathing. It was for tomorrow's movie, *North by Northwest*, and it depicted Cary Grant running through a cornfield from an evil crop duster bent on snuffing him out.

Ahead, under the marquee, a few insider traders stood smoking. And standing with them, discussing the NASDAQ index, was Eggers.

I approached the boy, put a hand on his shoulder.

"What are you still doing here?" I asked. "Is something wrong?"

"No," Eggers said. "I just thought . . . I kind of figured I might hang out with you for a while."

I had some big issues going on. This was my personal/leisure time. The last thing I needed was some grad student glomming on to me. I let my eyes dart to a distant point in the prison, as if some important business were calling me there. I exhaled with impatience, but Eggers didn't seem to get the hint.

"I've got things to do," I told him. "I've got places to be."

"Oh, sure, sure," Eggers said. "I understand, completely."

Yet he made no move to leave.

"Is there some special circumstance?" I asked. "I mean, is something wrong?"

"No," he said. "It's just—I don't have a lodge anymore. I don't have anyplace to go."

I slid my hands into the overalls. "Normally, sure, I'd love to. But I'm in prison here. I've got a lot on my mind."

He gave his normal Eggers smile, as if to say this was the answer he'd been expecting.

"Sure," Eggers said. "Sure."

"Any other time," I said. "Believe me."

"No biggie," Eggers said. "Forget I asked, okay? I never even asked." He took a couple of steps backward into the snow. There was a hitch of pain in the way he turned. This was the second time in how many nights that we'd parted this way, and it was awful watching him walk away again. It was truly pathetic. The kid seriously needed a few sessions with the counselors over in the psych department.

I was no professional, but I called out to him: "Wait. I suppose there's no harm in just walking together."

Eggers stopped.

I gave a throwaway gesture. "I mean, there'd have to be a couple of ground rules."

"Like what?" he asked.

"I've got some thinking to do," I said. "I can't very well do that with someone yakking in my ear."

"Are you saying—no talking?"

I shrugged.

Eggers shoved his hands into his parka and looked around, as if he were debating it. He must have thought he'd look spineless to agree to such a condition, at least too quickly. Really, though, it was a pretty generous offer.

"I guess I can live with that," Eggers said.

"Great, then," I said. "Let's start hanging out."

"So—does it start now?" Eggers asked.

"What?"

"The no-talking thing."

"You don't have to say it like that," I said. "It's just, you know, there are special circumstances here."

Eggers didn't say anything.

"I've got a lot on my mind."

Eggers was quiet.

Nothing, I could tell, would get him to talk now.

"Come on," I said, and began walking uphill, toward the top of campus. Eggers fell in beside me, the hood of his poncho pulled close around his face, and together we strolled past the old engineering building, a structure whose ivy had died and peeled away, though the trellises had left a ghostly, darker imprint on the walls. When the breeze swept by, you expected the ivy to shimmer, but it was no longer there. Eggers walked with me, crunching through a runner of fresh powder just off the sidewalk. Ahead, the snow-burdened branches of Douglas firs hung low and oscillating in the wind. As we passed, they tried to grab our ankles with their blind, groping limbs.

We neared the old campus broadcasting tower, galvanized with ice, and then there was the gymnasium, the repertory theater, and, at the top of the hill, the dome of the 1923 hand-crank Rawlins telescope. Eggers insisted on walking in my blind spot, silently pacing off my periphery, as if riding some invisible bow wave. In the corner of my eye, I'd catch a glimpse of his plodding booties, or the steamy grunt of his breath whenever he stumbled over a buried tree root. I'd be walking along, and just when I forgot about Eggers, there'd be a flash of shaggy fur beside me, or the ruffle of his game bag as it bounced with his hip. Yulia was coming, and what I needed was a plan. How could I concentrate with a Clovis hounding me?

Yet it was as if he weren't completely there, either. Whenever I looked over, Eggers' face was lost in his dark hood. Whenever I said "Eggers," Eggers made no response, as if he didn't even speak my language. It wasn't much of a stretch to imagine that Keno was cresting a hill with me, retracing ancient steps above a long-ago hunting valley. I knew this was Eggers pacing me, and not Keno. I knew Eggers was just acting withdrawn, giving me the silent treatment out of spite. And I wasn't even hoping for an answer when I stopped and asked him:

"Is she really going to come?"

Eggers stopped. Crossing his arms to ward off the cold, he faced me, though I couldn't make out his eyes behind all that fur. The whole campus was bordered by a sleepy, upper-middle-class neighborhood, and across the street were rows of brick houses, bought by people who thought they'd spend their golden years adjacent to the culture and vitality of a university. Some of these homeowners might have included the donors whose names were sandblasted off the buildings. Somewhere, buried between the sidewalk and that street, separating me from those normal families, was a cable that would sound an alarm if I crossed it.

"What other unseen things dictate our lives?" I asked him.

Eggers offered no opinion.

A simple step, I thought. I was one step away from how other people lived.

I considered again these sleepy houses. Frozen garden hoses were coiled stiff around spigots. The raised red ears of mailboxes stood suspicious and alert. The smoke from dark chimneys lifted, billowy and content, then, just above the evergreens, just out of view, raced away east. Somehow it was easier to believe in the hidden alarm than in the possibility that those homes were filled with families who were whole and happy.

I asked, "Is there really a buried cable?"

All that mattered, I supposed, was that we believed there was.

Then Eggers lifted a hand. He turned, slowly and strangely, as if guided by an unseen hand, toward the dark prison buildings. He took one step in their direction, but stopped. He peeled back his hood and cocked an ear.

Out there was a scampering sound in the snow.

From the darkness, a rocking figure began to emerge, long and trailing. Then it came clear: racing toward us was a team of six Pomeranians, harnessed in tiny leather traces, bounding through the snow. Chests plowing the powder, their little heads loped above pumping torsos, while the patter of white breath rose in fits. I looked around for Gerry and his kids, but they were nowhere to be seen. The Pomeranian named McQueen was in the lead—I'd recognize the snitty cock of his ears anywhere—and as they passed us, heading in and out of the prison lights, I could see they were pulling an empty wooden sled the size of a breakfast tray. Gerry had said he was going to increase his sales sixfold, and now it was clear that he was selling dogs by the team, probably working a buy-six, get-a-sled-free angle.

I turned to Eggers. "Love," I said. "Do you know it? Is it all they say it is?"

He regarded me. "I'm the protégé," Eggers said. "I'm the one learning from you."

The sound of the skids diminished, and the little sled slipped away, the dogs answering the call of an unseen driver who mushed them on with his ghostly voice.

Chapter Eight

The night arced high and cold, pulling icy black sheets over the prison. The sky was starless, the night infirm. Wind whisked inky and aluminum past my window. The chill penetrated the glass, radiating down to pool across the floor. Where was dawn? What good was the sun if it only came by every once in a while?

I rolled up tighter in my thin, penitentiary-issue blanket, but to no avail. The cold would not be stopped. It entered the room through copper wires and old weep holes. It worked its way into knotholes and sump fittings, was siphoned in through ducts and plumbing. It filled the voids in the cinder-block wall, made ice of my bunk's metal frame. The thick rubber backing of my ankle monitor was fat-tongued with cold, making the thing constrict enough to turn my foot nightingale-blue, to make my toes buzz like baby radio towers.

With some effort, I located my socks, both of them soiled, and slid them, one over the other, on my right foot, then stared at the ceiling, waiting for my foot to warm. First light was on the way; there was still time to sleep, but I'd had a dream, one bad enough to make me remember all the mistakes I'd made before bed. After Eggers left, I'd called my father, hitting him up to deliver my brown suit so I could look suave for Yulia's arrival. I kind of got going on a brag session, playing up how fine my new lady was, flying seven hundred miles to see me. But Dad's answering machine ran out of tape, and I was cut off before I even got to the part about Yulia's hothouse and my Siberian competition, a failed scholar named Ivan.

Next I called Trudy, waking her, and it's painful to admit, but I begged her to find Yulia's flight and pick her up from the airport. Finally, most shameful of all, I executed a masterpiece of folly—I called Farley, after midnight, to ask him for his sure-fire mushroom-soufflé recipe. When he answered, I heard Santana playing in the background, and it turned out he was not alone.

In my room, the cold seemed to radiate from everywhere: from the small metal desk, from the bulbless bedside lamp, from that lone wire hanger in the closet. Yet it was the dream that chilled my heart:

Artifact Number 8

It opens with me walking through my old house, now empty. Though all of Janis' possessions have been removed, I duck where her stained-glass lamp once hung. Where has she gotten to? I wonder. Suddenly I remember there is an extra room in this dream house, one hidden under the staircase. When I open the door, I find not Janis but our old dog, Roamy. It turns out that he wasn't hit by a truck after all. I suddenly remember that I'd left him here, years ago. All this time, he's been patiently waiting for me to come back—years and years of waiting. The part that really hurts is that Roamy isn't mad. He puts his paws on me and keeps licking my face. He can't stop—it's like he's trying to make up for all that lost time. I push the dog away and start running. I just close the door on him again and take off. I run in the dream—forever, it seems—until my ankle hurts, and then I wake, foot throbbing.

I had to get out of that room. I draped the blanket over my shoulders and stepped into the hall, which was surprisingly warm. Only my room, it seemed, was an icebox. I walked down the center of the dark hallway, and all those doors scared me to death. I kept thinking they would suddenly open—who would I find behind them?

At the end of the hall was a group bathroom and shower house. On the door was a list for latrine duty, with the names of others crossed out and mine written in. Past the bathroom was a communal kitchen area, and my name also led the coffeemaker detail, as well as dishwashing and floors. Gerry had put my name down for defroster duty on the big double-doored refrigerator, and I didn't even bother to check the list taped to the oven.

The kitchen opened into a group eating area, and on the

bulletin boards were activity sign-up sheets, to which my name had been uniformly added. I was now a member of the Christian Jubilee Choir, Books for the Blind, and Tax Tattlers, a program that offered free income-tax preparation services to the community. Beyond the food-prep area were several dining tables, aligned in a horseshoe so everyone could view a large projection TV that was housed on a platform built from fake lava rocks and maroon carpet. The set was tuned to a channel that showed nothing but the weather, and by this blue light I made out one of Gerry's kids. Before him, upside down on the table, was a wooden sled.

I didn't have much experience speaking to little persons, especially ones under the impression that I'd killed their dog. But I couldn't shake that dream. I tried not to think of the small, cold room waiting for me.

I neared the kid. "Whatcha got going on there?" I asked.

Looking up from the sled, he gave me the quick, recognizing glance that people reserved for the village idiot. Then he returned to the sled's runner, on which he was performing some delicate procedure. It's true that I had a blanket wrapped around my prison-issue pajamas, and I wore two socks on one foot.

"Saw your sled in action last night," I told him.

He shrugged.

"Very impressive," I said.

With the wax-paper modesty of an eleven-year-old, he said, "That thing? That was an assembly-line sled. That thing's for mama's boys in Nebraska. *This* is a racing prototype."

The thing did look fast and sleek. It was cut from a lattice of blond wood, and all the struts and braces were pulled tight by a cradle of rawhide as clear and taut as drumskin. There were no metal parts that I could see, and everything looked handmade.

I said, "So — who do you race?"

Almost defensively, he said, "Well, right now we just go against the clock."

"Right," I said.

"Mom never let us race the dogs the way they do in *Impossible Journey*. She said it was cruel to make them run around. But

Pomeranians were born to pull. They're an ancient and noble breed, you know."

"Of course."

"They come from Iceland."

"An ancient and noble place," I said.

He looked at me sideways, to see if I was making fun of him.

To assure him otherwise, I said, "I know you lost your dog."

He made a few passes down the sled's runner with a bar of wax that looked tacky and dry, like a withered scrap of soap you'd find in a gym shower.

Without looking up, he said, "No loss."

"I had a dog once," I said. "A long time ago. It can hurt pretty bad. I know you think I was the one who —"

"Forget it," the kid said, licking a finger and running it lickety-split down the runner. "We were going to sell that one anyway. Some dogs are keepers. With the rest, you just do your job and keep moving."

Where had this kid picked up such a philosophy? I hoped not from Gerry.

I asked him, "What exactly is your job?"

"I teach 'em to sit up and beg. They have to learn that, so you can slip their sledding harnesses on. McQueen does most of the work, though. The other dogs follow him. Gerry saved him, you know. Ever since Gerry brought him home from work, that dog's done most of the training."

The sheriff's station came to me, with its cell-full of dogs, and suddenly it made sense that Gerry was the one who had to put those strays to sleep. It suddenly fit why Gerry was more upset over losing a dog than he was over losing his job.

I shouldn't have, but I asked, "Does your mom know you guys were spending your days at the sheriff's station? Does she know you're here?"

"We're just hanging out till she gets back," he said. "Mom's on vacation."

"Vacation?"

"Yeah," he said. "At a dude ranch, a high-class one."

"A dude ranch," I echoed. "Can't say I've ever been to one of those."

"They call it the Lazy-R. They've got a fancy lodge with horses and fishing, you name it. Gerry says everything's first-class. At night they wash their steaks down with peach brandy."

The boy listed a few more of the dude ranch's amenities, including activities like making bullwhips and writing cowboy poetry, but there was no light in his eyes.

"You sure this is that kind of ranch?" I asked. "Isn't it more like a rehabilitation center or a convalescent home?"

He looked at me like he didn't know what the heck I was talking about.

"Your mother is recuperating, isn't she?" I asked. "I mean, wasn't there some sort of accident?"

The boy's look turned from incomprehension to uncomfortable vacancy. I wanted to grill him a little more about this supposed ranch that was open in the middle of winter, but I understood the kid was going through some hard times.

I tried to strike the right tone, a mix of casual and concerned.

"When was the last time you talked to her?" I asked.

He didn't say anything.

In the silence, you could hear Gerry snoring in one of the adjacent rooms.

From nowhere, an inmate strolled into the kitchen in his underwear—skin sallow, flesh pasty. I could tell he was a millionaire by the way he grabbed a gallon of milk from the avocado-colored fridge and stood in the light of the open door drinking for himself what was meant for us all.

The kid took the opportunity to pick up his wax.

"I've got to finish my sled," he said.

I took a long look at him. "You don't have any idea where your mother is, do you?" I asked him. "You don't know when she's coming back at all."

He seemed not to hear me. With his special wax, he began stroking the runner, methodically, the wax caking where he pressed too hard.

I went to the shower house. Under the urinal trough I found a stiff-bristled brush and a jug of industrial cleaner. I didn't have my shower sandals, let alone a sponge caddy, and forget finding any yellow rubber gloves. I just started scrubbing. Somehow that kid had gotten to me. Under the spray of old copper nozzles, I couldn't tell if I was crying or not. It felt like I was. Using the brush handle, I scraped at chalky green calcium deposits. Then I dug the bristles into the purple-black grout where microbial flagella clung as tightly as when they gripped the earth in the Precambrian era.

Normally, cleaning soothed me. I found solace in its sense of purpose and accomplishment, in the single-minded attention serious housework required. But I couldn't focus at all. Cold condensation dripped down from the ceiling. The lingering smell of kiwi shampoo and mango conditioner sickened me. *Kids*, I thought. They were born suckers. It made me shudder to think how lost and clueless they were. The way they looked at you, so blind, so trusting. They fell for any damn thing you told them. Then there was the neediness, the withdrawal, the tears. Who'd blame a mom if she did head off to the old dude ranch? Who wouldn't turn to a diet of cowboy canapés and nightly charades?

Under each shower nozzle was a depression in the cement where decades of human feet had worn the concrete, exposing an aggregate of sand and crushed river rock. I stood in these stations, polishing the tile, making the fixtures shine, dehairing the drains. I scrubbed until the first glints of morning light shone down through the vent shafts. I looked up, as if I could see pale sky through the lean ducts. High in a propeller plane, at that very moment perhaps, the most beautiful paleobotanist in the state of North Dakota was on her way to see me. Yet inside, where my stomach should be, there was only a hollow drop-off.

It was the same pang I'd felt after buying the Corvette. I had just published a book, one I fancied would shake things up in the intellectual world, and to celebrate I duffed five years of savings on a stupid car. After I paid for it, the shop in Sioux Falls kept the car a week while they installed the custom stereo I wanted, and mounted the rear spoiler and the window louvers. When a guy from the dealership finally dropped it off, he left the motor running, as if I'd dive in and race through town.

But all I felt was this: that no fool had ever so fooled himself, that self-suckery had now become an art. Babes, I suddenly understood, weren't going to start speaking to me—and they didn't. Colleagues wouldn't begin to respect me, as I'd fantasized. But what was there to do? I climbed in and drove around town all afternoon, revving the engine for nobody.

I moved to the commodes, which were filled with all manner of material, amber and otherwise. After I flushed them, though, you could see the porcelain bowls were passably clean. The toilet tanks, however, had never been touched, and when I lifted the lids, I found that beards of algae had grown deep into the water—they waggled, as if with wisdom, after each flush. I closed a stall door, took a seat on a toilet lid, and leaned back against the tank. Who did I think I was fooling?

In the bare light of a jailhouse crapper, I counted a thousand reasons Yulia would reject me. There were my bony wrists, so thin and flimsy that my hand could just about squirrel through the hairpin curve of a toilet trap. There was the fungal smell my scalp had picked up. These were obvious flaws, and then there were the ones that I couldn't see but she undoubtedly would. I was an expert at knowing when people *secretly* didn't want to be around a guy. I'd been trained to detect in my fellow humans those quiet inclinations to be some*where* else, with some*one* else.

After your mother leaves, you look back on things with sharper vision. You understand that those days she scanned the horizon, she wasn't thinking about the weather. You realize your walks to the post office weren't about your fascination with stamps, but some secret correspondence she was keeping, with someone far away. In retrospect, you remember which sections of the paper she read first, what distant radio station she spent forever trying to tune in. Flying a kite, she was the kite. Ice-skating, her tight turns were loops around the world. When I close my eyes and try to feel her now, it is not my mother's embrace that comes to me, not her hug, or the lap I sat on, but those interminable swing sets. After school we always went to the playground by the river. Even as a child, you know when the hands on your back are absent hands. To swing, you must face away from your mother, and she pushes you away, she pushes you away, but you keep swinging back. Her heart loses ground the longer this game goes on, until she is barely touching your back and you are barely moving, until her hands feel so faint, it's like she's pushing you from Paris. Listless in a swing, you toe the sand and watch the water as she finishes her cigarette. *You never step in the same river twice,* your science books say, and your mother is only a puff of smoke, passing over your shoulder.

So, after she leaves for good, your radar is on as your dad begins rotating through the parade of girlfriends that will eventually lead to Janis. After dinner, your father and a woman drink sherry in silence as you finish your ice cream, and you know when your company isn't preferred, you know they can't wait for you to go to bed. At the cinema, your father slings a jacket over his shoulder and leads a different woman to the lobby, where they will chat and gesture, where they will lean casually against the theater's big windows, touching fingers, waiting for you to watch the end of the movie reel. In a restaurant, you come out of the bathroom, and there are three half-eaten dinners around a table, some cash under a plate, and this means your father and some woman are already in the car, radio on, smoking. When you crunch across the lot, your dad's engine fires up, and as you climb into the back seat, he passes you a mint and gives you that look. The look isn't mean. It doesn't wish you weren't born. It doesn't hope you'll be gone tomorrow. It only wonders if you have to be right *here*, right *now*.

In this period, your father gives you books, literally, by the box. Once, he orders every book in the *Junior Geologist*'s summer catalogue. Sure, you read. But, for reasons you don't understand, you begin rifling through his possessions. While he's at work, you feel your way through the bottom of his sock drawer. You stand on a chair to inspect the closet's top shelf. Inside the breast pocket of his sportcoats, you find plastic swizzle sticks from bars you've never heard of. Your mother's nurse medallion, you discover, is something your father keeps in his medicine cabinet, beside his stomach pills. In a book, *Profiles in Courage,* you find one of your baby photos, except in this one there is a little puppy on a blanket with you. The puppy has a bow around its neck, but this dog you have never heard of. No one ever mentioned his name. You find a cache of condoms, taped individually to the bottom of the bedside table, and though you don't exactly know their purpose, it's clear to you, lying on the floor, looking up at them, that these have to do with the women your father dates. These are integral to the look your dad gives you as you take forever to finish that melting ice cream.

Cramped in the stall, my legs had gone to sleep. I had to lean on the toilet-paper dispenser to stand. I flushed the toilet under me, lest anyone think I was up to some monkey business in here, then walked stiff-legged to the common room, where I called Trudy.

When she answered, I said, "Trudy, I'm sorry. But this has been a mistake. You can't pick up Yulia. You can't bring her here."

On the other end, Trudy gave a long, exasperated sigh.

I was silent. I replayed Yulia's image over and over in my mind, looking for signs that she really didn't want to be with me. I couldn't detect any, but that didn't mean anything. It was my experience that it sometimes took a while to stumble upon someone's hidden reservations. If you spent enough time with someone, though, if you looked hard enough, you'd find them. It was always a matter of time. If I found them in Yulia . . . when I found them in Yulia . . . how would I stand it?

"Dr. Hannah," Trudy said, "you may not remember this, because it was late, but you called me about twelve hours ago."

"Things have changed," I said. "We'll have to go with another paleobotanist."

"What about Dr. Nivitski? She lands in a couple hours. What am I supposed to do? Take her sightseeing?"

"Can't you just not pick her up?" I asked. "I mean, she's an adult. She can take care of herself."

"I'm going to pretend this conversation never happened," she said. "You've been under a lot of stress. Anyone can see that. I'm going to meet Dr. Nivitski's flight at five, and I'm going to tell her how thrilled you are to have her consult on this project. Then I'm going to drop her off at the visitors' entrance."

This time, Trudy hung up.

Wrapping my trusty blanket around my shoulders, I headed for that icebox of a room, resigning myself to cold sheets and a cold mattress. This is how my father found me. I felt as if I'd only been asleep a minute, as if my eyes had just closed. Then he was shaking me awake. I squinted up at him, my teeth clenched with cold. He stood there, brown suit draped over an arm, looking at me—my bald head, my dishpan hands, the wet sock on my right foot. Though he was trying not to show it, I could tell he was dismayed. He went to pull off my wet sock, and when he found another wet sock underneath it, he shot me a look of moderate distress. From his pocket, he drew a pair of black wool socks, and after sliding these on my feet, he hauled me up to a sitting position.

"Arms up," he said, and pulled a white dress shirt over me.

When my head poked through, I got a good look at him as he worked my hands through the cuffs. His hair was thinning. There were a few liver spots on his scalp. His two new teeth looked wooden. He seemed, for reasons I couldn't put my finger on, very alone. But I was always wrong when I thought that of him. "Did you water the plants?" I asked.

He was working the buttons on the cuff vent. "Yes, I watered your plants."

"Did you play them some Latin jazz?"

"Sure," he said. "I danced them a marimba, too."

When he played me like that, I never knew what to believe. He was full of these little power moves designed to keep me off balance. They always worked.

He tugged my shirt this way and that, to center it.

"Relax," he said. "I watered your plants."

"Now you're really lying, aren't you? It would be like you to play the music and leave them dry."

"Look," he said, gathering the fabric of my slacks so they'd slip on easier, "I'm trying to help here. I'm on your side. Now, come on, lift those legs."

I complied, though I moved pretty slow, just to let Dad know I had a mind of my own. "You're wasting your time," I told him. "Plans have changed, if you haven't heard. She's not coming."

Dad didn't say anything. He just worked a pant leg over my ankle, then jammed on a dress shoe to keep the slacks from sliding off. This he repeated on my other leg, then began lacing.

"Did you hear what I said?" I asked. "Are you listening to me?"

When both my shoes were snug, he stood.

"All set," he said. "Just pull your pants up."

"I know how to pull my pants up," I said.

"Then pull your pants up."

A woman knocked on the door. "Is everybody decent in there?" she asked.

I pulled my pants up.

In walked the waitress from the Lollygag, though now her hair was down, and it was beyond black, full of sheen and depth. It was movie-star hair, rich enough to allow her to favor dark lipstick, wear a top that shimmered green, and carry a little extra weight.

Dad stuffed a wadded-up tie in my coat pocket. "I draw the line at other men's ties," he said, and tossed a thumb toward the woman. "You remember Lorraine."

A coffee cup hung from her finger. She swung it to show that it was empty.

I didn't exactly catch her name last time, but I said, "Of course. Charmed."

She handed me the empty cup. "Likewise, Professor," she said, a little playfully. "I was going to make you a cup, but that coffee station—really, it's a mess. Nothing personal. I mean, you do have quite a place here."

"The accommodations are temporary," I assured her.

She turned to my father. "Not much room for a party, I'm afraid."

I asked, "A party?"

Just then, I saw Farley walk past the door frame, headed down the hall. He wore one of those sharp suits of his, and he was carrying something in large oven mitts imprinted with red flames.

I followed in disbelief, catching up with him at the communal kitchen, where he was staring at the controls of one of the ovens. When Farley caught sight of me, he patted me on the shoulder and threw me a look that said, *What'd I tell ya, eh?* I could feel the heat of the mitt through my suit.

He said, "A cut above the county holding cells, huh? You hear any dogs barking? Smell any urine? It doesn't get any better than this. Here you've got your high-speed Internet access, your bowling league, and your"—he stopped, lifted his eyebrows—"conjugal visits." As if reminded of something, he shook off an oven mitt and withdrew a cassette tape from his slacks. This he slipped into my breast pocket, then patted its impression through the fabric. "I know you're an Eagles man," he said, "but give the Santana a test drive."

I pulled the tape out, examined it. "Farley," I said, "if this has anything to do with that call last night, let me apologize here and now. I was way out of line to—"

He turned to his casserole dish, sealed with aluminum foil. "Speak nothing of it, my man. I present one mushroom surprise, as requested," he said. With a note of conspiracy, he added, "I make the bacon bits myself. Trust me—the ladies notice."

I was always suspicious of sudden generosity. The rule of life tends toward the opposite. Still, I said, "This is too much, my friend. You didn't have to do this."

Farley shook his head. "What would you do without me?" he asked, not altogether rhetorically. I didn't mind. Against the tableau of an old kitchen, it felt as if Farley and I were family, standing in a place where, had we been brothers, we'd have talked late by the fridge light or met before dawn to make sandwiches before slipping out to fish under the morning star. There was a certain kind of kitchen that could always make you feel this: twin cocoa-colored ovens, an avocado fridge, and Formica countertops that had once been lemon-yellow. Throw in a stovetop whose burner pans were lined with tin foil, and some pull-out cutting boards that had long ago been resurfaced with handwritten recipes. What spoke more of family than an always-wrong oven clock or that lone Crock-Pot made from clear root-beer-tinted glass?

Farley leaned against the preheating oven.

"Amigo," he said, "you can do me one favor."

Then Farley mimed the zipping of a fly.

I looked down. Sure enough. I gave the matter some quick attention as Dad and Lorraine straggled into the kitchen. Behind them, the sun was setting through the tall windows of the breakfast area. Outside, the prison was canopied by mid-level clouds, yet the horizon was clear. The dipping sun shot brilliant light at us, slanty and intense.

Dad and Lorraine didn't say anything. They just stood in that sideways light, smiling at me. "What?" I asked them.

"Nothing," my dad said, though that grin was on his face.

I turned to Farley, and he had that stupid smirk, too.

That's when Eggers and Trudy came in, walking as la-di-da as Hansel and Gretel, as if they didn't have a care in the world.

"Hey, Dr. Hannah," Trudy said. She had her big sweater on and was wearing shiny clips to hold back her bangs.

"Howdy," Eggers said. He was carrying a party bowl of assorted potato chips.

Lorraine, out of politeness perhaps, grabbed one chip.

Farley shook his head. "Oh, that's vintage Clovis," he said. "Now, that's authentic. And here I'd been thinking that my ancestors had carried their Doritos in woven baskets on their heads."

This banter I ignored. I kept looking behind Trudy, through the door, to see if anybody else was coming. Perhaps Yulia was standing in the hall, waiting for the right moment to reveal herself to me. Maybe she was nervous about seeing me again, and was pausing to gather her thoughts. I took the time to adjust my shirt cuffs, to brush back my hair, though there was only stubble when I did.

I clapped my hands together, then rubbed them briskly. "Well?" I asked.

Eggers said, "Well, we brought the corn."

Trudy smiled. "Well, we're here," she said.

I walked past them and stuck my head into the hall. There was no one there. I looked at Farley, Dad, and Lorraine. I looked in the hall again. Had Yulia really not come?

"What are you looking for?" Trudy asked.

"Don't give me that," I told her. "What exactly is going on here?"

She looked like she didn't know what I was talking about.

"We brought the corn," she said. "Eggers brought some chips. We're here."

"I know you're here," I said. "Everyone in the world is here. Every Tom, Dick, and Harry in South Dakota is here. Where's Dr. Nivitski?"

Trudy said, "You told me not to pick her up. You called me and said—"

I threw my hands up. "You're telling me Dr. Nivitski is sitting at the airport alone, and you're all in here baking pot pies?"

"Hey, now," Farley said, "that was uncalled for."

"This isn't just about me," I said to Trudy, who'd crossed her arms. "Science is on the line here. Humanity is at stake. This goes beyond personal whimsy and potato chips. This is bigger than whether you can be troubled to pick someone up at the airport. I'd do it all myself, but I'm in prison here, if you haven't noticed. This is jail, in case you forgot what crimes I'm charged with."

Suddenly there was Yulia and a boy who must be her son, Vadim, standing in the doorway. I turned to Trudy and offered her a look of apology.

I approached Yulia, and we regarded each other. She wore tight dark jeans, snug as spray-paint, and a down ski jacket, powder-white. A red scarf wrapped her neck, and her hair was hidden beneath a cap of white sable. I neared her, so close it surprised me. My breathing sent white ripples through that ultrafine fur. Yulia's dark-brown eyes seemed depthless. Her pupils, fluctuating, hypnotized me.

I said, "I didn't think you'd come."

"Are you not pleased with my arrival?"

The wispy fur of her hat was something out of a dream, soft and undulating. The way Yulia's hair was pulled up showed the flare of her cheekbones, accented the cut of her jaw. Something daring rose in me.

"No," I said, "it's just that I can't believe I ever let you leave."

She threw me a look of exaggerated indifference.

"I am here in a professional capacity," she said. "I am hoping you are worth at least a tax deduction."

I knew the desire in her eyes. "Is that the only reason you came?" I asked.

"No," she said, "I also have frequent-flier miles. Soon they will be expiring."

Were there other people in the room? Was everyone staring at us? I didn't know. I saw only Yulia, her red lips, her white skin, the sparkle of her Russian dentistry. "You should travel more often," I said, "if it makes you beam so radiantly."

She looked at me sideways. Was she offended by my forwardness? Or was she basking in a compliment? "I notice you have denuded your hair," she said. "You look more severe. You resemble a man of intensity. And your eyes, I would say they appear more remarkable."

How Hope—fleeting, exhilarating—fortified me!

Yulia shouldered forward her son. "This is Vadim," she said.

The boy didn't look like Gerry's kids—those little truants were strong, scrappy things, composed solely of muscles and cowlicks. Gerry's kids, you could tell, were going to make it through the next decade on rash impulses alone.

No, Vadim was a solitary, brooding boy, thin at the waist, red about the nose. Trustful and half lost, he seemed unprepared for what life had in store, even though he'd had a dose already, traveling round the world, leaving his father behind.

I made a show of examining the boy. I placed my hand appraisingly on his shoulder and head. He wore a yellow parka that he'd nearly outgrown, and his hair, exhibiting none of Yulia's frizz, was cut in the manner of a bowl.

"So," I said, "this is the young scientist."

Vadim looked up. "You are the man with whom I chit-chatted?"

"Yes," I said, "we spoke. There will be some amazing science here tonight, I assure you. We are going to conduct an initial examination on a very important botanical sample."

I gestured largely, to show how meaningful our work would be, but Vadim's brown eyes were unreadable. He asked, "Is it not prudent to first wait for the results?"

Wise words indeed. They made me inspect the boy closer. To be Vadim's age, I knew, was to be plagued by unknowns.

Yulia patted Vadim's shoulder and squeezed once, to let him know she was there.

"Well," she said, looking into my eyes, "shall we see this corn, perhaps?"

Eggers cleared his throat. "We have some preliminary business," he said.

I'd forgotten Eggers was even in the room! How to speak of this night with anything approaching method, let alone objectivity? Dear guardians of tomorrow, I know not what future you inhabit when you read these words, what centuries or millennia have transpired. All I know for sure is that you all hold doctorates in anthropology, so you understand the principles of uncertainty at work in any version of the truth, let alone a saga soon to be stained by love and lust, as this one is. So I apologize in advance if I forget some particulars or lose track of any participants. As dedicated anthropologists, you will, I know, be especially offended at the destruction of an ancient artifact that I will shortly relate. I say only this: every thought and every action that shapes the rest of this wily and temperamental sojourn must be understood in terms of Dr. Yulia Terrasova Nivitski.

Everyone gathered around the kitchen island. The setting sun had purpled the room, and folks nibbled on orange potato chips from a festive bowl.

Trudy spoke up. "First things first, Dr. Hannah. We've been working on a project."

I looked to my father and Lorraine. I looked to Farley. If they knew what Trudy was speaking of, they gave nothing away.

"What is this project?" I asked. "What are you talking about?"

Eggers stepped from behind the counter. Dorito in hand, he gestured solemnly. "Dr. Hannah," he said, "I told you yesterday that everything in my lodge had been confiscated by the sheriff, but that wasn't exactly true."

Farley took a keen interest in this. He slid his casserole dish into the oven without taking his eyes off the boy. Trudy came forward to join Eggers. They looked at each other a moment, as if deciding how to proceed.

"One article of clothing was spared," Trudy said. "It was at the dry cleaners."

Farley just shook his head—he checked his watch to time the dish, but it looked as if he was taking note of the exact moment and place this statement was made. "Does anyone hear this?" Farley asked. "A Clovis using the dry cleaners? Is no one bothered by this?"

Eggers ignored him, strolled into the hall, and returned with a garment bag from the cleaners. "Here you go," he said, handing me a hanger that must have weighed thirty pounds.

I looked around the room, my eyes finally meeting Trudy's. "What is this?" I asked.

"Go ahead," she said. "Open it."

I slipped off the bag to reveal a grand coat, cut from the softest, richest pelt I'd ever seen. The pile of the fur must've been four inches thick. The coat closed with a set of toggles carved from antler that buttonholed into a rather smart-looking set of sinew loops. And the crowning glory was a large hood ringed with fleece cut from fur whose color and fluff I'd seen only in Pomeranians.

To Eggers I said, "I've never seen anything like it."

"I did the outside of the parka," Eggers said. He eyed Farley. "Using strict Paleolithic technology. I brain-tanned the hide, then soaked it in brine for three days. I smoked it, waterproofed it, then worked it soft with a hand loop. The panels were cut with obsidian flakes, and I did the seams with a needle shaped from a heron's beak. Trudy did the inside."

I laid the coat on the countertop so everyone could see, then folded it open to reveal an interior that was completely quilted and embroidered. The lining of the coat was a patchwork of fabrics, sewn into a large map of North America that depicted the Corderillan and Laurentide glaciers, which once extended from Siberia to South Dakota. All was glacial ice, except for a narrow gap that cut across Alaska and Canada: the route the Clovis followed to South Dakota.

Trudy joined me to explicate her work:

"American pilots in World War II used to sew maps of Europe in their coats," she said. "That way, if they crashed or bailed out, they could always find their way. Since this is a Clovis coat, I sewed in a map of America from twelve thousand years ago." She began explaining the different fabrics she'd incorporated. "The aqua satin is from a kimono my grandma sent me that was too short," she said. "The white canvas was cut from a cooking apron that Farley donated."

"It was my *lucky* apron, eh?" Farley corrected.

Her finger pointed to a patch of pink fabric and then a swatch of creamy velvet. "The pink came from one of Eggers' old polo shirts, which I found in the grad lounge, and of course you recognize the baby-blue of the old curtains that once hung in the Hall of Man. This velvet came from that big chair Peabody used to sit in."

I remembered that chair, all right. How many times had I sat in that old white chair in Peabody's office, listening to him speak of the grand excavations he'd been a part of? There was Folsom Creek and the Iowa Mounds. Peabody had worked the Manitoba Washouts and had personally met Ishi, a Native American whose California tribe existed completely on Stone Age technology until they were discovered and eradicated by land-grabbers in the year 1910. Ishi, the sole survivor, then walked to San Francisco, where he spent the remainder of his life trying to tell the story of his people to passersby who didn't know his language.

Trudy's words brought me back. "Only five arts are truly North American," she concluded. "Clovis points, Anasazi ceramics, quilting, jazz, and the blues. So this jacket is truly American."

I looked at Trudy. She'd somehow just synthesized nearly every important thing in my life into something beautiful and functional. I realized, right there, that her dissertation thesis would work, that she had the instinct and intellect to show the world how an ancient people's religion, art, philosophy, and physical needs were all met by a single object: a Clovis spear point.

Vadim inspected the coat. "What's this?" he asked.

He ran his hand over a pocket that had been sewn inside the breast. It was embroidered in cursive with the words "Open in

Case of Emergency." When I tried to open it, I found it was sewn shut. I looked to Trudy.

She smiled. "Open only in case of emergency," she said.

"What's in it?" I asked.

"Essentials," Eggers said.

I ran my hand over the pocket. There was something in there for sure, some sort of object, but I couldn't tell what. Was it hard or soft? Did I hear the crinkle of paper in there? I didn't try to guess—my brain was simply consumed with the beauty of the coat, the grandness of the gesture that brought it to me.

"Eggers," I said. "Trudy. I don't know what to say."

"We wanted to say thanks," Trudy added. "You know, for all you've taught us."

"It's just an *arigato*, that's all," Eggers said. "We'd been wanting to do something for you for a while. And when I heard a brown bear got hit by a train up in Glanton, I just had to get that skin."

"Glanton?" Farley asked. "That's thirty miles away."

Eggers shrugged. "It was no big deal. When you have the right fur parka on, you can walk forever. Besides, who would pass up a free bear pelt?"

Trudy said, "You should have seen the thing before I dry-cleaned it. The fur was all matted with blood. Don't forget it had been tanned with brains. And then Eggers used rancid grease to waterproof the backing."

"I don't know what to say," I said.

Eggers said, "You don't have to say anything. It's a gift."

Yulia ran her hand across the pile, the fur shining dark brown one way, almost silver the other. "Put it on," she commanded.

Here let me mention that, in my day, I was not a bad-looking fellow. I was broad of shoulder, lean of physique, though admittedly I tended to slouch. My hairline was respectable, and more than one woman had told me I possessed fine hands. Though I wouldn't say anyone had ever called me devilishly handsome, I could tell when certain women in the faculty senate cast an appraising glance my way. So, when I donned that bear parka, and stood to my full height, I can attest with a certain authority that Yulia gave me a look—a darting, up-and-down flash of the eyes—that suggested this evening might take a turn toward the salacious.

The coat made me feel large and stoic.

I clapped my hands twice. I needed to make a speech.

"Your attention, please," I said. "A toast is in order."

Lorraine shifted into bartender mode, pouring sodas from two-liter bottles into paper cups my father stoked with ice cubes. Farley took the opportunity to stick toothpicks in his mushroom surprise, and Eggers circled the Formica-topped island, pushing his prized potato chips on everyone.

When the sodas had gone around, I lifted my cup high.

"To my students, Eggers and Trudy," I said. All eyes turned to me, and there was my father, looking, for once, anticipatory and proud. Lorraine even seemed strangely at home with our company—it felt like she belonged. Farley sported an oven mitt, and at that moment, he was the brother I'd never had. As for Eggers and Trudy—I couldn't even look at them without getting choked up.

"To my students," I said again, but my lip began to quiver. Yulia cocked her head slightly, her eyes sending me support and understanding, and when I thought what a lucky man I was, when I took stock of all I'd been blessed with, the tears started to flow. I had to set my soda down and cover my face. Yulia put a hand on my shoulder. She thumbed the streams from my cheeks. This was happiness overpowering me. This is joy I'm talking about. I cleared my sinuses and tried to compose myself, but the emotion wouldn't let go.

"Here, here," Farley said, and everyone drank.

I'd never felt happier. To Yulia, I opened my arms for a hug. She looked a little surprised and tried to give me one of those lean-way-over-and-tap-you-on-the-back hugs. I knew all about halfhearted touching techniques. I was an expert at spotting those. When I got my arms around Yulia, I showed her a real embrace. I pulled her shoulders into mine. Through four inches of bear fur I could feel the pressure of her breasts as they struggled, fought, and then relinquished against me. Yulia said something rapidly in Russian, yet I understood her. When it comes to certain utterances between a man and a woman, no translation is needed.

I was on top of the world. I walked around the kitchen island to Eggers, who was going through all the cabinets, even though each door was labeled with a strip of masking tape that spelled out the contents inside. He was checking to see which Tupperware containers were airtight and which had matching lids. By the time I grabbed his shoulder, he was holding a frying pan in each hand, as if determining the heavier and more capable.

We both wore dark parkas. We were family. I admit I was still a little weepy. "Eggers," I said, "I want you to know how touched I am by this coat."

He set the pans down and, without really glancing at me, inspected some resealable freezer bags. "Sure, Dr. Hannah. You're the greatest. Don't sweat it."

He tugged the bags this way and that, to test their give.

I squeezed his shoulder. "Eggers," I said, "nobody's ever done anything like this for me."

Eggers set the bags aside and eyed a roll of plastic wrap.

"That's great, Dr. Hannah," he said. "Don't mention it."

He unrolled some of the wrap and stretched it to its breaking point.

I looked him in the eye and said, "Whenever I can be of service to you, anytime, anyplace, and no matter what engaged, I will assist you."

I don't know how Trudy's words came to my lips, but after I'd said them, I'd never felt better. It had reassured me immeasurably to hear those words from Trudy, but now I'd discovered it felt even better to speak them to others.

Eggers went back to the bags. He handed me a one-gallon freezer bag and asked me to hold it open while he poured half of the corn—about a kilo—directly from Keno's ball. Tiny and opalescent, the beads of corn shifted like tapioca pearls.

"That goes to Dr. Nivitski for research," Eggers said. "The rest is mine."

Corn in hand, I turned from Eggers to find my father and Lorraine. They were standing over the sink, talking. I couldn't help it. I was in such a mood that I said to them, "Whenever I can be of service to either of you, anytime, anyplace, and no matter what engaged, I will assist you."

My father just stared at me.

Lorraine said, "Well, good to hear. That's great news."

For spice, I added, "Believe me, I'll be there for you. Take it to the bank."

I felt like a million dollars. I downed a whole glass of soda and followed it with a fistful of chips. Vadim was standing there. I tugged the kid's yellow jacket.

An eleven-year-old with a missing parent can be a tough customer. I knew that.

Still, I said, "Whenever you need me, little guy, I'll be there. You get caught in a tough spot — I'm your man."

He looked up at me with an expression of cool incomprehension.

"Why do you say that?" he asked.

"You're a kid," I told him. "Kids need to know when people are there for them."

Trudy was right behind Vadim. I scruffed the kid's hair and stepped past him. Why hadn't I been telling people these things all along? When I neared her, I saw Keno's cracked ball on the table next to the chip bowl. Trudy was fingering it, inspecting it.

"Trudy," I said, "never has such a gift been bestowed upon me."

"It looks great on you," she said. "We were worried it wouldn't fit."

"Well, I have a gift for you. Whenever I can be of service to you, anytime, anyplace, and no matter what engaged, I will assist you."

"Oh, that's sweet, Dr. Hannah." She patted my hand.

When I realized I had just pledged her own vow back to her, I felt like an absolute idiot. The only thing I could do was strengthen the pledge even more. "Trudy, I declare, by way of gratitude, never to leave you when you need my aid, no matter how perilous your situation, no matter what personal risk I may incur."

I didn't want her to up the ante as well, and possibly refer to my pledge as "cute," so I quickly sidestepped her. I returned to Yulia, who still had a bit of a stunned look on her face. I handed her the bag, half full of corn. She held it up between us, examining the contents. "Here's the genuine article," I said. "This is a one-in-a-million find."

Did she want me to grab her again? Had her bosom forgotten me so soon?

"We shall see," she said. "I will have to get it into my lab. There it will be subject to many late nights of rigorous testing and strict standards."

I was no schoolyard kid when it came to the art of double-entendre. I knew exactly what the little lady was getting at. When she lowered the bag, I gave her, unmistakably, the eye. "Perhaps you could use a lab partner," I said. "A man with experience and ability, a man who has the endurance to take on a challenge, who will keep delivering and delivering until he unlocks the dark mystery and makes it burst with song."

Yulia leaned against the counter and shook the ice in her soda. "I have high-tech equipment for that kind of work," she said. "I would not waste man-hours in the lab that way."

I took a sip of my soda. "Are you saying you prefer to work alone?"

"Not necessarily," Yulia said. "Much of botany takes place in the field, where patience and attentiveness are required. This man you imagine—he would not begin as a partner. Starting as an assistant, he would have to listen and take direction. He would need to trust my judgment. In the hothouse is steam and convection. Bright flowers distract and delight, pollens intoxicate the senses, and botanical emanations prevent clear thinking. This man would have to know that, inside the hothouse, there can be only one boss."

Yulia looked me in the eye. I was imagining the dank work of germination. On my hands I felt the nectar of hybrid breeding—I downed my soda—I had to chew some ice!

She continued: "Scientists like us, Dr. Hannah, we wish to engage the world beyond observation and participation. We wish to make meaning of life, which takes time, discipline, and sacrifice. Certainly, when the *Beatificius gentillia* drip their once-a-decade pollen from the hothouse rafters, it is only human to strip the clothes. For the most part, however, this man you speak of would have to follow orders. He would have to find satisfaction in learning the ways of another, and when he finally wanted to become a partner, he would have learned when the time was right. By then, he would know how to ask."

Yulia looked to me for a reaction. I chewed my stupid ice and stood there stunned. Then she turned to speak to someone else. I took a step backward. I took another, until it felt as if I was watching the events before me like a movie. Yulia had told me the man I needed to become in order to be with her. And I froze.

That old sense of detachment came over me again. A few feet away, people drank sodas and ate chips. Conversations were made. Eggers put a skillet on the stovetop and sparked the burner. He poured a puddle of cooking oil in the pan and began making some sort of a speech that everyone in the room could hear but me. An invisible membrane separated myself from the others. Yulia was right in front of me, but unless I found the guts to become the man she needed, she might as well have been in godforsaken North Dakota.

Manning the stove, Eggers gestured largely, explaining his theory of why the Clovis, nomads who founded an empire of meat, might value corn. As the oil began to smoke and spit in the pan, he postulated that the Clovis would have popped their corn, rather than baking it and so on. He cited a few examples of corn popping in early petroglyphs. He listed the tribes who still popped corn in hot sand, and as he ran through the history of corn popping in the oral tradition, he began to remind me of myself at his age.

When hot oil formed golden waves along the bottom of the pan, Eggers hefted Keno's ball.

I knew Eggers could have offered a lecture. He could have explained that corn found in eighth-century Anasazi ruins had been successfully popped. So, too, had corn discovered at a Peruvian site dating to before Christ. He could have explained how kernels were designed to store moisture, and how moisture then turned to steam and caused the kernel to explode. Without moisture, the corn would've turned to dust ages ago. Eggers could even have confessed what I knew to be true, that his tenure as a Clovis had ended a few days ago, that his nontechnology pact was complete.

Instead, Eggers poured the corn into the hissing pan and

placed a lid on top. That shut people up. The room fell silent enough to hear the muted sizzle of the oil inside, and when Eggers shook the pan over the burner, everybody flinched but me.

Everyone stood there, staring at the pan, waiting for the first ping of fluffy white to strike the lid. I stood there with them, at the edge of the world they lived in. I could smell Farley's bacon bits through the oven door. I could hear Gerry and his ex–old lady's kids coming down the stairs before they even reached our floor. I could feel the radiating body heat of Yulia beside me. I was among this group of people, and yet I didn't believe something essential that all of them did: that people could simply come together and stay together. It seemed to me that what Eggers was really demonstrating was that it was easier to put your faith in the possibility that twelve-thousand-year-old corn could pop than in the hope that the person you needed also needed you.

The first ping of popcorn came as Gerry and his crew tromped into the common area, each kid holding a pillow half again his size. The kernel rang loud and clear; then the pan fell silent again. Was it a fluke? Had we imagined it?

The kids claimed the sofa and cued up *Impossible Journey* on the television as Gerry headed my way, casting an unsure glance toward my new coat.

"I got a bone to pick with you, Hanky," he said.

I stared at him, detached.

"Right now I've got a video to watch," he said. "But mark my words—you and I will have a little *mano-mano* before this evening is out. And this is not about skipping morning orientation or neglecting coffee-cleanup detail, both major demerits. This is about one of my boys getting it in his head that his mom isn't at the dude ranch. This is about someone telling him his mama's in a hospital. You have any clue who might've done that?"

Gerry went off to join the kids in watching that Pomeranian movie no one would shut up about. As the opening credits began to roll, the soundtrack swelled with some inspired French horns—sonorous, foreboding, yet somehow uplifting. This was the accompaniment we heard as Eggers' popcorn came to life, first crackling with the occasional volley, then bursting into salvos of Black Cats and repeating rifles.

Eggers turned off the heat when the old maids began to smoke. Opening the lid sent a cloud of steam to the ceiling, and we beheld a mass of grayish popcorn, the pieces smaller, fatter than I'd expected.

Farley spoke first. He studied that pan the same way he looked into the ice when we fished. "I'll give it a go, then," he said, grabbing a few kernels.

Farley chewed for a bit. There was a distracted look on his face. Eggers waited for him to say something, to give some sort of response, but after a while Farley only gave a simple affirmative nod.

Trudy tasted the popcorn next.

Eggers snarfed a little, then passed the bowl to my father, who refused.

"It always gets stuck in my teeth," he said. "I'll be flossing all night."

"Just taste it," Lorraine told him. "I will if you will."

Dad shook his head no.

Lorraine flashed her eyes toward me. "This is what your son does for a living," she told Dad. "This stuff is important to him. You want him to think you don't admire what he does?"

"I admire plenty of stuff about him," Dad said.

"Like what?" Lorraine asked.

Dad looked over at me. "Oh, all right," he said, and ate a couple of kernels.

When he tried to make Lorraine eat some, she laughed.

"No, thank you," she said. "My work is done here."

My father looked at me. "See what I put up with," he said.

When the bowl came to Vadim, he shook his head with some disgust and stood with his arms folded. Of course, he then looked around to make sure everyone noticed his aloof pose. "I see little science here," Vadim said.

I folded my arms as well. "I concur," I said. "Still, a scientist must gather data to truly analyze a situation." I grabbed a handful of popcorn and made a show of studying the kernels appraisingly, thoughtfully. I ate a few pieces. "Edible," I said to Vadim, offering him some from my hand.

He shot me a suspicious look, then glanced at the movie Gerry and the kids were watching. On the screen was an old cargo plane, flying high over snowy Canada. In the hold were a bunch of circus people and lots of animals. Pomeranians were frolicking, chasing each other around the seats. Suddenly a red light flashes, an engine flames out, and black oil begins streaking down the fuselage. It was the same old story of life. We'd seen it all a hundred times: things are going along fine, and then, for no reason at all, the unforeseen strikes and everything falls apart.

Vadim looked back to the popcorn in my hand. "No thanks," he said, and then slunk over to watch the movie, leaving me standing there alone, copping an adolescent pose for no one. Hadn't he heard my pledge? Didn't that mean anything to him? I sighed and ate the rest of my popcorn, which tasted like a long drive down a dusty road.

Yulia was looking sharply at Vadim, slouched on the sofa. She turned her eyes to me. Her look might have been apologetic, or she might just have been seeking my scientific attention when she engaged my eyes and put a kernel in her mouth. She held one hand up, authoritatively, and closed her eyes. For a long time, she just chewed. We all watched her. She was the paleobotanist on duty, after all. I loved the way her facial muscles moved, how they flexed and articulated.

"What's your opinion?" I asked her.

She opened her eyes. "What is yours?"

"I don't know," I said.

She studied me a moment, and then lifted her fingers to my face. Nails red, fingers lean, she placed one kernel in my mouth.

"Don't chew," she said. "Just wait. Wait, and we will test this Ice Age kernel."

I stood there, a spitty piece of popcorn in my mouth. I looked around the room. Farley lifted his eyebrows and went to join the party watching the movie. Yulia remained focused on me.

"Cooking has transformed the kernel's pulp," she said. "The initial starchy taste comes as the enzymes in your saliva begin converting sugars. Now feel the hull with your tongue. It should have the texture of cellulose. Note the bitter taste. That is from potassium and alkaloids, which give the outer casing its impermeability. This bitter taste suggests the seed was intact. At the heart of the corn is the germ, where the protein is stored. Here the texture is more oily, like a nut, and the flavor is slightly rich. When that flavor is strong, the seed is likely to be viable."

I opened my eyes—when had they closed? Eggers and Trudy were also watching the movie. Dad and Lorraine were nowhere to be seen.

"What is your opinion now?" Yulia asked me.

"I have much to learn about botany," I said. "And your assessment?"

"I conclude that perhaps you take direction well after all."

I studied Yulia. I wasn't so good at picking up on notes of conciliation, let alone invitation. Yet, in Yulia's eyes, in the way her coffee-dark irises fixed upon me and opened some to show me other colors—cumin and gold—there was some kind of welcome.

I buttoned the toggles of my coat.

I said, "Maybe I'll test this Ice Age coat, see how it performs in the elements. Would you join me for a promenade around the federal prison camp?"

Yulia looked to Vadim, who was sandwiched between the other kids on the couch. She walked over to him, said something, then grabbed her white jacket.

"Let us bring our minds to bear upon this coat of yours," she said.

Outside, the night was quiet and still. The cold was a force, a pressure you felt against your eyes, and along the frosted buildings the prison lights shone sodium and shrill, casting stiff, cement-colored halos off the corrugated roofs. The rising moon had its say, too—upon open expanses, in the branches of trees, its tincture recast the night in hues of indigo, iodine, and tulle.

We walked along a grated path. It was good to see Yulia's breath in the air again. I hadn't forgotten that. We passed a building where the prison choir was practicing. As we approached, they were doing the chorus of "Home on the

Range" before breaking into a sprightly "Buffalo Girls, Won't You Come Out Tonight?"

We stopped only once, so Yulia could souse her nostrils with saline spray. Her throat, when she leaned her head back, was the underside of white.

When we started walking again, Yulia pointed to the old observatory on top of the hill. She asked if it was operational. I said I didn't know, but we kept walking toward it anyway. Yulia's jacket had no pockets, so she crossed her arms as she walked. "Here," I said, and opened my coat, so the two of us huddled together under the fur. This made our steps awkward in a youthful way, and though I knew where I was and why, I ignored the criminals out smoking their evening cigarettes, I ignored that buried wire not far from our feet, and I pretended that Yulia and I were undergraduates, crossing a college campus by the river. I'd never written *The Depletionists*, I imagined. She'd never married Ivan.

The observatory was silo-shaped, with a lens window on the dome that made it resemble a lighthouse on the prairie. The door was small and metal, the kind you'd find on a ship. The hinges and handle suffered from disrepair, but inside, the heat was on and the light switch worked. In the warmth, Yulia pulled away from me, but for some reason I didn't panic. A circular flight of stairs rose to a landing, where a ladder led through a trapdoor in the floor above. Yulia climbed it first, and, watching her hips sway as she ascended, observing her legs pump above me, I became aroused. By the time she squeezed her buttocks through the trapdoor, my groin was fully involved.

The observation room was hemispherical, with plastered walls and hardwood floors. A lone notation desk sat beside the crank you used to turn the dome, and aside from a rolling chair, the room contained only a suspended telescope—longer, sleeker than you'd think.

Yulia sat in the chair and rolled to the eyepiece. She peered into it, squinting.

"What do you see?" I asked.

"I cannot tell," she said, adjusting the knobs. "The lens is fuzzy."

I knelt next to her chair, so our arms were touching, and

gave it a go. The image in the viewfinder was a haze. It looked gaseous and nebular, though we were most likely inspecting galactic birdshit.

"I don't know how to work this thing, either," I said.

Yulia rotated in her chair to face me. Right there, at eye level, her jacket hung open, and I witnessed the play of her breathing as it, ever so slightly, raised and lowered the hem of her shirt. Before me were Yulia's dark jeans, legs slightly parted. She put a finger to her mouth and studied me with curiosity and intention. She rocked forward and back in her wooden chair, deciding, it seemed to me, at least to entertain my advance.

I was close enough to smell her clothes, clean and womanly, and this was the point in the evening where a man could get premonitions of the events to come, where a guy might begin to think that, if he said the right words and conjured the right look in his eye, ardor was imminent. This is the point where the old Hank Hannah would've applied his magic touch. Moves would be made, garments would be shed, and after he'd paid a little lip service to the nipples, he'd locate the vagina, introduce himself, and attempt to speak its tongue.

But tonight, this prospect sent a wave of fear through me. Yulia would be flying back in the morning, and I didn't know when I'd see her again. Already I felt gripped by uncertainty and speculation. I'd spent my life learning to tolerate great unknowns, and yet of Yulia even the tiniest, most frivolous one seemed unbearable.

I took hold of the arms of her chair. I pulled her upright and close. "I have a question to ask," I said. "It sounds stupid, I know, but I need you to tell me where you rent your videos."

"You mean movies?" she asked.

"Exactly," I said. "Where do you rent your movies?"

A spark of amusement flashed on her face. "There's a little place in downtown Croix, a couple blocks from our house. An old man runs it. Mr. Wong."

"Do you walk there or drive?"

"If it is a school day, I stop on the way home. On weekends, we walk."

"Do you get old movies or new?"

"Myself, I prefer Westerns," she said. "For Vadim it is only space movies."

"This Mr. Wong, he runs the Chinese restaurant as well, doesn't he? I know how small towns work. Please, tell me your favorite dish, the one you always order."

She looked at me. "Why do you want to know all this?"

"I'm going to think about you," I said. "You're leaving in the morning, and when I wonder how you're doing, when you visit my imagination, I want to get it right. I need to know what your office looks like. I need to know whether you prefer linguine or fettuccine. What color is your toothbrush?"

She just looked at me.

I said, "I only buy clear toothbrushes, because they seem more sanitary. When I come home, I hang my keys on a peg below a picture of my stepmother. I wash my underwear separately. The presets on my stereo are all tuned to classic rock. Jazz drives me crazy, because I never know what notes they will play next. I don't recycle. I should, I know, but I don't."

I stopped. My breathing was fast, and I paused to search Yulia's face for signs she'd indulge me. She moved to rock back in her chair, and I let go of the arms.

"Mu shu pork," she said. "I like the angel hair, but Vadim only eats noodles with shapes, such as elbows and bow ties."

I smiled. "That was perfect," I said. "We couldn't have had a better start."

Her face was fixed somewhere between flattery and amazement.

"Start?" she asked. "You want more?"

"I want it from the beginning," I said. "I want to take it from the top."

The closing credits of *Impossible Journey* were playing when we returned, though nobody laughed at the Pomeranian outtakes. The kids had fallen asleep, and the adults were teary, especially Farley and Eggers, who had reddened, stoned eyes and stupid smiles, even as the tears ran. The popcorn bowl was empty, and the room reeked of mushrooms and cheese.

Gerry stood, the venomous expression he'd had earlier

replaced now with some brand of sadness and inspiration. Pieces of Keno's popcorn clung in the folds of his shirt. These he brushed to the floor. "You'll find yourself on cleanup duty," he told me, and began rounding up the children.

People roused themselves, stretching and making for the bathroom, mumbling their goodbyes and good nights until we were alone, Yulia and I and her son, who was curled up asleep on the couch.

Yulia stood watching Vadim sleep. She shook her head. "I used to just pick him up when he was like this," she told me. "When he was little, I would scoop him up, and only later, when we were home and I was putting him to bed, would he wake."

"What hotel are you staying at?" I asked.

"The Red Dakotan," she said. She looked deep into my eyes and smiled. "The third floor. The bedspreads are blue. On the wall is a painting of a riverboat. Through the window you can see the dam and the frozen lake behind it. What is the name of this body of water?"

"Lewis and Clark."

"Yes," she said. "The explorers." She nodded at her own recognition, then pulled my arm, to get me to lean over. "I will kiss you now, before we wake him up."

Later that night, alone in my cold room, I sat up in bed. A fever had gripped me. My ribs were quivering, and when I tried to stand, I nearly went down. On the sheets, I saw I'd left a sweat angel. When the saliva began pooling in my mouth, I knew I didn't have much time. Nearly naked, I ran down the hall to the bathroom, wondering if I'd make it. When I burst through the door, Gerry and his kids occupied all the stalls, so I was forced to vomit in the sink I'd cleaned that morning. That's how we finished out the night, the six of us. You'd think you were done retching, but then you'd hear a child vomit or smell the contents of another man's stomach, and you'd start anew. No one had even turned on the lights. We voided our stomachs by the red glow of the backup lamps, which hung silently in all public rooms, waiting for the right emergency to turn themselves on.

Chapter Nine

I will now attempt to tell a joke:

A banker must take a business trip. Before he leaves, he asks his neighbor to help watch his home and family while he's gone. Days pass, and after the banker calls home to find no answer, he rings the neighbor.

"How are things going?" the banker asks.

"Just awful," the neighbor says. "First of all, your cat died."

"Oh, God, don't say that," the banker says. "Man, that hurts. Did you have to say it like that? Couldn't you have eased the blow a little? Maybe you could have started by saying the cat wasn't feeling well. Or, better yet, you could have said the cat was playing in a tree, and the cat was having the best time of its life chasing a squirrel higher and higher through the branches, until it got stuck at the top. Maybe you called the fire department, who brought the ladder truck, and a rescue worker went to the very top, and could almost reach the cat, but at the last second the cat slipped and . . . You know what I'm saying. You could at least tell me they took him to the vet and there was a struggle."

"You're right," the neighbor said. "Gosh, I'm sorry."

"God, my wife must be a wreck," the banker said. "How is she?"

"Well," the neighbor began. "Your wife was chasing a squirrel in a tree . . ."

As you can see, I am not so much the jokester. Humor is a poor mode of discourse, and I discourage it now. My point, however, is well illustrated. I have set out to speak the tale of the end of my culture, and I must admit I am more like the banker than the neighbor. There are grim scenes ahead, and perhaps it is true that I have become carried away with the details of this story in a feeble attempt to postpone relating what I now must. Now the dark ink must flow.

It was a normal week at the prison after Yulia left. The fever that gripped us was savage, to say the least, and, concerning my gastrointestinal tract, it took no prisoners. Luckily, the illness left as quickly as it struck, though my lips remained red and swollen and a certain darkness lingered under the eyes. The only other calling card was a cough that would not go away. Misfortunes happen.

Artifact Number 9

I found it best to shift my focus to the tasks at hand, and get to work. There was a terrific amount of cleaning to do. I procured some yellow gloves and a couple squirt bottles, then made a crash cart to hold all my cleaning gear, one I could wheel anywhere. Farley had filed several motions concerning jurisdiction and precedents, and he hoped to have some "results," whatever those would be, in the coming weeks. I cleaned in the mornings, tackled my correspondence to Yulia midday, and, evenings, I donated my services as a tenor in the Club Fed Follies, as the boys called themselves. The group's signature number was the doo-wop hit "Cathy's Clown," and I was the only one who could nail the falsetto refrain.

After these first days of regaining my strength, I decided it was time to begin my rotation as a reader for the blind. The prison had a model program in which books were read twenty-four hours a day, broadcast on AM radio across the Midwest and southern Canada by way of the old university radio tower. One of the inmates came down with the flu, so I was given his slot—prime time, just after the dinner hour each evening.

In the afternoon I went to the library, looking for a candidate to read that night. Conrad and Melville came to mind, though I knew Trudy would be on my back if I didn't pick a female author. I couldn't exactly name a book I'd read by a female writer, so I surfed the stacks, curious to see what these woman novelists had to offer. At one of the reading tables, I saw Gerry, head bent, a host of books about dog sledding spread before him. The only thing I'd ever seen him read was a pornographic periodical named *Shaved Sniz*, but here were journals of the old

Yukon postal teams, racing through fields of snow so deep only the tops of trees could be seen. One of the Iditarod books looked interesting, as did *Winter of Darkness, Summer of Light*, which contained grand pictures of Russian researchers crossing Antarctica via high-speed, stripped-down dog sleds. I saw that Gerry had traced one of these pictures out of the book, except that, in front of the sled, instead of huskies and malamutes, he'd drawn a chain of little dogs, three dozen deep. In the book, the Russians' faces were both fine and hale, which made me think of Yulia, and I slipped off before Gerry noticed.

It took me a while, but in the subbasement I found Yulia's book, *Gender Dander: Reproductive Strategies of Extinct Pollens*. I read the first paragraph, and though the writing was certainly stimulating on an intellectual level, the words lacked voice and rhythm, that ineffable thing I referred to as "it." Of course, it must be noted that English was her adopted language. On the back flap I found the author photo. Here was a Yulia from many years ago, a bit fresher of face perhaps, but no more beautiful than today. In the picture, she leaned against a giant Russian computer, tape reels spinning. Her hair was trimmed in a wild bob, the frizz of which stood nearly sideways. Her neck shone sleeker with shorter hair, more articulate, and her eye shadow was perestroika-blue. I've never been much of a breast man, but one couldn't help being impressed with the way they were outlined by the casual drape of her lab coat.

I affirm here my great respect for books, research materials, and libraries, yet I had no choice but to tear that photo out and slip it in my pocket.

Rummaging further through the stacks, I made, by chance, a surprise discovery: a copy of *The Depletionists* stared down from a high shelf. A wave of panic ran through me. Only the most obscure research libraries had purchased editions of my book, which meant this copy had to have been a donation from someone who'd attended my one local book-signing, held years ago in the annex of USSD's audiovisual department. But who had pawned my book upon the prison library? Who had abandoned my words to criminals? If inside there was an inscription to my father or a label that read *Ex Libris Peabody*, I wouldn't be able to go on.

I opened the spine, which complained all the way. The loan card was blank—never been checked out. On the title page, there was an inscription. In my own handwriting, it read, "Laura—may this humble tale of the indomitable spirit of humanity inspire you to chase your own dreams, whatever size they may be." In a script both bold and flourished, I'd signed it "Yours, yours, yours—Hank 'The King of Spades' Hannah."

Still, the book was a rare find. Few were printed, and too, too few made it into the hands of the general public, exactly the people who needed it. The common people were the readers I dreamed of when I wrote the thing, people who'd talk about it at their local coffee shops and town-hall forums. I wondered, how many times did the blind of the Dakotas get to hear works read by their authors? Who else could fully interpret the nuances and inflections of my prose? Who else knew the thesis of the sequel? What other reader had twenty-seven boxes of supplementary material to the books they aired?

Book in hand, photo in pocket, I stopped by the Warden's Residence on the way back to the dorm. Discovering *The Depletionists* had inspired me to try a little flint-knapping, and I remembered all the mineral samples here. I had some time to kill until Farley cleared up the legal mess surrounding the ridiculous charges against me. By making a few spear points, at least I could pretend I was still a scientist. Kicking around in the snow for a nice piece of chert, I found a hunk about the size of a melon. Using everything I had in me, I hefted a meteorite high above my head, and if you ever want to feel the engine of the universe, send a meteor smashing down on a chert core, the slivers of which you'll later chip into razor-sharp Stone Age knives.

When I reached my dorm room, a strange visitor was waiting. He wore pleated khakis and a mint-green turtleneck, probably cashmere, over which he sported a fleece jacket. His hair was trimmed in a crisp buzz cut, and his feet were clad in flashy new tennis shoes. I had a strange feeling he was a former student. I confess I didn't always read my students' final projects, so I was nervous whenever they approached me—often they wanted to talk about lame papers from years ago. I walked past this young person, as if to grab a glass of water. When he followed me into the common area, I knew he'd been a student. He caught me at the sink and delivered this cryptic message:

"They've opened the other one," he said.

At the sound of his voice, I was sure I knew him. I looked at his watch, which was pretty sharp, one of those titanium self-winding models, and I studied the small hoop in his ear. But they didn't strike any notes of recognition. I noticed his fingernails were speckled white from mineral deficiencies. His jaw was clean-shaven, his eyeglasses were new and hip, but his skin was weathered, and no barber can trim off ringworm.

"Eggers?" I asked. "Is that you?"

Eggers did a slow turn to show himself off.

"What do you think, Dr. Hannah?" he asked. "I mean, check me out." He hopped on one foot, to show me a sneaker. "Nikes, my man. These are freakin' Nikes. I'm walking on pillows here. I'm strolling through clouds. No more broken toes. Goodbye, festering nails."

More than just the clothes had changed. His whole demeanor was different, as if he'd traded in cool and capable for cocky and posturing. I tried to remember that quiet, earnest kid who once sat in the back of my classes, asking no questions. Where was the solemn young man who, in the doorway of my office one afternoon, looked more as if he wanted to propose Jesus to me than living on Paleolithic technology for a year?

"My word," I told him, "I can't believe it's you."

"Watch this," Eggers said. He jogged in place to demonstrate his sneakers. "You can't believe the instep on these things. My arches are singing."

In the face of absurdity, practicality took hold. I said, "You aren't going to wear those in the snow, are you? You'll freeze your feet off."

"You thought those leather booties were warm?" he asked. "The doc says they're why I don't exactly feel my extremities so well. That and a minor case of rickets. Let's see him find sources of vitamin C in the winter. Compared with my dentist's to-do list, though, the rickets is small potatoes. All that orthodontia, all those years in braces—shot to hell."

"Who are *they*," I asked Eggers, "and what have they opened?"

Eggers checked his watch. "Okay," he said, "more about the dentist later. Now it's time to turn on the TV."

He grabbed the remote control and hopped over the back of the couch, landing on a stack of cushions. Sprawled so, he flipped through the channels. With a haircut and a trip to the dentist, this could be Keno, I thought. In my lectures, I tried to impart a sense of connection to the peoples of antiquity, a sense of the humanity that underlies the very notion of anthropology. But there's no substitute for direct observation. It was clear that, given a polo shirt and a pair of sunglasses, Keno could ride the Dragon at Glacier Days, throw some blackjack at the Thunderbird, then book a flight for Florida and just slip away into America.

When the local news came on, Eggers set the remote aside.

He said, "The footage is from this morning, but the evening news always replays it."

On the screen was a program entitled *Parkton 7 Action Report*. In the world update, a forest fire gripped Eastern Europe, a Russian pyramid scheme had collapsed, and, like twisters crossing open water, twin columns of civil war walked tall and storm-faced across Africa. Locally, there was a warehouse fire, a funeral-home lawsuit, and a couple of lost dogs.

"Here we go," Eggers said.

On the screen came a typical powder-puff public-relations segment for a local ground-breaking ceremony: there was footage of a big ribbon being cut, and then a tedious shot of several guys in white hard hats and business suits pretending to push shovels into the frozen earth. There were a few sound bites from a speech—the bright future, partnerships for tomorrow, and so on.

"Eggers, please," I said, "is this what you've been doing with yourself? Did your year as a Clovis impart to you nothing but a love for Nikes, Doritos, and the couch?"

"Calm down, Dr. Hannah," he told me. "Watch."

On the screen came a shot of the thunderbird logo, and I realized this was an expansion celebration for Phase II of the casino.

The *Parkton 7 Action* anchor then cut "live" to a *Parkton 7 Action* reporter. The two women looked identical to me—lots of puffy hair and bright suits. On the screen came a standard Native American purification ceremony, held in the casino's parking lot. Cedar and hemp were burned, an Honor Circle was maintained, and there was a very serious execution of the Dance of the West Winds. When one of the Elders entered the circle and appealed to the Great Spirit, I needed to know what he was saying.

"Eggers," I said, "turn it up, would you? Pass the remote."

"Shh," Eggers said, trying to figure out how to work the thing.

The volume went up, but all you could make out was the babbling of the *Parkton 7 Action* reporter's voice-over. I stared at the Elder. It was time, I knew, for the sacrifice, but instead of offering the Winds objects of previous good fortune, like proven arrows, musical instruments of particular sweetness, or heirlooms with strong medicine, the Elder hefted Keno's other ball.

Suddenly the camera panned to film the assembled crowd. Just when Keno's ball was about to be destroyed in an act of sacrifice, we were given images of the geriatric gamblers, convention-goers from the American Meat Wholesalers Association, and a fleet of sleeping tour buses, their parking lights outlining them in the cold mist. When I needed to hear the Confirmation of Elders and see which dance they chose, I was instead forced to watch off-duty meat cutters and guards from Club Fed as they fed their fat kids cotton candy and Indian fry bread. That's what drove me crazy about television—you could never see the images you wanted to see. I stood. "Eggers, I can't take this shoddy videography!"

"Please, Dr. Hannah," Eggers said, "control yourself."

Finally, the camera did one last pan of the ceremony. The dancers, of course, were moving under trance, and members of the Honor Council wore gazes that come only when one contemplates the millennia. The Elder, after appealing to the sky with force and purpose, simply smashed the ball against the pavement before moving on to conduct his other duties— sanctifying the circle's perimeter with handfuls of flax that quickly blew away, and making appeals to the wind that swept the circle's four corners. That was the end of the segment, but as the camera cut to the reporter's pitiful summary, we could see in the background something that nearly made us jump out of our seat: a cloud of grainy black dust issued forth from the smashed ball, looking like instant coffee as waves of it took to the wind, blowing in streaks down the line of spectators. The cloud smudged ties, blacked faces, left old people coughing and meat wholesalers shaking out their collars.

The reporter signed off, and Eggers killed the television.

"That black cloud," I said, "what could it have been?"

Eggers said, "If you ask me, that was meat—blood and meal weathered down to an oily dust. That was what remains of a raw mastodon flank. Take a look at the bottom of my game bag if you want a lesson on meat desiccation."

The Egyptians were the ones who came to my mind, the way they removed a human's vital organs before burial. These organs were placed in individual clay jars marked with the appropriate insignia of the god intended to watch over them— liver, Isis; heart, Anubis; lung, Amen-Ra—so the body could retrieve them in the afterlife. But I didn't tell Eggers that. I didn't outwardly muse that it was Keno's organ meat floating up the noses of meatpackers, that it was the blood of the best animal-killers on earth that had gritted their hair and gotten under their skin.

What shocked me was that it was over. A door to the past had closed, right before our eyes, and the horror I felt was magnified by the fact that we witnessed it as a rerun. Of course, what we couldn't know there, on that couch in the prison rec room, was that the opposite had really happened: that what we'd really witnessed was eternity's icy door opening wide. "Is there any way to know?" I asked Eggers. "Will we ever figure out what that cloud was?"

Eggers put his new shoes up on the ottoman. He rubbed his hair, then gave his wrist an almost imperceptible shake. This little tic was something I'd noticed during his days as a Clovis, but only now did I understand that the gesture was meant to wind the movement inside his perpetual watch. "Negative," he said.

My dear colleagues, were there any anomalies that would help you, so far in the future, to figure out the exact day on which these events took place? Was there an odd weather disturbance that might leave a long-term mark? Were the sun and moon engaged in some rare dance, or did the planets align in an unusual pattern that might allow you to trace this day from your distant vantage? Negative.

I had been feeling pretty spunky about my debut in the broadcast booth, but as evening came on and I walked toward the signal tower, I did so contemplatively, staring at my feet, the fur of my coat scampering in the wind. Of course, I couldn't have known that things had forever changed. A scientific opportunity had been lost, certainly. Some insight into the past was irretrievably gone. It didn't matter that it was in the name of greed, gambling, or quality meat. That was the way of the world. The loss I felt was more personal. It was as if I'd come close to meeting an aged relative from the Old World who then expired on the crossing. As long as Keno reclined in a grave, and someone wanted to know her story, she was alive. And now, after waiting thousands of years for me to come find her, she'd died. I'd spent my life shining a flashlight into the universe, trying to back its mystery up a few steps with the weak beam of my inquiry. Well, it was the universe's turn to put me on my heels.

The broadcasting booth looked not unlike a grad student's cubicle — cement walls, carpeted partitions, and pipes above that rattled with every toilet flush. I'd expected a big microphone and fancy instrument panel, one whose displays would flicker with my every word. There wasn't even a sound team. Instead, there was only an old white guy who sat me down in front of some obsolete language-lab equipment and clamped a pastel-blue headset on me, the kind with the loopy cord. He broke the news that my readings wouldn't be archived, that no tapes would be made for posterity. My words would simply be beamed out into the world, and they'd never come back.

When the red light flashed above me, I opened my book, folded back the front matter, and looked at the first sentence, which was a long and lofty metaphor comparing humanity to a wildfire that would consume the fuel of the earth until it burned itself out. The flashy, sophomoric bravado of hooking the reader with an opening shock made me cringe. I began with the second line instead: "So, when examining pre-Holocene Paleo-Indians, we must follow a twin-pronged strategy of examining the fire of Clovis lithic hunting technologies with the fuels of North American megafauna."

I can't say I got past the first page or two on that opening night of reading. I had many asides and interjections planned, but whenever I dove into an anecdote, it felt forced and clumsy. And all the gossip I inserted about rival anthropologists ended up sounding catty. I would read and jabber, read and jabber, and soon I couldn't tell what I had written and what I was ad-libbing.

Before me in the sound booth was a Bible, a book with way more ancient tribes than mine, not to mention convoluted family trees and unpronounceable names. Still, the book had some poetry going for it, and more than one cliffhanger. Talk about reversals of fortune. As I read *The Depletionists* into the microphone, I lifted this Bible, flipped through its illustrated pages. Another prisoner must have read this during his hour, and the thought of sending scripture out into the dark prairies was somehow soothing to me.

As I droned on about Clovis hunting technologies, I flipped through the Bible, looking at all the color plates, paintings in watery pastels of blond angels cavorting with bearded prophets. One picture near the end was nothing but ringing trumpets and flaming chariots, shining cymbals and thrones of gold. The Bible, it seemed, occupied most of its time describing the manifold kingdom of the afterlife, with all its rings, rooms, levels, and layers. The Good Book told you what songs the angels sang and how many steps led to the seat of the Holy Ghost. Over and over, the dead had it made—all was glory and light. Halos, harps, lapis, and linen were standard issue. But there was little real news of our loved ones—where did they sleep, and how did they occupy themselves? Isn't that what we, the people left behind, wanted to know? Isn't that why we point our telescopes skyward—to catch some glimpse among the firmament of the glitter-dust of the soul? Why else did people watch sunsets, if not to observe the contrails of the heavens cross the horizon line of the earth?

And what of the rest of us stuck here below? Why did the prophets make no provision for the living? And why is heaven an either/or situation? Should we just pretend that souls are swept cleanly to some golden afterlife—that, of a mother or lover, not even a crumb remains? I *know* that people leave shadows behind. I *feel* the traces of the departed—in the stillness of my room, just before sleep; in the moans of ice on the water; in the shine, dusty and spectral, flashing off a digging trowel. So—why won't the Bible give us the coordinates of where to look in the sky? Why doesn't it tell me the frequency I need to hear the voices of the departed? What are we supposed to do? Use our dang imaginations?

And why does no one ask of a lover or friend, *Tell me, if a piano falls, or your car rolls over, how will I find you?* Why doesn't anyone simply ask, *Where will you leave some of yourself when you're gone?* How come no one grabs a parent, before Dad's heart attack, before Mom's stroke, and asks, *Where will I feel your presence? Where should I stand, what object should I touch, what language should I speak when I say I still need you?*

And why did I not ask this of Yulia? Why did I waste my breath querying her over what bulbs she had planted? How could I fritter important time away, wondering what flowers would rise from her garden come spring? I needed to implore of her, *If you leave me, what will evoke you?* I should have demanded, *Tell me what movie I should watch, what tune I should sing, what book should be open on my chest when I wish to fall asleep and dream of you.* Tell me, dear colleagues of tomorrow, tell me that in the future these are questions no one's afraid to ask.

In the broadcasting booth, a red light flashed, which meant my time was up. On the table before me were a Bible and my book, both open, and I realized I hadn't been reading either of them, that, lost in thought, I'd been broadcasting silence to the blind of the Dakotas, and because only silence came back, I had no way of knowing how long it had been going on.

Over the next couple days, they began killing the pigs. I can't say any of us thought too much of it. There was some new kind of swine influenza going around the Midwest, they said, and it was true: people were starting to come down with a nasty bug. Some of the guards had called in sick, and Gerry was working round the clock, which was fine by him. Plus, in the last couple years alone, we'd seen news images of Europeans slaughtering cattle in the tens of millions, and Hong Kong had killed every chicken in its principality, by lots of a million a day.

When they first lit the swine fire, I was sitting on the dorm steps, attempting to shape a piece of chert into a spear point. The evening was clear and still, with the setting sun teetering on the horizon, its light limp, urine-tinted, and coming right at us. Through this, the smoke rose vertically, with dark billows breaking free.

Several prisoners drifted out. Hands buried in their blue jumpsuits, they studied the blaze. Someone said the National Guard had left the armory in Rapid City for parts unknown. Other people who had watched the news said the sickness started in meatpacking plants. Fifteen million hogs, someone said, were being slaughtered in Iowa alone. Bacon was being pulled from the shelves. Hospitals had opened quarantine wards. As they were talking, an old prisoner coughed, and everyone took an instinctive step away.

They went on and on—what was rumor and what was true? I didn't need any news, let alone speculation. The night was clear enough that the truth was before our eyes: at all points on the horizon, bright sparks of light were igniting in towns like Doltin and Willis, like Hollister, Glanton, and Langley. There was to be a Holocaust of hogs, and, unfortunately for the pigs of America, their Auschwitz, Dachau, Bergen-Belsen, and Birkenau already existed. The dark aria of pigdom, I knew, would soon be finished, and I figured that, within the week, they'd be importing fresh little piglets from places like Portugal and New Zealand. What I didn't know was that when the oven bricks glowed white-hot at Hormel they'd glow for good, and I'd soon be stoking the flames.

Eventually, Gerry joined us in the cold night air. He looked at the assembled prisoners as if searching for some petty infraction he could berate them for, and, finding none, he turned his attention to me. He toed through the various samples of stone I had spread on the steps.

"Don't these look just like the pretty rocks in the warden's garden?" he asked.

I didn't respond. Whatever I said would earn me push-ups, and then there was the fact that I was flint-knapping chert, a difficult stone to work, and I was shaping the initial blade line, the most critical part. Holding the chert in a flap of buckskin, I chipped my way from the tip to the base, using an antler to strike short, deep cuts.

Gerry sat beside me and picked up a piece of obsidian. "You think you know everything, don't you, Hanky?" he asked. "You think everyone else is a stupid little doofus." Copying my motions, he began fashioning the stone—cleaving off larger, convex chips with strikes to the edge, and then lining the cutting surface with teeth in a twisting, pressure-flake maneuver.

We watched the fires, which had been ignited only an hour or two before, and still smelled mostly of fuel. Though we couldn't yet feel the heat on our faces, the columns cast deep shadows, the turning air inside corniced with the black carbon of fat and blood. Gerry picked up stone-blade technology faster than anyone I'd seen. He really had the knack, especially when it came to obsidian, which even Clovis probably wouldn't work in a low-light situation. Gerry was basically playing with black glass in the dark. I offered him a piece of chert, which was white. He shrugged this off and kept working, occasionally watching my technique, occasionally casting an eye to the growing fires. Though Gerry had no idea how to make a spear point, he somehow knew that strikes to the base would broaden the biface and that sharpening the tip should be saved for last. He didn't understand the need to flute the point or to segment the tail so it could attach to a spear. Yet the cutting edge he had going looked ready to butcher a mastodon.

And, instinctively, he employed a brilliant and dangerous technique: instead of laying the blade flat in his hand as he sharpened it, he stood it on end, so one side of the spear point rested against his palm as he chipped the other side straight on. This move was so dangerous, I'd never seen anyone try it. It was like picking up a double-edged razor by the blades, rather than the plane, yet it allowed Gerry to sharpen with more control and accuracy than I'd ever imagined.

"You know obsidian makes the sharpest blade on earth," I told him. "Sharper than any metal. Its edges regularly flake down to a width of five microns. That's the thickness of an anthrax spore."

The stars were coming out, and in the fading light, we could see that the growing plumes, now dark brown and maroon, were glowing inside from superheated mists of grease that burned as they rose. These plumes swelled like anvil clouds whose heads, when they reached the stratosphere, raced off with the jet stream toward blackness. Sometimes, low booms came from within the flames, which made the inmates ooh and aah.

As the dark wore on, I could only see the prison lights glinting off the obsidian's faceted surfaces. At last, Gerry finished the blade, the final sharpening of which he must have done with his imagination. It wasn't a spear point, really; it was a chunk of rock with two dastardly sharp edges, dangerous and invisible. I was afraid he'd try to place it in my hand.

"There you go, Hanky," he said, holding the blade up. "I know you think you know everything, but you don't. You don't know about me or my old lady or her kids. I've had to do some fast talking all week to erase what you did. I invented a dude-ranch rodeo, and those kids wanted to know every damn thing about it, like what kind of bulls did they have and what color were the clowns. I had to make up a thousand stupid things to keep them from worrying about their mother. And guess what? I just talked to the docs, and they say they're going to take her tube out tomorrow. I'm the first person she's gonna see. That's going to spark her memory, I know it will. That will make her start talking again."

"Look, Gerry," I said, "I'm sorry, I wasn't trying to butt in. It's just—"

"You did butt in," he said. "And you don't sound sorry."

"Kids, they're funny. They want to hear good news, but deep down they always know the truth. In the long run—"

Gerry gestured with the blade. "They taught us crap like this in the Boy Scouts," he said. "They taught us how to make a compass from a needle. In the long run, did I ever end up needing one? Did I ever have to make a teepee in life? No, but stuff like that got me out of the house, got my mind off things. For a while, I could be a kid. That's what I needed, some time away from all my old man's troubles. Kids need people to protect them, to let 'em be kids. That's what I'm doing, Hanky. I'm protecting them."

Gerry flicked the blade out into the snow. "So stay out of it," he said, then cast one more glance at the fires before trudging up the icy steps to his dorm.

In the distance, there was a large flash. It swelled, a low boom following, enough to make the windows hum, and then a warm glow came. They'd ignited another pig fire, the initial mushroom of which created its own wind. It looked as if someone had crossed a cyclone with an oil-well fire, as if an inferno were being sucked to the sky. The sight was raw and beautiful enough to lure people from their homes, to make prisoners and administrators float down from their cramped rooms. Those first few days were like that, filled with awe and electricity. Disbelief hadn't even begun.

On that night, all the citizens of Parkton were drawn to the red glow. Families in the street marveled at the way lava flows of burning grease raced for the Missouri. Old people wanted to witness the sulfur-yellow smoke of incinerating hooves, to speculate, hands over mouths, upon each crackle and boom that sounded from within the flames. Whenever the dark curtains of smoke parted, the fire inside stunned us. Leaping, the flames were streaked blue-green from kerosene and fat, and that same light, corporal and marine, counted coup upon all our faces, prisoner and pilgrim alike.

Breakfast was otherwise normal. The eggs, I'd say, were undercooked, though I understood some people liked a little yolk sac to run through their food. The bacon I usually devoured with relish was gone; instead, there were two soggy strips of imitation bacon, pressed into shape from soy by-products. I ate quickly, thinking of all that I had to do that day—there was correspondence to be conducted, a couple dry runs were in order for my evening broadcast, and my fingernails had been shamefully neglected. After I bussed my table and stacked the tray, I headed for the cafeteria exit, where an old-timer handed me two sandwiches. He was handing everyone sandwiches.

Outside, Sheriff Dan had a small fleet of pickups waiting.

We were driven in groups of six down the hill, and no alarm sounded when we crossed the buried wire at the edge of campus. We drove toward the fire, the trees becoming more ashen, the roofs less snow-laden, yet things appeared normal enough that when we neared the river I felt a chance the driver would turn upstream, toward USSD and my home. Instead, we veered toward Hormel, whose expansive parking lots, when we entered them, were dark under black clouds, and smoking embers fell like comets from the sky, plinking off hoods and windshields. Red cars were gray. Yellow cars were gray. And there we were, cruising toward the angry roar of the pyres.

Only when our caravan stopped and we were ushered forth did we understand the true volume of the flames. Cloaked inside the general drum and rumble, there were other percussions. From the tall yellow flames came the higher-pitched *clap-clap* of air, pulsing with the flare-ups. There was also something vascular to the fire, not the beating of a heart exactly, but more of a gassy murmur, like the swooshy flow of blood. And of melodies there was no shortage: deep inside the core were gas releases whose wheezy hasp sounded almost like the colorfully sketchy reception you'd get from Japan, say, or Senegal, on a marine-band radio.

And as for the smell, I would soon come to be on intimate terms with the aroma of the pressure-cooked contents of hog stomachs. For now, the wind spared us. A tide of air, cold and cutting, raced straight for the inferno, shuttling food wrappers and white plastic bags, making antennas, fence slats, and old hunting caps bend toward the flames, like ears leaning in for savory news. The wind was enough to make pant legs clap, to rattle the cigarettes in people's mouths. I caught a page of newspaper flying by. It slapped my hand, let me read the headline "Governor Orders Calm" before it was stolen toward the flames. Suddenly, from the direction of the fires, a smoldering pig came running. Pigs normally trotted around, ears jingling, surprisingly light on their hooves. This pig careened off parked cars, bolted between bumpers. As it passed us, you could see that the fat on its back was exposed and sizzling.

Up until then, I'd been thinking about sanitation. It was obvious we'd been conscripted into some manner of lousiness, and I was wondering if we'd get rubber boots and gloves, if we'd have surgical masks and, I hoped, some kind of eye protection. But when that pig ran smoking past me, I understood that an engine of death had been started, and it looked wholly unsatisfied by everything it had been fed thus far.

A young deputy approached the guys from our truck. He was one of Sheriff Dan's boys, and I could tell he'd been itching for a juicy emergency like this all of his nineteen years. He lined us up, then handed each of us a "drag stick," which was just a wooden pole with a steel hook on the end. His tone was so serious and considered that he'd certainly copied it, from church or a movie perhaps. He asked, "Who here is a leader of men?"

He appraised us a moment, then stepped in front of me.

Was he crazy? I shook my head no.

One of the other inmates stepped forward.

"I'm a vice-president for Merrill Lynch," he announced.

The deputy gave him an approving, paternal smile. "You're just the man we're looking for," the deputy said. He handed the VP a metallic, flame-retardant suit and began leading him toward the pig fires, where conveyor belts were lifting twenty hogs a minute up to the blaze. I never saw the VP again.

I was placed on a "drag crew," which meant that several times an hour a semi trailer of pigs would back into the yard, at which point Sheriff Dan's boys would shoot all the hogs, sometimes by walking among them, often by firing through the slats of the flatbed. Shell casings bounced off the guard rails as hogs inside skittered and slipped in their own blood. It took far too many bullets, in my opinion. When the deputies were done, we lowly inmates would climb into the trailers and drag the hogs, one at a time, to a loader bucket poised at the back of the flatbed, which would hoist the hogs high and drive them to the conveyor belts. Was more grisly work ever conceived? Was a grimmer plan ever undertaken? Certainly, but none I'd ever seen firsthand. Wounded hogs writhed and shuddered under the spell of death, and even hogs who'd lost their brains pedaled their hooves in slow circles, like blind newborn puppies.

When the wind shifted, it would rain black oil that coated everything with creosote. Offal froze to your boots. When a bullet struck the casing of a hog skull, a shimmy of dust would lift, and the animal's head would buck, thickly, as if it were nodding ye-e-s or no-o-o. The pop of the police pistol and the knock of bullet meeting bone are different sounds. "Knock" is the only word I can use. Think of a single, hard rap on a hollow-core door. That knock of death, higher-pitched than you'd think, had a knotty lack of resonance, and the sound seemed to emanate from the animal's entire skeleton, as if the shock wave clacked through all the bone sockets.

Despite all this, I can't say I truly questioned the project. All those hogs were bound for awful fates anyway, I figured, and this kind of animal control had become routine: Earlier that year, ten thousand white-tails had been culled from New England to arrest the spread of deer ticks infected with Lyme disease. Then there was the mass poisoning of central-African bison to prevent the spread of rinderpest. And doves and pigeons all along the Eastern Seaboard had been thinned to stem the West Nile virus, which incubated in birds before being spread by mosquitoes. The CDC even claimed to have invented an avian virus that would kill infected birds.

Only once on this first day did I near the area where the men in silver suits toiled. We'd just dragged another truck, and when the loader driver backed away, a wounded hog went wild in the bucket. I rode along in case the pig made a break for it. Bucket raised to block the intense heat, we drove the load to the conveyor belt's hopper, and only in the moment when the bucket lowered and the hogs spilled into the hopper's paddle wheels could the blaze itself be directly seen. Still-bleeding hogs tumbled wholesale into the pyre, their bodies landing on the bloated bellies of the blackening hogs below. Ribs by the thousands glowed like sticks of light. Most hogs burned inside out, flames spewing from open mouths, and when their intestinal cavities burst, organs spat segmented and steaming, unfurling like rubber hose.

At the end of the day, our faces were black. When the last tractor-trailer rig backed out, we were ready to get back to Club Fed, where we intended to fight for the showers, eat like mules, and drop into slumberous dreams that this nightmarish day had never taken place. I didn't have time for any of this slaughtering business. I still hadn't prepared for my broadcast. Yulia was expecting my phone call. We had chorus practice to go to — opening night was less than two weeks away!

But no trucks came to pick us up. Instead, we were led into Hormel's main rendering floor, where cots lined the dormant disassembly line. Since all the hogs went straight to incineration, the room was a ghost town, dark and cold, reeking of antiseptics. My cot was between the gut carts and the giant autoclave that sterilized all the knives. On the wall above me was a display case that contained a cartoon drawing of a cross-eyed hog trying to eat a shopping cart, below which was mounted an assortment of the curiosities discovered inside porcine gullets: several spark plugs, tin cans, the remains of many shoes. There were jars of nails, and ball bearings and a surprising amount of glass. The oddities went on and on, as did the cartoons, and I felt truly awful for the poor pigs — condemned from birth, slaughtered wholesale, then subject to postmortem ridicule. Didn't anyone know that the boar was one of the few animals that the Clovis couldn't eradicate? No animal, it seems, was safe from the Clovis, not horses, sloths, llamas, camels, capybaras, pronghorns, or even pampatheres. Only two large mammals escaped the Clovis' eradication frenzy — the bison survived because of sheer numbers, and the boar exists today because it is savagely smart and beyond formidable when aroused.

Here we were asked to sleep, and sleep was what I wanted, achromatic and comatose. We were fed little tins of army rations, food that stood oily and stiff on my plastic fork, and then I lay back on my canvas cot, in a room full of men on canvas cots, only to stare wide-eyed at the metal roof. It wasn't that the ghosts of ten million hogs kept me awake. It was the opposite: I felt a total absence of life.

And who could sleep with hot bone chips raining down on the tin sheeting above? What human would slumber with smoking pig teeth bouncing off the windows, let alone the *pock-pock* of semi-automatic gunfire coming from town? When a pyre would surge, it shook the steel girders, setting aswing the butchering gear hanging above me. Pneumatic saws rocked from bright-yellow air hoses, and chains of hooks tinkled and winked as they swung in the dark. Then there was the coughing. The soot and smoke had played hell with my bronchial passageways, and I lay there wheezing, clearing my throat, pretending, like everyone else, that I didn't have "it," this illness we were attempting to stanch.

What I did was this: I closed my eyes and traveled a great distance. I emptied my mind until all was white. Moving through this white, I came upon a house made of crystal. Inside, the air was warm and steamy. Crickets played a simple melody. Here, too, were many metal instruments, but these all shared growth as their purpose. There was a copper watering can, dimpled on its surface. Brass tanks held nutrients. Hand shovels and rakes hung shiny from hooks on the wall, and a pair of silver pruning snips sat closed-mouthed on a bench. And, of course, there was green. I parted tendrils and fronds, trailers and vines, heading deeper into a room diffuse with glowing light. Condensation dripped like tonic from panes of warm glass. The smell of loam, thick and fecund, rose from the shelves of plants. In the back of the room, shrouded by ivy, was Yulia. She wore only her white sable hat, and she'd been waiting for me. When I neared, she held aloft a Chinese takeout box, one side stenciled red with a large-combed rooster, the other bearing a golden fish, recumbent in a pagoda pond.

From this, with golden chopsticks, Yulia fed me mu shu.

When I said *mmm*, she said, *I am your fortune.*

Thus my days in the Hormel plant went. I worked another shift on the drag crew, but as men got sick and were trucked in a slow stream to the infirmary downtown, I got transferred to different details. One the men called "shake-n-bake," and another was "scrape-n-rake," a crew whose particular duties I'll spare you, except to say that sixteen hours on the dumb end of a de-bloating stick and you'll be hoping for the infirmary yourself. Of course, a hospital was a surefire place to get sick, but I had "the cough" already, and I couldn't help fantasizing about clean sheets and sponge baths, about adjustable beds, fresh-cut flow-ers, and chocolate pudding. I mean, a few weeks on your ass with the flu is not the end of the world. I even imagined that Eggers, Trudy, Dad, Farley, and I would all get sick together, that we'd recline in adjacent beds with thermometers in our mouths, arguing over the motivations of characters in daytime soap operas.

Though we'd started with at least a hundred men, by the fourth night there were only a dozen of us left, all with lousy coughs and low morale. We ate C rations in our cots as men mused to one another in the dark. One man espoused a grand corporate-conspiracy theory behind "this so-called disease," and he even itemized all the companies that would profit from the hog disaster. A pair of men sank into unbridled nostalgia, trad-ing reveries about vintages of wine they had known, the clarity of water off certain Mediterranean beaches, or the succulence of various cuts of sushi. There were the hopeful, too—strong, grown men nearly paralyzed with hope. Teams of lawyers, the hopeful claimed, were at that moment filing motions of cruel and unusual punishment. As they spoke, calls were being placed from very important people. Writs of pardon were being drafted. Helicopters were en route to whisk them away!

I tried to think of something I could say to these men. I seemed able to endure our hardship better than most, and though I generally thought little of the assembled embezzlers, insider traders, and profiteers, did I not regularly preach that they were people, too? I decided against pointing out the three-legged race they were running with speculation, nostalgia, and hope. I also passed on describing for them the great paradox of life, that for someone truly to reside within you, they must be wholly unavailable, and therefore we were not alone.

Instead, I chose to hit them with the twin fallacies of hu-manity. Lying back on my cot, arms crossed over my chest, I announced to the dark cutting floor, "It is a common mistake for people to believe they live in times of great change, and it can only be vanity to think your lives, compared with the last several million years of humanity, are of great account. And take heart in the knowledge that only a fool thinks he knows when his life has reached its high and its low."

A ration can, still wet with fish oil, flew across the room, striking me on the ear.

Chapter Ten

The next morning, we were roused from our cots, and half of us were helped into the infirmary truck while the rest, the last six able-bodied men, were ushered into a white pickup. The truck was driven by a deputy whose name I can't remember, a stocky guy who wore a military green biohazard mask that covered his nose and mouth with a creepy, snoutlike filtration canister. It was the first person we'd seen wearing any special kind of protection, and we all looked at each other like, *What the hell?*

We rolled south, through the kind of open country that, on afternoon cruises in the Corvette, made me let the V-8 off its leash. Six of us jostled in back, everyone red-faced and freezing but me in my fire-blacked, blood-matted Clovis coat. Bare tree limbs waved against the sky, and farm implements stood to their ankles in snow. The farms were big on decorative windmills that pumped no water and grand doghouses that housed no dogs. I noticed the cattle were clustering around the barns and stock sheds, a sign of bad weather ahead.

I remember we were just driving along when I saw the first body.

As we headed down some road, it could have been any road, there it was, a human form, face-down in the snow. I did a double take—a man in a red hunting jacket was sprawled in the snow. I turned to the other inmates. They were all huddled together, trying to stay out of the wind. "Did you see that?" I asked. Nobody looked up, though I knew they'd seen a dead man beside the road. How could they miss it? I pounded on the rear window and yelled at the deputy to stop, but he just drove on. That person in the snow had met his end here, alone in this gully, and his family at home would never know what became of him.

You poor bastard, I thought, and on down the road we went.

Soon, we pulled onto a tractor path whose twin, rutted trails were iced over. We fishtailed across a farm demarcated only by the yellow insulators on the cattle fence, and finally the deputy stopped beside a Quonset hut that reeked of chickens. The structure was as big as an aircraft hangar, and you could hear a million chickens in there, gargling away. We got out of the truck, and the deputy handed us all short-handled hoes. The instrument was similar to an adze, with a long curved blade at one end of the handle, and a loop of leather to sling around your wrist at the other.

Artifact Number 10

I looked from the blade to the deputy. It was quiet, save for those chickens. "Surely you don't expect us to —"

The deputy slammed the tailgate shut. "You should be thanking me," he said. "Some of those other prisoners — their work hasn't been so pretty."

"You mean, less pretty than incinerating hog corpses and hacking live chickens to death?"

The deputy looked me square in the eye. "Yes," he said.

From the farmhouse, an old man appeared, his mouth wide open, as if he was ready to shout something. He was wearing overalls, and his white hair flopped in the wind. He hailed us with a raised hand, though he was wheezing too hard to speak.

The deputy turned to Bondurant, an inmate I'd dragged hogs with. He was supposed to be an honest-to-God billionaire, self-made through motivational speaking. "Go see what the hell he wants," the deputy told him.

Bondurant didn't move. Mind you, this was a guy who hooked pigs in the neck like he'd hooked pigs in the neck before. Bondurant told the deputy, "I know what the old man wants. He wants us to not kill his damn chickens. I don't want to kill them, either, not with this thing, not without a mask." He held up the hoe. "Forget chickens. Where's *our* masks?"

On the heels of that, another inmate said, "Yeah, where's our masks? Cheese and rice, I'm an accountant here. I've got to have a mask."

I didn't want to pull rank or anything, but I had a Ph.D. "Yeah," I chimed in.

From behind his mask, the deputy said, "There aren't any masks."

There was a tense moment. It felt like something bad was about to happen.

Bondurant threw his hoe on the ground. "Well forget these things," he said. "Let's just torch that hut and get out of here."

That's when the old man walked up. His mouth was wide open. He held a hand out as if to halt us, but the palm was glistening with the brightest, pinkest blood you've ever seen. He covered his mouth when a fit of coughing came, then lifted his hand, asking us to *stop, please stop,* because no matter how hard he moved his lips, the words wouldn't come out. I took a couple steps toward the old man, till I was close to him. His turning, spectral eyes took me in. Ghostly and wide, his cloudy pupils said, *Enough.* When he breathed, a mist of brilliant blood spotted my glasses. Warm and pink, it freckled my face.

The deputy grabbed my shoulder. His eyes were intense, and that dark-green mask shuddered as he spoke. "Forget the old man," he said. "Your pal's right. We burn them."

"I thought it was the pigs," I said. I was a little shaky. I couldn't stop looking at the dots on my glasses. "The pigs did this, right? But we got rid of the pigs."

"Word came from upstairs last night," the deputy said. "They say it's probably a domesticated bird. They thought it came from the pigs, but now it's likely a chicken or goose or something."

"A bird?" I asked. "It doesn't sound like anyone has any idea what's happening. There's lots of birds. It could be any bird."

The deputy shook me. "Look," he said, "forget about chickens. Forget turkeys and tweeties and every duck in Peking. This isn't about one chicken hut. This is about *us.* Either we beat this thing or we don't."

Bondurant said, "There is no infirmary, is there?"

"No infirmary?" I repeated. I was light-headed. "Of course there's an infirmary."

The deputy was quiet.

"There has to be an infirmary," I said. "Where else would the sick people go? Where else would they recover?"

Nobody said anything for a moment.

Then the deputy spoke up: "Just get the kerosene."

That's how Bondurant and I ended up walking the length of the chicken coop, pouring kerosene on the floors. I was crazy, I tell you. I was sloshing it everywhere. They stacked the fresh eggs—a hundred eggs a flat, stacked fifty flats high, a whole wall of stacks—and these I sloshed with kerosene. Every egg glistened when I was through. And those stupid birds just watched. They weren't even scared of us. Their dumb little heads nodded expectantly at everything we did, as if we were about to sit down and read them a story in which chickens got doctoral degrees and went to heaven. We soaked the whole place and then locked the door.

The deputy was the one who lit the match and tossed it through the dormer window. There was quite a flash. Sheets of metal flew off the building. A charge of smoking feathers rolled out. The deputy got the worst of it. The concussion blew his hat and mask off and knocked him down. When he stood up, he was holding his ears. "What?" he yelled at us. "What?"

That's when Bondurant raced for the woods.

Yellow snarls of smoke flashed through gaps in the metal siding, and we looked from the deputy to Bondurant, running full-bore for the tree break.

When the deputy's eyes cleared, and he came to understand what was going on, he didn't chase after Bondurant. Instead, he yelled at us: "Did you hear the rasp in his lungs? That's a ghost running through the woods. Nobody survives it. That's a dead man. I promise you, that man will be dead before the moon rises tonight."

I bent over, breathing in and out, listening. A couple of the guys looked at me, but I didn't care. I could hear it, down there in my lungs. I was sure I could.

We returned to town with the Rolling Stones blaring. In the truck bed, none of us spoke. Several patches in the road were red and green with spent shotgun shells. We maneuvered around an abandoned car, doors open, then slowed as we passed a burning farmhouse, the entire downstairs of which was a stream of orange, while above, all was roiling black. We heard the discordant jangle of a piano falling through an upstairs floor and crashing into the parlor below. No one fled these flames. No one watched them burn. No one tried to extinguish them.

We came upon a man crouched in the gully, firing a deer rifle at the telephone poles and power transformers. If he was shooting birds, I couldn't see them. Near the outskirts of town, a helicopter, rigged with crop-spraying arms, flew low overhead. The mist it laid down looked milky and sweet but tasted like mosquito repellent when it finally floated in. Crossing the Jim River, two women were struggling over the bridge. They tried to flag us down, and when we didn't stop, one threw cans of tuna at us.

The dark laughter of gunfire rose as we entered town. Short pistol claps alternated with long rolls of rifle fire. Askew on the corner of Clark and Pine was Bill Hasper's taxi, with its "In Case of Rapture" sticker in the rear window. Bill's head lay sideways against the steering wheel, as if he were listening to an important message from the cruise control. He was clearly dead. On his face was an expression that said, *Wow.*

Outside the new middle school, a team of men with pistols ran down the street, shooting at everyone's rooftops. And any of us who were planning on jumping out of the truck and making a break for it sank lower in the bed at the sight of another string of armed people running backyard to backyard, jumping people's fences.

Cars roamed aimlessly, and random houses were on the ground, smoldering. Every so often, there was a person or two down in the snow, or slumped over a vehicle. Strange how it was possible to view these neighborhoods as almost normal. One could choose to observe the seasonal decorations hanging in windows. Doors that stood open could be seen in a welcoming way. Newspapers sat on porches, people's mail flags were up, and recycling bins sat at the curb, awaiting their midweek collection. Even a human sprawled in the open could be imagined fixing a testy sprinkler or inspecting the underside of a car for that loose muffler bracket.

At Broadway, we hit the first roadblock. A deputy in a dark mask held at bay a woman in a suit who was demanding passage. She was waving a stethoscope in his face. Behind her, an old man in a sedan revved his engine as if preparing to ram the deputy's cruiser. When we neared, the deputy waved us through. With that mask, I couldn't get any real look at his face, though there was something personal in his wave to a fellow deputy, suggesting he'd been standing out there a long, lonely while.

When we reached the intersection of Douglas and University, there was a fire truck parked sideways, blocking the downtown's main entrance. With this thing in the way, no one would be able to reach the firehouse or city hall, let alone the sheriff's station. With the road blocked, you couldn't get to the park, the university president's house, the Red Dakotan, or any of the businesses, not to mention the Odd Fellows building.

The deputy honked, and for a few minutes we just sat there, listening to the shooting going on in the center of town. The gunfire was too much to believe. It was silly how many guns were going off. I grabbed hold of a kerosene can, just to steady myself. Finally, a young fireman came and backed up the truck enough for us to enter. He wore yellow fire-gear, and was finishing a hamburger. He thew the white wax paper on the ground and licked his fingers as he fired the engine up and dropped it in reverse.

The town square was the gateway to everything I'd known in Parkton. It was home to the old movie theater, the courthouse, and Glacier Days. From here I could walk to my office, my home, to Trudy's grad dorm, and just about anyplace Eggers might be sleeping at the time. Yet it felt as if we were entering the Coliseum when the deputy pulled forward. The streets glittered with spent bullet casings like Coronado's Seven Cities of Gold, and so many windows had fallen into the street, we could have been entering the fabled jewel mines of El Dorado. The truth, once the light shifted, was not so pretty.

Though plumes of smoke rose from all quarters of town, two fire trucks were also blocking the downtown's other entrances, with the pumper covering Main, and the ladder—cherry picker extended as a sniper nest—controlling Park. We drove slowly toward a makeshift command center at the corner of the square, where all the park's ducks and geese lay dead in a heap, and most of the city's municipal workers—sewer workers, ambulance drivers—were eating hamburgers, grilled by the young man, obviously conscripted from Dairy Queen, who'd brought me a burger on the day I was first arrested.

In the park, two teams of men were attempting to flush the keening ravens from the trees. The only plan was to pour boxes of cartridges into the sky. After an initial volley of lead went up, the men followed the birds as they swept low, toward the old carousel by the fountain. Beyond the shooting, chips of brick flew off the downtown buildings, circles of paint leapt off car fenders, and an entire row of windows dropped from the bank. The statue of Harold McGeachie, "The Farmers' Farmer," took a gut shot. Only one bird fell, and heads lowered in unison to reload.

We pulled up to none other than Sheriff Dan, standing near the hamburger grill, talking into a radio, gesturing with his thermos. Some other men wore their masks around their necks or on top of their heads as they ate, but Sheriff Dan had none on him. Our driver stopped, got out. He took a few steps toward the grill.

Sheriff Dan glanced at us. "Is that it?" he asked the deputy. "Is that all of 'em?"

The deputy nodded.

Sheriff Dan shook his head. "Any of them sick?"

The deputy grabbed a hamburger bun. "How the hell should I know?"

"Well, put them to work cleaning up those birds," Sheriff Dan said. He looked like he was going to go on, but then he paused, looking up to the sky. He peered into the blue above, squinting, then drew his revolver. "Get ready, boys," Sheriff Dan said. "He's coming by again."

Other people drew their pistols.

Sheriff Dan pulled an extra box of bullets from his back pocket. "Until someone can verify that chopper's one of ours, we take him down."

Suddenly, that little helicopter swooped low over the park, pearly mists curling out behind its prop wash. Bug-eyed, the chopper hot-dogged in, its black bubble windows expressionless, then banked like a dragonfly, spraying us all good, before it zoomed away over the library. Sheriff Dan cracked off six quick shots. A half-dozen men followed suit. If anybody hit the thing, I couldn't tell.

Sheriff Dan told the deputy, "Now get those convicts to work."

That spray was already settling into the trees, and those ravens had about five minutes until they would start dropping from the branches.

We got out of the truck. The ground was littered with brass shells, and the way they rolled under your feet, it was worse than walking on ice. The other guys started hauling rakes and hoes and kerosene, but I approached Sheriff Dan.

"My father's in that building," I told him. "And I need to see if he's okay."

Right then a fireman yelled, "Power's out again."

Sheriff Dan looked up to the traffic lights, which were off. "Cowards," he said to no one in particular. "That's just great. That's all we need. Deserters." Then he lifted his radio and yelled into it, ordering someone to find those dam-keepers, drag them back to the turbines, and get the power working again.

He turned to me. "Sorry, Professor, but nobody crosses quarantine lines."

"I don't even know if he's alive," I said. "I have to see him."

Sheriff Dan looked at me. "I sympathize," he said, "but we have a situation here. It takes everybody. I'll thank you to respect those quarantine lines and join the officer here in disposing of those birds."

Hadn't anybody read *The Black Chronicle* of Cardinal Ignatius, or Defoe's *Journal of the Plague Year*? Quarantine lines didn't save Rome in 1347, and the shutting up of houses only made things worse for London in 1664. Any ghost can tell you that pestilence carves its own swath.

"Sheriff," I said, "cutting people off from each other is no way to help those in need. Guaranteeing that the sick suffer alone is not a public-health policy."

"Objection noted, Professor," he said. "But we've got procedures to follow."

Sheriff Dan was already returning to his work. He cradled his radio against his shoulder so he could talk as he reloaded.

For some reason I stopped him. I grabbed his coat.

Some of his bullets spilled to the ground.

"This park used to be full of squirrels," I told him. "They're all gone now."

He squinted at me, trying to determine if he should be angry or amused. "Is that so?"

"Yes," I said. "My student Brent Eggers secretly snared and ate them—a pretty clear violation of park ordinances." In the park, the other team of men began firing into the trees as the birds, now stunned, struggled to fly. Sheriff Dan didn't flinch at the shots. "I suppose," I continued, "that you'll be issuing a warrant for his arrest."

He couldn't help cracking a smile.

"Ease your conscience, Professor," he said. "I think I can look the other way."

"That's not all," I added. "My other student Gertrude Labelle was the one who speared the hog at Glacier Days, and I further confess that I was not only a witness but a conspirator."

"You maybe haven't heard," he said. "Pigs no longer exist."

"There's more. In addition, despite my lawyer's plea of 'not guilty,' I am responsible for tampering with a human burial."

Sheriff Dan indicated a Subaru in which several frozen corpses were piled, stiff legs levitating out the back, arms locked together in ways that seemed oddly tender. "Okay," Sheriff Dan said, running low on patience, "you are hereby absolved of improper conduct at a gravesite."

"Thank you," I told him, "but my point is that, when it comes to enforcing the rules—"

He lifted a hand to stop me. "Please," he said, "I can see the case you're making, and you're right—the rules have changed. I am attempting to save this fair town. Law and order itself is under threat. Measures are called for, and, rest assured, my decisions are in accordance with Judge Connelly and of course your very own warden — God rest." Sheriff Dan waved a hand toward some men by the hamburger grill, though many of them wore those snouted masks that obscured their faces. He picked up his bullets and dropped them in the cylinder of his revolver. "When we get out of this mess," he told me, "I guarantee you may go where you like. Until then, consider yourself called upon."

From behind us, a fireman yelled, "Looter."

We turned to see a young man down the street, stumbling out of an abandoned market with plastic bags in his hands. I couldn't tell if he was falling or running or what, but by the time he'd made it to the curb, the men around me had brought their revolvers to bear, and in a hail, they'd wheeled their guns empty on him. As he fell, you could see bullets in the distance tearing the bark off trees and whitening the windows of parked cars. Law and order!

I ran to him. I found him on his back, alive, his unseeing eyes staring at the bright sun. One of his plastic bags contained video-movie rentals and a bottle of Chardonnay, unbroken, while the other spilled open with frozen dinners. Crouching, I realized I knew him. Though his name escaped me, I recognized him as the young drama professor at the university. Lord, how I felt for those sissy-foot English-department types. Their whole lives were fantasies. Their whole existence took place between the lines of obscure poems. And now look at what had happened. For some reason I was mad at him. I wanted to pound on him for getting killed over a few foreign films and a bottle of white wine.

He coughed. His mouth was red inside, and his hands were red from coughing. He looked toward me, but I can't say if he saw me.

"Don't try to talk," I said. "They shot you. Those beasts shot you."

He was looking right at me, but when I waved my hand, he didn't seem to see it.

Voice faint, he asked, "Where?"

"What does it matter?" I asked him. "They shot you. They shot you, and you're going to die right here, in the middle of this stupid street."

That red mist was coming out of his mouth, and he could barely breathe, but he tried to sit up. I pushed him back. "Lay down," I said. "You're dying."

"My play," he said. "Find my play."

"Don't talk," I said. "Save your energy."

I don't know why I said that. I'd maybe seen it in a movie. Then he started to go. I mean, you could see him go—the color drain, the muscles slacking. I'd never seen that before. But there it was. Still, he wouldn't shut up. "My play," he said. "It's on the shelf, beside my bed."

He was going to go any second, I could tell. I mean, this guy was dying.

"Shut up," I said. "Quit talking."

With like his last breath, he asked me, "Do you know any CPR?"

"No, damn it, no," I said. "I always meant to learn."

He took this big, rattling breath, and as he exhaled, he spoke:

"In Act IV," he said, "erase the cruel words that Lonnie speaks. He doesn't mean it. I know that now. Don't let him turn his back on Susan, either. Have them embrace. That's how the scene must end, with them embracing."

He said this, then—bang—he was dead! It all happened—the head roll, the eye glaze, that weight coming to his limbs—but those are just the things that catch your eye. They're nothing compared with that lifting you feel. He just lifted away.

I looked around. I can't even tell you what I was looking for. Sheriff Dan and those guys were eating hamburgers. The other inmates were raking up dead birds and burning them in neat piles, like last season's leaves. The light off the Odd Fellows building was coppery, and I knew my father was in there. It's hard to explain the buzz in me. I mean, things looked the same, but I saw them different. Suddenly it was clear that Sheriff Dan wasn't really quarantining the town. He wasn't quarantining anything. This was a last stand. The city workers were circling the wagons to keep the citizens out. People were dying all over town, and these guys had a cooler full of sodas. They were tearing the corners off ketchup packets and squirting it on their hamburgers. Suddenly it was obvious to me that they were all men. Where were the women? Where were the other women who worked in the courthouse, women like Janis? Would they have let Janis through the gates? Or would she be left to her dark fate out in our fair town?

I started going through the professor's pockets, looking for his identification. I didn't know what I'd do with it. I just needed know who he was. I'd tell his story, maybe. It would matter to someone, what became of him. To someone, that story would be everything in the world. I started rifling through his pockets, looking over my shoulder at all those guns and burgers, and then a funny thing happened. I couldn't find any of those bullet holes. I couldn't find one place where this kid had been shot. I rolled him over and felt under his jacket. I checked his feet, even, but, no, all those bullets had missed. Sheriff Dan and his boys had missed every time.

I stood. The Odd Fellows building was across the town square from me, about a block-and-a-half sprint through the dormant trees. On the horizon, dark stands of snow clouds were moving in, but for now the sun was direct and bright. Most of the snow and ice had melted, so the ground would be firm. In the cherry picker above the courthouse hung two firemen with binoculars and rifles. To get through the trees, I'd have to move sidelong past twenty or thirty pistol barrels.

To the drama professor, I said, "I'm sorry about what happened to you, but I have to go."

Then I bolted. I crossed the street in a couple big strides, tried to slalom when I hit the tree trunks, running in and out of them, branches whooshing past my head. For a while, it was easy. I leapt twin park benches, then leaned hard as I rounded the fountain. My arms were pumping, and I kept telling myself that I was strong, that all of Gerry's push-ups had helped me, that dragging hogs would serve me now. But the truth was, I felt anything but strong. My lungs felt like I'd inhaled a fistful of thumbtacks. With every breath, I kept looking for the spotty blood to start coming out of me.

I cut through the playground equipment at full speed.

When I heard a booming voice yell, "Hold your horses, Professor," I tucked and rolled under the jungle gym. The sand was half frozen, and I paused there, breathing hard. When I got up and started running again, the bullets began.

There was lots of banging going on at the edge of the park, but I didn't look. Sure, the guns were loud, but they were way over there, and the bullets were right here. I guess I'd had it in my head that the bullets would be invisible things, that, unless one hit me, I wouldn't know how close they'd all come. But you could hear every one of them. Most of them sounded like a finger snap. *Snap-snap*, they went. *Snap-snap-snap*. Some bullets came by like *sssst*, while others went *wooo*, just the way kids sounded as their roller coaster plunged at Glacier Days. When slugs went through the holly, sharp leaves flew past my face, and you'll never forget the smell of a bullet sizzling through a chinaberry bush, Christmassy and fresh.

Passing the carousel at the other end of the park, I entered the open street and poured on everything I had. All the wooden carousel horses got peppered—*thuck-thuck*, the solid hits sounded like, with a *thwack* whenever splinters flew. The last stretch was without cover, down an empty street, but here the bullets stopped. I don't know if the deputies were reloading or if they'd lost interest, but there was only the sound of my shoes as I clapped past the old Bijou Theater and the Red Dakotan, then burst through the brass doors of the Odd Fellows building.

I had to rest, I needed to collapse, but there in the lobby was an old guy on one of those red couches, and he was sprawled out as if watching the television mounted above. The TV was dead, though, and the sound of his green oxygen bottle hissing on without him made me not look too close. I just went for the stairs.

On the top floor, I found my father's door locked for the first time. I pounded on the big metal door, and when it didn't open, it took me three tries to wheel out the combo. I heaved the door wide, and there was my father, golf club lifted in self-defense, standing on the far side of the room, framed by those large coppery-tinted windows.

"My God," Dad said, "you're alive."

I couldn't breathe. I had to bend over. "Yeah," I told him, "I'm alive."

I'd never felt so alive.

Dad lowered the golf club. "You've got it, don't you?"

Hands on my knees, wheezing, I nodded. "I've got it."

"Well, what about your asthma?" he asked. "You probably just need your inhaler. You've always had problems breathing."

I looked up at him, shook my head no.

Dad just stood there, as if he couldn't move. I walked to him, and he started shaking his head. I put my arm around him, and all he could do was shake his head. Through the window was the Missouri River Valley and the main hog fire, still raging, though squat now and more intense.

"I didn't know if I'd see you again," he said. His eyes were clear and wide. "I went to the prison. No one's there. The rooms are empty. There was no one to tell me anything."

He really was upset. Deep down, I could tell, the man was really hurting. I wanted to tell him to relax, to calm down, that everything would be okay. But I couldn't say anything like that, because on the outside my father was as calm and collected as could be.

"There's nothing on TV," he said. "They just play reruns— old shows, soap operas, twenty-four hours of reruns. The radio stations are on, but they're all broadcasting the same old swing dance music. Now the power's out. And for some reason, they stopped the dam. I take it you've seen what's happening down there in the streets. I've watched it all from up here."

"I've been through town," I said. "I've seen it. But I don't know what I was looking at."

Dad said, "Think what's happening in big towns like Omaha and Des Moines. Just look at what's left of our town. You know what's next, don't you? You know what they're going to use those fires for." He grabbed the back of my neck and pulled my head to his chest. "I didn't know if I'd see you again," he told me.

I was too tired to feel anything right then. I just looked past his shoulder to that fire. Within its white core, there was much movement—objects deep inside the furnace would suddenly incandesce, then rise, hover, and turn in pulpits of heat. These were the ashen husks of hogs, burned free of weight, light as carbon, floating round and glowing like paper lanterns. My mind kept trying to imagine what human bodies would look like in that convection, but I wouldn't let it.

I said, "I have to find my students."

Dad turned to me. "Is that what you want to do?" he asked. "You don't know how much time you have. You know I'll help you, but you may not have much time. I was talking to this man on the street. Sure, he was coughing, but he looked normal, and then, all of the sudden—"

"Dad," I said, "tell me what're you going to do."

"I have to find Lorraine," he said. "I have to know."

I looked again to the river, where a mile-long ash shadow covered the banks. The open water was fouled by runners of oil that blacked the current and washed rainbows of animal waste upon the ice. Like pink buoys, bodies bobbed in the eddies. They'd bloated large enough to tear any clothes off, and they turned and rocked in a river that was slowly running away.

"Whatever we do," I told my father, "we do it together."

"There's a snowmobile in the basement. I can get the key."

"Everyone out there has a gun."

"We'll go tonight," he said.

Before our eyes, we witnessed that little helicopter swing too near the hog fire. When its mist of poison floated down to the flames, that whole section of the sky exploded, and the chopper disappeared inside a cylinder of blue flame.

While we slept, the snow clouds rolled in, a slow-moving, snow-burdened front that worked through steady accumulation, so that nine or ten inches could fall in a day without your really noticing. Dad and I shared the bed, fully dressed under a mound of blankets. My sleep had grown accustomed to the syncopation of distant gunfire, but the snow slowly hushed this. Eventually, all you could hear was the moaning of ice loosened by the falling river, and the quiet progress of snow.

The room was black when we roused ourselves. In the dark, I couldn't see my breath, but it was there. Without speaking, we gathered our gear. Through the windows, you could only see the muted glow of some fires burning unabated.

In the basement was a trailer that held the snowmobile. Once the tarp was removed, the thing looked pretty mean, with large, forward-facing air scoops and an anodized suspension. I held the flashlight as Dad connected the battery and primed the carburetors.

"Do you really know how to drive this thing?" I asked.

Dad answered, "Do you?"

"That wasn't the question," I said. "So —whose rig is this?"

Dad hit a red button and the engine fired up. "It's ours," he said.

This engine didn't purr. The exhaust was high-pitched, full of raps and pings, and oily smoke hung in the air. You could tell it was high-performance. We waited for it to warm up. The basement was pretty much a cinder-block parking garage, enough for twenty cars maybe, with a cement ramp up to Main, which meant, once we backed it off the trailer and got it out on the street, we'd somehow have to make it through one of Sheriff Dan's blockades.

I don't know if it was the sound of the engine or what, but a woman suddenly stood up. Suddenly, there she was. It made me drop the flashlight. She must have been sleeping in one of the cars. "There you are," she said to me. "I've been looking for you." When I grabbed the light and shone it on her, she was walking toward me, wearing a sweatsuit with one of those quilted robes over it. I started to back up.

"Tony," she said, "I've been waiting all this time. Where have you been?"

The woman was older, and she looked drunk or drugged or something. She wouldn't stop walking toward me. I was circling away, but she kept coming closer, her arms out to me. When she coughed, red spittle came out.

"Get that thing going," I told Dad.

I was shining the light right in her eyes, but she didn't even see. She put a palsied hand on me, and I pushed her away. I mean I shoved her good.

"Come to me, Tony," she said. "I've been right here, all this time." She came at me with her arms open and those zombie eyes. "Don't you love me?" she asked.

"Get away from me," I told her and knocked her down. Dad had the snowmobile pretty much backed off of the trailer, but I yelled at him, "Get that damn thing going."

He revved the engine and whipped the tail around, the steering skids scraping along the cement. I jumped on, and I wasn't going to look at her again. She was Tony's nightmare, not mine. I killed the flashlight, and we raced up the dark ramp by memory.

Headlight off, we rolled across the sidewalk, felt the track drop into the street. Dad turned left, but it was so dark there was no way of knowing for sure where we were headed. The square was completely black. The snow was thick and steady enough that light wouldn't travel too far anyway. I dragged my foot—there were maybe four or five fresh inches on the ground. We were idling along about the speed of a trot, and we could've run into anything, anything at all. Though you couldn't see them, people were out there. We heard a slam—a trunk or a tailgate, you couldn't tell—and there was some kind of distant chatter. Certainly they could hear the *brap-brap* of our engine.

Soon, I started to hear a certain sound out there. It was transient, so I couldn't put my finger on what it was. There was a hissing aspect to it. Also a mechanical whir. Though it was dulled in the thick air, its source was up ahead, and we didn't dare turn on our headlight. I imagined a large robot ahead in the darkness, a thing with hydraulic arms and ram presses for feet. This sound would stop and start, hiss and whine, and when it sounded like it was right ahead, Dad stopped. The sound stopped, too.

We idled a moment; then Dad clacked the snowmobile into reverse, backing up a few feet. The sound was unmistakable now. It neared some, and paused. I whispered to Dad, "Hit the light."

When he did, we saw, hovering in the air before us, two men with biofilter masks and rifles. They were suspended above the ground in the cherry picker, its long boom extended sideways across the square. I screamed and threw my flashlight, hitting one guy in the neck, which scared the crap out of them.

Dad gunned it. We tore one wide loop around the square, chasing the bouncing white cone of our headlight. Through this light wheeled bullet-ridden cars, half-looted stores; in front of the pet shop was a pile of blackened birdcages, all of which must have been thrown on a fire with live parrots, macaws, and lovebirds inside. There was a stack of men in various uniforms, piled like cordwood to be burned in the morning, and the last thing we saw before we shot the two-foot gap between the wall and a fire truck was an empty Chardonnay bottle, standing upright on the pump truck's chrome fender.

Without goggles, the wind cut at our eyes as we booked across the USSD campus and followed the river past the hog fires to the edge of town. In the orange light, frozen cattails stood smudged with black, and regarding the river ice, I'm here to tell you that blackness can illuminate—the soot-stained ice sheets were strangely glowing as they sprawled into the oily, color-flashing river. Though bodies were beached along this shore, we raced on. Though the hog loader was parked beside dump trucks whose tires sagged under heavy loads, we didn't pause to investigate what use they had now that hogs were extinct. We didn't consider what business the remaining inmates had been up to when they called it a night and made for their cold cots.

Soon, we were flying across cornfields in the general direction of the casino, and the Lollygag Motel. "Hold on," Dad said, and I wrapped my arms around him for all I was worth. He put the engine in high gear, tearing so fast through the ice and corn stubble that the headlight was worthless. He turned it off. I couldn't believe the balls he had to ride open-throttle into complete black. I imagined the casino where I thought it should be—without electricity, it was only a black cube against a charcoal sky.

Can you feel condemned and liberated at the same time? Can you sense that death awaits even as you marvel at how you're cheating it? I decided I had nothing to fear—my father was an expert at converting darkness into speed. I leaned forward and put my head sideways across my father's back and closed my eyes.

At some point, we hit something in the dark. We were bound to. If it was a rock or a post, I don't know. The snow-mobile lifted, and we were ejected. In the darkness, there was no stage direction. I flew, I tumbled, but I did not lose consciousness. I heard my father's body hit the ground hard. Somewhere near me, I could hear him moaning. He'd cracked a couple ribs, and there was a hitch in his voice. With each breath I could tell he was wincing. He called out my name, and though I could tell it hurt his ribs to shout, I didn't respond right away. It sounds weird, I know. My ankle was sore. I was jammed funny in the snow. Yet I didn't answer. Over and over, my father called my name. He'd busted out the crowns on his two front teeth, so there was a whistle to his voice, but I didn't care. I listened as he felt his way through the snow. I was silent as he cursed himself. He made a series of oaths to the heavens or the universe, and I didn't want to spoil it. I didn't want it to end.

When he found me in the dark, he grabbed me and pulled me up to him.

"I've still got you," he said. "You're still here." He shook his head, then broke into fretful, nervous laughter. "Twice in one day," he said. "I thought I'd lost you twice in one day." He sat there laughing, a forced, painful laugh that lifted his shoulders, that made him grimace from his ribs. He put a hand on my chest and with his other mitten wiped his eyes. "Oh, God," he said, clearing his nose and shaking his head. "Oh, God, twice in one day."

When I think back on this night, I remember it ending with those words.

Of course, other things fade from your memory. Rest would not come until we had finished our business. And our night would not be over until we had pulled ourselves together and made the mile-or-so walk to the Lollygag, where we would discover Lorraine, much as we'd feared we'd find her. I had wanted my father to grieve for a year now—to empathize with Janis' worsening illness and to feel her loss after she was gone. When we reached the motel and my father found Lorraine, I finally got my wish. He began weeping, uncontrollably, inconsolably. Helpless before his shuddering grief was how I spent the rest of the night. Right away, I knew I was wrong in wanting to see this grief. I knew no person should feel such pain. Yet what was started could not be stopped.

No, in my memory, the night ends with a snowmobile on its back. It concludes with the two of us finding each other alive in the purple and tan of a cornfield, clutching each other's coats for all we were worth, as if our hands and shoulders were finally admitting what our voices would not—that we were all we had.

Chapter Eleven

The next morning, my father and I collapsed from exhaustion. The sun was cresting the horizon when we made our way to the room we'd shared the night I sank my car. After kicking in the door, we even slept in the same beds. I'd never kicked open a door before. All it took was one boot, right above the knob. I'd always felt safe behind locked doors, but locks, I discovered, only locked you in.

I can't say if I slept. The room was literally frosted, and somewhere in the hotel, a dog was barking. Returning to this setting, with its musty drapes and scratchy sheets, made it feel as if I'd stepped into the past. I knew the television wouldn't work, yet I couldn't shake the feeling that if I lifted the remote control *Jeremiah Johnson* would be playing, that with the push of a button, I'd see Robert Redford dressed for the year 1870.

The cars in the parking lot meant other rooms contained other Lorraines—humans slumped in chairs, curled on floors, or reclined in tubs of water grown cold. Looking at the ceiling, I could sense the chalk line of a person in the room above. In other rooms, I imagined the dead the way thermal cameras see the world—with everything reduced to green and black: the energy of the living glowing through walls and doors, vibrant against an eternal, inanimate night. The only life in the building was that dog, trapped in a room with its owner, now only the signature of the person, a formless dark disruption, a void where a person should shine.

I rose to wash my face. I couldn't remember the last shower I'd had. It had been a week since I'd even removed my Clovis coat. If the water was hot enough, I might even forget the things I knew we'd encounter in the day ahead. When I opened the faucets, nothing came out. I felt like an idiot. Of course there was no water. In the mirror, my face was black and oily. Nervously, I inspected the interior of my mouth. There was no red. I exhaled forcefully against the mirror a few times, but there was no misting of blood. Relieved, I engaged the commode, and after I'd fully employed it, the thing, to my horror, would not flush.

When Dad woke, he wanted breakfast. We laced our boots and walked through the tiny lobby to the lounge, which, fortunately, was empty. It was a relief that no humans had chosen to spend their last moments in a place adorned with plastic bottles of Popov and dirty bean-bag ashtrays lining a Formica bar.

When we approached the short-order grill, Dad stopped.

This grill had fried a million chicken wings, hashed out countless patty melts, and had started the days of too many men with the beer-and-eggs special.

I asked him, "You sure you want to do this?"

"Not really," he said.

On the counter were chips and jerky. Beyond that were doughnuts under glass.

I said, "We can grab a bite and go."

"No," he told me. "Lorraine would want us to eat. If she were here, she'd cook us the works."

At the grill, Dad ignited the propane burners. He rounded up some bacon and partly frozen eggs. I thawed orange juice and began grating potatoes. We'd eaten such breakfasts a thousand times. Janis insisted that Saturday mornings begin with big, lazy breakfasts. So we crisped our bacon and grilled toast with a practiced familiarity. Cracking the last eggs, I wasn't thinking that such a breakfast would never again be eaten. Dad just whipped the whisk the way he always had, and I measured out the flapjack batter with my usual scientific sense of proportion.

We sat at the same counter, on the same stools, and dug in, eating quietly, sopping up everything with quarters of pancake. The cold juice stung the stumps of Dad's front teeth, and the

Artifact Number 11

way food kept gumming up there bothered him greatly. Those teeth would soon blacken, I knew. I felt bad for him, knowing they'd have to be pulled.

The potatoes were crisp, the muffins buttery. We'd garnished the plates with slices of orange, and those, too, we ate. You would think nothing could discombobulate a guy more than eating this meal, on these stools, in the house of the newly dead, where you kept having the urge to pass the salt to someone who was no longer there. Yet Dad was right. It felt as if we were all eating together.

Dad lifted a fork to his mouth. He took a big bite, then chewed some.

"Janis always put pecans in her pancakes," he said.

"That's right," I said. "She did."

I grabbed a handful of mints before we left. Dad partook of several toothpicks. Outside, the snow was untouched by man. The road wasn't cleared. The steps hadn't been salted. You couldn't even see the outline of the parking lot, let alone where the road was, and only a plow would be able to move through snow that was fifteen inches deep and falling. We stepped off the porch as from the Apollo moon lander—my first footfall sank shin-deep.

Walking away, I realized I had some unfinished business. That dog was still barking. We went down the motel looking for it, kicking door after door. When we found the thing, it turned out to be a little collie. I stuck my head inside the room. There was a big bundle on the bed. The sheets had been stripped from the other mattress, and this person was slumped under double comforters.

"Hello," I said, like an idiot. I stood there a moment, then closed the door.

Outside, the dog assumed a crablike stance, then crapped a half-moon across the parking lot. After that, it was a ball of energy, tongue lolling. You'd never seen a dog jump like that. Dad and I turned toward town, calling the little guy, hoping he might make for good company on our grim walk ahead. When I whistled, he instead dashed toward a snow-covered blue pickup, where he hopped in back and sat waiting.

The road we walked looked like this: There was a plain of

white as far as the falling snow would let you see, and the blacktop was indicated only by two cattle fences whose bottom wires had been buried by the growing drifts. There were no trucks on the road, no cars in the ditch, and with that slow, steady snowfall, it looked as if we'd never see another person.

We stopped at the first place we came across. It was one of those creepy old farmhouses, the kind whose rooms had pitched ceilings, whose tornado cellars made you think of abandoned children, and whose backyards promised forgotten, unmarked wells. In the driveway, a pair of tricycle handlebars stuck out of the snow, red tassels and all. The roof gutters were choked with dead birds.

We knocked, then kicked the door in. Two Labradors raced out. They ran through the snow, digging out black wings.

In the kitchen, a transistor radio played static.

"Hello," I called.

"Anybody home?" Dad called.

Dad examined several firearms on the table, but none of them had bullets. Then he went for the fireplace. There, displayed above the mantel, were two pair of snowshoes from a previous century. I didn't think it was possible, but we sat on the leather sofa to buckle them. While I was adjusting the straps, I kept looking at the ceiling, as if at any moment the homeowners would come down. When we had the shoes on, Dad and I clacked them on the floor, then did a slow loop around the downstairs. The snowshoes didn't feel too bad. As I passed the kitchen, I turned that awful radio off, and only then did Dad and I hear the sound coming from the bedroom. We stopped, looked at each other. The sound was rhythmic and creaking.

I slowly walked to the bedroom in my birch-hoop snowshoes. When I opened the door, I saw a husband and wife curled under the blankets of an old sleigh bed. Cough-drop wrappers were everywhere. Beside the bed was a mechanical swing, a battery-powered thing that rocked back and forth on plastic arms. In it was an infant, its head flopping forward and back, forward and back.

"What is it?" Dad whispered from the hall.

"Nothing," I told him, then closed the door. I didn't have the guts to go near the thing and turn it off, and for that, a dead child would forever swing on in my mind.

When we left, the dogs were playing tug-of-war with a frozen raven.

We walked along the tree break to the next farmhouse. A dog was inside, trying to scratch its way through the door, but I didn't want anything to do with it. There was no way I was going in. I mean, through the front window you could see a woman was right there, on the couch, dead. She had a box of tissues and a remote control, and she was frozen solid. The blood on her face had blackened, and the frozen blood seemed to have glued her hand to her mouth at an unnatural angle.

I waited while Dad went inside. He didn't call hello. I didn't hear him opening and closing any doors. There was only the clacking of his snowshoes, the *tikka-tikka* of dog claws following him, and finally the emptying of a bag of dog food on the hardwood floors. Still, it took Dad a while to return.

When he came out, he was holding his ribs, so I knew something had made him breathe heavy. "What?" I asked him. "What'd you see in there?"

He left the door open for the dog, then started walking sideways down the porch steps. I followed him. "You must have seen something," I said. "What was it?"

"Nothing," Dad said. "Forget it."

That's how it went on our way through town. We were compelled to check the houses, and every time we did, the hope of survivors was tempered by the reality of what we found. More than once, we heard a shutter swing shut or saw a piece of siding flap in the wind and rushed to someone's aid, only to find the person frozen stiff. The only public service we seemed to provide was freeing the trapped dogs of Parkton. That no one had made provisions for the dogs confirmed my suspicion that no one understood the severity of what was happening.

In Samuel Pepys' journal entries of England's great plague, there are innumerable accounts of the horrific variety of human death. The London plague took months to spread, and in the extended panic, Pepys witnessed victims hallucinating, begging for exorcisms, and throwing their children from rooftops. One man ran through Crambly Market with a hot poker, stabbing passersby in the neck. Pepys described persons performing primitive surgeries on themselves, and documented in detail the fanatics of Roland Hall as, one by one, they took turns burning themselves alive. The doomed souls of South Dakota, however, simply curled up in bed, drank lots of fluids, and drifted off.

As we moved from house to house, there were ghastly sights, but the ones I remember were not the bloody or the visceral. In one house, I saw a fish tank that was frozen solid. The expanding ice had busted the glass to the floor, so there was only a rectangle of water, sitting on a table. The goldfish had died right away—they were all locked in the top inch of ice, belly up. But deep inside you could see the blue-red of neon tetras that had circled and circled in the shrinking pocket of water until they were all bunched in the center, where they'd frozen solid. Also in this cloudy, distorted ice were various tubes and some colored gravel, a string of plastic plants, and a tiny sea diver. The beautiful impossibility of it stunned me. The life-and-death of it spoke to me. The way existence was reduced and compacted, the way the tetras still schooled at the end, frozen mid-turn, bright as a Christmas ornament, seemed a model of the universe.

We saw people who'd died holding telephones, eating diet foods, looking at pornography. There was an old woman who cradled a red bong. But the bodies that spooked me most, that reside still in my memory, were the ones you couldn't see. The closer we got to town, the more people seemed to have died outdoors. In driveways and on sidewalks, we came across contours in the snow that suggested humans were below. These white mounds may or may not have been the shadows of buried people. Scariest was the way your denial was allowed full discretion. I'd see a small snow-drifted form, and I'd tell myself, That's not a child down there, the snow's just buried a bicycle or perhaps a guitar case. Another such hump might simply be a pool raft, I'd think, or possibly a kayak. My mind could make up anything in its efforts to stop the inevitable: picturing all the people I knew who might be below—Jill Green, who ran the library reference desk; or Mike Magnason, proprietor of Video Utopia, where I was a preferred member.

To tell the truth, we didn't need to go house to house to convince ourselves that everyone had been taken. Walking deserted streets, moving through empty neighborhoods, you quickly get used to seeing corpses. They're so clearly soulless, so utterly void of humanity, that they're just empty vessels. Soon, of bodies, all that mattered was the scale—a family here, a dozen there, a bushel, a mountain, a million. What you can't get over, amid all the human bodies, is the total absence of humanity, the sheer lack of its force and energy.

Like power lines without voltage running through them, the world looked the same but was missing its crackle and buzz. Gone were voices. Missing were music, cooking, and the shouts of children. The ice-skating pond, usually white with the calligraphy of skate blades, was instead a mirror that mirrored only empty trees. From the Karate House came no shouts of *Hai, hai,* as teenagers snapped their white *gi*s with each punch. The parking lot was full when we passed the Lutheran church, yet it felt hollow, in total want of prayer, and the bay windows of the senior center, normally filled with old people, were void of the crochet club and bingo hour. Never again would I see shrunken, ancient couples executing a brisk foxtrot, samba, or Virginia reel. The energy of humanity was simply gone, and that lack was everywhere: in the silence of a phone lifted from its cradle, in the stunned blankness of an interstate, in the stillness of television antennas, and the way you could somehow feel that the hydroelectric dam had gone off-line, three miles away.

We walked down Poplar Street, past River Drive and Meriwether. Where were we going? What excursion didn't have a human interaction as its destination? Nearing the USSD campus, we passed the Everland Cemetery. How ridiculous the headstones looked, with their ordered spacing and uniform rows, as if the dying had stumbled toward their appointed slots and dropped into Grave L-19 or RR-124. What a laugh—as if the tablets of death could be sorted as simply as abacus beads. We saw an elk walking through the rows. It was a grand thing, with a tawny winter coat that tended toward coffee at the throat, and a muzzle that was nearly black. These were reclusive, wary beasts, so it surprised me to see one walking calmly through town. Only once in a great while did I lay eyes on an elk—occasionally, a herd would try to swim the Missouri, and one of them would invariably stop to rest on one of the sandy islands. From my office window, I could see when one got stranded. I'd watch it pace and fret out on the shoals, wading chest-deep until it felt the current and halted. When it lifted its head to call the others, the ones who'd swum on, I felt I could hear that mournful bray. This elk paused at a mausoleum, where it sniffed some plastic flowers. It rutted its antlers in the slats of a gazebo, then moved on.

My father and I behaved less nobly. We were more like the dogs being set free: stunned, curious, wandering stupidly from house to house, inspecting everything, recoiling at every false alarm. On campus, the backup generators were going, which meant that the emergency lights would shine another day or two. It also meant the central heat exchangers were functioning, and as we walked past the administration building, you could already smell the decay of warm bodies in the dorm rooms. All those students gone, every one of them gone, and I hadn't even learned their names.

I made for the river, the square of the Missouri I thought of as mine. The snowfall was steady. When we crossed the white of Central Green, there was only a dome of visibility that centered on us—objects entered, stayed a while, then vanished. Snowy park benches came into view, inscribed in memoriam with the names of dead donors; it seemed unthinkably creepy to sit in them. Already I felt the cold of Janis' monument out there in the white. Suddenly the idea of placing a monument to the loss of a single life sickened me. How could such an elaborate marker commemorate the passing of just one person, whereas the population of South Dakota had only this glut of snow as testament that they'd ever lived?

Dogs raced past us, feathers glued to their faces.

I steered Dad wide of where I thought Janis' plaque must be.

Always, I'd striven to lift the veil of the dead, but that spirit now left me. Now I was happy to see only a surface of white, to snowshoe onward in ignorance of the assembled citizens and songbirds of Parkton below my feet. Teams of dogs rummaged through the snow. When we didn't see them, we heard them, and when we didn't hear them, we came across the hollows they'd dug to ferret out some manner of dead thing.

When we reached the riverbank, the Missouri was gone.

"My God," Dad said.

"I never," I said, shaking my head.

The river had simply run away, leaving a deep, empty channel at the center of which was a brook no bigger than Keno's. For some reason, the snow in the riverbed didn't stick, and here, between pools of trapped water, was Sheriff Dan's infirmary. Here were hundreds of corpses, thousands of corpses. The bodies that had begun to decay before they'd been cast into the river marked the old waterline. Bloated and pink, they'd swelled large enough that their limbs didn't touch the ground. They looked like pieces of inflatable pool furniture, beached along a rocky shoal. And the bodies that had been dumped frozen and wholesale into the water had sunk to the river's icy floor and now lay exposed in the stiffening mud. Ropy and drawn, these poor souls appeared almost natal, as if constructed from discarded twists of umbilical cord. Darkened clothes and uniforms clung to dislocated limbs—arms stood tall and wild behind people's backs, boots appeared to be laced on backward, and necks, it seemed, could do anything.

The utter stillness of this field of bodies was punctuated only by great reserves of gamefish clustered into small pools. The humps of large carp mooned from the water, the cartilage of their lips gobbling the surface for air. As other fish rolled and paddled, whiskers and spines would flash, and all the while small white perch leapt from the wells, only to land in the mud or, worse, in the cold crotches of humans. Desperately, the little fish would struggle to flop back in again.

How can I accurately describe the amount of death? How can I grab you by the shoulders and shake this death into you? In his best-seller *Journal of the Plague Year*, Defoe included the daily death tallies of London's great plague. He gave the locations of all the mass graves, and detailed how many thousands were dumped in each. Still, later generations grew to disbelieve his descriptions, preferring to think them fiction. Not until the Nazi bunker bombs fell in World War II was the veracity of Defoe's accounts confirmed. The explosions opened graves the size of auditoriums, making it snow calcium and rain a porridge of rancid bonemeal. A single buzz bomb sent a cloud of remains up from Brixton Square that rained thirty thousand skulls down upon the good people of London.

The sight of these people before me in the river was so disturbing that I didn't have full control of my thoughts. Someone's glasses were in the mud, and I thought, *Those are my glasses.* I thought this even though my glasses were right there on my face! Some corpse must have gone into the water clutching a cane, because the horn of a walking stick poked from the mud. I thought, *I know that cane, that's Peabody's cane;* then some of the bodies started to resemble Peabody. If you looked close enough, some of the bodies seemed to move slightly, maybe in the corner of your eye, like they were barely breathing and needed you to blow more life into them. When you looked straight on, they were dead, but sideways, maybe, just maybe, they were alive! But I didn't care. I wasn't wading into that mud! Then I heard them breathing—very light, then stronger, then it turned into a *shh* sound.

Shh, it said. *Shh.*

In my mind, this sound mutated into the hushing skids of Gerry's Pomeranian team, the one I'd heard that night at the prison, mushed on by the hand of a ghost driver. That's how strange I felt. That's how your mind can play tricks on you when the Ultimate is unrolled before you like a rug.

I clapped my hands on my head. How could the river have left us?

Dad kept asking practical questions, just talking to the air. "Why would they close the spillways?" he asked. "If they wanted to take the dam off-line, why wouldn't they just open the gates and let the turbines spin free?"

Who cared? The river was gone. Soon, I knew, it would be gone in places like Kansas City and Baton Rouge. I pictured those places without their rivers. I pictured them strewn with bodies, and only then did it come to me that those cities were gone, too. Only then did I nod my head at the knowledge that Florida was perhaps gone, as was Paris. Only there, beside an empty river, did I realize that, wherever in the world my mother was, she was dead.

That shushing, sledding sound came again, like a vibration in my ears.

I put a hand on my father's shoulder.

"I know," he said. "I know."

I bent over and lost my stomach in the snow. It made my face shudder. Saliva ran from my mouth. I ate a handful of snow. My nose was dripping, and my eyes were wet and out of focus. When I closed them, I saw nothing. Now, all these years later, I understand that what made my shoulders heave, what made my hands grip the fabric of my pants, was a welling sense of relief: I finally knew what had become of my mother. So the pain I felt wasn't grief occupying me, but the beginning of its eviction. Ease—peace, even—had begun.

Dad put a hand on me. "Breathe," he said. "Remember— steady and even."

I exhaled as deeply as I could, then drew in sharp air.

When I stood, Dad dusted me off. "That's better," he said. He kicked some snow over the vomit, then turned me from the river. The two of us stood there, staring at the white lawns of a university. "Big breath," Dad said.

I inhaled till it rattled.

"Much better," Dad said.

"I'm okay," I told him. "I can do this." Backs to the river, we began walking, our snowshoes following the trail they'd broken before.

I'm not one to believe in signs. If there is a grand blueprint to existence, our lives are no more than the little round shrubs with which the Architect adorns the corners of the plan. Still, I won't try to lessen what happened next.

We heard motion and panting. There was the hiss of skids, and then, as if out of an old movie, several dogsleds raced through the haze at the edge of our vision. They were merely dark outlines against the snow, but there was no mistaking the swatting sounds of paws plunging through crusty snow. Your mind can't make up the cracks of a mushing whip upon the backs of dogs.

"Ahoy," I shouted.

The lead sled stopped, and the others followed. The figures, for they were only figures through a drifting veil, set their snowbrakes and, turning our way, lifted dark goggles to observe us.

I don't know why I'd shouted "Ahoy," but, stupid as it sounded, I shouted it again.

Dad and I began to trot toward the drivers and their steaming dogs.

In the distance, an arm waved, large and sweeping.

We began to run, a high-kneed gallop to keep our snowshoes from snagging in the powder. The main sled was harnessed with six dogs, and had piled on its litter coils of rope and all the nets from the campus volleyball courts. The little sleds were rigged with two dogs each, and they were packed with dog toys, things like Frisbees, squeaky balls, and tugs.

"Gerry," I shouted.

"Hanky," Gerry called back.

Running toward me, Gerry shouted, "Dogpile." When he'd closed the distance he sprang high, and once again tackled me. I went back into the snow, then one, two, three, four children jumped on me. The point of the exercise seemed to be to smother people experiencing acute respiratory distress, especially by way of rubbing snow up your nose and then having children set their smelly little butts on your face. When this greeting was over, they helped me stand.

"How?" I asked Gerry. "How is it possible?"

Gerry was so happy that tears streamed down his face. "See?" he told the kids. "See, I told you there were people still alive. I told you the radio wasn't lying." He rubbed all the kids on their heads. "I told you your mom's okay," he said to them. "I told you she's just fine."

"Where are you guys going?" I asked Gerry. "Where are you headed to?"

Gerry and the kids had racquetball racquets tied to their feet. We were in a circle, all our snowshoes toe to toe. "I knew it," Gerry said. "I knew it. Tell them, Hanky. Tell them how things are going to be okay."

I looked at the kids, all bundled up in their winter gear. Which were which, which were boys or girls, I couldn't tell. They just stared at me.

"Things are going to be okay," I said, but it was so feeble, so lacking in feeling, that I attempted a cheery "Don't worry" to bolster things.

"You hear that?" Gerry asked them. "That's a professor talking. He's a very smart man. If he says things are going to be okay, things are going to be okay."

The littlest kid started crying.

"What's going on, Gerry?" I asked, trying to ignore the children. "What are you doing out here? What's with the nets and ropes?"

Gerry looked at me. "Tell them how their mom's going to be okay."

Everything got quiet.

"Gerry," I said, "it's time to stop pretending. You've been by the hospital, haven't you?"

But Gerry didn't flinch. His sharp blue eyes didn't even flinch.

"Go on," he said. "Tell them how people at the dude ranch are okay. You must have heard that people at the dude ranch are just fine. I know you did. Tell them how their mom's just fine."

"Come, now, Gerry," I said.

"Don't keep it a secret," Gerry said. "Go ahead and tell them."

I looked to Dad. He shook his head, *No, don't do it.* Then Gerry locked in my gaze. For a long moment, we looked at each other. When his blue eyes flashed to the river, I knew what he meant. He meant, *Look at all the death around us; help me keep this death from penetrating these children.*

And then there were the kids. They cocked their heads, waiting for my answer.

"She's okay," I told them. "You mom's gonna be A-okay."

"See?" Gerry said. "You heard it from the professor. You heard it for yourself." He passed out some candy bars to the kids, then started talking about his dogs. "You're wondering about the Pomeranians," he told me. "Well, the Pomeranians didn't work out. Given enough time, maybe. In a couple more months, we might've really made it work. There's no more capable canine, you know. No dog is more cunning. But on short notice, we simply needed stronger dogs." Here Gerry nodded at the Akitas, shepherds, and mastiffs harnessed in the traces. "It was not for lack of vision. We had the breeding camp. The training system was in place. Show me finer studs."

He went on and on about the dogs, but I didn't listen. I'm sure it did not escape your notice, anthropologists of the future, how I committed one of the gravest crimes of humanity: the giving of false hope to children. No doubt in your time the penalty for such a crime is stiff, and I willingly accept any punishment posterity deems fit to levy upon my memory. Let me say only this—the circumstances were extraordinary, and forget not that you are all descended from me, that I myself am the source of your laws.

"You mentioned the radio," my dad said. "What did you mean with the radio?"

My poor father. With his teeth, it sounded like he was saying "wadio."

Gerry pulled out a transistor radio. He slowly tuned the AM dial along its spectrum of static until it came upon a voice: "I repeat—this is the city of Parkton, United States," the voice said. "If you receive this signal, we are monitoring shortwave, citizen's-band, and military frequencies. If you receive this signal and you are capable, transpond this message toward Okinawa."

The voice was Trudy's.

I turned toward Club Fed, though I couldn't see a hundred yards in that snow. "It's the prison radio," I said. "The backup generators must be running."

"I don't understand," my father said. "How?"

A thought came to me. I turned north. I walked a couple steps. All was white, but I suddenly knew that out there somewhere, Yulia was alive.

"Gerry," I said, "I need you to get us to that prison."

He nodded. "You bet, Hanky," he said. "Just help us catch a couple more dogs. We were chasing two malamutes when we found you."

When we reached the prison, I was covered in dander and had red claw marks up and down my forearms. The dogs I drove had lived lives of willfulness and indolence, and they did not take to the harness well. Behind a full dog team, I drove a little sled with the child named Pat on my shoulders. I kept getting kicked in the face with racquetball racquets, but he was a good kid—trusting, quiet, and he leaned with me in the turns. The dogs did not want to run the last uphill leg across the prison grounds, and I had to lay it on with a willow switch to get them to dig.

"I'm sorry, doggies," I yelled at them, "but I need everything you've got."

I put some sauce on the switch—*that* set their paws on fire.

When we neared the base of the broadcast tower, I set the snowbrake while the dogs were still running, a move that knocked them off their feet. Holding Pat's ankles, I ran forward with the inertia. Pat wrapped his arms around my neck as we burst through the door, and I nearly killed us both trying to run up stairs in snowshoes. When we reached the broadcasting booth, it was empty. In the blue plastic control panel, a cassette tape was playing in an endless loop. I looked around for any sign of Trudy—a lipstick, a gun, a hot-rod magazine—but found nothing. Along the edge of the console, however, was a sprinkling of crumbs. I pressed my finger into them and in-spected the ones that stuck—definitely some kind of chip had been eaten here. I licked my finger, but couldn't guess at the variety.

I lowered Pat off my shoulders and hooked him under an arm.

"Are those Dorito crumbs?" I asked.

He, too, licked his finger and tasted. Eyes closed, he scrunched his face. He seemed to sense the gravity of the situa-tion, but still he had to shrug.

"Can't say," he said.

Outside, Gerry and my father were pulling up.

When Gerry had set his snowbrake and dismounted, he said, "Easy on the dogs, Hanky. You're not dealing with highly trained animals here. These are house pets."

Dad set the snowbrake on his sled. When he lifted his goggles, he said, "What, were you trying to lose us?"

Gerry grabbed a box of treats from his litter. "Haven't you ever heard of the reward system, Hanky? When dogs do good, dogs get treats." He started passing out dog biscuits, paying no attention when a Chow Chow nearly took his finger off.

Oh, it was easy for Dad and Gerry to act like charter members of the Dogs Are People Too society. These particular curs had yet to taste the frozen flesh of a human corpse. They would, though. The hundred-thousand-year friendship between man and dog was but a brief interlude, a cheap affair in the history of both species, and in a week or two, these dogs would join thirty million of their canine brethren in sharpening the teeth of forgotten instincts on the hocks of human loss.

Looking down, I realized I was still holding a child under my arm. When I set him down, he put his arms out for me to pick him up again. Instead, I began pacing in the snow. If my theory was correct, Yulia was alive and well in Croix, North Dakota. To drive to her in a car, I'd need to travel west to Sioux Falls, catch Interstate 87, then head north to Fargo on roads that would take me five hundred miles out of my way. The snow was two feet deep already, and another foot might drop before this weather front moved on. It'd take two weeks for the roads to melt clear, and I wasn't waiting two weeks. The only other possibility was driving the whole way in a snowplow, at five miles per hour. Imagine the stalled vehicles and various obstacles blocking those thousand miles. And snowmobiles were out of the question—even if I did figure out how to drive one, what about breakdowns and fuel scarcity, and a dozen other ways to get stranded in rural North Dakota? Only two things were clear: First, the shortest route to Yulia was to follow the Missouri straight across the Dakotas. Second, of dogs there was no shortage.

I turned to Gerry. "I have a hunch," I said. "If it's correct, I'm going to need a sled, a big one, the best sled you've ever made."

Gerry asked, "A hunch about what?"

"Do you still have your workshop set up?"

"Well, sure, Hanky."

"Can you make the sled or not?"

"Sure, I suppose," Gerry said. "What's this about?"

"You've got three hours," I told him.

I turned to Dad.

"I'm coming with you," he said.

"We're off, then," I told him. "Gerry, you've got three hours."

Next to the broadcast building was the clinic. Dad and I kicked in the door—it took both our boots. Inside, all was quiet and low-lit. The floors were polished, and the brushed stainless-steel cabinets shone red under a single emergency light. Clean butcher paper covered the beds, and several examination instruments waited patiently in a cylinder of blue antiseptic fluid. Ten thousand people had died within miles of this room, and not one bandage had been dispensed.

The next building was the armory. There was no getting in that door, but Dad boosted me up to a small reinforced window. Inside was a sort of prison cell. Behind its grated doors were the prison's guns, hanging orderly along hooks and racks. Spread across the checkered floor, however, was a chaos of empty ammo cans. It was the same story everywhere: the city was choked with firearms, but there wasn't a bullet left on earth.

The cafeteria reeked of rotting enchiladas, and the indoor swimming pool had bloomed a fabulous green. The post office got to me more than anything—bin after bin of letters stood waiting for hands that would never receive them. Eggers and Trudy were nowhere to be seen. On a longshot, Dad and I went to check the vending machines that had replaced the Unknown Indian.

In the basement, everything looked normal except for a

ceiling-mounted strobe light that overwhelmed the cheery machines, with their beeping sounds and flashing LED panels. The machines seemed so sad and pointless. Here they were, standing at the ready to minister to the desires of humans, but they had no idea. They didn't have a clue. Dad pulled out some change. Newly minted quarters shone foolishly in his palm. He inserted them carefully into the slot. Was this the last machine we'd ever use? The last money? Two granola bars dropped, and we began munching them as I studied the inventory. In all of the machines, a certain product was missing.

"Find a clue?" Dad asked. He had to bite and chew with his back teeth.

"They've been here," I said. "They're in this prison. But where to look?"

Dad said, "We're looking for a young man, right?"

I nodded.

"You said his parents are out of the picture. So he's pretty much been on his own in the world, as you and I often were in our respective upbringings. We know such a person cares little for material things. He's not interested in money or conveniences. He's learned to be self-sufficient, and perhaps even feels at home in times of trouble. He's not seeking security, as most people think of it."

"Go on," I said.

"Well, what does this person want?"

"He wants connection," I said. "To be close to other people."

"Enter this young woman. Enter Trudy. These two—are they, you know, are they a thing?"

"It's possible," I said. "Probable."

"I know *probable*," Dad said.

"You say that like we should be checking all the cots and mattresses," I told him. "You're forgetting about Trudy. Her four years of high school were spent in four different countries. Her father is a Louisiana Creole. Her mother's half Japanese and half Korean—figure that one out. We may never understand where Trudy's coming from, but the term papers she writes are about connecting to a history that predates modern ideas of culture, that comes long before the labels people place on her now. So—she's not just after a roll in the hay, Dad."

"Don't get defensive," Dad said. "I'm just saying if those two are alive they're together, and they're here. This place makes too much sense. It used to be a college. It's in the center of town. The radio tower's here. It's the only place that isn't littered with bodies."

We finished the granola bars in silence. Our snowshoes melted puddles on the floor. I stared into the vending machines. Little galleries of delights, were they any different from the emporia of Rome or the bazaars of Baghdad? One of the machines sold only sundries, like razors and sewing kits. Here, for a mere dollar, you could buy a packet of fancy cologne or a little box of dog treats—artificially flavored to taste like meat, shaped to simulate bones—for the lapdog you brought along to your white-collar prison.

"One thing we know for sure," Dad said, "they think they're the last people on earth. What do people do for fun in this prison?"

"Watch movies," I told him.

The theater, when we entered it, looked like something out of Hitchcock. A tight, vertebral staircase spiraled up to the projectionist's booth, and in the lobby was a little sitting area furnished with the props of old Parkton College plays. A Victorian settee and a Greek daybed framed a Louis XIV coffee table. These were separated from the snack bar by a Japanese screen, as if Tokugawa, Marie-Antoinette, and Pletheus held salons here to discuss Orson Welles.

Crossing the lobby, we heard Cary Grant's staccato voice, followed by Ingrid Bergman, breathless and deceptive. The film was Hitchcock's *Notorious*.

We parted the curtain, and sitting alone in a field of seats were Trudy and Eggers, feet up on the next row. Above them on the screen was Hitchcock's South America, a place filled with exiles, inhospitable terrain, and long-hidden love.

Even in the dark, you could tell Eggers was wearing the kind of parka they'd sport down the runways of Paris. It was cut from a flashy silver material, and the thing was covered with zippers that were bordered by strips of highly reflective yellow.

Dad whispered, "What does she see in him?"

"What is his secret?" I whispered back.

We walked down the aisle and stood on the runner at the end of their row. They were only six seats from us, but they were totally wrapped up in the movie. This is the point where I was supposed to say some cool John Wayne line or something, but I couldn't think of anything. I just watched the two of them. It was the scene where Cary Grant realizes that Ingrid Bergman has been poisoned, and when Grant races up the staircase to her, Eggers and Trudy held their breath. Their fingers were interlaced, and, looking at their profiles—Trudy's strong cheekbones and almond eyes, Eggers' sharp jaw and sweeping brow—I had to give the couple their due.

"Great jacket," Dad said to Eggers. "You looking for a job on an aircraft carrier?"

They turned. Trudy called, "Dr. Hannah!"

Eggers was the one who leapt from his seat to embrace me first.

"We thought you were dead," he said. "We thought everybody was dead."

Trudy rushed me, arms wide. Her eyes were wet from the movie. "We went by your house and your office. Jesus, have you seen campus? Have you seen what's happened?"

"How?" Eggers asked. "How did you make it? How is this possible?"

I lifted a hand to halt them. If they said one more word, if they held on to me a second longer, I was going to break down and cry. "Listen," I said. "In due time. Things will come clear in due time. Right now, we have to find Farley. If he's alive, then Yulia's alive."

"What?" Eggers asked. "What are you talking about?"

"I'm not finished," I said. "This next part is very important: I need to know whether or not you saw Vadim eat the popcorn."

Eggers shrugged. "I don't know. I don't remember it."

"The popcorn," Trudy said. "Of course. Keno's corn. We all ate it."

"Trudy," I said, "did you see him?"

"No," she said, still shaking her head. "Cooking the corn must've somehow killed the disease. It must've inoculated us."

I turned to Eggers. I grabbed him by the sleeve of his fancy imported jacket. "Tell me this," I said. "And by God answer me straight, boy: can you or can you not fly a helicopter?"

"No," he said.

"Okay," I told them. "We improvise. Come on, we've got dogs waiting by the woodshop."

"Waiting for what?" Trudy asked.

"To take us to Farley," I said. "I think I know where Farley is."

We parked our sled teams next to the lake. Though the dogs were tired, they were restless in their lanyards, wearily eyeing lake ice that growled and moaned. The lake had risen ten feet at least, submerging the boat ramp, leaving floating docks pinned underwater by their tethers. Without circulating water, the lake was colder, more ice-choked. Slabs of white busted up at odd angles, rising jagged and treacherous. As these sheets abutted and broke, new pieces bobbed up and froze like tombstones, welded in place with scars of clear water.

The four of us stood there, Eggers, Trudy, Dad, and I.

We raised our mittens to scan the ice. All the fishing shacks had been crushed and pulled under. Only stray boards and occasional bits of hardware shone against the white.

Trudy was the one who spotted Farley, a fuzzy speck far out on the lake.

"Ahoy," I yelled.

We all listened for a response, but he'd gone a great way out, and the snow and wind swallowed everything. On the count of three, we cupped our mouths and shouted, "Farley."

Everyone has a Heroics Bone, the source of fear-induced valor and idiotic acts of daring. You know it—it's that nervy vertebra in your lower back, the one that plays hell with your bladder and prostate. While we listened for Farley's response, I looked at Dad and Trudy and Eggers. They were all would-be lionhearts. When we heard nothing but our echo back, I preempted their obligatory chivalries:

"Let me go," I said. "The man will listen to me."

A normal spill on the ice would result in some accidental urine and seven days of heating pads. This ice was waiting to grab you, freeze you white, then fold you up like airplane luggage. What made it most dangerous was its beauty and playfulness. There was something jocular about the way sheets of it raced downstream to the lake, then nose-dived below the waiting ice or rode upon its back. Great slabs of it would tumble, surface like whales, then bob like bath toys.

But people weren't exactly falling down to block the path of my possible death.

"Be careful," Trudy said. "It looks pretty awful out there."

"Yeah," Eggers added, "watch your step."

Only my father cautioned me against going. "There's no need for this," he said. "Your friend will come off the ice when he's ready."

"He needs me," I said.

Dad clapped me on the back. "Okay," he said. "I understand."

Eggers gave me his sledding goggles, and Trudy closed the toggles of my coat.

"You might want to take a few dogs with you," Eggers said. "If you fall through the ice, they can pull you out."

I looked at those loafy dogs. Labs stood with drool frozen to their chins, and a Saint Bernard wept mucus. Kicking down the doors of my neighbors, I'd run across plenty of dogs like these. Invariably, they were the ones who, upon the deaths of their masters, scratched open the cabinets, ate all the dog biscuits, then jumped on the bed to sleep off their tummy aches. And you don't want to know what the little dogs did.

"I'll take my chances," I said. "Eggers, Trudy — I'm sending you two on a mission. This afternoon brings with it the beginning of a perilous journey, and I'll need you two to secure my provisions. Meet me back on campus, at Central Green."

They stood there nodding. "Get going, then," I told them.

I turned to Dad.

"I'll wait here for you," Dad told me.

"So be it."

I set out upon the ice, avoiding places where the snow had piled, trying to find sure footing, hopping from one piece of clear ice to the next. I tried to keep my eyes on the horizon and, by way of baby steps, both my prison-issue boots under me.

Frozen inside the ice was lots of trash—white napkins, crumpled brown sacks, and patches of black that looked like roofing tarpaper. As I made my way toward the center of the lake, there was more refuse in the ice, but most things I couldn't identify. I came across only one human. He was entombed about a foot and a half down, so it was hard to make out detail. Because the ice had fractured and migrated, I saw his feet first, then about ten inches away were his shins. His knees were snapped clean, as were his femurs, and this kind of cross-sectioning went on. Above his midsection, nothing was in attendance.

It was easy to get turned around on the lake. You couldn't see far enough to make out landmarks, and the monolith of the dam, which could always be counted on as a frame of reference, was now merely a curtain wall above the ice. Snow blindness was a problem—yellow spots haunted my peripheral vision. Once, neglecting to watch my footing, I stepped into a pool of open water, only to realize it was perfectly transparent ice, transmitting the true black of below. And only when I fell did I realize those pieces of frozen trash were birds. There were millions of them, all the birds that I'd have seen littering the landscape of Parkton were it not for the snow.

In the light through the ice, I could discern each filament of even the blackest feather. Pink marrow was visible in even the tiniest bones of broken wings. I could make out the fluting of nearly invisible quills. I'd never been so close to birds. They'd always been up in trees or at great heights. Now, when they were inches away, just past my cheek, they were locked away behind ice. With their nautilus beaks, the red rings of their feet, and the flecks of color in their eyes, there was no denying that each one of them was a ravishing thing. If the history of humanity has been the history of extinguishing other forms of life, it's hard to say whether we have been evolving. The Clovis built an empire of meat, and their parting gift to the earth was to leave it thirty-five species lighter. And our last gasp was to eradicate hogs and birds. The Clovis outdid us in the variety of their extinctions, but we had them in terms of time. The hogs were gone in two weeks, and whatever happened to the birds—a poison, a nerve agent, a virus?—took place in two days.

Farley, when I finally neared him, held a tilt-up rig like a fishing rod and was sitting on an upturned bucket. Slumped, he focused his eyes on the line in the hole.

"Farley," I called, but he didn't look up.

When I neared, I saw another bucket sitting there, as if waiting for me.

"Farley, it's me. Hey, buddy, I'm here."

When I sat on the bucket, Farley glanced up, but only for a second.

"Not you, too," Farley said.

"Are you okay? It's me, Hank."

"Are you Hank? Or more to the point, eh—are you the ghost of Hank?"

Ghost of Hank? "I'm alive, Farley. I'm here to help."

Farley started reeling in his line, turning the handle slowly while pinching the water off the incoming line so his tackle wouldn't freeze.

"I left these buckets out here," Farley said. "And here they are. Everything else is gone, the warming huts and ice shacks, but the ice left these two white buckets."

When the hook came up, I said, "Looks like they stole your bait."

"I didn't bait it," he said. "Isn't that funny? You wander around knee-deep in death all week, and a guy doesn't have the heart to put a cricket on his hook."

"Farley," I said, "you don't really think I'm a ghost, do you? I know you're Native American and all, but you realize I'm really here, talking to you, right?"

"I've seen a lot of ghosts this week," Farley said. "My old man would talk about spirits and that kind of business. That stuff was never for me, but I've seen ghosts now, a lifetime's worth of them." Here he pulled out a cough drop. "I was sitting here thinking, What if I'm the one who has left the world of the living, and now I'm in a place where I'm the only one? Does that make me dead? Am I the ghost, Hank?"

"Give me the rod," I said. "I'm going to stick that hook in my finger. Maybe blood will prove this is me, Hank, the guy you used to eat lunch with at the cafeteria, the guy you'd let copy off your exam papers. Give me that hook, and I'll show you alive."

I thought Mr. Wouldn't Hurt a Cricket would wave that notion off and take me at my word. Instead, Farley handed me the rod.

I found the fishhook and lined it up with my fingers. After careful examination, I decided on the pinkie finger. With that little silver hook poised to draw blood, I said, "You think you're funny, don't you? You're going to make me do this. Tell me this first, do ghosts bleed?"

"I don't know, eh," he said. "They might. They might bleed more than people."

I shook my head. "You are in some kind of state," I said. I set the fishing rod down. "You would make your friend stick himself in the finger, wouldn't you? Well, now you're just being silly. Now it's time to snap out of it. I have a journey to make, my friend, and I can't leave with you out here on the ice."

Still Farley sat there. He shifted the cough drop in his mouth.

I stood. "And what if you are a ghost, Farley? Then what? You going to sit out here and fish forever? I can tell that you really haven't thought this afterlife thing through. Loneliness and a bucket—that's as far as you've gotten on your own. And say I am a ghost. I happen to be the one ghost on earth out here talking to you. I happen to be the only spook who cares."

Farley stood. "Jeez, Hank, do you always have to be like that?"

"Be like what?"

"Oh, bring your bucket," he said. "We'll use them for flotation if we fall through the ice."

Once we were off the ice, I sent Dad and Farley to the library for topographical maps and river charts, and then I sledded home to University Village. I hadn't been back to my apartment, and when I walked up the steps to the courtyard, everything looked ominously the same. The professors who shared the complex with me were a closed-shade, locked-door bunch, and their disappearance from the earth left not a trace. I felt my pockets for keys and panicked when I remembered they'd gone down with the Corvette. But when I got to my place, it was wide open. On the door, above the busted deadbolt, was Eggers' calling card: a shoe print with a Nike swoosh.

Snow had drifted in, and all of Janis' plants had gone limp before freezing. I'd been in a lot of houses lately, and what struck me about my apartment was that it looked more like a motel room than a home. In the bedroom, I went through the hampers until I found some good clothes for the trip, ones that seemed durable and warm. These I stuffed into the washing machine, and only after I'd added detergent did I remember there was no electricity.

That move left me with little to pack. I pulled my carry-on bag down from the shelf, and into this I threw socks, undershirts, and drawers, and a toiletries bag stuffed with dental floss, Q-tips, and my liquid antibacterial soap. I thought the carry-on bag was a pretty good choice—compact, sturdy, with wheels and an extendable handle. I also packed the cast of my mother's leg, the photo of Janis, and Peabody's bottle of bourbon. I looked around my house, thinking there must be something else to take. I looked at my rock-and-roll collection. I opened and closed drawers in the kitchen. I studied the tools hanging beside the hot-water heater. All of those items looked foreign and worthless to me.

Professors of tomorrow, as you excavate the empire that was America, you'll find a million unusual objects to puzzle over. Don't bother. Make no theories concerning the purpose of a Slinky. Postulate not over flip-flops. I've made sketches of selected objects that no longer exist, and I include these only because they have a certain bearing on the drama I deliver to you now. So, please, muse not over food dehydrators, subwoofers, and blow-dryers. Waste no time attempting to understand golf carts, greeting cards, StairMasters, and car alarms. Ignore high heels, cycling pants, pet cemeteries, carpeted cat condos, videotapes of child birthings, and anything you stumble upon that is cryogenically frozen.

I left the door open on my way out.

This time, when I reached the prison the dogs needed no special prodding to race uphill. Their backsides remembered the way. At the workshop, Gerry had a grand sled waiting. The runners measured out at eleven feet, and the litter, nearly eight feet itself, was capable of carrying a driver, a passenger, and a few hundred pounds of gear. Inside, the kids were putting the final touches on the dog harness, a chain of lanyards tailored from seatbelt webbing and anchored back to the sled with two long copper cables. These had been the grounding cables for the workshop's lightning rods. The rig was so large I'd have to use the snowbrake to steer it.

"It'll take thirteen dogs to pull her," Gerry told me, marveling at his own creation. "But I wouldn't advise mushing through any electrical storms."

Roaming through the shop were a few dozen dogs that Gerry and the boys had captured. They were big, goofy-looking things with no idea how their lives were about to change. One kid moved from dog to dog, cutting off collars with tin snips. The collars went into a pile not unlike the one on Sheriff Dan's desk.

"You really think these dogs are up for it?" I asked.

"I've got a randy bitch for the lead," Gerry said. "Putting a female up front is an old Eskimo trick I read about. The male dogs will follow her to the end of the earth. You'll pull five miles an hour, fifty miles a day, guaranteed. The question is—are you up for it?"

"That doesn't matter," I told him. "I leave from Central Green in an hour."

"That's the spirit, Hanky," Gerry said. The kids were saddling up the first dog, an Irish setter with a case of the shakes. "You hear that?" he called to them. "The professor's going to go see his old lady."

From the Hall of Man, I retrieved the bones of Keno's hands and placed them in a large Ziploc bag. Upstairs, in my office, I dug Peabody's old bullwhip out of the closet and stuffed it under my belt. From the coat rack, I grabbed my university regalia—the robes, hood, and mortarboard I wore at graduation ceremonies to grant degrees to my students. Packing these things was a no-brainer. Next, however, I was faced with a hard choice.

When it came to Junior, I had to admit there was no way all twenty-seven boxes were going to fit on the sled. I stared at the stacks of paper, a life's work. It would have been easy to get all soggy thinking about wasted years of my life, but the more legitimate fear was that I was about to strand myself hopelessly in North Dakota, where I was likely to perish. That thought kept me sane. Plus, I had been given a gift not everyone received, not the young playwright dying in the street, not the old man trying to save the chickens he'd raised from eggs. I was the one with an opportunity to salvage what I could of a life's work.

I narrowed the boxes down to the most essential fourteen, which I humped one at a time down the stairs and lashed to the sled. It took a lot of bungee cords. I didn't save the scientific studies that were most crucial in supporting my argument. Instead, I saved the data that were gathered under the most extreme circumstances, and would therefore be more difficult to replace in whatever future was ahead. These included ice cores recovered from three miles beneath the Greenlandia Ice Sheet, gas samples gathered from metallic balloons cruising the lower ionosphere, and sulfur-to-CO_2 ratios in molten lava harvested from the Colvenas Trench, at the bottom of the Pacific.

It was only a short ride to Central Green, where I would make my departure. The sled was overburdened and kept threatening to spill. Whenever the dogs got rebellious, a taste of Peabody's lash was needed to secure their allegiance. I almost got weepy crossing campus—there are few things more difficult than leaving your home, and it makes no difference whether that home is a palace, a prison, or the playing fields of death. As I mushed, I tried to think of the words I might speak to my friends, family, and students. I didn't want to get speechy, but I hoped to convince them to set aside their worries for me. Certainly I was scared silly, but I felt called to do something. My whole life I'd been chasing the inaccessible and unavailable. But things were different now. Yulia needed me, Hank Hannah, and not any other person in the world. She needed me, and I would go to her.

The dogs hadn't even begun to froth when I halted in the

middle of the quad. I looked around, then checked my watch. No one was there to see me off. Not Eggers and Trudy, who were supposed to outfit me. Not my father, not Farley.

I checked my watch again. Remembering Gerry's reward system, I gave the dogs some biscuits. I adjusted the straps on my boxes. The most dangerous chapter of my life had arrived, and no one could be troubled to see me off. I paced up and down in the snow. Could anyone be counted on? Were humans even capable of being true? I kept practicing the address I was about to give, but the more I went over it, the more I rehearsed the words, the more hollow they sounded. Out in the white, wild dogs circled and pawed. Somewhere beyond my vision, mastication was taking place.

Finally, several dog teams approached. When their drivers pulled up and lifted their goggles, however, I saw it was not my father or Trudy, but Gerry and his kids. Their sleds were packed, and the kids were equipped with foul-weather boots and proper snowshoes. "We're coming along," Gerry said. "The kids want to visit their old lady after you visit yours."

There was no irony in Gerry's voice at all. It was as if he'd convinced himself that the woman he loved really was alive, that she was off at a dude ranch having a high old time. I looked at those kids, glassy-eyed with the hope of seeing their mother. Just the idea of a bunch of kids being dependent on me gave me the willies, let alone taking them down a road that would never lead to their mom.

"I appreciate the offer," I told Gerry, "but I'll move faster alone."

"Oh, it's no bother," Gerry said. "It's no trouble. There's not much for us here, and we're happy to help pull some extra weight."

Wouldn't those kids quit looking at me? I wasn't the one who'd been feeding them lies. I didn't electrocute anybody's mother.

"There's no way," I told him. "You can't come. I'm finding my own old lady."

Gerry said, "Hey, who do you think just built your sled, Hanky?"

Farley pulled up, dogs howling. Dad was in the litter. He

threw me a handheld GPS tracker. "We don't need maps," he said. "The satellites still work."

"Dad, Farley," I said, "I'm glad you're here. Someone needs to tell this guy he's not coming with me. Tell him this is a one-man mission."

When I looked at the sled Dad and Farley were driving, though, I could tell that it, too, was outfitted for travel through cold country.

"Hey, there, now," Farley told me. "We're all coming with you, eh?"

Dad shot me a look that said, *Get real.* "You can't do this trip alone," he said.

I addressed all of them: "This trip will be long and perilous. There'll be great obstacles, unforeseeable dangers, general loneliness, and little hope of success. I can't ask anyone else to risk their lives. I can't be responsible for that."

I was starting to scare the crap out of myself. Talk like that was really weirding me out. I had to get out of there; luckily, Trudy and Eggers were sledding up.

Trudy set the snowbrake, and Eggers jumped up from the litter, wearing all his old Clovis gear. It was a nice show of solidarity. His richy-rich parka and perpetual watch had been replaced by buckskin breeches and a big Clovis coat.

"Sorry we're late," Trudy said. "Last-minute shopping."

When I went to their sled, there weren't any supplies.

"Where are my provisions?" I asked. "What am I supposed to eat for the next two weeks?" On their sled were several shoeboxes, and a whole raft of potato chips. "What is all this?" I asked, staring at the chips. They were suddenly incomprehensible to me.

"Easy, Dr. Hannah," Eggers said. "We got some goodies for you, too."

"I don't want new sneakers," I said. "I need staples. Rice and flour. Meat."

"You don't need provisions," Eggers said. "I lived for a year without provisions. We'll find stuff along the way."

"I've got news for you," I said. "You're not going along." I started rifling through the stuff they'd brought. There was a Frisbee, a box of dog treats, and a new set of barbecue tongs. "I can't eat any of this," I told them. I picked up a golf club. "What the heck is this?"

"It's only a nine iron," Eggers said. "So I brought one club. So kill me."

There was a large sack from the pharmacy. I tore this open. It was filled with hundreds of little discs, each disc ringed with little white candies. "You brought candy? I asked you to do one simple thing like keep me from starving, and this is what you come up with?"

Trudy snatched the bag from me. "These are my birth-control pills," she said. "If I'm going to be the last woman on earth, I'm not taking any long trips unprepared."

Gerry said, "Hey, now, you're not the last woman on earth."

"Yeah," I said, "you're not the last woman on earth. That's what this trip is about. That's what I'm about to kill myself trying to establish. But it doesn't seem like anybody gives a crap about that. This is just a big picnic to some people."

Eggers lifted his hands. "What say we lighten up a little, Dr. Hannah? How about we go easy on the negativity? Maybe Trudy and I got a little carried away, but you're really not one to talk when it comes to packing dogsleds. You've got about six hundred pounds of computer paper there, and that suitcase is designed for overhead bins, not long-distance mushing."

I walked to my sled and lifted the snowbrake. I said, "I'm sorry, but this is something I have to do. If I've misled anybody, I apologize. If I haven't lived up to your expectations, well, so be it. I figure it will take me two weeks to find Yulia and at least two to get back, assuming the snowpack holds. Until then."

"Why are you taking Junior?" Trudy asked. "If you're coming back, why are you taking your research with you?"

I didn't have an answer for that.

I simply said, "I'll see you in four weeks."

Farley threw a thumb toward the lake, though you couldn't see anything through the falling snow. "If water starts coming over the dam," he said, "it's only a matter of time till the abutments erode. Town might not even be here in a month."

I stepped onto the sled runners. When I lifted my whip, the dogs stood.

"Dr. Hannah," Trudy said, "what's wrong? What's gotten into you?"

"Listen to me," my father said. "Do not do this."

Eggers came up to me. "People stick together," he said. "Do you remember the night you taught me that? I didn't know that. I'd made it to graduate school without learning that. *You don't turn your back on the people who need you.* That's what you said to me. Those are the words my own father never taught me."

"Yet you went off anyway," I told him.

"Well, I was wrong," Eggers said.

Gerry's kids were giving me this spooky look. It was blank and expectant, and they were relentless with it. I had to leave right then, I had to get out of there while I still had an ounce of resolve, or I would simply crumple. I turned toward the river. I popped the whip, and held on tight when the sled lurched.

"Dr. Hannah," Eggers called after me, "this is a low-down and lonesome thing you're doing."

Chapter Twelve

Racing through the riverbed, I barely glanced at the corpses. I thought of them all together, as a single entity. *You sad bastards*, my mind said to them, *you poor stooges*. My vision was blurry. I kept wiping my eyes, but honestly, I couldn't see a thing. "Hya," I yelled. "Hya!"

The snow had begun to settle in the Missouri bed, but it was thin, and believe me, you knew when the skids hit a "bump." Here's where all the dogs were, some lying casually across river-softened corpses, lifting their muzzles whenever they needed to horse down soft tissue, while others were re-cumbently engaged in digestive naps. When I raced through them, though, they took great interest, agitatedly charging me in little bluff-runs as I crossed the channel. They spread out into flanking lines that paced me on either side, just beyond my vision through the snow. I hadn't gone a quarter-mile before my hamstrings were burning from holding on so tight. Every bump was a near spill. Each drift we punched through shook the pulp in my teeth.

The thirteen canines that pulled my sled were terrified of the newly wild dogs, and soon I realized my prodding wasn't needed—those dogs were mad to get out of that river of death. We emerged into the woods on the far bank, passing the ancient riverboat docks, and swinging wide around the great pipes of the county irrigation pumphouse. We entered thicker trees, and, to keep my mind off the madness I'd undertaken, I focused only on the snow, the runners, and the train of dogs ahead, curving through the trees. I could still hear wild dogs out there, echoing our movements. Their panting lope was un-mistakable, and that devilish little language of theirs, the yips and whimpers they plotted their attack with, couldn't have been more sinister.

Before I describe the remainder of my journey, let me say, first, that I'd only worked with sleds for one day, and this was my inaugural experience driving a sled of this size. Second, the dogs were quite suspect to begin with. I'd detected more than a little passive-aggression in their eyes, and their disposition vacillated between longing for sweets, and fleeing with terror at the slightest development, let alone being hunted down by packs of their wild compatriots. Finally, and I'm sure this was an honest mistake, Gerry's kids had managed to get a fair amount of wax on top of the skids, making the footing quite treacherous.

We mushed through quiet fishing camps along the opposing rim of the lake, places where families had planted stands of white pine and spruce to freshen the air on their weekend stays. The occasional cabin, log-cut and compact, was the kind of re-treat that I imagined the blind of South Dakota living in when I read to them over the radio. Cutting through an open meadow, I made out the bounding motions of a pack of dogs as they tried to box me against the water. Behind me I heard the gargly ex-citement of some beast. I kept looking over my shoulder, but I only made out rushes of fur through the trunks. If it was a chase dog or some kind of straggler, working on his own initia-tive, I could handle him, but if I was dealing with yet another pack, things could turn grim. Over my shoulder, I saw that, yes, about a hundred yards behind me, a full complement of dogs was closing.

I turned forward just in time to see my dog team disappear under a low-hanging branch. It caught me square in the chest, and deposited me on my back in the snow. It felt as if the pine needles had brushed the skin off my face, and my cheeks burned with the witch hazel of pine resin. The tree hadn't been a large one, and above me it swung from the impact, shaking off stiff clumps of snow. When I sat up, I saw the last of my vanishing sled and the wag of the dogs that pulled it.

I heard a jingly-jangly sound. It was rhythmic and almost soothing.

Usually when a pack of dogs is bounding headlong to maul you, you're on higher ground or at least standing tall. Now I was at their eye level, and I saw them — nostrils wide, haunches rolling — as would a toddler in a playpen. Their bodies stretched and balled, dug and flew, and each time their paws clapped the snow, it sent a shudder through their fur. I remember thinking, *How shimmering are these coats, how singularly they flow.*

I scrambled up the puny tree that had dethroned me. It really was a pitiful thing, leaning this way and that as I stepped from branch to branch. I couldn't get more than six feet high without its threatening to topple. The mongrels surrounded the trunk, and, tails awag, began making fusillades at my feet. One black standard poodle had my number. Twice he latched on to my boot, and nearly brought me down by way of the rubber sole. Had I been wearing tennis shoes, all would have been lost. The dogs were quite active in their assaults on my ankles, but I grew brave enough to feel my ribs for breaks (none) and to look for signs of my sled (none). That dog team was out there, barreling on without me. What a sight it must have been. Imagine seeing that driverless sled charge toward you, led by a team of frothing, wild-eyed dogs running from the raw history of the last hundred thousand years, all charioteered onward by the hands of extinct humanity, hands that had at their grasp a whip, a bottle of bourbon, and the power to grant doctoral degrees.

The dogs began making running starts to lunge farther up the tree. Then a sheepdog raised up and gave the trunk a bear hug. Its vocal cords had been snipped. It threw a tantrum of barks my way, yet all I heard was a hoarse, tracheal pant.

"Ahoy," I shouted into the woods.

I pulled the Global Positioning System tracker out of my pocket. It was the size of a transistor radio, but it had no communications abilities that I could see. I turned it on. "Acquiring Satellites," it flashed. On the screen came a depiction of our globe, with a flashing dot in the Northwestern Hemisphere. That was me. I pressed the zoom button. The flashing dot appeared on a map of North America. I pushed zoom again and again. I flashed in South Dakota, in Parkton County, and, to my dismay, I realized I was technically still within the city limits of Parkton. I pushed the mark-map button and put the thing away.

Afternoon wore on, cold and still. The color spectrum shifted to dark green, with long shadows of dirty purple. An Airedale had done a ditty on my calf, and a collie drew blood. If you know the lonely sounds of wind vibrating your clotheslines or a gust cycling through a leaf-burning barrel, if you've heard the breeze play the bones on the rusty tines of an upturned fan rake, then you know where I was. You know what I saw when I gazed from that tree upon a birdless America. That's the state I was in. That's how low I was. The thought crossed my mind that it was my coat that was driving these dogs mad, that they could smell the Pomeranian trim on cuffs and hood. It actually crossed my mind to take my coat off, the one thing I had left, the thing that Eggers and Trudy had made for me by hand, and throw it to the dogs in an effort to appease them. "What's wrong? What's gotten into you?" Trudy had asked me as I insisted on going off on my own. The question kept cycling in my mind.

I'd never throw that coat to the dogs, but the GPS cartography had gotten me thinking. I loosened the top toggles on my coat and pulled it off, steamy and leather-smelling. I opened it and fanned it across the branches. There was a map of North America, embroidered by Trudy, with a star exactly where I was. And there, on the inside breast, was embroidered "Open in Case of Emergency."

I tore loose the stitching, and from this pocket removed a photo of Eggers, Trudy, and myself at last year's Parents Weekend mixer, an affair to which none of our parents came. This was back when Trudy had just won her Peabody Fellowship, and Eggers, clad in a black suit, was about to begin his dissertation as a Clovis. I had to wipe my eyes with the back of a mitten. I dug deeper in the pocket and pulled out dental floss and Q-tips. My students knew me! They really knew me. But there was something else in the pocket. I withdrew a piece of buckskin, and before I even unfolded it I knew what it contained. I nodded my head. *All this time,* I thought. Through my prison stay and escape, through brown infernos and the harrows of ice, I had been carrying Keno's spear point the whole time. It burned pink in my hands.

Right away I got to work. I found a limb about an inch thick, and this I whittled from the trunk with the spear point. I stripped the small branches, cut a deep notch at the end, and, after seating the point, I secured it with several hundred wraps of floss. It didn't take long for our four-legged friends to make another foray toward my legs, but now I was ready to redden a few muzzles.

From deep within the woods came a voice. "Dr. Hannah," it called.

The dogs all turned to look.

"Ahoy," I shouted back. "Ahoy, ahoy!"

Through the thickets came several dogsleds. Trudy and Eggers were in the lead, with Gerry and his kids on the next sled, followed by Farley and my father, mushing together. Driving up, Trudy dismounted with the momentum. She had a box of dog biscuits in her hand. Eggers set the brake and followed, brandishing the golf club. She slung the whole box of biscuits out, broadcasting them across the snow. Uniformly, the dogs went for them. Trudy walked toward me, shaking her head at my pathetic state. "Remember my pledge to aid you?" she asked. "Remember 'no matter what engaged'? This one doesn't count. This was too easy."

Eggers was laughing. "That is the saddest spear I have ever seen."

Trudy put a hand on her hip. "Dr. Hannah," she said, "just about every decision you've made on your mission to rescue Yulia has ensured that we'd have to rescue *you*. Is that what you really wanted, for us to come save you? Well, here we are. We've dropped everything. We came for you. Next time, just ask. When this little trip is over, the real problems begin. That's when I have to find a way to Okinawa."

I leapt from the tree. My legs had nearly gone to sleep up there. Leaning on the spear, I nodded to Trudy. That's all I could do, nod that I understood.

Eggers said, "Let's get out of here before the biscuits wear off."

We followed the tracks of my departed sled. Of its cargo, only three items had bounced free along the trail: my university regalia, a bottle of bourbon, and a lone box of research, which, when I inspected it, turned out to be my most prized data—the Greenlandia Ice Sheet results. Fate is not always so cruel as she seems. The sled, it would turn out, was something we'd never see again. The dogs, I must presume, were lost. And the precious research remains at large, waiting for your discovery and excavation, my colleagues of the next millennium.

We broke camp a few miles upstream. There were cabins and fishing lodges in the woods, but we passed them by. Who could rest on such sofas? Who could approach coffee tables laden with dog-eared Christmas catalogues and half-sipped cups of herbal tea? We stopped in a clearing near the bottleneck of the lake, and our camp consisted of parking the sleds in a circle, igniting a green fire, and staring at each other as we ate from cold tins of franks and beans, which were Gerry's contribution to the endeavor.

We were too indifferent to unharness the dogs, and we watched blankly as Gerry's kids played a game called "school bus," whose only rule was a three-elbow limit. Farley had brought a complement of five-gallon buckets. These we sat on, hands extended toward the cold fire. It was late afternoon, still an hour till dusk, yet already dark thoughts had set upon us. Each person, you could tell, was taking stock.

Farley asked, of no one in particular, "Is a puffin a penguin?"

Eggers said, "A puffin's an aquatic bird, but I they're different somehow. I think puffins live in Iceland, while your typical penguin is Antarctic."

"Well, they're birds that live in the middle of nowhere, right?" Farley asked. "Surely the penguins are okay, way down in Antarctica. How could the puffins be gone, out there in Iceland?"

Dad said, "How about parrots, deep in the jungle?"

Gerry said, "I've been thinking. There are a lot of missile silos in North Dakota. People go down in those things for months at a time. I bet there are scads of people down there. I bet they don't even know what happened."

Eggers sucked his plastic spoon clean and pointed it at the sky. "Isn't there a team of scientists up on that space station?"

"What about remote weather outposts?" my father asked.

"What about submarines?" Farley responded.

"And islands," Trudy said. "People have to be okay on islands. If all the people exposed to the disease are dead, then there's no one left to spread it. Let's say a person went to an island, a person like me — do you think I would infect the people there?"

We fell silent. When the smoke blew in your face, the sap in it made you cry.

"You know what I keep thinking about?" Trudy asked. "I keep thinking up questions to put on my Arc-Intro exam. I'd only written half of it, and I keep thinking 'Humans are descended from (a) Neanderthals; (b) Cro-Magnon; or (c) Unknown.' And now there's no exam. There's no school. And all the students are —"

I stood. "Stop this," I told them. "Stop this idle speculation."

It had been a hard day, and I didn't want to give anyone grief, but this speculation would lead to nostalgia, and then regret, and everything was downhill from there.

"None of you knows anything about what happened," I told them. "You have no idea what you're talking about. Trudy and Eggers — you're doctoral candidates. Since when do you form hypotheses without first gathering data? Haven't I taught you to confront the unknown with industry and self-application?"

Eggers said, "We *were* doctoral candidates. Now my dissertation was for nothing. My university doesn't even exist. Anthropology doesn't exist."

I pointed a finger at the boy. "Police that kind of talk right now," I told him. "Look at the pathetic fire you built. Observe its lack of heat. Notice how the wind blows right through it. That's what you learned from your dissertation? You want a Ph.D. for that? And, Trudy, I've seen you throw a spear, yet you settle for cold beans from a can. What happened to the woman as artist and hunter? As for the rest of you: Gerry, is this how you treat dogs, leaving them hungry and wet in their traces? My friend Farley, now is the time we need someone to go fishing, and you sit on a bucket, contemplating penguins?"

Here my father looked at me, waiting for his admonition. He had to settle for a drink order. "There's a bottle of bourbon in my litter," I told him. "We could all stand to have someone fixing drinks."

And so we rallied. In the soft light of sunset, I followed Trudy to one of the country cabins. There a deer pawed through crusty snow, looking for forgotten onions in a dormant garden. Crouched behind a tree, Trudy readied her weapon. Then she stood. When the deer looked, she froze. In plain sight, Trudy advanced on the deer, pausing each time it lifted its head. When it lowered its muzzle to the snow a final time, she punched its side with an atlatl dart, traveling a hundred miles an hour. The animal dropped directly, though it took several minutes to die. Prey animals possess the trait of self-pacification in the face of death; a peace comes over them, then they depart wide-eyed, and, I believe, feeling little pain.

Trudy put a knife to its throat. Together we waited for the animal to stop breathing. "It's time to say thanks," Trudy said.

The animal had the finest velvet covering the base of its horns. I touched this.

"I'm sorry for what happened to you," I said. "But thanks a lot."

It felt a little weird saying thanks to a deer, but it was definitely better than not saying anything at all. When those big eyes reflected no light, Trudy drew the blade.

Together, we field-dressed the animal, wrapping the guts in the hide to carry back to the dogs. We could see Eggers' fire a quarter-mile away, but the closer we came, the more the flames were settling toward coals. Eggers was at work on a roasting spit, and Gerry had rigged a tripod for the fish broth, which smelled clear and pure, even though we had to listen to Farley's lament at not having the sage, butter, and sherry necessary for consommé. Gerry's kids staked out the dogs, and then reveled in hacking up the guts and tossing them into open mouths. Dad had scrounged up any containers he could find to serve the drinks. All we had was bourbon with a spoonful of snow, but he fancied up the delivery. He handed Trudy the bottom half of a plastic soda bottle, saying, "Your cosmopolitan, m'lady." My bourbon and snow came in the red plastic cap to a shaving-cream can. "Martini, double and dirty," he said.

We sawed the venison off as it cooked, but what won me over was the broth, which consisted of nothing but sides of perch fillets, a pinch of salt, and whole stalks of winter dill. We spoke only of today—which dogs were unruly, and how the mushing order would be shifted tomorrow. There was talk of whose muscles were more sore, and much debate over the sleeping arrangements. For dessert, Gerry's kids treated us to a show. There were several knock-knock jokes, a push-up competition, and then they sang a winded version of "Old MacDonald Had a Farm," with key words switched to carry the motif of flatulence. We skipped the ghost stories.

Finally, before Farley and Eggers brought out the wacky weed, I rose, calling Trudy and Eggers to the fire. In the crackling light, I stood them side by side.

Farley, Dad, and Gerry rose from their buckets as I produced my regalia. The robes were not at all shabby for having taken a spill in the snow. I put them on, the heavy velvet draping blue and dark brown at the cuffs and collar. Even Gerry's kids stood in a row, their ribby, hipless bodies long-limbed in the firelight.

When everything was in order, I greeted Trudy and Eggers. "Welcome," I said.

I shook each of their hands, then lifted my arms for silence.

"I've devoted my life to anthropology," I told them, "and all of my work has come to no tangible end. My book no longer exists. I have little hope of researching another. My theory that the Clovis vanished as a result of resource depletion has been dealt a serious blow by the contagion we have witnessed. Am I a failure? That's for the future to decide. It is of no matter to me. That's not the reason I became an anthropologist."

The fire was warm on my back. My students' eyes were attentive and expectant.

"A few basic questions have been behind all of my work," I continued. "Throughout my life, I've wondered, *Can people just vanish? What makes them leave? Where do they go?* To test whether the answers to these questions were true for the people closest to me, I asked them of the most inaccessible people on earth. The reason I spent my spare time fashioning Clovis spears and tools was so I could come closer to knowing the Clovis' hearts. Did theirs contain the same stuff as mine, I needed to know, or were there people who were different, who, as with the wave of a hand, could do what is unthinkable to another? I wanted to know what reason on earth the Clovis had for leaving the lands of their birth, traveling into a dangerous and unknown land, with little hope of return. Standing here today, on the brink of a similar journey, I'm beginning to understand such motivations. Have I solved the riddles of the Clovis?" I shook my head no. "Do I feel closer to them? Yes."

I removed my robe and draped it around Trudy.

Over Eggers' head, I placed first my hood and then my octagonal mortarboard.

"Gertrude Labelle and Brent Eggers, never have I had the honor of guiding such bright and original students. As of late, our roles have begun to reverse, and I feel more under your tutelage, which is the natural order of things. I hereby proclaim you doctors of anthropology. I charge you first to discover the questions that underlie your passion for discovery. Seek these answers, not esteem and acclaim. Second, remember the words of the Pima anthropologist Tohono: 'Unearth the heart, then the bones will speak.' Finally, I charge you to go forth and propagate the science."

With that, I again shook their hands, and many congratulations ensued. Another round of drinks was produced, and the celebration was a grand one. It really was a fine night. Trudy asked if she and Eggers could make a speech. "You have many speeches ahead, Dr. Labelle," I told her. "But tonight, we make only toasts, and they're all aimed at the two of you."

Eggers and Trudy wanted to swap a few stories from the past, and I indulged them. In these stories, the humor was derived from some goof-up or boner that they always attributed to me. Dad and Farley joined in, and it seems everyone on earth had a story in which I looked like an idiot. Still, we were having a fine time of it. Gerry gave little sips of bourbon to the kids, and joined in the laughter. When he opened his mouth, I braced myself for a ridiculous tale from Mactaw High.

But instead he told his kids, "This is just what it's like at a dude ranch. Your mom's probably camping by a fire just like this one. Wait till we tell her about the swell time we're having."

Things became quiet.

Dad looked at his drink.

Farley said, "Maybe I'll turn in."

Gerry's kids simply stared blank-faced at the flames.

For those kids, the fire contained a light of possibility that shone on none of our faces. That's what I thought about when I finally drifted off to sleep, the way those kids turned away from talk of dude ranches, the way they managed not to see all of us sloshing the last of our drinks in the snow. Instead, they let the fire hypnotize them. Lowering their lids somewhat, they released themselves to its endless sleight-of-hand. Within the glow, you could see yellow fingers roll flashy quarters down burning knuckles, or, deep inside the coals, make out the shuffle of white-hot shells. And if you were patient enough, if you waited and watched, you would receive a message from the fire, in that sign language peculiar only to dying flame.

In the morning, I could smell nothing but Farley's feet.

I rose before the others and washed my face—the skin was raw from my accident. I flossed, employed the use of four Q-tips, then went to the sled, where I found my box of Greenlandia Ice Sheet data. It was the only paper we had. The first dozen pages were meaningless introductory notes, so I tore out a few sheets and put them in my pocket. I was a man of routine. I required privacy and concentration. So I headed for the woods to get some personal time before the others were up.

But when I crept past Gerry, curled up with all his kids, I saw his eyes were open. His face was dark from fire smoke, and his eyes were troubled.

I knelt beside him. Peaceful kids dozed around him, but I couldn't tell if they were really asleep or pretending to be asleep, as I often had in the presence of adults.

"You have to tell them," I whispered.

His eyes fell away.

"Gerry," I whispered, "they already know. If they don't,

they suspect. You're the one who's pretending. Face it—the charade is for you, not them."

His voice was barely audible. "Maybe she was one of the lucky ones. What if she—"

"You didn't go see her in the hospital, did you?"

Gerry shook his head.

"Listen," I whispered, "they need you. You're a father now. They're not going to sob, if you're worried about that. There'll be no bawling. Trust me, they'll just be stunned."

Gerry looked at me. "You're a professor," he quietly said. "They'll listen to you."

I shook my head. "No one can do this but you."

"You could be there," he said. "What if you just stand there while I do it?"

I shook my head.

Gerry closed his eyes, pretending to be asleep, too. He scrunched his face up in pain, then relaxed. "Okay," he said, "okay." I left him that way.

We broke camp and began our trek along the river. Lacking a sled of my own, I switched off among the three teams, riding in turn with Trudy and Eggers, Dad and Farley, and Gerry and company. The morning was clear, but by lunch a fierce wind descended from the north, flapping our clothes and gear. A burst of hail drummed us, hard as Christmas candy, followed by an afternoon of murk. The skids made a pocky sound moving over the hail. Whenever we came to a wire fence, Farley dismounted with his cutters to let us through. More than once, there were cows at these fences, their legs buried to the pasterns in the snow, their feed bins long since empty. Cows I stared at anew. Their whiskers moved like oars as they chewed tall stalks of river weed, and they seem somehow solitary, even in herds—a very human trait, it seemed to me. Their eyes I'd always seen as vacant, but now there was something ancient and seaworthy about them. We often went to great lengths to fell game on our trip, but never did it occur to us to butcher one of these lost, humble beasts.

We encountered no living humans. A flotilla of burned

boats drifted past, and for a while train tracks paced the river, leading to a stalled Amtrak special that gave me the willies. A couple passengers still leaned against the windows, and you'd think they'd been rocked to sleep by the scenery and locomotion, were it not for the crystalline sprays of red on the glass. When Europeans colonized this hemisphere, 93 percent of the indigenous population died, from the tip of Chile to the Hudson Bay. But this process took many years, and the culprit was an all-star team: smallpox, cholera, typhus, diphtheria, typhoid, rubella, measles, and mumps. The Clovis disease only took ten days to devour everyone in sight.

And what a poor form of life it was. By consuming the kindling of humanity in one stroke, it burned itself out. Anything that rages so, quickly flickers. The successful forms of life are the parasites, the ones who bleed their environment to optimal exploitation, who stunt everything by taking a lion's share, who leave their hosts alive but shriveled.

We fed the dogs and took an early supper near a motorhome park that appeared suddenly by the river. The awnings were out on the recreational vehicles, and plastic chairs had been blown about by the wind. Little dishes pointed toward quiet satellites, and a couple of the rigs wore multicolored wind socks and weather vanes whose blades were cut from sprightly-colored cans. All the inhabitants, we knew, were below us in the snow. Spring, grisly spring, would come!

I wished I could give those souls a proper farewell. I'm not talking about putting names to headstones. Names are the least telling information about a human. I wanted to document that they had *been*. I wanted a narrative of each person—his last meal, the tattoo inside her hipbone, the possession he clutched, and whether she was alone when the end came. Though their lives had been lost, their stories still lingered, and *now* was the time to study the remains. Now the site would yield the freshest data. I had the skills and the inclination, but, sadly, not the time. Passing by, all I could do was mark the location on my GPS map.

I only hope that you, future anthropologists, are well under way in your excavation of this calamity. I dream that one day you'll account for all its victims. What a grand project, to exhume every human lost in the catastrophe, but are you not capable of it? Wouldn't a society consisting of anthropologists take this task as its central focus? And why stop there? Why, in a golden age of anthropology, would it not be possible to account for everyone, for each person who's ever been, since we first stood tall in Africa? If you have not already attempted to do so, I charge you to open the graves, drain the bogs, and sift the shores. Find everyone, ever, and record their existence in a giant book you shall call *The Register of Being*, the volumes of which you shall house in a building here named the Hall of Humanity.

That night, we camped near an ancient levy by the river. Only when Eggers climbed it in the moonlight did we see that it was a Native American burial mound, so large and complex we knew it was meant to be viewed from space. The next night, we camped where the river was deceptively broad, and we unknowingly placed our lean-tos and litter awnings out on the ice. We didn't realize it until late, when the fire melted through the ice. In a steamy, ashy shush, it disappeared. The embers died like shooting stars under our five-gallon buckets as the current swept them away.

As we moved farther north, the temperature dropped. The slightest cloud would cause the snow to ice over, reflecting things with dazzling clarity. A few moments of direct sun meant you were mushing through ice porridge. How my senses were alive. Had I never heard the clack of bare tree branches in the wind? Did I never before notice the scent released when a wood-boring beetle drilled into birch? Passing along the river with the sun straight up, you could make out the gold fillings and diamond earrings on fat corpses, lodged under shelves of ice. On the back of an enormous woman, I saw the green-orange tattoo of a Japanese carp.

Dog breath, rhythmic and misty, ushered us on.

My greatest proof of the afterlife was the fact that the land wasn't haunted by a billion souls. You didn't feel their weight moving through the woods, or see the light of sunset distorted by the slow, vaporous march of the newly dead along the horizon. Tree limbs weren't laden with the departed, faces didn't shimmer back when you knelt to drink meltwater, clouds weren't fleshy with human forms. The world was thin and light, crisp as newspapers blowing over the snow, sharp as the aqua flash of sunlight through power-pole resistors. Were the souls of the lost sharing the earth with us, their energy would traverse it in squalls of dark weather, filled with warm, electrical rain. Their energy would melt the ice.

Previously, it was my belief that humans left a signature on earth, a certain resonance that could be felt. Now corpses confirmed the opposite. Desiccated corpses cast their purply, deflated corneas not upon angelic light but on the freezing rust of Farm-All plows. Their cracked, withered ears heard not the calls of loved ones, but the dry whistle of fence wire. Of this contradiction, I can only offer the following: People need people, in life and beyond. When the earth was full, souls gravitated here. And now that it is empty, they have sought solace someplace else.

On the fourth day we passed a sign that read "Entering Central Time Zone." How bizarre it seemed at first—*moving into another arena of time*—but the idea grew on me. In this new time zone, the river seemed to behave a little differently. The Missouri was flowing faster, I believed, though I couldn't be sure, because we were sledding hard upstream, and when things floated down—a beer keg, a bloated horse, a dog on a piece of ice—they already appeared to be marching double-time. We made camp near an old train bridge. Here we were sure something was up. The river looked leaner and faster, the water taking on the cocoa color of silt scoured from the channel floor.

Eggers and Trudy walked out upon the trestle. They dangled their legs above the water. Gerry and Farley were off foraging, and I was pulling baby-sitter duty. I sat on a bucket, directing the kids on how to dig birds out of the snow in order to harvest their tail feathers, which I attached to the base of at-latl darts. There was an irony I didn't like in removing the feathers of birds and asking them to fly again, in the service of killing other animals. But I didn't mention this to the kids. When I looked up at Eggers and Trudy once more, they were swinging their legs, and that simple intimacy made me think of Yulia.

I'd gone a long way in defeating my weaknesses on this trip.

I'd conquered my desperate hope that Yulia was alive by simply deciding she was alive. And it was with knowledge that I defeated speculation: I knew what Yulia's house looked like. I knew what foods were in her cupboard. So, when I imagined — over and over — entering her hothouse and lowering her to my bearskin coat and demonstrating the Celsius of my passion, the copper watering can by her side and the shiny tools on the wall weren't products of my imagination, but real pieces of her life, pieces she'd given me. It was Vadim who haunted me. It was his yellow jacket I constantly saw in my peripheral vision.

One of Gerry's kids pointed a black feather at the river. "The water," he said.

Before our eyes, the river began moving visibly faster.

We set down our quills to watch, and we didn't chase after them as, one by one, they blew away. The water was really moving. You couldn't take your eyes off it. Soon, it was sucking itself from its own banks, retreating into a deep channel of accelerating froth. Entire ice shelves cracked off and were thrown downstream like panes of glass.

"What is it?" a kid asked.

"I don't know," I said.

The water was *literally* sprinting, faster than a man could run. Trees, barrels, boats, docks and piers — anything that had been drawn into the channel simply shot past us. Humps and valleys formed along the river's surface, like a dragon's back, and you could hear a deep rumble as the current pushed large, unseen boulders along the bottom of the channel. The bridge pilings began to vibrate against the rush of water, and by the time white spray was blasting off them, the trestle's black girders were shuddering.

"Run," I yelled to Trudy and Eggers.

"Run," the kids shouted. They didn't understand why, but they knew something was terribly wrong. "Faster," they called when Trudy and Eggers made for shore.

"What is it?" the biggest kid asked. "What's happening?"

I looked at him. "The dam's gone out in Parkton," I said.

The kids looked downstream, though we were hundreds of miles away.

Another kid asked, "Is everything okay there?"

"Parkton is gone," I told him. "I'm sorry, but everything there is gone."

The oldest boy nodded his head, as if he understood what "everything" meant, but he didn't. How could he imagine the prison being washed away, the university, and the casino? Could he picture ten thousand bodies surfing the wave's crest, or conceptualize the river casting the ivory dice of a million hogs' teeth? In that frothy wall of water turned poker chips, Odd Fellows bricks, chained-up hot rods, and the warden's meteorite. Roiling along would be the glitter of bullet casings, the glimmer of spectacles torn from people's faces, and the life's work of Hitchcock, unreeling in ribbons of celluloid a hundred miles long. Deposited across the cornfields of Iowa and Kansas would be titanium turbine blades, white-roofed school buses, and the statue of Harold McGeachie, "The Farmers' Farmer," perhaps dropped side by side with Janis' plaque. Liberated was the man who was cemented alive while constructing the dam. Freed finally were the lake's petroglyphs, appearing suddenly, as if carved in one night.

The train trestle, after Trudy and Eggers left it, dropped to its knees.

There was nothing to do but sled on, following the exposed plains of mud where the shoulders of the river had been. The retreating river exposed rocky outcrops, some of which looked excellent for fossil hunting. I marked on my GPS unit a rare outcropping of ochre-colored rock from the Devonian period, the age in which the first tetrapods crawled forth from primitive seas. That night, a mist rose from the mud that smelled of turtles. From camp, I heard an owl call, but I figured it was Farley having one over on me, so I didn't tell anyone.

We moved through the Sioux Reservation, windy and quiet. If only they'd harbored an atavistic gene of immunity, passed down from Keno, there would have been some delicious justice. But no, the reservation was windy and quiet.

Over the next week of sledding, I came to understand the power of Trudy's theory. I'd always seen a simple elegance to her postulation that spear points were the Clovis people's chosen art form. As we made our way into North Dakota, I saw firsthand how art and necessity are the same thing in primitive technologies. There was art to the way you'd shape a new sled strut. There was art in the way you stacked kindling for a perfect fire—airy enough for ignition, yet tight enough to produce a hot, compact burn. When I carved a ladle for our broth pot, I couldn't help whittling the face of a Pomeranian into the stem, just to give the kids a kick. There was even art, Eggers taught me, to butchering an animal. You didn't just disassemble the thing, the way I'd imagined—slicing all the muscles into steaks and fillets. Instead, you studied the animal's anatomy, and after saying thanks, you traced the tendons to the joints, then snipped them there, so the sinew wasn't wasted and the bones revealed their uses. You learned to remove the liver so perfectly that you could see your reflection in the hepatic membrane.

We'd been gone nearly two weeks when Gerry called for a day of rest for the dogs. I wanted to push on, but when Gerry showed me how tender the pads of their paws had become, I understood. We stopped on the lee of a small hill. We all had our routines at this point. Gerry began pulling off harnesses and putting the dogs down for the night. The kids teamed up for firewood. Dad got to work on the sleeping quarters, while Farley began assembling the menu. At this time each evening, Eggers and Trudy would splash doe urine on their arms and legs, then set off to hunt. If they returned late with a certain symbol painted in blood on each other's faces, I figured they'd had sex.

I was the guy who got the fire going, drew a pot of water from the river, and, once it started simmering, went fishing with my father in the last light. Our culture had ended, the people who called themselves "Americans" were no more, but the fish of South Dakota cut us no special slack. The night we rested the dogs, my father and I returned with one measly perch, nothing more than seasoning for the water. Coming back from the ice, we could see the fire in the distance, playing on people's faces. The moon wasn't up yet, but its light was in the sky.

"What do you think the afterlife is?" I asked my father.

We were walking close. Our snowshoes kept clacking.

"You mean, like heaven?" he asked.

"Could be," I said. "Could be anything you want it to be—heaven, paradise, something else."

He thought about that. "Well, if afterlife means to keep living on after life is over, don't you think that's us? Aren't we doing that?"

I neared the fire with that thought in mind. If this was the afterlife, it was a place where you performed hard work for a good cause, with those who populated the center of your life. I'd have had another person or two with us if I could, but you can't just order up an afterlife like a tuna-melt special. You don't get to bargain. If there's no Corvette, so be it. If there are no martinis or shrimp bowls, so it goes. The voices of our friends were reflected large off the hill. They were big-spirited people with much to give. We were embarked on a grand endeavor, together. Nearing them, I wondered if there hadn't been a way to make something like this happen before. Couldn't we have made our lives matter more during our before-life?

We rested and ate leftovers. When the dogs were finally harnessed up again, they wouldn't budge. They planted their feet against the traces, and even if we'd still had Peabody's whip, I doubt it would have worked. I assumed the dogs had been spoiled by their rest, figuring we'd have to run the indolence out of them all over again. But when we finally shouted and prodded them forward, the crest of the hill showed us what the trouble was. Below was the city of Croix, and roving snowy plains between us and its small-town streets were gangs of feral dogs.

At the sight of those wild, sidling beasts, our sled dogs whimpered and moaned. There was no end to their fretting—they stammered forward and back against the leather, swiveling their heads round to one another for support.

"We're here, aren't we?" Gerry asked.

"Yes," I said, rather triumphantly. "We've made it."

"Okay, then," Gerry said, and began letting the dogs go. He said, "We appreciate your services," to each dog as he unbuckled its lead, and that marked the last time I ever saw humans and canines working together. That was the last time dogs ever lent a paw to help us with anything. The surprising thing, what really blew me away, was how each dog, instead of running away, bolted downhill to join the packs of loose dogs. *Good riddance*, I thought, though I didn't say it. Nobody wanted any more of my predictions that dogs would become the bane of humanity. Time would bear me out.

The University of Northwestern North Dakota clock tower was visible, and that's where we were headed, even though we'd have to cross a shallow pan of fields where the dogs were engaged in mischief. Gerry led the way. The hill was a big one, so he pointed his sled in the right direction, told the kids to hold on tight, and trusted gravity to get them most of the way to the university. Once they were off, Dad and Farley lined their sled up with Gerry's tracks, and Trudy brought up the rear, with Eggers and me crouched low in her litter.

Things started out okay—we floated nicely for a few yards—but I had no idea how fast a sled could go. We were tobogganing! All I could think of were those roller-coaster cars plunging through Parkton's downtown during Glacier Days. We stayed gripped to the tracks of the sleds ahead, and never had I felt such velocity.

You could hear Gerry's kids wooing and wowing their way down the hill as we advanced upon what looked like the town junkyard below. At a certain point, however, their shouts of joy became screams of panic. "Look out," my father yelled from the litter ahead. The wind had my eyes all teary, so it was only too late that I understood where we were really heading.

The city of Croix had developed no system for the burning of animal carcasses, and we were barreling at breakneck speeds toward acres of frozen hogs, poured who knows how many deep in the marshlands below the university.

Gerry's sled burst upon the hogs, clacking along stiff bellies and backs until the sled dumped and all were thrown. Dad and Farley bailed at the last moment, tumbling through sprays of white, but it was too late for us. We were riding it in.

Eggers and I braced ourselves as we pounded down upon the brown mass and rattled out upon the plain of them, yellow hooves beating the struts off, exposed ribs tearing loose our crossbars. The sled finally tipped, and we were battered out upon the icy blue meat. Eggers had a blackened eye, and ribs I thought were healed reasserted themselves. There was no regrouping. We all began making our way to the other side, to the lawns of UNND. We had to get out of the field of pigs. Mostly, they had been shot. Mustard-colored ice dripped from holes in their bodies, and ice—liver-red and tobacco-brown— froze them together into one mass. The lug soles of our boots left prints in their skin.

Just when I'd gotten used to hogs, I discovered that, near the end, Croix had taken down all its beasts. Horses, sheep, goats, and cows lay upon the terminus of the heap. I'd endured almost the whole stretch without breaking down, but right at the end, four little petting-zoo donkeys nearly broke my heart.

On the other side, I didn't wait for the others. I called to them and, receiving their thumbs-up, forged on ahead. Though Croix had been a smaller town, the mayhem here was worse. Cutting across campus, I could see down the side streets. Signs of final horrors were everywhere—barricades, bodies under cars, bullet holes all over. The campus was vaguely familiar, and I made for the agriculture department's hothouses, the only buildings on campus lacking layers of snow.

At the main nursery, I burst through the doors. For two weeks, my central occupation had been to bar from my imagination all the horrible possibilities that could have befallen this place. I'd kept at bay images of the glass broken, the plants wilted, the structure burned or washed away. As long as it survived intact in my imagination, Yulia was alive, Vadim was alive.

And here I was. Inside, a propane space-heater kept the place warm. The bulk of the building was filled with rows of experimental crops; the wings contained exotic plants from the world over. The aisles, however, were packed with houseplants, regular-looking things, in all different pots. You had to duck under the canopies of overgrown ficus plants and squeeze past the fat arms of rubber trees. There were junipers in terra-cotta pots, and poking from an urn were the nosy trumpets of a creeper. I even had to fight several spider plants hanging from overhead racks. As I waded through all that damn greenery, it suddenly dawned on me that Yulia had gone door to door, as my father and I had, except she'd rescued the houseplants of Croix.

"Ahoy," I announced.

Through some baskets of bamboo, I made out movement. I began running down the row, and when I emerged at the other side, I saw Yulia and Vadim seated on stools at a pruning table, eating a lunch off of white paper.

"Dr. Nivitski," I yelled, "it's me."

Yulia wore a white smock. Her hair had gone wild. She held a can of soda in her hand. When she turned and saw me, she stood. She wore no eye shadow, no lipstick, and her face looked aged and puffy.

I pulled back my hood and lifted my goggles. I suppose I was no Soviet Romeo, either. I walked a little funny because of my ribs. I hadn't bathed in a month. The winter sun had shown me no mercy.

"Finally," I said, "Yulia, I finally found you."

I began walking toward her, arms out. I sought to lock her gaze, but her eyes were desperately flashing from my clothes to my arms to my beard to my hands, and they would land no place on me. "It's Hank," I said. "Hank Hannah."

That's when she ran. She exclaimed something drastic in Russian, and ran.

I guess I didn't understand what was going on. I went to Vadim. From where he sat, I could see the last glimpse of Yulia as she ran down a row of seedlings, smock flowing behind her. She stopped at some sort of root cellar, bent down to open the doors, and shut herself inside.

Vadim was eating a slice of frozen pizza.

"She won't be out for a long time," he said.

"Doesn't she know it's me?" I asked him. "Didn't she recognize me?"

"You came through the dogs, didn't you?" Vadim asked me. "How did you get through them?"

"What?"

"I don't ever go out there alone," he said. "Professor Winslow went out there alone, and he never came back."

"Who's Professor Winslow?" I asked.

"This was his hothouse," Vadim said. "This is his pizza."

I brought the boy with me to the cellar, where, indeed, the

insulated doors were locked. It looked like they stored plant bulbs and seeds down there.

"Yulia," I shouted through the doors. "It's Hank Hannah from South Dakota. We've come to rescue you."

There was no response.

Vadim was drinking a soda. "She doesn't speak English anymore," he said.

"Yulia?" I called. "Yulia?" I turned to Vadim. "Talk to her," I said.

"It won't do any good," he told me.

"Then tell me," I said. "What's Russian for 'We're here to help'?"

"She gets like this," he said. "The longer you yell, the longer it takes for her to come out."

"Doesn't anything work? Won't anything bring her out?"

He shrugged, sipped his soda. "You don't happen to have a *Draculunus vulgaris* on you, do you?"

The rest of the gang came panting in, calling my name. When I apprised them of what had happened, Farley looked at the door hinges and the frame and said, "We can have this thing open in no time."

Eggers said, "I bet Trudy can pick the lock."

"Hey, hey," Gerry said. "You can't just drag her out of there. The woman's alone in there, afraid. She's got to come out on her own terms."

Vadim sat on his stool, eating pizza.

Trudy said, "Let me try to talk to Yulia," she said.

"Yeah," I said, "that's a good idea. That's worth a try."

I pictured poor Yulia down there in the dark. I remembered the way she described herself in that speech: as a girl, suffering first from terrible allergies, then caused further pain by the doctor who was supposed to help. I had to get Yulia out of that cellar. I had to show her that I was here to help, that I would never hurt her.

I went to Vadim. He was wiping his mouth with a napkin. Some kind of eerie, casual disconnection had taken hold of the boy.

I asked, "Where can we find one of these *vulgaris* plants?"

"This was a kind of joke," he said. "The *D. vulgaris* is one of the rarest flowers in the world. They bloom only at night, along the South China Sea."

"There's got to be some other plant we could bring her?" I asked.

"We saved all the plants."

"Well, then, we'll dig one up," I said.

"Out there?"

"Yeah," I said, "out there."

I grabbed a bucket, and we walked to the hothouse door, where we closed our coats. Vadim grabbed a gardening spade off the wall. It had a long, lean blade, and I could tell this was what he carried to ward off dogs. He waited for me to choose a tool. I grabbed a pickax and leaned it over my shoulder. "Where to?" he asked.

Outside, I tried to head away from the ugly portraits of town. A couple knolls overlooked the Missouri at the edge of campus, and I figured there had to be some shrubs or something up there.

Vadim was petrified of dogs. His cool, collected posture quickly disappeared. Watching him constantly scan for marauding dogs made me realize this wasn't a single morning's work. My entrance into the lives of these two people wouldn't be as simple as the rescue scene I'd imagined. There wasn't going to be a dinner where I regaled Yulia with stories of hardship, kept filling her champagne glass, and later claimed my passionate reward. I didn't even know Yulia that well, and it would prove true that she'd gone a little mad from the events depicted, as testified by some of her behavior later in life. But I held her in my heart, and would stay with her all my days, even if a great many of them were trying ones. If love dictated only in Russian, I would learn that thorny tongue.

Since the boy owned no snowshoes, he stumbled often, and each time he fell, his first thought was to defend against advancing dogs. Before, he'd been a smart, brooding boy, prone to silence and introspection. Now, after what he'd experienced, I wondered if I'd ever get through to him.

We were making for the highest spot on the hill. There were some little chinaberry bushes poking out of the snow.

"I know you're going through a hard time," I told the kid.

He didn't answer.

"I've brought you something," I said. I produced Keno's point. "Dogs are afraid of this," I said. "I've scared many dogs away with it. Keep it in your pocket. They'll smell it on you. They'll keep their distance."

I placed the point in his hand. The thing would save his life come spring, after we'd all set out for Okinawa. Now Vadim seemed impressed mostly with its beauty, with the pink light coming from its edge, but he looked indifferent to my claims of its potency. I'd expected a few of his science-minded questions, like *How can dogs smell it?* or *How does it work?* But such questions were dangerous. From them, it was only a short hop to other questions, like *Where is my father?* and *What will happen to me now?*

I knew where he was at — it seemed impossible that mere inquiry could protect you from the unknowns swirling about like cast-nets. It seemed unthinkable that simple questions could prevent you from being forever drawn into the seine purse of doubt. But one day, that would change. One day, he would separate himself from what he felt, so "this hurt" would become "that hurt," and once that happened, once he learned to step outside the cloud of his loneliness and examine loss with scientific eyes, then words and names would begin to work for him. Then he'd be able to tell his story as if it had happened to someone else, which is the only way you can speak the story of your life and still survive when it ends.

The ridge, when we reached its rounded peak, was stunning. A gray wedge of cold front cut against the horizon, and in the sun off the water, the light was intense. I tried to find the smallest chinaberry out there, one that would fit in our bucket. That chinaberry smell always made me think of Parkton. I pulled out my GPS unit and marked the spot. Its batteries were failing.

With the pick, I scraped snow away from the little plant until I found frozen soil. I began chipping at the earth, breaking a little dirt loose with each stroke.

"You gonna help or what?" I asked Vadim.

"This isn't going to work," he said. He stood there, watching me dig. "She will not be impressed by this weed."

It was pretty hard not to hurt the roots in the frozen dirt, but I did my best. The plant smelled good on my hands, and I've always liked the shape of those little blue berries.

Vadim wouldn't let up. "What makes you think she will like that plant? There are a million plants just like it. What makes you think that one is special?"

I just kept digging. When my face started to shine, Vadim joined me, and soon we had a passable hole. Soon we had a plant in a bucket. I looked at that hole. It was a good spot we were at. I didn't quite understand Vadim's resistance, but we'd turned our first corner here. I pulled out my GPS unit. I wrapped it in the buckskin I'd used for Keno's point, and together Vadim and I buried the thing. If this story has reached you, fellow humans of the future, then you have no doubt found this and all the other artifacts I have left for you. Perhaps some sort of historical marker now stands where Vadim and I stood that morning. Perhaps such monuments to our deeds litter the landscape from here to Asia.

Certainly, of course, there will be those in the future who have found a way to hold me responsible for the very calamity that we here survived. I trust the thinking persons among you know foolishness when you hear it. Always there are lesser scientists who, for lack of a good dissertation topic, will spend several years researching such cockamamie ideas. Their goal is not truth but celebrity, and their means are incendiary sensationalism. I've said enough on the topic already; suffice it to say that, over the last million years, the fates of the cultures of the world have always been the same: dust. Anthropologists don't erase cultures; we remember them.

Other decisions, I'm sure, will fall under some scrutiny. In teaching Gerry's kids, a duty that fell solely to me during their long march toward doctoral degrees, I instructed them in Latin at the expense of Greek. I perhaps overstressed the Enlightenment, and I confess that I pretended the entire twentieth century didn't occur. As to my rendition of feminism, I tried my best. Vadim was to outclass all students before him, earning his Ph.D. in record time, and when his thirst turned from humanism to popular culture, I readily admit the inaccuracies I may have passed on in my depiction of the movies, songs, and literature of the day.

That bank of clouds was still gnurling its way across the horizon. They looked like glaciers to me, slow, determined, unearthing everything buried before them.

"So how long does she usually stay in the cellar?"

Vadim shrugged. He'd been doing fine while occupied with digging, but now fear again gripped him, and he looked down upon the town with weary eyes.

I said, "I'm going to say a couple things to you, all right?"

Vadim looked at me. He nodded.

"All those dead people in the streets," I said, "they're not people anymore, so don't be afraid of them. Their spirits have gone someplace else. I haven't figured out where yet, but I've been doing a lot of thinking on it. Your father is probably with the spirits. We won't know for sure until we get to Vlotovnya."

Vadim looked past me, to the town and hog fields beyond. He was still listening, though.

"These are only words to you now," I told him. "It will take your whole life to understand what it means to lose your father. Someday, though, I'll teach you how to tell his story. In the future, I believe everyone's story will be told. Right now, it's not possible. For now, all we can do is tell one story that has a part of everybody."

I indicated the cloud front on the horizon, pointing to the sooty wisp of its leading edge, as well as the ice-blue within. "I will never leave you," I told Vadim, "though everyone's time must come. When mine comes, you can look at a cloud like this, and you will feel me there. I'll leave a part of myself there for you."

I stood. The cold air was sharp against my ribs, but the sun was really something off the snow. You could about see forever. It's funny—I'd always pondered what had made the Clovis leave their homes and ancestors to make their crazy journey, but it had never occurred to me how they must have felt when they got there. They'd risked everything, and suddenly, emerging from the ice, they discovered a new world, a continent that was entirely unpeopled. What ran through their veins when they were confronted with such a possibility? What first words did they speak when they stared into a land that knew not their echo?

That morning, with my hand on Vadim's shoulder, I felt I knew.

"Come on," I told him. "It's time to get your mother out of the cellar."

We turned from the depopulated plains of North America. We weren't going to found an empire here. We had other plans, ones that included Canada, Alaska, the Bering Sea, and the Kamchatka Peninsula. We were headed to Okinawa next. My life's work had yet to begin, and the journey ahead would shuttle us off this continent by the same route that had brought the Clovis, thus concluding humanity's twelve-thousand-year camp-out in North America. The trip wouldn't be so hard. We'd taught a thousand students how it went. It was a story we knew by heart.

Acknowledgments

The author wishes to thank the entire Harrell family, without whose generosity and tireless support this book could not have been finished. Specifically, I am indebted to Dr. James Harrell, the Honorable Gayle Harrell, Jennifer Sobanet, and Melinda Johnson; and nothing is possible without my wife, Stephanie Harrell—you are my perpetual orbit, my flight, my fuel, my gravity.